WHEN SECRETS KILL

A Novel By:
Rick Claeys

When Secrets Kill is a work of fiction. Names, places, websites, dialogue and incidents either are products of the author's imagination or are used fictitiously.

To every young girl, young boy, woman or man, who has ever been sexually abused, whether it is by a stranger, a person in a power position, or worse, a family member; there is no excuse, ever, whether it is by force or coercion. I feel your pain. Don't stay silent! Tell someone because it is wrong!

ACKNOWLEDGEMENTS

When I started this endeavor, I had no idea that it would take all of 13 years to finish. It has been a journey of ups and downs, of computers crashing and luckily having had the presence of mind to print everything out as I went along. Yes, I have typed this three times! Without the support of my wife, Pat and children, Celine and Caitlin, my loving parents, Elizabeth and Gilbert, and friends, you know who you are, who have pushed me along through the years to finish the manuscript, it would still be an unfinished mystery. My wife would still bug me about "who done it".

To Deb Gallmon and Tyler Mitchell and their wonderful family who introduced me to "small town Georgia", thank you.

PROLOGUE

The events that took place that summer were beyond what anyone in the small quiet town had ever imagined; a dormant, southern town, unmarked yet by the dangers of the Big City. The citizens knew about crime and injustice; they read the big city papers and watched the evening news. Never once did they consider the possibility of Big City crime coming to their town.

It was July, just past Independence Day, and everyone in town was still euphoric about the cook-out the mayor of the town had held. Magnificent fireworks lit up the sky for over an hour following the cook-out. The heat of the summer made everyone move slower than they usually did, and the ceiling fans in the homes rattled a little harder as the blades were turning full speed. The old schoolhouse hosted the Children's Bible Study School during the summer. Everyday, it was a handful of children listening to Mrs. Montgomery, a retired teacher, and playing with the few older girls who volunteered to keep the little one's happy and out of trouble while school was out. At night, after their parents returned home from work and supper was finished, they sat down, watched television and talked over the events of the day. Then it was bedtime and the little town felt dormant. Except for the sounds of crickets and frogs, the town was quiet from any noise. It had been this way for two centuries, ever since the town was founded in 1795. Stuttgart was a peaceful town, a town where you could still leave your door unlocked, a town where neighbor still helped neighbor; a town hidden from evil, or so it seemed?

Seventeen years earlier:
Susan sat on her bed, naked, her knees pulled up to her chest, her arms wrapped around her legs. Her face was red and tears were running down her cheeks. Where he had grabbed her by the arms, she could still feel the pain and knew she once again would have to hide the bruises that were inevitably going to develop. She laid her head sideways on her knees and stared at the wall connecting her room with her sister's room. She had heard the door to her sister's door open a little while ago and heard the muffled begging. Susan cried harder. She had known her sister would be next. What had

they done to deserve this? Why was he doing this to them? She heard a muffled cry come from her sister's room. Susan knew that he was holding her mouth closed with one hand while he was controlling her arms with the other. She knew he had forced her to sit on her knees on her bed and that he had just pushed his manhood inside her. He would now be relentlessly pushing in and out of her young body, not caring whether he caused her any pain or harm. It would never take him long to reach his climax. Having satisfied his sick desires and pleasures, he would get off the bed, put his underwear and pants back on and walk casually down the stairs back into the living room to watch the evening news before retiring to bed.

Susan thought about telling what was going on in their house, but he had threatened both her and her sister with physical harm if they ever told anyone. He controlled their bodies and their mind. How were they ever going to escape this nightmare? It had been going on for about a year now, ever since her body had started to develop. Susan figured that her breast starting to grow had been his sign that she was ready. Ready for what? Ready to be his sexual play toy? Ready to be raped night after night by the one person who was supposed to protect her? Ready to have her young body violated and bruised by the one person who she should feel safe around?

Was there no way out of this nightmare? How long was this going to go on? The rest of their lives? She was scared of what he would do to her if she ever told anyone. Would he kill her if she told someone so his dirty little secret would not see the light of day? Would he harm her sister as a show of what he was capable off? No! She could not tell anyone! She had to keep quiet and live the nightmare until she was old enough to leave. How long would that be and how much more of his abuse would she be able to stand? Susan didn't know. She was trapped in a living nightmare of which there was no escape.

1.

Stuttgart, 2 miles. The sign stood on the side of the road, half toppled over with many bullet holes in it. The signs of bored youth on Saturday night, who, with the help of a few cans of Budweiser, thought they were invincible. The man in the black convertible slowly shook his head and smiled. Nothing had changed since he had left Stuttgart five years ago. The fields were covered with corn, cotton and peanuts, the orchards with peach trees and pecan trees. The peach fields were busy this time of the year. Migrant workers filled the fields, picking and collecting peaches from the heavy-laden branches; a good year for peaches. Mr. Knox would be pleased this year. The Knox family had been growing peaches for four generations. They were one of the wealthiest families in the area and provided summer jobs for the local teenagers. James Knox IV was currently in charge of the company. He had replaced his older brother Samuel, who had died in a plane crash about 6 years ago.

The black convertible reached the outskirts of the dormant town. The cotton gin, the local five and dime, the gas station, they were all there just the way the man in the car remembered them. It was late in the afternoon and the locals were gathered at the gas station, sitting on seats removed from some early model van and transformed into a bench for afternoon chatter. All eyes followed the car as it drove on, leaving a small cloud of dust behind. When the car was out of sight, the locals continued their chatter, each wondering who that young man was and what he might be doing in their little town.

The rush of the afternoon commuters was over at "Langston's Gas & Food". Though small, Stuttgart was located on the intersection of two major highways which brought commuters from Atlanta to their respective country hideouts. When the Department of Transportation decided to move traffic away from the centers of little towns and built new highways around them, Stuttgart lost the through traffic from North Georgia to South Georgia and the traffic from the Northern States to Florida along Highway 41. DOT made sure that traffic flowed a whole lot better; however, it destroyed the businesses that benefited from the through traffic. Phil Langston, who was just beginning his gas station in town when the new

7

highway was built, sold his store and moved to the intersection of Hwy. 41 and Hwy. 76. With the arrival of the new better-paved highway came the rise in property value and land taxes.

Phil invested everything he had in the new store and for the first decade barely survived. He finally could pay most of his debts off and recently was doing better. He had bought a new Dodge Ram pick-up for himself and a Ford Explorer for his wife. Pam Langston had stood by her husband through the hard years. She struggled to keep food on the table for her family. She aged quickly during those years. However, the last few years, people in town had noticed that she was smiling more often and that she was looking younger. At 44, Pam enjoyed hearing the comments about looking younger. After 18 years of hard work, the gas station and the just recently added restaurant were doing well. As more and more city slickers moved to the country, escaping the pressures from the big city, business was picking up and stayed busy.

Today was no different. It was just after six o'clock and the last of the commuters had left the store. Phil was 46 years old, a little less than six feet tall. He had a medium-built body and started to have some gray in his hair. He had piercing blue eyes that did not miss anything. He was gentle in his movements and reflected that same gentleness with his customers. More than once he had to go into his office and ball his fists after a dissatisfied customer aired his feelings and opinions. He was in his office right now. He wasn't balling his fists or cursing a customer, he was counting the revenues of the day. At six o'clock every day he pulled the registers and counted his revenues. He had the cash register drawers sitting in front of him on his desk. The door to his office was closed. No one in the store would see what went on in his office. Not only did he lock the door during the time he counted the money, but he also kept a loaded 357 Magnum handgun on his desk. In the 18 years he had been in business, he'd never been robbed. The last few years, however, a few of the other gas stations in the surrounding area were held up and Phil decided to get the handgun just in case. As he counted the money, he kept a close eye on the store through the surveillance cameras. Phil had a large TV screen in his office to which the cameras were connected. He did not solely rely on his employees to keep an eye on the store. It was not that he didn't trust his employees but when you have people working for you, they think about themselves and not you or your place of business. Some of the town's people called him over-concerned, but Phil knew that one day he would be glad that he kept an eye on everything.

Pam was in the kitchen cleaning up. She was 5'-8" tall, slender built was ash-blonde hair. She had high cheekbones and slender lips. Wrinkles started to form around her eyes and the hardship of difficult years showed. She was in charge of the kitchen and restaurant and called it rightfully hers. She handled everything from supplies, to cooking the food, to making sure the customers were satisfied. Phil had told her that she could try the restaurant and see how it would work. They would close it down if it was not profitable. That was 5 years ago. Pam had managed to make the restaurant into a profitable business. At lunch she would attract the locals by serving quality country cooking at a reasonable price. Once word got out, "The Country Kitchen" as some called it fondly, became the regular place to have lunch. In the afternoon, the commuters would pick up quick nutritious take-out food. She had her regulars with the commuters too. There was a construction worker who lived about 10 miles south of the restaurant. He was single and enjoyed much rather eating Pam's cooking than the microwave dinners he had in his refrigerator. Then there was the couple that worked for Delta. They lived just West of Stuttgart and stopped to pick up their dinner daily. Throughout the day, truckers would stop to fill up their trucks and take a break from the road. They nestled themselves in the wooden booths and relaxed while taking a quick lunch or dinner, or just drinking a hot cup of coffee.

On Saturday evening, Pam had started a tradition of baking Pizza. She had hoped the teenagers would be interested in coming to eat pizza before going out on a date or whatever it was today's teenagers were compelled to do. At first it didn't pay off, but then Pam had the brilliant idea to provide specials on the pizza after the High School football games. Both football players and fans would make the short distance to the restaurant to come eat pizza. From then on out, the restaurant had become a popular hangout place for the local youth on Friday and Saturday night. Adding a jukebox and some video games made it all the more popular.

"Langston's Gas and Food" had 4 employees. Two who

helped work the morning shift and two who helped work the evening shift. One of the evening shift employees was Michelle Murphy. She had just graduated high school and was getting ready to start college. She was a slender, tall blonde who had been a cheerleader in high school and who had won the local beauty pageant. She had an outgoing personality and could strike up a conversation with anybody who passed through the gas station. Michelle was cleaning up the outside trash cans, a job she thoroughly despised. But it was part of her job and she dutifully slipped on the rubber gloves every evening and disposed of the trash and garbage the customers left behind. It was a hot, muggy day and the smell of the trash was especially nauseous that day. Flies, gnats, mosquitoes, and wasps were swarming around the trash cans and dumpster. Armed with a spray can of bug repellent, Michelle managed to get the trash bags changed and put into the dumpster. When she turned around from the dumpster ready to head back into the store, she saw a black convertible drive into the parking lot. The car was covered with dust. Michelle noticed the license plate, something Phil had taught her to do just in case they had a "gas-up- and-run" customer. It was a Virginia license plate, "DIM V A 1". She shrugged her shoulders and walked inside the store. Probably another Northerner on his way to Florida, she thought as she started her clean-up routine inside the store.

  The driver of the black convertible walked in. He was well over six feet tall with broad shoulders and muscular arms underneath them. He had a full head of dark hair. His blue eyes looked around the store, taking in everything in sight. He was wearing blue jeans and a T-shirt with worn sneakers underneath. He walked up to the counter and pulled out his billfold to pay for the gas. Brenda, the cashier looked the man over.

  "Hi, I've got 30 on pump 4," the man said as he handed her a credit card.

  "Hi to you too!"

  Brenda slid the credit card through the processor and took another good look at the man.

  "Here you go," she said as she gave the man the receipt. "Please sign at the bottom."

  The man signed the receipt and kept the yellow copy.

"Tell me, is Phil in?"

Brenda looked at him with questioning eyes.

"He's in the office. Can I tell him who's calling?"

"Tell him it's the Flemish Lion, he'll know who it is."

Brenda went to the office and knocked on the door.

"Mr. Langston? There is a gentleman here that would like to see you. He told me to tell you that it's the Flemish Lion."

"The Flemish Lion! I'll be damned!"

Langston came out of the office, making sure the door locked behind him and made his way to the counter.

"Dimitri Van Acker! Where the hell have you been hiding, you son of a gun!" Langston said, grabbing the man by the hand and shaking it vigorously.

"Hey there old man, how are you doing?"

"I can't say I'm doing all that bad."

"Yeah, I would say so. I like the addition to the place."

Langston pointed towards the restaurant.

"Best improvement we did since we moved here. Pam's running the place. She's making some good bucks at it too. Come, let me show her what the cat dragged in."

They walked towards the restaurant when out of the corner of his eye, Dimitri Van Acker saw the young woman cleaning up the aisle to his left. He turned towards her and let out a slight whistle.

"Michelle, is that you?"

Michelle Murphy turned to face the man addressing her when she realized who it was.

"Dimitri!"

She hastily made her way towards him.

"Dimitri, how are you? What are you doing here? Why didn't you tell us you were coming? How long are you going to stay?"

With a bombardment of questions, she made it to Van Acker and slung her arms around his neck. He in turn wrapped his arms around her waist and they gave each other a long intense hug.

"Look at you," Van Acker said, as he took a step back and admired the young woman in front of him. "You were a whiny, little girl when I left here, and look at you now. You're a woman. I must say, the pictures your mother has sent me don't do you any justice."

11

"Oh please, stop it, Dimitri. You're much too old to be flirting with me. Besides, I already have a boyfriend," she teased.

"You mean I drove all this way for nothing?"

"Sorry, but I'm sure a couple of my friends would be interested."

"Great, I can't wait to meet them," Van Acker teased back.

"Well, I guess I'd better get back to work before Mr. Langston gets upset with me and lets me go."

"Don't worry, sweetheart. Phil and I go back a while. I'll put in a good word for you!"

Van Acker winked in her direction and planted a solid fist in the shoulder of his friend.

"Come on, old man, let me go admire that old lady of yours."

"Watch it, you no-good..."

Pam Langston had overheard some of the conversation in the store and had walked in from the restaurant.

"Dimitri, you sly fox, you! Come here and give me a hug."

"Hi, Pam," he managed to say, looking a little flushed in the face as she grabbed him and pulled him close to her. He could feel the contour of her body against his chest. His face darkened a little more.

"Tell me, what brought you back to this godforsaken place?" Finding his composure, the redness drained from his face and it reclaimed its older color.

"I'm moving back," he said. "I've seen to much ugliness in Washington. It's time for me to settle down and become a small-town lawyer who handles land title searches and an occasional dispute about a dog barking on the wrong side of the fence. I don't want any more murderers walking into my office and paying me drug money to stay out of jail or out of the chair."

"You know, we already have a lawyer here in Stuttgart," Langston informed Van Acker. "I hope that old Tom won't be too upset that you show up to give him competition.

"Yeah, he's such an egocentric jerk," Pam added. "If it doesn't go Mr. Sutton's way, it doesn't go at all."

"Tom Sutton, you said?"

Van Acker rubbed his hand through his hair.

"Sutton? Isn't he the one who married the oldest Knox girl

right before I left?"

"He's the one," Langston said.

"Well, that'll be just fine. I'm sure I'll get to meet him real soon. I have my first appointment tomorrow morning with his wife's sister, Susan. I gather, it'll get interesting around here real soon!"

"Dimitri, is something going on over at the Knox'?" Pam asked inquiring.

"I don't know yet. A couple of months ago, Susan wrote me a letter. She got my address from Helen Murphy, and wanted some legal advise about a certain matter. I called her up and asked her if it was a pressing matter, that I was moving back in a couple of months. By that time, I had decided moving back down here, and told her that when I got back in town, I would come visit her and talk face-to-face with her about the matter. I didn't know until you told me that Sutton is also a lawyer. I might have my hands full with this deal."

"Don't you think it's strange that she would come to you all the way in Washington to discuss a legal matter with you, while her brother-in-law being a lawyer himself lives just 2 houses down the street?"

"It does seem strange to me, but like I said, I didn't know she had a lawyer in the family."

"Didn't you two used to go out?" asked Langston.

"Yeah, we dated for almost a year until she broke up with me and told me she had found someone else. Hell, I guess that's been about 7 years ago now."

"You know, she's still single. Rumors have it that she's a bit of a nymphomaniac," Langston said winking at Van Acker.

Van Acker, looking around, obviously not feeling at ease talking about his potential client, shifted the direction of the conversation.

"Pam, do you have any of that good country cooking left?"

Pam looked at her husband and they both knew not to press the Knox issue any further now.

"Come on, let's see what we can round up for you."

Pam made Van Acker a platter and he gratefully sat down in front of it and started eating. When he was through he asked Pam how much he owed her and she waived him off saying:

"This one is on the house, my friend. We're just glad you're

13

back."

"Well, I appreciate the gesture. I'm sure, you'll see me around."

"We count on it." Pam said, winking at Van Acker.

"Phil, I've got to ask you something. The old Brannen place, you know, the Victorian house on Main Street, is that house still available?"

"Yeah, there was a couple from Atlanta living in it, but they decided to move back and just put it up for sale about a month ago. You interested?"

"Maybe. Just thought I'd ask."

"See you around buddy."

"See ya, Phil."

2.

Susan Knox was sitting on the couch in her living room. Her mind was not on the magazine in her lap, but on what she was about to start and how it had all begun. At eighteen she had moved out to join the Army, only to return six months later, discouraged and upset with the way she had been treated by senior officers and fellow soldiers as well. She made claims of sexual harassment and of being mistreated. She never did file any official claims to the armed forces and the whole Army ordeal quickly dissipated. When she came back, she did not want to move back into her parent's house and her father agreed to build her an apartment above the four-car garage. The apartment had a kitchen, a bathroom, a bedroom and a living room. The kitchen and living room were one big room divided by a bar, which Susan used as a dinner table. The bedroom was just big enough to fit her queen sized water bed. The apartment was perfect for just her and whomever she might bring home to spend the night. Even though Susan was 30 years old and single, she did not have any trouble attracting companions. She was a petite woman who barely stood 5'2" tall. She had long red hair, green eyes and a milky white skin with many freckles. Her face was delicate and almost sculpted. Her body was shapely and she kept it trim by running at least 5 miles every day. To support herself, she worked as a secretary for Dr. Earl Scarboro, the town's doctor.

Susan was trying to focus on the magazine in her lap when there was a knock on the door. She looked at her watch. Almost 9:30. She was not expecting any visitors this evening. She instinctively grabbed her .380 and walked towards the door.

"Who is it?"

"Let me in Sue, it's me!"

She opened the door and let the man in.

"What in God's name are you doing here at this hour?"

"I had to come see you. I need some relieve!"

"You had another fight?"

The man nodded his head as he dropped himself down on the couch.

"I can't stand that woman anymore! Every time I want to make love to her, she tells me no. I just don't know what to do

15

anymore!"

"Well, I'm sorry, but you knew what she was like when you married her. I still don't see why you went through with that marriage."

"The only reason I married her was because she was so damn proper and churchgoing. It was perfect for my political career."

"And what are the good citizens gonna think when they see you come over here day after day?"

"Sue, I've been coming over here since before I married her, and no one has found out yet. I think I'm damn good."

"Well, I've got some news for you, buster. I don't want you to come around anymore. You wanna visit socially, that's fine. But don't come over here any more pushing your sexual wants and needs on me. I'm not going to do it anymore!"

"You can't do this to me! You can't just kick me out after all these years," he said angrily.

The man stood up walked towards Susan. He took her by the arms and pulled her to him. Susan tried to break loose from his grip.

"I'm telling you, Sue, you can't do this to me. I've got to have you!"

"Let go of me. You don't want me to scream. I promise you, I will!"

Scared suddenly, he let go of her arm. He didn't want her to scream and alarm her parents. With his head down, he walked towards the door. He opened it and looked behind him at Susan.

"Please, Sue, don't cut me loose."

Susan stood by the bar and looked at the man. He was close to tears and it was a pitiful sight. A grown man, a pillar in the community and deacon in his church, standing there close to tears because his mistress cut him loose; she loved it. She finally stood her ground and she loved it. As the man walked down the steps, she ran to the door and decided to stick the dagger deeper into his heart.

"Hey, Tom!" She said, loud enough for him to hear, but low enough so her voice would not carry into her parent's house. "Kiss my sister for me, will you?"

She walked in the house and closed the door. Through the window, she watched as her brother-in-law walked back towards his own house. A smile appeared on Susan's face. Free of number one.

Three to go!

3.

Tom Sutton walked home in disgust. His tall stature seemed small under his plight. He stood just over six feet tall with a medium built body. His hair was thinning fast and gray was appearing around his sideburns. His once lustrous black hair was no longer. At 35, he was starting to loose his youthful appearance. He still had the muscular tone to his body, which had made him popular with the girls while attending college. While in law school, he loved to show off in nothing but sneakers and shorts while playing football or Frisbee with his fraternity brothers. He had a quick mind and a well-trained tongue, and he was never short of female companionship. He excelled in Law School and made his way to the top quickly. He worked for one of the most prominent law firms in Atlanta. Norwick, Chatham & Sloan had been good to him. He passed the bar exam and was well on his way to make partnership with the firm. Then he met Julie Knox. She was the first woman he went out with that did not bed him on the first date. As a matter of fact, she did not bed him till they were married. Julie had a strong moral character. She was a beautiful blonde with a magnificent body. She had big blue eyes and a tanned skin. She made most men turn their head to take a second look. She was the daughter of a peach grower somewhere from around the middle of the State. Sutton knew he wanted to enter politics someday and decided that a proper, churchgoing woman would be perfect to stand by his side. Visiting her hometown, he saw his opportunity to enter into politics on a local basis at an early age. He was not in love with Julie. However, he needed her for his own personal benefit. After 3 years with Norwick, Chatham & Sloan, he left the firm and established T. Sutton, Attorney-at-Law in Stuttgart. He married Julie, became involved with the local Baptist Church, bought one of the grandest houses in town and quickly became a popular figure in Stuttgart. Even though Tom Sutton had not set foot into a church since his parents quit taking him when he was just a teenager did not matter. A skilled talker and quick thinker, he established himself in the church and became a deacon. Soon he was involved in the county and was elected to the Board of Education just 5 years after he settled himself in the community.

Little did the people in Stuttgart know who the true Tom Sutton was. He had many affairs in the 5 years he'd been married. He kept several mistresses, one who was his sister's wife. He had wanted to bed Susan the first time he laid eyes on her. After being in Stuttgart only a couple of weeks, he managed to get Susan by herself and he tried to make the moves on her. Susan, who was willing to sleep with whomever paid her attention, let Sutton have his way with her. By the time he married Julie, Tom Sutton had spent many nights in the arms of Susan. Sutton loved having the proper, strict moral wife, who thought her husband held the same high ethics as she did. He also loved being able to walk down the street at night and make love to her sister. Julie had not turned out in bed the way he had hoped she would. She disliked sex and when they did have sex, it was the same over and over. She would just lie there and close her eyes while he came down on her. He didn't care. After all, she had a wild and wanton sister down the road willing to do and try anything. Thus he kept the affair alive, even though it became more difficult to convince Susan of their relationship. Of late, she had been refusing his advances.

Walking down the street, back to his house, he was confused. For five years, he had been able to get sexual satisfaction any time he wanted it. Now, it was all over. He stopped in the middle of the street and looked back at Susan's home. He shook his head and continued his walk back home. When he reached the house, he walked up the steps of the porch and walked in the door. Julie was sitting in the den, watching television. It was some religious program and Sutton shuddered. Julie called out to him.

"Tom, we need to talk."

Sutton ignored her and walked to the bar where he poured himself a drink.

"Tom, I said we need to talk," insisted Julie.

"What is there to talk about? I would like to be close to my wife and I can't get her in the bedroom!"

"Tom, you know that I don't like it," she said turning away from his stare.

"So what am I supposed to do then? Walk around till I bust? I'm tired of going in the bathroom and talking cold showers, damn it!"

19

"Tom, maybe we should do something about it. Maybe you're right. Tom, I love you. I just don't feel comfortable having sex."

"What do you mean do something about it? I've been telling you for years to do something about it. Get some magazines, books that show you and tell you about sex. Buy a damn Hustler and read the stories in them. They might just turn you on!"

"You know I don't want that filth in my house. I would never stoop so low as to read those magazines."

"Then what do you want to do about it?"

"I was thinking about going to see a marriage counselor. Maybe we can get some help that way. Tom, I don't know why I'm the way I am. Don't you think it hurts me not feeling right about making love to my husband? Don't you think I don't want to make passionate love to you? I know it can't be easy on you. I'm just glad that you're so faithful to me. Many men would have gone somewhere else to satisfy their sexual needs."

Sutton almost spit his drink clear across the room when she mentioned him getting sexual pleasure somewhere else.

Julie continued:

"Please help us to find a solution for this problem, Tom. I want to be a perfect wife for you. I want to bear your children, raise them, and see them grow up, with you. I don't want you to leave me. I love you. Please help me!"

Sutton was dumbfounded. Never before had Julie wanted to talk about the problem. Tonight of all nights, she felt that they needed help. He just stared at her and didn't know what to say. He was just about to respond when the phone rang. Julie answered it.

"Hi Sue, how are you?... I'm fine... Yes, I've been crying... You know, the bad thing... No, I don't think I'm ready to deal with it... No, he doesn't... Tomorrow?... When?... Yeah, I'll be home... OK, see you then."

"What did Sue want?" Sutton asked, feeling uneasy.

"She just wanted to see if I was OK. I called her earlier. I wasn't feeling good and wanted to talk to her. She just called back wanting to know if I felt better."

"What was that about "the bad thing"?" he asked in an investigative tone.

"Sue knows about my... problem with sex. I refer to it as the bad thing. You know, Sue has a problem with it too. Hers works the opposite. She wants it all the time. Isn't that strange?"

Sutton couldn't help turn a shade darker. Quickly, he recomposed himself.

"Really? I didn't know. I mean she has quite an array of men visit her, but I never associated it with wanting sex."

They both remained quite. They looked at each other in silence, each of them with their own thoughts. Julie walked over to Sutton and wrapped her arms around him.

"Let's go to bed, honey. I... I want to make you happy tonight."

Sutton swallowed hard. He knew what was to follow. He didn't say a word but took his wife by the hand and let her upstairs to the bedroom. Twenty minutes later, the lights dimmed.

4.

After leaving the gas station, Dimitri Van Acker drove back into town. He had arranged with Kelly Murphy to spend a couple of nights over at her place till he could find a place of his own. She had given him directions over the phone and he drove straight to her house. Kelly lived in a double-wide mobile home about three miles from her parent's house. Kelly was 24 years old. She was the oldest daughter of Allen and Helen Murphy. Van Acker had lived with the Murphy's while he was attending law school at Mercer University in Macon. They had treated Van Acker as one of their own. Van Acker had grown found of Kelly whom he considered his sister. He treated Michelle with the same respect; however, their relationship was not as intense as with Kelly. Kelly was a beautiful young woman with short brunette hair, a small round face with brown eyes and small pouty lips. She was about 5'4" with a slender body. At twenty two she had moved out of her parent's house. She worked full-time for Tom Sutton and went to college part-time.

Van Acker honked the horn as he drove up in the driveway. Kelly Murphy opened the door and ran out to meet Van Acker. He barely had enough time to get out of the car.

"Dimitri, hey! How are you?"

She wrapped her arms around his neck and hugged him. Van Acker in turn put his arms around her waist and returned the favor. He gently kissed her on the forehead.

"Hi, sis, I'm doing fine. How are you?"

"Great, now that you are here!" I've wanted to see you for so long. Gosh, I can't believe you're finally here."

"Well, I must say, it's good to be back."

"Come in, I've got some supper cooked up."

Van Acker looked surprised but didn't say anything. He was not about to get Kelly upset and tell her he already ate.

"All right, let me just get my suitcase out of the trunk. I'll be right there."

"Okay, I'll be making you a plate."

As Van Acker got his luggage out of the car, a Sheriff's patrol car drove by. Van Acker looked towards the car. He could see a woman deputy Sheriff behind the wheel. The car slowed down.

The deputy looked in his direction. There was recognition. The car stopped, backed up and drove up into the driveway. The deputy stepped out of the car.

"Dimitri, is that you?"

"Hope! How are you?"

"I'm fine. When did you get back?"

"I got back today."

"Gee, I don't know what to say. It's been so long."

"Yeah, it has been a long time; perhaps too long."

"Are you for real? Do you really mean that?"

"Hope, I know you had a crush on me when I still lived here. I must admit that I always liked you."

"You never let on that you liked me. Why?"

"Well, I don't know. I enjoyed going out with you, but you were mostly gone for months at a time. Remember, you had a career in the Navy."

"Yes, I did. I got out as soon as my six years were up. When I came back, you were gone. They said you went to Washington, DC to play big city lawyer."

"I did. I'm sorry I never got back in touch with you. I lost touch with my roots here in Stuttgart. It took some time before I realized that I had been a jerk not contacting anybody back here. But now, I'm back."

"Well, I'm glad that you're back. Listen, I've got to get back on the road. Where can I reach you?"

"I'll be staying with Kelly for a couple of days. Hopefully by then, I can find a place of my own. If I'm not here, just ask Kelly where I'm at. She'll let you know where to find me."

"All right, maybe we can get together and pick up where we left off, if you don't mind, that is?"

"I was hoping that you'd be around and single."

"Well, I'm around and single. I'll see ya." Hope laughed and got back into her car.

"Bye, Hope."

Kelly had walked out the door and silently watched Hope and Van Acker. She smiled at Van Acker when he turned around to walk into the house.

"See you got a date already."

"Yeah, I'm kinda glad that she's still single. I really liked that girl. I still have her picture with me from when we went out together. Can you believe that?"

Kelly didn't answer but instead changed the subject.

"Com'on, let's get something to eat."

Van Acker sat down and ate his second meal of the evening. They were quite and didn't say much, both enjoying each other's company. He couldn't finish his plate and apologized for it explaining that driving all day make it to where he couldn't digest food too good. Kelly shrugged it off. He helped her with the dishes.

"Kelly, what do you know about Susan Knox?"

"Susan? Why?"

"She wrote me a letter when I was still in Washington. I called her and she told me that she needed some legal advise."

"Dimitri, her brother-in-law is a lawyer. I work for him. Mom works for him. Why doesn't she go see him for legal advise?"

"Yes, I found that out tonight at Langston's."

"You went to see Pam and Phil?"

"Well, I had to get gas for the car. I saw Michelle there. She's become quite the young woman."

"Yes, she has."

"Anyways, what about Susan?"

"All I know is that she works for Dr. Scarboro. The rumor is that she has no lack for male companionship. You know what I mean?"

"Okay, so she gets around. Otherwise, there's not much there, right?"

"No, not really. I do know that Michelle doesn't like her. Susan has made the moves on Michelle's boyfriend a couple of times."

"Who's Michelle's boyfriend?"

"Bryan Scarboro, Dr. Scarboro's son."

"I guess she met him at work?"

"Yes. Right now he's home for the summer. He goes to Columbia School of Medicine. Michelle just started dating him this summer. Mom and dad don't approve of her dating him because he's seven years older than her."

"Seven years? What has gotten into Michelle?"

"I don't know, but I know that he's not good for her. He's toying with her. He knows that she's young and attractive and I guess he's trying to get into her panties so he can brag about it when he goes back up North to school. I know that he was at Susan's the other night. I came back from going to the movies with a friend and his car was over at her house."

"So Bryan is playing it more than one way."

"You could say that."

"Does Michelle now about Bryan and Susan?"

"She does. She was all upset about it last week. He had canceled a date with her, saying that he was tired and would go to bed early. Later that night, Michelle and a friend drove through town and saw his car at Susan's house. He told her that they were going over some records from his dad's practice when she confronted him."

"Did she believe him?"

"I don't know if she did or not. All I know is that she needs to stay away from him. He's trouble."

"Well, that gives me little to go on. I guess I will have to play it by ear. I have a meeting with her tomorrow."

"You don't play around, do you? One day in town and the practice is booming," she said punching him in the arm.

"Listen, Kelly, have you thought about my offer. I would like you to be my secretary. I probably won't have much to do at first, but I sure could use some help getting started. I'm thinking about buying the old Brannen place. If I remember correctly, there's a big room in the front that I could make into my office and I could remodel it to where I could have a waiting room across the hall."

"Dimitri, I've thought about it. The answer is yes. I want to get away from Tom Sutton so bad. He's been trying to make the moves on me. That hypocrite, I swear. He sits in the front pew in church and sings Hallelujah, but at night he prowls the streets. He thinks nobody knows. There are plenty of people that know that he sleeps around. Poor Julie, I don't know why she wants to stay with him."

"Well, I'm glad you decided to come join me. If you want to you can go ahead and give Mr. Sutton your notice and by then hopefully, I have the house and my furniture from Virginia will have come in."

25

"I'm looking forward to working with you, Mr. Van Acker," Kelly joked. What you gonna name the practice?"

"I think I'll call it "Van Acker, Esquire"."

"I like that."

Van Acker looked at his watch. It was close to midnight.

"Listen, Kelly, I think I will turn in. It's been a long day. I'll see you in the morning."

"Good night, Dimitri."

Van Acker kissed her on the forehead and gave her a hug.

"I love you."

"I love you too, Dimitri."

Each went to the respective bedrooms. Before he turned of the light, Van Acker wrote down some notes in his logbook. This promised to be an interesting adventure.

5.

The morning sun woke Susan Knox. It was Saturday. Even though it was the weekend, she still had to go to work. Dr. Scarboro was open on Saturday mornings, a service to the town he had started when he first opened his practice. Besides work, she had a full day ahead of her. Dimitri Van Acker was supposed to come by today and go over her legal problems with her. She had to go see her sister, and she had to get rid of Bryan Scarboro. These thoughts filled her mind as she took a shower, put on her make-up and got dressed. She put on a conservative dress. She had to look proper to meet Dimitri. In the kitchen she grabbed a banana and walked out the door. When she reached the bottom of the steps, her father walked out of his house.

"Good morning, Susan."

"Good morning, father. How are you this morning?" she said in a cold tone.

"I'm all right; getting ready for my morning jog."

"Well, have fun. I've gotta run. See ya later!"

Susan got in her car and drove off, leaving her father in a cloud of dust.

"Damned woman," James Knox mumbled half loud.

Susan worked as Earl Scarboro's secretary. She kept up with his appointments, ordering supplies, billing the patients, filing insurance claims, and taking care of collections. She had worked for Dr. Scarboro for about four years now. In the morning when she got to work, she made a pot of coffee, brought in the newspaper and put it on Dr. Scarboro's desk. She then started going through the previous day's patients and entered their information into the computer. Those who had not paid yet were printed a statement. Next came filing insurance claims. That was the bulk of the work. A lot of the patients would not have medical insurance and could not afford to pay the doctor's bill, and would file through Medicare and Medicaid. Filling in and reviewing the Medicare and Medicaid forms kept her busy the rest of the morning. Once the patients arrived, Susan had to concentrate between doing her paperwork and making sure the patients filled out the proper forms. In the afternoon, when the mail had come, she would sort the mail, and mark the payments. She would review the statements that were supposed to have been paid by that day. Then she would write reminders to those patients who had not yet paid. Most patients paid within the allotted time, however once and a while some needed a reminder. And yet others needed to be threatened with their statements being handled by a collection agency. Dr. Scarboro let her leave to go home around 2:30. That would give her time to go by the bank and make the deposit for the day. After Susan left, Dr. Scarboro's wife Mary filled in for a couple of hours.

Today was a little different. Bryan Scarboro, Earl Scarboro's son was supposed to be assisting his father. Bryan was in his second year of Medical School. He was going for his general practitioner's degree. During the summer, he helped his father, whenever he felt like it. When Susan arrived at the office, she started her routine. She went into the kitchen to make coffee. Busy with her task, she did not hear the door to the kitchen close. With her back to the door, she could not see the man approaching her from behind. Susan finished putting everything in the coffeemaker and turned the unit on. The man was standing right behind her, less than a foot away. Susan turned and screamed. The man quickly put his hand over her mouth.

"Will you shut up!" the man said.

Susan, recognizing who it was, composed herself and nodded yes.

"What do you think you're doing?" she said, noticeable agitated.

"I thought I'd surprise you," the man said.

"Well, you got what you wanted. Just be happy that I recognized you in time and didn't hurt you. I would hate to have to risk your chances of fatherhood."

"Don't worry. You wouldn't hurt me."

"Don't count on it. Move!" she said pushing the man out of the way.

Susan went into the waiting room and unlocked the door. She walked onto the front porch and picked up the newspaper. When she walked back in, the man was sitting behind her desk.

"Bryan, what do you think you're doing?"

"I bet my father doesn't even know how to work one of those." He pointed at the computer.

"Don't bet on it. Your father knows exactly what goes on in

that computer. He's the one who showed me how to use the program when we first got it. Don't underestimate him."

"Susan," he got up and took her hand in his. She pulled her hand back. "Are we still on for tonight?"

"As far as I know, we are."

"Good, I've got a surprise for you."

"As a matter of fact, I have one for you too."

"Do I have to wait until tonight to find out what it is?"

"Bryan, would it be a surprise if I told you now that it was?"

"All right, I'll wait."

"Are you going to help your father today?"

"No, I don't feel like it today. I stayed up too late last night. You know what I mean?"

"Well, if you're not going to work, I suggest that you let me do my job and get out of here."

"Wanna get rid of me? All right, I can take a hint. I'll see you tonight at seven."

"Bye, Bryan."

Bryan Scarboro left his father's practice. Susan shook her head. She wasn't looking forward to tonight.

6.

When Dimitri Van Acker woke up, it was well into the morning. He looked at his watch. 9:36; he rubbed his eyes and got up out of bed. He looked out the window. Kelly had already left to go to work. Even though it was Saturday, Sutton made her work a half day. Was it possible that he had that much work? Van Acker seriously doubted that he did. Since he was the only one in the house, he walked into the living room in his underwear. He turned on the television and searched for a news channel. Living in the country, Kelly did not have cable. Obviously, she could not afford satellite as the only channels he found were the three networks. Cartoons on all three! In disgust, he turned the television set of. He made his way into the kitchen. On the table was a note.

> *"Dear Dimitri,*
> *I've gone to work.*
> *Please make yourself at home.*
> *I have cereal in the cabinet above the stove.*
> *There's milk in the fridge.*
> *I'll be back this afternoon.*
> *I love you,*
> *Kelly."*

Van Acker smiled and pushed the note aside. Cereal! He couldn't remember the last time he had eaten cereal. In DC, he would have breakfast in the café on the main floor of the building where he worked. Once in while, he would have a business meeting over breakfast; but cereal was not a breakfast item on his menu. He was hungry and decided to try his luck anyway. He opened the cupboard and found about six different kinds of cereal. He chose the one he thought to have the most sugar in it. He needed to get started. He had a meeting with Susan Knox at four. He also needed to stop by the farm and see Allen Murphy. Van Acker sat at the table staring in front of him while eating his breakfast. He was putting his schedule into his mental memory bank. He finished his breakfast, put the dish in the sink and washed it out. He got his personal items out of his suitcase and checked out the bathroom.

He took a shower, shaved and got dressed. It was a hot summer day and when Van Acker walked out, the heat overwhelmed him. It was almost lunch time and it felt like 100 degrees outside. Instantly, Van Acker could feel sweat forming on his body. He got in his car and turned the A/C to max.

"I should have stayed up North," he said out loud.

He made his way into town and turned onto Main Street. If he remembered right, the Brannen house was located at the edge of the city limits. He slowly drove towards his destination. Soon he saw the house. It was as grand as he'd remembered. It was a late 19th century Victorian style house. It was two stories high with a high-pitched roof. It had a wrap around porch with two round areas that protruded from the rest of the porch. The round areas had their own roof over them. There was elaborate detailed woodwork on the porch. The house extended back onto the property and had been in the Brannen family since it was built. When Mrs. Brannen died about seven years ago, the house was put up for sale. Since then the wood siding had not been painted and was visibly peeling. Some of the screens in the windows were torn and a few shutters were missing. Van Acker stopped in front of the house. He looked at the "For Sale" sign. Miller and Jones, Realtors. He wrote down the phone number. The Realtors were from Macon. He reached for his cell phone. It wasn't there. He then realized that he had taken it out of his car the night before and forgot to bring it along. He'd see if Allen Murphy would let him use the phone to contact them.

When he was ready to leave, he looked in his back mirror to see if anyone was coming and noticed a white Cadillac parked behind him. The driver stepped out of the car and walked over to Van Acker's car. The driver of the Cadillac was tall and had thinning hair. He was clean cut and despite the heat of the summer, wearing a two-peace suit. Van Acker was cautious and quickly pulled his .45 from underneath the seat. He had made a special scabbard that held his handgun under his seat. Without much trouble he could grab the gun and have it in his lap when he needed it. A few times, it had saved him from being mugged. The man tapped on the driver side window. Van Acker lowered his window, stopping about two inches from the top, enough so he could hear what the man had to say; but also to be secure should the stranger try to reach inside the car.

"Tom Sutton is the name."

Van Acker wasn't surprised. He was sure Kelly must have turned in her resignation already and must have mentioned starting to work for him. Sutton was egocentric from what Pam Langston had told him. He must have felt threatened and wanted to check out his competition. Van Acker planned on playing the game along.

"Nice to meet you, Tom. You don't mind me calling you Tom, do you?" Van Acker made a point to make sure Sutton noticed the .45 being put on the passenger seat.

"No, not at all. And you are?"

"Oh, I'm sorry. Seems I've lost all my manners. Dimitri Van Acker, principal of "Van Acker, Esquire".

"I thought so. I can tell you right now, Van Acker," Tom Sutton said, pointing a finger at Van Acker. "You don't stand a chance in this town. There is no room for the two of us. You will go back to DC with your tail between your legs."

"Well, I'm glad we got that straight. But, I think I'll give it a shot anyway. I've already got one client."

Van Acker was contemplating telling Sutton about his appointment with Susan Knox.

"One client? You'll need more than that to make it!" Sutton chuckled.

"Hey, I've gotta start somewhere. From what I understand, you had to get married to a well-known local gal to get your practice started. Seems I've got one up on you. My client didn't even know I was moving back here. You know, you might not be as popular as you think you are, Sutton."

Sutton's face reddened, his eyes turned into slits, and the smile disappeared from his face. Van Acker took advantage of the situation.

"Well, Tom, it was a pleasure meeting you. I've got a house to buy. See you around."

Van Acker drove off; leaving Sutton standing bewildered on the side of the road.

"I'll get you, Van Acker! Don't think you can just waltz right in here and take over. I'll show you!" Sutton shouted at the car.

A couple of pedestrians walked by and looked at Sutton with wondering eyes. Sutton realized what a spectacle he was making of himself and made his way back to his car and sped off.

7.

"Mom, I'm telling you, I know what I'm doing!"

"I don't know. He'll have a hard time getting started against Mr. Sutton."

"I know he will. But think about it, if he doesn't get support from the people he trusts and counts on, he will not make it for sure."

"I know what you mean. I hope you're making the right decision."

"I am, mom."

Helen Murphy looked at her daughter with admiring eyes. She was taking a big step going to work for Dimitri Van Acker. Leaving her job at Sutton's would probably mean a pay cut. That's what Helen was afraid of. Working for Sutton gave her a chance to make more than she would anywhere else in town. And now, she decided to go work for Van Acker. She hoped her daughter was making the right decision.

Helen Murphy was 43 years old. She was of average height and was medium built. Giving birth to two children had given her a little bit of a stomach, but she had been able to keep it to a minimum. She had hazelnut brown hair that started showing some gray. The last six years had been rough. Her husband's farm had suffered during the latest recession and they needed some extra income. She had made the decision to go back to work. Tom Sutton had been looking for a legal aid and she took on the challenge. She was making enough to help her husband with the bills during the difficult times. When the farm started recovering from the recession, she decided to stay on with Tom Sutton. He had told her that she had become an integral part of his business and that she was doing an excellent job in helping him prepare his cases. Tom Sutton also offered her daughter Kelly a job as his secretary. Kelly had thought long and hard about starting to work for Sutton. In the end she decided that it would give her an opportunity to get some of her bills taken care off and maybe enroll in the local college. From there she would see where life would take her. Helen had encouraged her daughter to come work for Sutton. Even though her husband didn't think that mother and daughter working together was going to work out, they beat the odds and treated each other as co-workers rather

33

than mother and daughter. They left their work at work and when they went home, they starting acting as mother and daughter again.

This morning was different. When Kelly Murphy had pulled her mother to the side and told her about her decision to quit Sutton's and to go work for Dimitri Van Acker, a look of worry swept over Helen's face. Helen had tried to persuade her daughter to change her mind. She was sure Van Acker would understand if she decided not to work for him. He would find someone else as his secretary. There were other women out there looking for a chance. But Kelly had stood firm. She told her mother that she worked for Sutton for the money, and she didn't like Tom Sutton. Helen did not understand why and Kelly said that this was not the time or place to discuss why she didn't like Sutton. She would tell her mother later. After their talk, Kelly continued to type up her resignation. She had given it to Sutton when he had asked her to type something for him. He had retreated to his office. A few minutes later he came back out and asked Kelly why she was quitting and whom she was going to work for. Kelly told Sutton about Van Acker's offer and that she had taken him up on it. Without saying so much as a word in response, Sutton left the office distracted.

Helen came over to her daughter's desk.

"I think that upset him."

"Which part, the part that I'm leaving or the part that he's getting competition?"

"Kelly? What's wrong? Tom is a good man, a good employer. You should appreciate that!"

"Yeah, I should appreciate it. I wonder if you would still appreciate him if you truly knew him, mom."

"What do you mean?"

"Honestly mom, has he ever made a move on you?"

"No! How can you say that? He's a happily married man!"

"Mon, wake up! He's not the faithful husband he wants everyone to believe he is. He screws around. He's even tried to make a move on me."

"Stop it, Kelly! It can't possibly be true. Not Tom!"

"Remember when he called me in the office a couple of weeks ago. How long was I in his office? Twenty minutes! It took him five minutes to dictate the letter he wanted me to type. The rest of the time he was making the moves on me. Commenting about how gorgeous I looked that day. How he loved the way my hair was making my face look like an angel. How my dress made my body curves come out so perfect. He wanted to know what I was doing that evening, if I had any plans. I just had to let him know, he would arrange to come over and appreciate those curves. That's when I walked out. That's when I decided to work for Dimitri."

"Kelly, is everything you just told me true?"

"Is what true, mother? That he made the moves on me and tried to get in the bed with me? Yes, it's true! And it is true for countless other women around here. And why do you think he wants us to work this weekend? The case he's working on is not coming up for another couple of weeks. I think he's looking for a date. And you'll be the one he'll approach. Mark my words!"

Helen sunk down in her chair, put her elbows on her desk and dropped her head in her hands. All color had drained from her face.

"Kelly, I need to know for sure. I need to know if he really is like you say he is. Not that I think you're lying about it, but sometimes actions, words, can be misinterpreted."

"All right, mom. Let's set him up!"

"Okay, let set him up. And if what you say is true, then I'm walking out with you."

"Thanks mom. That would mean a lot to me. And if you walk with me, I think I'll write an article in the Gazette about Tom's excesses."

"Make sure you have evidence or he might just sue you for libel. You know, he'll blame Dimitri for all of this. Make sure that before you write any articles or do anything to attack his character, you talk to Dimitri. Let him know what's going on."

Helen looked at Kelly with wondering eyes.

"Kelly, how do you feel about Dimitri?"

Kelly chuckled.

"How do I feel about Dimitri?" A smile developed on her face. "I don't know. I guess I still look at him like I would a brother."

"I was just wondering. He has been gone for a while, and... Well, you know..."

"Yeah, I know. I must admit that I do feel attracted to him. But I don't know if the feeling is mutual." "You know, Kelly, I love that he'll be back in town, but I still haven't figured out why he wants to come back here to practice law. He's not going to make half of what he would where he was."

"Maybe money is not his biggest concern. Maybe he wasn't happy doing what he was doing. Maybe he felt trapped in the big money world and wanted his freedom back. Maybe he's tired of being played like a puppet. I don't know. But he told me last night that he's tired of being a defense lawyer for murderers and drug dealers, no matter how much money there is to be made from it."

"I just hope it won't throw our lives into too much distress."

"What do you mean? I was going to leave here anyway. I have an application in over at TRW. They are looking for skilled computer analysts. I have two more semesters left in school and I'll have my degree. Whether Dimitri showed up or not, I was going to leave."

Helen walked over to Kelly and gave her a hug.

"Honey, I hope that whatever you do, you do the right thing. Now let's get ready to set Mr. Sutton up and see if he's really what you say he is."

Kelly hugged her mother and smiled.

"You'll see."

8.

It was right at 12 o'clock when Dimitri Van Acker drove up to the big white farmhouse of the Murphy's. Allen Murphy's truck, an older model green and gray Dodge Ram, was parked by the hanger where he kept his tools and equipment. Van Acker got out of his car and walked the short distance to the hanger. The hood of the truck was raised. Murphy was doing some mechanic work to the truck.

"Mr. Murphy?" Van Acker said with a very official tone to his voice.

Murphy raised himself from underneath the hood and looked at the man addressing him.

"I'll be damned. Dimitri! How are you doing fella?"

"I'm all right, how about yourself, you old rascal?"

"I can't complain. You look good."

"Thanks. You don't look so bad yourself. Lost some weight since the last time I saw you."

"I've been needing to loose some weight. Got to where I just didn't feel good anymore."

"So how are things around here?"

"Things are just about the same as before you left. We're doing better here at the farm. Chicken prices finally picked up some, plus I've been able to pay off most of my debts. I'd say, we're finally sticking our head above water."

"Man, I'm glad to hear that."

The conversation stopped for a moment as both men thought about the next part of the conversation. Murphy broke the silence.

"Dimitri, from talking with Kelly, I understand that you're going to open a practice here in town. Tell me something, what kind of law is it you'll be handling?"

"Well, I hope to be handling some land cases, land disputes, title searches and the likes. But if the need arises to take on other civil matters like divorce and God forbid, murder, then I'm geared for it. Hell, drug and murder cases where about all I handled in D.C."

"So you passed the bar exam here in Georgia?"

"Yep, I passed the bar in Georgia before I left to go to D.C. I had an offer from a law firm in Atlanta, but they weren't what I was looking for. I had wanted to move up North and D.C. looked pretty good. Besides that, I was hoping to get involved in some politics there, but after getting my butt kicked a couple of times I've decided to come here and try my luck in small-town USA."

"You thinking about running for office around here?"

"Hell, Allen, I don't know. Do you reckon I stand a chance? We've got big shot lawyer Sutton to content with. Ain't he the big political hero around here?"

"Hey, listen, I didn't vote for him! Helen may be working for him and think that he's the best thing since sliced bread; but I know a little bit more about his comings and goings to know better. I'm sure you'll find out soon enough."

"Well, I've had a run in with him earlier this morning."

"You did? Where at?"

"I was over at the old Brannen house writing down the Realtor's phone number when Sutton came up to my car. He said I wouldn't make it in town as long as he was around."

"Sounds like Sutton. You know, he thinks he's the only one that can handle the law around here. And he has many folks convinced. He's got a slick tongue and a quick mind. He'd be perfect for a used car salesman."

"I guess you could say he's made from the same wood as our President, right?"

"Don't even get me started on him!"

They both started laughing. President Woodbury was as slick as they came and was able to talk his way out of any scandal he got involved in. The list was long, but the most recent one had him in a bit of trouble and the Republican Congress was trying hard to get him impeached. How he was going to get out of having sex with an intern inside the Oval Office remained to be seen.

"Allen, listen, do you mind if I go use the phone? I'd like to call the Realtor about the Brannen house. I really would like to get my hands on it."

"Go right ahead. You know where the phone is."

"Thanks, Allen... Hey, Allen, do you want to get some lunch at Langston's then?"

Murphy thought for a moment.

38

"Be glad too. Give me a couple of minutes here to get the truck back together, and I'll be ready to go then."

Van Acker went inside the house. It had not changed a bit since he lived with the Murphy's. Everything was still as spotless as ever. Everything had its place and nothing was out of place. He couldn't understand how Helen did it. Working full-time and keeping a tidy house like this. He grabbed the cordless phone and sat down at the kitchen table. He dialed the number.

"Yes, my name is Dimitri Van Acker. I'm interested in the house you have for sale in Stuttgart on Main Street."

"Are you talking about the old Victorian house, sir?"

"Yes, that's the one. I was wondering if I could have a walk-through?"

"And when would be convenient for you, sir?"

"I guess as soon as possible. How does this afternoon sound?"

"Hold on just a minute, let me check the schedule."

Van Acker looked around the kitchen while he was waiting for the voice on the other end of the phone to come back. Lot's of memories came back as he absorbed the surroundings. He had lived with the Murphy's for four years. Four years, he had been part of the family. It had been four good years. He remembered birthday parties and holiday gatherings. He remembered Kelly coming home one night from a date, when he was up late studying for a test. She had tears and mascara running down her face. She had sat down and told him that her boyfriend had broken up with her that night. He had taken her in his arms and comforted her. He had been a brother and best friend that night. From that moment on, Kelly had come to him with all her problems. He was part of every relationship, every broken heart, her loss of virginity, everything, whether he wanted to be part of it or not. Van Acker smiled. They had been good years.

"Sir?" the voice on the other end of the phone was back.

"Yes, I'm still here."

"Mr. Jones can meet you at 3 o'clock, would that work out for you?"

"Three would be perfect. I'll meet him at the house. Thank you much."

"Thank you."

Van Acker hung up the phone. He sat at the table and stared in front of him.

"I sure hope I'm making the right decision," he said half loud.

He had failed to see Murphy come in the house.

"Don't tell me you're having second thought about taking me out for lunch! I'm mighty hungry."

Van Acker jumped.

"Allen, I... I didn't hear you come in." He looked flustered.

"Are you alright?" Murphy asked worried.

"Yeah... yeah, you just surprised me. I was thinking out loud"

"Come on. Let's go get some dinner. We'll talk there."

Murphy put his hand on Van Acker's shoulder and squeezed gently. The gesture made Van Acker feel better. He knew that no matter what, Allen would always be a listening ear and source of advice.

9.

It was after lunch when Tom Sutton returned to his office. He had driven around town worrying about Dimitri Van Acker. He just couldn't understand why a successful defense lawyer from Washington D.C. would come and establish himself in the backwoods of Stuttgart. Sure he had ties around here, but even so, he had to start his business from the ground up. With him as his competition, he would have a hard time. The people loved him. Sutton smiled as he walked into his office.

"Good afternoon, Tom," Helen Murphy said as he walked in.

"Good afternoon, Helen. Still here?" he asked as he looked at his watch.

"Yes sir, I decided to catch up on some paperwork."

"Do I have any messages?"

"No, it's been a quiet morning."

"I guess Kelly is already gone? She was supposed to type up some reports for me."

"She left about lunch time. I think she'll be back later this afternoon to finish those reports for you."

"Well, anyhow. It doesn't matter. Today is her last day anyway. I hope she realizes that she'll be back knocking at my door begging for her job. I just hope that she hasn't been replaced by then."

"I hope not. I hope Dimitri can do well here. There should be enough room for the both of you."

"That's where you're wrong, my dear. There is only room from one lawyer around here, and it's me. That Van Acker fellow will realize that soon enough."

Sutton made his way into his office. He shut the door behind him. He had been so preoccupied with Dimitri Van Acker that he failed to notice that Helen was not wearing the same outfit as she had that morning.

Helen hurried to the backdoor. There, Kelly was patiently waiting. Helen and Kelly had planned for Helen to be by herself when she tried to see if Tom would make the moves on her. Kelly had hurried to her mother's house and picked out a short black skirt, a white see through blouse and a pair of black seamed nylons. She had quickly run by her house and picked up her miniature tape recorder and soft cloth elastic garter belt that Kelly had rigged up to hold the tape recorder.

"Come on in, he's in his office."

"I heard him carry on about Dimitri and how I'll be back begging for my job."

"I hope he's wrong."

"I hope I'm right."

Helen's face went gray.

"Come on, Mom," Kelly whispered, noticing the concerned look on her mother's face.

"It's show time."

Kelly gave Helen the miniature tape recorder and the cloth belt.

"Put the garter belt around your thigh. It's got elastic in it so it will stay in place. Then put the tape recorder here in this little pocket. Now, listen Mom, those top two buttons are the one's that you need to push in for the tape recorder to start working."

Kelly pointed at the record and play buttons.

"The recorder is set to activate only when there's sound. So only your conversation with Tom will be on the tape."

Helen raised her skirt and put the garter belt on. She made sure it sat snug up against her body. She then put the tape recorder in the little pocket on the inside off her thigh. She lowered her skirt.

"Perfect. You can't tell you're carrying a recorder. Now, just before you walk in, raise your skirt and push the buttons down."

"Okay, I know how to do that. I just hope this will work."

"It will, Mom. I will walk outside and call you on my cell phone. Then you'll go in to his office and tell him I'm not coming back and that you will have to get his notes to type up the reports. When he's through dictating the reports, ask him if there's anything else. Make sure, when you get up that you're leaning over some and show him your cleavage. He won't be able to resist!"

"I don't know, Kelly. Do you really think he'll make a pass on me?"

"Yes, especially if you tell him that you'll be home by yourself tonight, that Dad is going to the ball game, he won't be able to keep his hands to himself."

"We'll see. Now, go and get out of here."

"I'll be outside when you need me."

"Okay."

Kelly made her way out the door and ran to her car, which was parked a block away from Tom Sutton's office. She opened the door and grabbed her cell phone. She dialed Sutton's office number. Helen answered it on the first ring. As planned, Kelly would not come back that afternoon. Helen hung up the phone and swallowed hard. She waited five minutes for Kelly to make it back to the office. When the muffled knock on the door came, Helen knew it was time. She got up and walked to Sutton's office.

"Here goes nothing," she whispered.

She knocked on the door.

"Come in."

Helen pulled up her skirt, pushed the correct buttons on the tape recorder, and straightened her skirt back out and walked into Sutton's office.

"Yes," Sutton said, without looking up from what he was doing.

"Eh, I, eh, just got a call from Kelly. She, eh, said that she, eh, won't be back this afternoon."

"Oh. Why?"

"I, eh, asked her, but she, eh, didn't give me a clear reason. She, eh, seemed confused on the phone. Since she won't be back, I guess that I'll take down the notes for your reports."

Sutton finally looked up from his notes. His eyes moved up and down over Helen's body. Hmm, not exactly a super model. Not bad though. A little heavy around the waist. Not too much. Hell, why not. She might be wild and desperate like most married women were. He licked his dry lips.

"Are you ready to take down the notes now?"

"Yes sir, if you're ready."

"Well, let start."

Sutton grabbed a stack of papers from the tray on his desk and sorted through them while Helen grabbed her notepad and pen. She was nervous. She sat down in front of Sutton's desk and crossed her legs. Her skirt being short, it crawled up her thighs as she sat down. With her legs crossed, she was showing Sutton more than she

43

wanted. But she had to be sure. Sutton started dictating his reports. Outside the window to his office, Kelly was looking in. She was praying this would work and she could convince her mother that Sutton was a womanizer and always looking for his next kick.

It took about 15 minutes for Helen to take down Sutton's notes. She got up. Accidentally she dropped her pen. This was not part of the plan, but it gave her an excuse to bend over without having to be obvious. She bent through her knees to pick up the pen. As she lowered herself, Sutton raised himself out of his chair and leaned forward over the desk just enough to be able to look down her blouse. He licked his lips again. He liked what he saw. He lowered himself as quickly as he had gotten up. Helen got up and bent over to straighten her skirt.

"Helen?"

Helen felt the blood rush to her head as her heartbeat sped up.

"Yes, Tom?"

"Are you and Allen doing something tonight?"

Not expecting the question, Helen had trouble finding her words.

"I... I don't think that... eh." She composed herself. "Actually, I'll be home by myself. Allen is going to the Braves' game in Atlanta. And Michelle, well, she'll probably have a date or go out with some of her friends. Why?"

"I was just wondering. Thought we might get together or something. You know, you and Allen and Julie and I. Maybe play some cards?"

"That would be great. Maybe some other time?"

Helen was turning to walk out the door.

"Wait, Helen. Why don't you sit back down? I'd like to have a little conversation with you."

Helen's heart started to race again. She turned around and made it back to the chair. She sat down. As she did, she watched Sutton's eyes closely. They were focused on her thighs, specifically where her skirt was crawling up on her legs. She could only imagine that her panties were showing and that Tom was drooling over the view he was getting. She hoped that he would not notice the tape recorder strapped to the inside off her thigh. She closed her eyes. How was she going to continue? Kelly had been right. She looked up and found Sutton's eyes.

"Tell me, Helen. How is it; or rather how was it, to have two children? Was it hard to raise them?"

"Well, it was hard at times. But it was worth every minute. I must say that I'm lucky and have two good children that have not given me too much trouble while growing up."

"To me, most mothers who give birth to a couple of children, have a hard time keeping their bodies in shape. But look at you, I mean, you don't show that you bore two children. How did you do it?"

"Tom, I don't know where this conversation is going. I don't feel comfortable talking about this."

"I'm sorry. I guess this is personal. But the reason I'm asking, Julie and I are trying hard to get a baby, and we have all these questions."

"Perhaps I should talk to Julie about how to keep a body in shape after delivering babies."

"I told her that but she said that she doesn't feel comfortable talking about that with other people. She asked me if I could ask you."

"Well, I don't know, I feel uncomfortable talking about it with you."

Sutton got up from behind his desk and walked around to where Helen was sitting. He positioned himself behind her and put his hands on her shoulders.

"Now, Helen, you know there's nothing to be uncomfortable about."

He started massaging her shoulders. Kelly who was looking in was getting furious. She should have grabbed her father's camcorder to record this.

Helen was moving back and forth in her chair. She felt more nervous than ever. She hoped that Kelly was nearby because if Sutton made a move to fondle her, she would scream for help.

"Tell me, Helen," Sutton asked in a low voice bringing his mouth closer to her ear, "does this make you feel more relaxed?"

All Helen could do was nodding her head.

"I enjoy giving a beautiful woman like you a relaxing massage. There's nothing better for the senses."

"I don't think this is proper, Tom."

"Let me be the judge of that. I want to talk some more. Talk about how you keep that body of yours in shape, the way you keep your breasts so firm. Did you breast-feed? I bet you did."

His hands were moving away from Helen's shoulders and making their way to her breasts. Helen was frozen. She thought she would be able to react, but she was frozen.

"Why don't you stand up, Helen. I'd like to admire that shapely body."

Helen hesitated but slowly got up. At least his hands were away from her breasts. She looked towards the window. She hoped Kelly was there, close by, and ready to come in when she needed her.

"Now, let me take a look. You know, Allen is a lucky bastard, and to think that he'll be away tonight. What will you do? What will you do to get satisfied? I tell you, I'll be glad to come over and see if I can help you out with that."

Helen realized that it was time to get out. She started walking towards the door. Sutton grabbed her by the arm.

"You don't know what you're missing. I've been eyeing you for a long time now. I thought that you'd swing around. I guess I was wrong. But please, don't let that affect your professional opinion of me."

His eyes were small and he had a smile on his face.

"Why don't you take the rest of the day off? Consider my offer for tonight. You have my number. I'll be glad to come over and keep you company and let you fill me in on breast-feeding and other exercises that keep your body trim."

Helen was crying. She pulled away from his grip and hurried out the door. She grabbed her purse and rushed out into the street. Outside, she looked for Kelly. She didn't see her. Helen ran to her car and reaching it, leaned up against the door and vomited. Kelly came running from behind the building.

"Mom, are you alright?"

Helen just shook her head affirmatively as she tried to compose herself.

"Now do you believe me? Now do you see what an animal he is? We've got to stop him, mom."

"I know sweetheart, I know. But he's slick; he'll make it

46

seem like nothing happened. He'll make it sound like the conversation was interpreted the wrong way and that I was overreacting."

"Mom, we've got him on tape talking about your breasts and breast-feeding. How he would like to come over and help you get satisfied."

"Kelly, all he did was make a pass at me!" He'll be able to wave it off as that and nothing else. Sexual harassment won't even be considered. He's not making it seem that I need to do those things to get a raise or something like that. All it will be to him is an embarrassment."

"You're telling me you won't do anything about this; that you will just shake it off as a bad experience? Mom, he was in there making the moves on you, against your will. If I'm not mistaken that could be construed as rape."

"Honey, he didn't rape me. All he did was make me feel very uncomfortable. I'll think about this over the weekend. If I feel that I cannot handle this one episode then I'll quit. Otherwise, I'll go on."

Helen pulled up her skirt and removed the tape recorder.

"Here, do with it what you want. But please, don't upset the normal order."

Helen opened the door of her car and got in.

"Did I hear you right? Do not upset the normal order? Damn it, mom! The normal order around here is Sutton pushing his way around with women whenever he feels like it! Maybe to you that's just uncomfortable, but to me, it's a crime!"

Helen was crying louder now. She looked at her daughter and didn't know what to say. Kelly was right. It was wrong what Sutton had done. But what would happen if they exposed him. It would ruin so many good people.

"Kelly, can you come over tonight?"

"Yes, I'll come over. If Dimitri doesn't have any plans, I'll bring him over too."

"Okay, honey. I'll see you then."

"I love you, mom. I won't let anybody hurt you."

"I love you too, sweetheart."

Helen closed the door to her car and started the engine. With tears running down her cheeks she drove off.

Kelly stood and watched her mother's car disappear. She was angry. Still a smile began to appear around her mouth.

"You don't know what you just did, Tom Sutton." She looked at the tape. "This will come back to haunt you."

10.

It was right at three o'clock when Dimitri Van Acker met with Mr. Jones to look at the Brannen house. After he had lunch with Allen Murphy at "Langston's", he had gone back to Kelly's and made some final notes for his meeting with Susan Knox. He had also gathered all the financial information he needed to take with him to his meeting with the realtor. The firm which he worked for had given him a parting gift or rather incentive of $100,000.00 with the hopes that he would reconsider leaving them. They had told him that they would keep his position open for one year. Should Dimitri decide to come back within the year, he would not lose any of his benefits. They were even willing to keep his healthcare plan running for the year. With that in mind and the $100,000.00, he knew that he could get started with his practice. During his years with the firm in Washington, he had been able to put a lot of money in savings. He did not waste money like most of his counterparts. He had lived in a small 3-room apartment the whole time he had been in Washington. His car and computer were the only excesses he had. The car was paid for and so was the computer. The rent of his apartment and utility bills were his only concern. So with his savings and the parting gift, he felt he stood a chance of making it. If he didn't make it, he hoped it would be within the year; that way he could always move back to Washington.

He met Mr. Jones on the front porch of the house. Albert Jones was at least fifty pounds overweight and in his mid 50's. He was well over a foot shorter than Van Acker was, but was about three times as big. Despite the heat, he was wearing a black three-piece business suit. Sweat beads were visible on his forehead and he seemed slightly out of breath.

"Mr. Jones?" Van Acker asked as he made his way to the porch.

"That's right. And you must be Mr. Van Acker."

"Right. It's nice to meet you."

"Likewise."

Albert Jones pulled a key from his pocket and opened the door. He motioned for Van Acker to go first. Van Acker walked in and waited in the hallway for Albert Jones to walk in. He looked around. There was a staircase to the left of the front door going to the second floor. To his right was a large room with big windows looking out onto the porch. They walked down the hallway. Under the staircase was an arched opening that lead into a large open room. To the right of the room were sliding doors. Van Acker walked into the large room. It had 12-foot ceilings and elaborate wood moldings everywhere. The floor, just like all the other rooms in the house was hardwood. He walked through the sliding doors. Another room presented itself. Again the tall ceiling and wood molding were prevalent. To the back of the room, he could distinguish the kitchen. The cabinets in the kitchen looked rather new and he decided the previous owners had remodeled the kitchen. A dishwasher and double door refrigerator were signs of the remodeling. To the right of the kitchen next to a door that led to the backyard was a smaller room. He walked in it and found a washer and dryer. He walked back into the kitchen and the room next to it and opened a door which Van Acker found led him back into the front entrance. He walked into the hallway and found a door to his left and right. He opened the right hand door and discovered a half bath nicely tucked away under the stair landing. The door to his left led into yet another large room. Walking into the room the wood flooring and molding again made an impression on Van Acker. To the front of the house, sliding glass doors opened into the front room. He looked at Albert Jones and smiled.

"I like this!"

"Not many people dislike houses like these. They are masterpieces. Don't build them like that no more, though. Trouble is, these days, is the upkeep. Everybody's too busy to take care of 'em."

Dimitri agreed and eyed the stairs.

"Let's go take a look upstairs," Van Acker said. He couldn't help but chuckle at Jones' sales pitch about the house being a masterpiece.

They walked up the stairs onto the landing. There was a landing all around the stairs looking down into the entrance. A baluster railing secured the opening. Van Acker took the railing in his hands and shook on it vigorously. It barely moved.

"I'm glad this one's sturdy. I would hate for anyone to lean up against it and fall down."

"You're right. That would be some fall," Jones said agreeing.

Van Acker walked around on the landing. The front of the house on both sides of the landing revealed two large bedrooms. Next to them, towards the back of the house were two smaller bedrooms. In the middle, right in front of the stairs was a large bathroom with a double sink, tub and shower unit. All this was renovated when the couple from Atlanta moved in the house. Van Acker made his way back downstairs, Albert Jones close on his heels, sweat pouring down his face by now. Van Acker found the thermostat to the heating and A/C unit. He turned the A/C on. Outside in the back, they heard the compressor kick in. A few minutes later, cool air was filling the house. Van Acker look pleased as he smiled at Jones.

"Well, what do you think, Mr. Van Acker? Do you like the house?"

"I like it. Now for the really hard part; how much would this set me back?"

Albert Jones grabbed inside his briefcase and pulled out some paperwork.

"Okay, let's see. The owner wants to get $95,000.00 for the house. Of course, since it's been on the market so long now, they told me over the phone this morning after you called, that they would be willing to come down on the price some. If you would make a suitable counteroffer, they might be willing to negotiate."

"Mr. Jones, I think that I would like to make a counteroffer of $80,000.00 even. Should they decide not to take my offer, then I'm willing to consider their price if the wood lap siding gets stripped and painted, the screens in the windows get replaced, the walls inside get new paint and the shutters get replaced. At that point, I'll be willing to settle for $95,000.00."

"Do you know what mortgage company you will be using for this purchase, should the deal be agreed upon."

"I have already taken care of the money. All you will need to do is fax the paperwork to my mortgage company in Washington, D.C. and they will handle it from there. If we can agree on the price this afternoon, and get the paperwork faxed to them by closing time, we may have this deal closed by the middle of next week. Do you think that would be suitable for you, Mr. Jones?"

Jones was speechless. Usually a deal of this size could take weeks before it closed. The buyer would likely have to battle it out with the mortgage company to get the necessary funding for the deal. But this man in front of him had worked the details out even before he considered buying a house. He wished all of his customers were like this. A faint dream he decided.

Van Acker smiled. He had obviously caught the poor realtor off guard. He had already made arrangements with a mortgage company back in D.C. to have money in case he decided to buy a house. He was pre-approved for $150,000.00 with a 20% down payment. All he would have to do is fax the paperwork on the buy to them and within a couple of days the deal would close. If he could get the house for $80,000.00 with a 20% down payment, he would have enough money left to fix the house up and buy some new necessary office furniture. He would be able to move in by the middle of the following week. Just in time for his moving van to arrive.

"Well, Mr. Jones, can we call the owner and see if my offer is acceptable?"

"Give me a couple of minutes. I need to run to the car and get my cell phone. I'll be right back with an answer."

"Please, do."

While Albert Jones was making his call to the owner, Van Acker walked the house one more time. He was imagining how he would furnish the rooms and how to paint them. The front room to the right of the front door would make a perfect reception and waiting area. The room next to it to the back of the house would become his office. He would make a door opening from that room into the kitchen area; or maybe into the dining room. The middle room on the left side of the house had become the dining room in Van Acker's mind. He would be able to access that area from his office without having to come into the hallway or waiting room. He liked that idea.

Upstairs, he would use one the large front bedrooms as his own. On the other side, he would connect two bedrooms and make it into a private study and office area. The other bedroom he would keep open for storage and his exercise equipment.

While Van Acker was reflecting how the rooms would be used, Albert Jones made his way into the room where Van Acker was waiting.

"I talked to the owners. They are willing to let the house go for $82,500.00 as is and they're not willing to settle for $95,000.00 and take care of all the repairs."

"Um...$82,5," Van Acker stroked his hand through his hair and rubbed his chin pretending to think about that number, knowing that he would be a fool not to jump at an offer like this. "Well, Mr. Jones, I do believe that I could handle that. I think we have us a deal. Why don't I give you my mortgage company's information and let you get on your way to fill out all the necessary paperwork. If there's anything you need to get signed, here's my cell number. You can reach me at that number anytime."

"Thank you, Mr. Van Acker. I'll get back to the office and start the paperwork right away. Would there be anything else we can do for you, sir?"

"No, I believe that will be all. Let me know when you have the buy closed out and I'll come by your office, sign the paperwork, and pick up the keys."

"That's sounds good, Mr. Van Acker. I'll let you know as soon as everything is in order."

"I thank you, Mr. Jones. It was a pleasure meeting you and doing business with you."

Albert Jones shook Van Acker's hand and waggled to his car. Van Acker stood on the front porch and smiled as he saw the short overweight man get in his car. He had a place to live and run his business from. Now he needed to find clients. That reminded him. He looked at his watch: 3:45; he had fifteen minutes to make it to Susan Knox' house. He walked down the steps of the porch, turned around to take one last look at the house and got in his car. With a smile on his face he drove off, eager to meet his first client.

11.

It was 3 o'clock when Susan Knox knocked on the door of her sister's house. She was calm. She knew exactly what was going to happen next. At work, Susan had been absentminded and was happy that it had been a slow day. She had a lot to do today. Meet her sister, meet Dimitri Van Acker and then get rid of Bryan Scarboro. She had mentally gone through the meeting with her sister. She knew exactly how to handle the situation. It wouldn't be pretty.

Julie Sutton opened the door and they gave each other a hug. They walked into the living room and sat down on the couch. Julie looked pale. She nervously rubbed her hands back and forth over her legs. Susan sat back and relaxed.

"You know, Julie, you should get out more often. Sitting here in the house is making you look pale. Get out in the sun and get some tan. Throw on a bikini and take a swim in the pool. You have that big pool there in the backyard and the only time anyone swims in it, is when we have a family reunion."

"Susan, honey, you know I wouldn't feel comfortable going out there in the backyard in a bathing suit, much less a bikini."

"I don't see why you wouldn't, I mean, it's not like you don't have shrubbery everywhere to hide behind."

"I'm not like you, Susan!"

"Damn right you're not! I'd be out there naked, for all I care."

"Don't you talk like that! God will strike you one of these days."

"If he was gonna strike me, he'd 'a done it a long time ago, sis. That's one reason I want to talk to you this afternoon."

"Are you finally willing to recommit yourself to God?"

"No, I'm not talking about God or Church. I'm talking about the way I am and the way you are."

"You mean why you sleep around and enjoy having sex with everybody and their brother and why I'm here hiding away afraid and scared to even let my husband touch me."

"Exactly! You know why we're the way we are?"

"Yes, because Daddy couldn't keep his hands off us."

"You, mean, 'cause Daddy couldn't keep his dick away from our mouths, pussies and asses."

"I wish you wouldn't talk like that, but yes, that's what I meant."

"Now listen, Julie, something terrible will happen because of that. It involves you and it involves me. I don't know yet how everything is gonna work out. I'm meeting someone this afternoon to see if there's anything we can do about it."

Julie started to say something but Susan cut her off:

"Wait till you hear me out. I know that it has been a long time ago that all this happened. I guess he stopped doing it to me when I was about 15. He kept you going for a while longer because he knew you were weak and wouldn't fight back. But he knew I would talk. That's the last thing he needed. He bought his way out of my talking. He gave me $50,000.00 when I turned 18. I walked out and joined the Army. But I was damaged goods, Julie. I was a slut. I got kicked out of the Army for sleeping with every recruit I could get my hands on. One commanding officer found out and was going to take advantage of it. He made me his secretary and I gave him what he wanted, every afternoon of every day that I was there. I can't even count how many blow jobs I gave that son of a bitch. That was until he hit me one day. Said he wanted it rough, wanted to play a game, pretend he was raping me. God he was a sick son of a bitch."

Julie started crying. She had her head in her hands and her body was shaking.

"Do you want to hear more, sis? Oh, there's so much more. There are more stories about sex, debauchery and acting like a cheap whore and tramp. Do you know what I did when I got out of the Army? I was out 4 months before I came back home. I went to New York City. I wasted all the money Daddy had given me. I bought drugs, Julie. I smoked pot, shot heroin, snorted coke, smoked crack, you name it and I did it; till the money ran out. I was hooked. I needed to get high and the only way to get the money was to work the streets. I became a hooker. Here I was, 18 years old, walking the streets in short skirts and tops barely big enough to cover my tits. When I couldn't make enough on the streets, I started working the peep show parlors. I sat in front of glass boxes showing off my body, rubbing my pussy and spreading my legs for men behind the glass who were jerking off their silly little dicks. All the while picking up the dollars they slid into the slots. I bought my drugs and needed more. In a clear moment of thought, I called Daddy and asked for more money. He said he would come and give me the money himself, wanted to see how I was doing. Like he cared! All he wanted was to see if he could get inside my panties one more time. So he wanted to know what Army base I was one and I had no choice but to tell him what was going on. He came and got me. Dragged me back to this godforsaken hole under the promise that if I came back, I could live above the garage until I met someone whom I was going to marry. I would do as I pleased as long as I stayed off drugs. I promised not to tell anyone as long as I was allowed to live above the garage, not pay any rent or utility bills."

Julie who had stopped crying was now listening in utter amazement.

"Susan, you did drugs? You were a hooker? How come I never heard this and why are you telling me now?

"Julie, I'm telling you now because now is the time for you to hear. I cannot tell you yet about what I'm planning on doing. I know this much though; because of what daddy did to us, I'm a slut. I'm no better than when I was in New York. I just don't get paid for it now. Not only am I a slut, but I'm sick. I have a disease because of what I did in New York. All that sleeping around and doing drugs caused me to get a STD. I'm afraid it's one of the worst one's too."

"What... what are you saying? What... what do you have?"

"Julie, I'm telling you that I've got AIDS!"

"No! No! No, not you! It can't be true. Susan, tell me, please that it's not true. No!"

"I'm sorry, Julie. I found out a couple of weeks ago. I was feeling ill, was getting these lesions around my vagina. I thought I had herpes at first. So I had some blood tests done. It came back positive for HIV."

"God, Susan, that's awful!" Julie blushed as she used God's name out of context. She was so surprised and taken back by the confession her sister gave that she didn't care.

"Julie, there's one more thing. You'll probably hate me forever if I tell you, but I've got to tell you now that I know I have

AIDS." Susan looked down at the ground and started crying herself.

Julie moved closer and put her arms around Susan.

"What honey, why would I hate you? You're my sister. I could never hate you."

"Oh yes, you could," said Susan wiping tears from her cheeks, smearing mascara over her face.

"Julie, Tom and I have been lovers since before you got married to him. The only reason he wanted to marry you was to have a proper churchgoing wife that could stand by his side when he entered politics. He came to my place to get his sexual kicks because he couldn't get them at home. I know, it's bad, and I'm sorry this all happened, but I have to tell you this because more than likely he's got the virus too and now, maybe you have it too."

Susan was crying uncontrollably. She didn't dare look her sister in the eye.

Julie was sitting on the couch frozen. She still had her arms around her sister. She had turned white as snow. Slowly, she managed to get up. She looked at Susan. Susan looked back at her. Julie slapped Susan right across the face, leaving her palm print on her face. Susan just locked her teeth and took the slap. She knew she deserved it. God, if only she could turn back to clock. But it was too late. What was done was done. She had finally done the right thing and if she thought that Julie was just going to accept it, then she had been dead wrong.

"Get out!" Julie shouted as loud as she could. "Get out, you fucking whore! Don't you ever set another foot in his house! You will burn in Hell for this!" Julie started to pace the living room.

Susan got up from the couch and walked towards the door. For the first time since she started her affair with her sister's husband did she feel some guilt, some remorse. But it was too late. She realized that now. She turned towards Julie.

"Julie, I know I did wrong. I should have never started that affair. But you know whom you should be mad at? That's Daddy! He's the one who screwed up everything. You fear sex because of what he did. Well, I crave it. The more the merrier. You know what having HIV means to me? It means that a lot of people in this county may also have HIV all because of me. I can't remember all the men I slept with since I came back from New York. There's no telling how many people will die a slow horrible death because of me. Am I a murderer? Or am I just the medium by which the murders will take place? Think about that for a minute. I'm not saying what I did with Tom wasn't wrong. Hell, I know it was wrong, but it was fun and it was sex; hot, steamy sex. That's all I wanted. That's all I ever want!" Susan stopped for a second to wet her lips and take a breath.

"But you know, there's one person out there that respected me for the woman I was, and who wasn't looking to get a quick lay. There's one that did not have sex with me the whole time we went out. I'm meeting that man this afternoon. He's a lawyer. I'm going after Daddy. I can prove what he was doing to us, Julie. I can Goddamn prove it! I have videotapes; I have stuff on videotapes! He doesn't even know I trapped him. I knew what he was doing wasn't right. I taped him with you. I was hiding in the closet and when he was coming down on you, pounding your precious little body, I taped it. I set up a camera in my room. I knew when he was coming to get me. So I turned the camera on and taped him with me. I taped him coming down and pounding away at me with his dick. I know I was wrong, but damn it, I have a disease that's far worse than HIV. I have a disease that caused the other disease and I'm not going to sit by and rot away while he's acting like nothing is wrong, like nothing ever happened. He's going down Julie. Be angry with me; hate me all you want. I understand. But, I'm begging you, help me. Help me tear him down! Help me expose his dirty little secret. People will die because of it. You may die because of it! There needs to be justice and I will need your help to make justice prevail."

Julie, who had stood with her back turned towards Susan, slowly turned around. Tears were running down her cheeks. Her arms were hanging lifeless beside her body. She looked as if all her strength had left her body and she was ready to collapse.

"Hate me for the rest of your live, Julie. I don't care! I deserve it!"

"STOP!" Julie screamed.

"Stop!" Julie took a deep breath and seemed to regain some of her strength.

"Susan, I will never forgive you for what you have done. As my sister, you should have never slept with my husband, no matter when, or what, or how. But, you're still my sister. I will always love you, no matter what. I will help you. I'll do whatever it takes to get that sick bastard behind bars. What I hate more than hating you, is to hurt mamma. She's going to suffer the most out of this. Her life will be branded. She won't be able to show her face in public. She may have to move. We may have to move. But I will fight with you, side by side. And after it's all over, I want you out of my life. After this whole damn thing is finally settled, then I want you gone as far away as you can possibly go. And when Judgment Day will come, then I'll see you again. You *will* go to Heaven, Susan. I know that. You'll go to heaven because you, just like me, have been in Hell already. Daddy will go to Hell, not you. Now, get out!"

Susan opened the door and walked out. Julie looked out the window, her eyes following her sister walk across the street. She wasn't crying anymore. She had a look of bitterness on her face; a look of hate. She hated with a passion. Never before had she felt like this. She never thought she could ever hate, but now she knew.

12.

Dimitri Van Acker arrived at Susan Knox's apartment right at 4 o'clock. He straightened out his hair and tie as he walked up the steps to her door. Susan greeted him at the door.

"Dimitri," she said with a big smile on her face, "how are you?"

"Hi, Susan, I'm fine. How are you doing?"

"Why don't you come in and have a seat while I tell you how I'm doing."

Van Acker walked into the apartment and had a seat on the sofa.

"So, tell me Susan, what legal advise is it you need that your brother-in-law cannot take care off. The only thing I can think off is that maybe it has to do with him."

"Boy, you jump right in, don't you?"

"I'm sorry, Susan, but I am used to jumping right in. In DC, you cannot afford to wait to get a case going, because there are so many other lawyers in town. Let's start over, okay?"

"All right, Dimitri. So tell me, how have you been doing? You look good. Better than ever I would say."

"I've done all right. I enjoyed working in DC, but I couldn't face myself in the mirror in the morning. God knows how many crooks are still on the street because I got them off on a technicality or because I could turn the facts around. The partners in my law firm loved it. They had rich clients. Contractors, politicians, investors, Realtors, you know."

"I see. Listen, would you like something to drink?"

"Yes, I'd like that. What do you have?"

"I have tea, soda, or beer."

"I'll have a beer, if you don't mind."

"Coming right up!"

Susan grabbed two Budweiser out of the refrigerator and sat beside Van Acker on the couch.

"So, what you're saying is that as a lawyer, you specialize in cases where your clients are guilty?"

Van Acker nodded his head affirmatively.

"Then you go out and gather information and research the law books and find technicalities on which your clients can be dismissed. Am I right?"

"You're right. However, gathering information and doing research is only part of the game. Selecting a jury that is favorable to your client helps too. Let me give you an example. In a case of a rapist, the worst thing you can do as a defense lawyer is to allow women on the jury. Also fathers with young daughters are a no. It's important to have a jury that is not partial with the victim in trials like that."

"Let me ask you something. Let's say that you were the prosecuting attorney, instead of the defense attorney, would you be able to choose a jury in the same manner?"

"Well, yes. You see, jury selection is a battle between the prosecution and the defense on selection jury members favorable to their case. In all jury trails concessions are made on both ends. However, it is important to have specific questions for specific jurors. Reading the bios on the jurors is not enough to form an intelligent opinion on which juror is acceptable or not for your case. Asking the potential jurors questions can help you release a juror's passion. For instance, in a murder trial, asking a juror what he or she thinks about someone who murdered an old helpless woman during a robbery can give you the following: I hope he burns in Hell! Then ask them if they should get life in prison for that. If the return answer is that he should fry on the chair, you have a definite Capital Punishment proponent. As a defense lawyer, you try to get that juror dismissed. As a prosecutor, however, you would want that juror in a jury seat."

"So it's a cat and mouse game between the two parties and whoever gets the most favorable jurors can win the case."

"Not always. It's important to have a smart jury. A smart jury, no matter how much in your favor, will analyze the facts and testimonies. They will look at that, rather than what they believe. It's up to the defense lawyer to create reasonable doubt. If one or two jurors are convinced that there's reasonable doubt, they can swing the rest or you can have a mistrial. You always hope for a unanimous jury, however with a split jury, you know that you'll be back in court going through the whole process again."

"Gee, I'm glad I'm not involved in all that lawyer mess."

61

"So, tell me Susan, why all this interest in courtroom antics?"

Susan looked at Van Acker, smiled, and then looked down at the floor. She took a big gulp from her beer.

"I'm interested in it, because, real soon I will more than likely become part of the antics."

"Why don't you go to Sutton and get the answers to those questions. He should be as familiar with them as I am. At least he makes out to be like he is."

"Dimitri, I cannot go to Tom. My legal problem involves my whole family. I suspect that Tom will probably be on the opposite site of where I am."

Tears started to well up in Susan's eyes.

"But why me, Susan? I mean, you were willing to go all the way to DC to find you a lawyer. Why didn't you look into a local lawyer?"

"I wanted you, because I know you; because we had something at one time that I have never been able to understand. You know my family. I wanted someone who had a little insight in the way things are run around here. And besides, now that you're going to be living in town, you're the perfect choice."

"Susan, you know that was just a coincidence. No one knew I was coming back except the Murphy's. You probably couldn't afford me if I still worked for my old firm."

Susan looked away from Van Acker and wiped a tear from her face.

"Tell me Susan, who all does this problem of yours involve?"

Susan turned back to Van Acker and grinned.

"To tell you the truth, honey, I don't know. It's a long story. But I will give it to you as short as possible."

"I've got time."

"Let me ask you this, are you charging me yet?"

"No, I think I'll consider this your initial advice session. No charge, should I decide to take the case, then I'll start charging. I'll let you know what my fee will be as soon as I make a decision."

"That sounds fair."

"Are you ready?"

"Yes, I am. Let me start with the most serious problem. I found out a few weeks ago that I'm infected with the HIV virus. I'm progressed to having full-blown AIDS. My life expectancy is fewer than 3 years."

Van Acker's jaw dropped and he stared at Susan in disbelieve.

"Susan, how did you come to have the virus?"

"I had sex with whoever wanted to give it to me from the time I was 18. I did drugs, shared needles, you name it."

"This might seem like a stupid question, but why? What drove you to do these things?"

"It's not a stupid question. I mean, here I am, a well-to do daughter of a prominent farmer. I'm 30 years old and still single. I have a job as a secretary for a doctor. Not the picture you would imagine, is it?"

"Well, career wise, I don't think there's to much people can say. You're beautiful, 30 years old and still single, now I can see why people would start talking, especially around here."

"I know what you mean. Anyways, to answer your question about why I did those things, I had never paid to much attention to it. The only thing I knew is that I loved sex. I wanted sex all the time. That's what got me kicked out of the Army. I know I never told you that I was kicked out. Everyone thinks it was because I was harassed. It wasn't. I spread my legs for every soldier who was willing. Then after they kicked me out, I went to New York. There I got involved in drugs. I needed money. I started working the streets and the peep show parlors. Eventually, I asked daddy for money and he brought me back here. Once back in town, I had several affairs. Most of the men were still single, but I've lured several married men into my lair too."

"What you're trying to tell me is there might be many people out there that are also infected with HIV because of you."

"That's right. But to answer your questions about why I can't go to Tom with my problem... Well, he's one of the married men that I had sex with."

Van Acker whistled.

"I understand now."

"No, you don't. There is a different twist to the story; something that no one could ever imagine!"

"I'm listening."

"Julie and I were both sexually abused by our father. From the time we were starting to develop, he fondled us, he made us masturbate him and give blowjobs to him. When he thought we were ready, he had vaginal and anal sex with us."

"Susan, that's a big accusation. Why have you never told anyone about this before?"

"I thought the pain would go away. You see, the reason I want sex all the time is because of my experience when I was a child. Julie is the opposite. She hates sex. She's afraid of it because of what he did to us."

Van Acker looked at her with wondering eyes.

"If I ask Julie if her father sexually abused her, she will give me the same answer, right."

"I know it seems unbelievable that we never said anything. But I'm sure that many young girls never told anyone. I've tried to tell mamma a couple of times, but she never wanted to talk about sex with us. It was like this big taboo thing, you know. Talking about sex would make you go straight to Hell if you believed my mother."

"I know what you mean. I've never seen a country where the subject of sex is so taboo. And yet, this country out of all the civilized countries in the world has the highest rate of teen pregnancy. There are more sexual crimes committed in this country per capita than any other country. So yes, I know where you're coming from."

"Well, anyway, about your concern about the strong accusation, I have proof. I have videotapes of him abusing my sister and of him abusing me. I've held on to those just in case I ever needed them. You see, he's supporting me like he would a mistress. I want to charge him with whatever I can charge him with. I've heard about people getting charged with assault and attempted murder. I want to go after him with the hardest possible charge the State will allow. And I want you to represent me. I'm sure that he'll approach Tom to defend him. But I know that Tom is no match for you. So what do you say?"

Van Acker rubbed his hand over his chin, thinking about what Susan had told him.

"Susan, I will need some time to think about this. Give me a couple of days. I'll do some research. Once I've got my computer, I can tap into my old firm's data bank and see if they have any information whatever on incest and AIDS as it relates to attempted murder, etc. I know that if you gave anybody else the virus, they might come after you, especially if they smell money. If you take this thing to court, the newspapers and TV stations will have a field day with this. You need to think about that. Also, can your father get a fair trial in this county? Or better yet, can I get an unbiased jury in this county. You father is well known, Tom is well known. If I take on this case, I will need to jump through a lot of loops to get a conviction. At best, you can ruin your father and see everything he worked for go in the ground. At worst, your name and reputation will be worst than it is now."

"Wait a damn minute! How do you know how my reputation is?"

"Look, people are not stupid. They see guys come and go. You're not married, but some of the guys coming to visit you are. People put one and one together. Most of them come up with the right answer. So, what I'm saying is, I need to study the preliminaries before I can let you know if I'll take the case or not."

Van Acker got up out of his chair and walked in the kitchen. He threw the empty beer can in the trash.

"Susan, when we were going out, how come you didn't try to get me in bed? If you were so eager to have sex and couldn't hold yourself back, how come you never tried to persuade me?"

"I don't know. I guess it's because you showed me so much respect. You treated me like a lady, not some cheap tramp that was easy to get in the bed with. You were different from the rest. You weren't looking for a sexual relationship."

"Then why did you break up with me? There was nobody else, was there? You just couldn't stand that I didn't make a move to the bedroom!"

"No! No! I broke up with you to protect you! I knew I couldn't commit myself to just you. I tried! I really tried! But the last couple of weeks before I broke up with you I was back doing my old tricks. I needed it, Dimitri! I needed to feel the physical love!"

"Susan, there's no love in just the physical. Love starts as an emotional aspect of a relationship. The physical is a result of the emotional. You cannot just go to bed with someone and say you love

65

them. Sure it feels good and brings satisfaction, but it's not love. It's lust. You lust for someone. You don't love them. I loved you, Susan! Believe me, I wanted to take you to bed so many times but I didn't because I respected you."

"I'm sorry. But maybe it was for the better that we broke up. I wouldn't have been a good wife. I would have cheated on you, Dimitri."

"I'm glad you finally have the guts to tell me. I was hurt after you broke up with me, especially since I had no clue what had happened for you to break up with me. But, that's all in the past now."

"I'm sorry if I hurt you, Dimitri. Listen, I'm glad you're back."

"I hope it's the right thing I've done. Susan, I've got to go. I will start my research and I will let you know next week if I'll be able to do something and if I think we'll have a case. I will call you on Monday to let you know what my rates are."

"Money is of no concern to me, Dimitri. I've got a good bit put aside."

"All right, I'll be in touch."

Van Acker walked out the door. Susan leaned back on the sofa and sighted. She was exhausted. It had been a trying day. And it wasn't over yet. She still had to deal with Bryan Scarboro. Susan closed her eyes and dozed off.

13.

It was a little after five when Tom Sutton drove into his driveway. He had recovered from the turn down he'd received from Helen Murphy. He figured that she would not call him that evening. He went ahead and made other plans. He had called an acquaintance in Macon and he would meet her tonight. He'd tell Julie it was a business dinner. She'd believe him, of course. Besides, she'd have the house to herself and didn't have to worry about him wanting to fulfill his marital duties. He was looking forward to tonight. When he walked in the door, Julie was sitting in the living room, looking him dead in the face. The hate she had felt earlier was still there.

"Hi, Julie, how are you doing tonight my darling?"

He walked over to her and kissed her on the cheek.

"Tom, we need to talk."

"I sure hope it's not about what we talked about yesterday. I don't want to think about that anymore. Besides, I have to hurry I've got a business dinner to attend."

"You're not going anywhere till we talk. Sit down!"

"Don't put on that tone of voice with me, woman. I won't have you tell me what to do!"

"Oh really? And who's been telling me all this time what to do? Who's been keeping me locked up in this house all this time while you are out, God knows doing what?"

"What's that supposed to mean. Are you suggesting that I'm sneaking around behind your back?"

"No, I'm not suggesting anything. I don't need to suggest. I know what you've been doing all those evenings that you were gone. Dinners, receptions, and whatever else you could think off! I know what you were doing!"

"Is that so? So what was it I was doing?"

"You were out catching a Goddamned disease!"

"Julie, what are you talking about?"

"Do you know what I found out this afternoon?"

"No, I don't have the slightest idea. Why don't you fill me in and walk me out of the dark."

"I found out that you've been having an affair for over six years, Tom."

"What? Me? An affair! You're out of your mind, Julie! You have for sure lost it now!"

"No, I've not lost it. Remember Susan was supposed to come over this afternoon and talk with me? Well, she did. She talked. She told me everything. How you and her were lovers before we even got married. You were sneaking around behind my back while we were engaged. And stupid I didn't even notice it!"

"That's a damned lie, Julie! I don't know what your sister is up to, but it's a damned lie!"

Sutton was starting to lose his cool and his face turned a little redder.

"A lie? Okay, it's a lie? Susan is lying to me? Susan is trying to hurt me on purpose by telling me lies about you and her doing the wild thing behind my back? I don't buy it, Tom! You know something else, Tom? Do you know what else she told me? She told me she's got AIDS. AIDS Tom! Goddamn AIDS!"

Tom Sutton's face was no longer red. All the blood had drained out of his face as soon as he heard the word AIDS. My God, if it were true. If Susan really had AIDS, she could have given it to him. And he could have given it to Julie and to... My God! All the mistresses he's had. He tried to compose himself.

"Susan's got to be lying, Julie. There's no way she could have AIDS. It cannot be true!" he said, his voice reaching a higher pitch than normal.

"Why are you so worried, then? It's just my sister. It's not like she could've given it to you by shaking your hands. Or maybe...? That's right! She could have given it to you because you were screwing around with her! You fucking son of a bitch!"

Sutton was on the defense. He'd never heard his wife curse in all the time he'd known her. Here she was, swearing like a sailor. He had to get the situation back under control. There was no telling what his wife would do.

"Julie, please, calm down. Susan is not telling the truth. She's lying! I've never done anything with her. I've always been faithful to you, no matter how hard it has been. You've got to believe me, Julie. I've never cheated on you!"

"Oh, stop it, Tom! I believe my sister! I've had a good while to think about this, and I was wondering how many other women besides Susan that you've been with. How many are there, Tom? How many?"

Julie's voice was reaching higher pitches, as she grew more and more furious with her husband.

"I don't have to listen to this verbal abuse. I will not continue this conversation. I have never and will never have sex with any other woman besides you. If you believe different, you'll have to prove it. You'll have to prove that I've been unfaithful."

"I will!" Julie said with confidence. "And now, Tom, I want you out of my house. I want you gone. I'm going over to mama and daddy's house and when I come back in about an hour, I want you gone. I want all your stuff out of this house. Anything left will be burned. I'll have fun watching it go up in flames."

Tom Sutton looked at her in disbelieve. She was kicking him out. He walked over to her and tried to take her in his arms.

"Don't touch me! You touch me and I swear I'll charge with domestic assault! Get out!"

Julie rushed to the door and ran down the steps into the street. She turned around. Sutton was standing in the doorway.

"Julie, please, come back in the house. You're making a scene. Come on, honey, get back in here. Let's talk about this."

"There's nothing to talk about, asshole!" Julie didn't care there were some unexpecting witnesses to their conversation.

"Julie, please come back in. We can work this out!"

"There's nothing for us to work out, Tom. Maybe you can call one of your sluts and work it out with them. What are they going to say when you tell them you may have AIDS?"

The people in the street started whispering to one another. As soon as they heard that Tom Sutton might have AIDS, they were gathered in little groups.

"Julie, don't go around spreading these lies. People, please, there's nothing here to see. She's having a little trouble today."

Sutton was looking for damage control so his name would not be smeared too much.

"You can go to Hell, Tom Sutton! That's where you belong! Remember, you better be gone when I come back, or we'll have us a great big bonfire in the yard tonight!"

Julie spun around on her heels and ran towards her parent's

house. The people in the street were talking. Fingers were pointed at Sutton. Eyes were focused on him. There was speculation going on among the citizens. Sutton could feel their eyes burning him. Quickly he closed the door. Once the door was shut, he leaned up against it and slid down. What was going on? Damn you Susan! Why did you have to tell Julie? Why?

"Why, Susan, why?" he screamed out.

A few of the curious outside the house heard his voice. By morning, the whole town would know. Everyone would know that Tom Sutton might have AIDS and that it had something to do with Susan, Julie's sister!

14.

Susan Knox jumped up from the couch. She looked around, bewildered. She had dozed off and had slept faster than she had like to. She looked at the clock: 5:30. The phone was ringing. She hurried to the receiver and answered it.

"Hello?"

"Susan?"

"Yes?"

"It's me, are you alright?"

"Oh, hi, yes. I dozed off. That's all. What's going on?"

"I was wondering if you were free tonight. I'd like to come over and have some fun."

"Listen, I don't think it's a good idea for you to come over anymore."

"What do you mean not come over anymore? You don't like me anymore?"

"It's nothing like that. I just don't think that I need to see you anymore; that's all."

"I don't buy it, Susan. What's going on?"

Susan ran her fingers through her hair. She looked much older suddenly. Wrinkles formed around her eyes. Her mouth was pressed shut. Her lips were white and she clenched her teeth.

"I have a confession to make."

"All right, let's hear it."

"You probably know this... at least you should. If you don't, then you're stupid to think that it couldn't be true."

"Would you get to the point, Susan?" The voice on the other end of the line sounded anxious.

"Listen, you're not the only guy that comes over here and has fun. There are others, several others. And because of that, I just can't see you anymore."

"I'm not stupid, Susan. I know there are others, but why the change suddenly? Why won't you see me anymore?"

Susan didn't know what to say. She had to tell him. She owed it to him, especially a man in his position. He'd find out eventually anyway. It might be better if he'd find out from her than from someone on the street. He would be devastated. He'd be mad with her. She couldn't blame him. He didn't deserve this. He deserved better. But it was too late. The damage was done. She would try to save his reputation. Don't call him to the witness stand if it came to that. If he didn't testify, he would not expose himself and would be able to keep his reputation. He could resign for health reasons.

"Susan? Are you still there? What's going on? Susan?"

"I'm still here. I don't know how to tell you this. But, you will hear about it eventually. I may as well tell you." She swallowed. Tears started welling up in her eyes. She cleared her throat.

"Tell me what, Susan?" The voice on the other end started to shake. There was obvious concern. Not only did Susan say that he would find out eventually, by someone besides Susan. It had to be serious.

"I'm sick."

There was laughter on the other end of the phone.

"Honey, you're sick? That's nothing to worry about. We've all been sick before!"

"Would you just listen?" Susan said. She was getting angry. "I'm not just sick. I'm seriously sick. I'll be sick for the rest of my live."

Susan lowered her voice as if to make sure that no one would hear besides the person on the other end of the phone.

"I've got AIDS."

There was a long silence on the other end of the phone. Susan waited. She knew what was going on. A man on the other end was slumped down, probably sitting in his chair, the phone in his lap. His face would be white as snow, all the blood drained from it. The face would have signs of concern, fear, anger, and disillusion all at the same time. She felt pity. He had no fault in any of it. Like so many other men who had no fault. They were all victims, victims of her immorality; victims of her past.

The voice on the other end finally came back.

"How long have you known?"

There was anger in the voice.

"A couple of weeks."

"Weeks? Did you say weeks?"

"Yes."

"Damned, how is this possible? Where does that leave me? Do you know what this could mean to my career, my name?"

"I know. I'm sorry this happened." Susan was crying.

"I should have known better! I knew you were a cheap tramp! I wish I'd never met you! I'll get you for this! I hope you will burn in Hell!"

The phone cut off.

Susan collapsed on the couch. What a day! She had hoped to put off this conversation a couple of days. To no prevail. The conversation found her. She was expecting a different result. She had hoped for compassion, understanding. Not the rage and anger that had been hurled her way. She had never seen him mad or angry. Tonight proved different. There was a lot at stake for him. At least he wasn't married. Still, he was the mayor of Stuttgart. Susan sighted, two down, two to go.

15.

"Com'on Michelle, hurry up. I don't have all evening. I've got to go to that social tonight, remember?"

"Oh shut up! Give me some time. I'm new at this, remember."

"In about twenty minutes, you'll have all the experience you'll need!"

"Don't flatter yourself. You're not the only stud on the market!"

Bryan Scarboro was lying on the bed, anticipating Michelle Murphy's emergence from the bathroom. They had planned this afternoon on the spur of the moment. He had begged Michelle to go to Macon with her. He had a surprise he told her. On the way to Macon, he had produced a bottle of Tequila. Michelle who had never been into the drinking scene while in high school was curious to try it. She had gulped away a good bit when they made it to Macon. She felt loose and was willing to try anything. Her mind was polluted and her actions would not be rational. Scarboro had hoped that would happen. Since he had laid eyes on Allen Murphy's youngest daughter, he had wanted her. He drank himself some courage on the way to Macon, taking a couple of shots of the Tequila himself. He had rented a motel room. He knew what he wanted. He didn't care how he got it. Michelle had thought it to be a great idea. At 18, she was still a virgin. She had always been pure at heart and thought. She went to church every Sunday and swore she would not have sex before marriage. Today, the alcohol was washing away her ethics. She was succumbed to her emotions, rather than to her rational. Scarboro had played it perfect. He knew that a young girl like Michelle had to be aching to find out what sex was all about. He felt he had to be the one. So here he was, lying on the bed with nothing on but his shorts and being visibly excited.

Michelle opened the bathroom door and entered the motel room. She had taken off her clothes and was only wearing her bra and panties. The alcohol was still working, however the effects were decreasing. While in the bathroom, she had started second-guessing her actions. She knew what she was doing was wrong. But Bryan was so sincere. She knew that she could hold on to him. As she walked towards the bed, she held her hands in front of her panties. She blushed as she noticed Bryan's eyes running up and down her body, pausing at her breasts. Unwillingly, she felt her nipples stiffen and a warm feeling was starting to develop between her legs. A smile appeared on Scarboro's face.

"Look at you! I never imagined you'd look this good. You are positively gorgeous."

Michelle blushed a deeper red.

"Thank you."

"Come here," Scarboro coaxed her. "Come here, and sit on the bed right here."

He padded his hand on the edge of the bed.

"Let me make you feel even better."

It wasn't long before they were in each other's arms, naked and rolling around on the bed. It was the first time in her life that Michelle had been with a man. She enjoyed it. She felt wonderful as Scarboro entered her body. The stories she had heard about having sex hurting the first time around had not come true. Apart from the slight discomfort of Scarboro pushing through her hymen, the whole experience had been wonderful. At least at that exact moment it didn't hurt. That Scarboro had not worn a condom and had not bothered to pull out when he reached his climax did not cross her mind. She'd been on the pill for a couple of years now, just in case she ever fell to the temptation of having sex. She was glad that she had made the decision to be on the pill. She was sure that she would not get pregnant. She didn't think about the other consequences that unprotected sex could cause.

16.

Gerald Radcliff was sitting with his hands in his lap staring blindly in front of him; his eyes fixed on the television set. He was not seeing or hearing anything of what was displayed on the screen.

Gerald Radcliff was a middle-aged, overweight man. His once black hair had begun to gray prematurely, and at age 48, he was completely gray. His steel blue eyes saw everything that went on around him. He was a broker by trade. In his younger days, he had raked in numerous diplomas and certificates from various colleges and universities. He was an expert in his field. He had made a lot of money in the brokerage business. He was well known in the community. Everybody felt sorry for him. Radcliff had lost his first wife just after two years of marriage to a drunken driving accident. His second wife had left him after just one year of marriage. He had been heartbroken. He decided to remain single and just play the field as they called it. He involved himself in various local organizations and decided to enter politics. Three years ago, he became mayor of Stuttgart. He was suited for the job. He was intelligent, had time to invest in the job and was a community minded individual. The people enjoyed having Radcliff as a mayor. He made efforts to construct a playground, improved the athletic fields, and started planning a city park. No one had ever seen him angry or upset. He was always cheery and happy. Tonight would prove different.

After Radcliff had slammed the phone down, he had rushed through his house like a madman. He had paced through the living room, slamming his fists together. He had knocked a ceramic lamp off a table next to his chair. Pieces of the ceramic were scattered everywhere. He didn't bother to clean up the mess. Eventually exhausted, he had sat back down in his chair.

Several hours had passed when Radcliff finally got up. He needed a drink. He grabbed a bottle of whiskey from the cupboard and planted it on his mouth. Again, he started pacing through the house, steadily emptying the bottle of whiskey. He walked into the bedroom. His eyes fell on something. He slung the bottle of whiskey to the side. It hit the window and crashed through it. Broken glass from the window covered the floor. Radcliff grabbed the object. His .44 Magnum. He stroked it with his fingers, the cold steel running shivers down his spine. He opened a couple of drawers and finally found the bullets to the gun. He filled the clip, pushed it back into the gun and smiled. The mirror on the dresser reflected the smile, a contorted, sick smile. He started laughing, louder and louder.

He would teach her, that slut. No one could do this to him without suffering the consequences. He stopped laughing. His cheeks dropped, his lips pursed together and his nostrils flared as he took a deep breath. His eyes had turned to slits and the light of the bedroom made his blue eyes look even colder. He pushed the gun between his stomach and pants and rushed into the living room. He found his car keys. He looked around the room, then rushed out the door, got into his car and drove off.

17.

It was right at seven o'clock when Bryan Scarboro showed up at Susan Knox' door. He was satisfied with himself. He had managed to get Michelle Murphy in bed and teach her all about love making. Now he would complete his evening with Susan. He was looking forward to her passionate love making. The woman was a total nymphomaniac. He had never been able to satisfy her. She wanted more, all the time. He smiled as he knocked on the door.

Susan Knox had managed to take a shower and put on some make-up after her conversation with Gerald Radcliff. She didn't know whether she could handle another confrontation tonight. She had put on blue jeans and a black T-shirt. She did not want to appear inviting to Scarboro. She took a deep breath as she opened the door.

"Hi, Bryan, how are you?"

"I'm feeling as wonderful as anyone could possibly feel, darling. How are you doing? You don't look so hot tonight!"

"I'm doing fine. I must say, I've felt better."

"You're not coming down with anything are you?"

Susan sat down on the couch and looked away from Scarboro.

"No, I'm not coming down with anything."

"Good. I'd hate to come over here for nothing." Scarboro smiled.

He's as arrogant as Tom, Susan thought, thinking about how she could break the news to him.

"Com'on, give me a smile. Whatever it is, it couldn't be all that bad, could it?"

He sat besides her and put his arm around her shoulder, leaning his head towards her neck. Susan pushed him back and got up.

"Wow! What fell in your grits this morning?"

"Nothing, all right!" Susan snapped.

"Hey, I didn't come here to fight; just to have a little fun, with my main lady."

"You are so conceded, Bryan Scarboro. Do you think that I'm so stupid to think that there's nobody else in your life? You spend 10 months out of the year away at college and you're trying to tell me you're not sleeping around up there? Who do you take me for?"

Scarboro was taken back by the sudden attack on his character. He knew she didn't think that, but he was just kidding around, trying to loosen her up. Confused he scratched his chin.

"Susan, I'm sorry I upset you. I don't think that you're stupid. You're right; I do have my share of fun while I'm in college."

"Do you know what you're doing when you're with some new, innocent girl, not yet primed in the ways of sexual pleasure? Do you know what you're spreading?"

"What are you talking about? I'm not spreading anything other than some cute girl's legs."

"You think that's funny? I'm not talking about spreading some young innocent girl's legs. I've never seen you put on a condom with me. I can only guess that you don't put one on either when you're with somebody else. Am I right?"

Bryan turned scarlet.

"Well..., you see..., I do wear them sometimes."

"Bryan, my dear Bryan. Sometimes is not good enough. One time without protection is enough to catch something."

"Susan, let me get something clear here. You're trying to tell me something, right? Something that's not easy for you to say?"

"Yes, you're right. I am trying to tell you something, and yes it is not easy for me to say."

"Whatever it is, I can take it, Susan."

"It's funny, Bryan, because the last person who found out, did not take it so good. Before I tell you, however, I want your promise that you will call whomever you've slept with since the first time we had sex. You need to promise me that you will tell them what I will tell you. Promise?"

Scarboro turned pale. He knew it had something to do with a STD. All he could do was nod.

"Bryan, I'm sorry, but I'm infected with the HIV virus. Actually, I've got full blown AIDS."

Scarboro leaned back in the couch. He closed his eyes and rubbed his face with his hands. He looked at Susan as he tried to place his hands on his legs. They were shaking violently. He had

79

lost his composure, lost his nerve. The cool, calculated, scared of nothing Bryan Scarboro had lost it all. Finally he responded.

"How long have you known?" he asked Susan in a low voice.

"A couple of weeks. I've been celibate since then. I expect the same from you. No more sex Bryan."

"You can't ask me not to have sex anymore!" Scarboro interrupted her.

"Bryan, think about this. This is serious. I'm telling you to stop having sex until you see a doctor and have an HIV test done. If you're negative, that's good. But that doesn't mean that you can just sleep around again. You will need to be tested every six months for the rest of your life! If you decide to have sex with anyone, please wear a condom and tell the person that you may have contracted the virus. If they still want to have sex with you, then do whatever you want. I wouldn't. I've learned my lesson."

Bryan Scarboro was listening to Susan's lecture. She made sense, but his needs were cut short.

"It's just not fair, Susan. Just because you contracted the virus and might have given it to me, I have to quit being with a woman? My whole life is ruined!"

"I know! So is mine, Goddamn it! But those are the consequences of the actions we take, Bryan. We make decisions in life that sometimes will bite us in the ass."

"When did you become a psychiatrist? Don't tell me you listen to that woman on the radio. Dr. you know the one with that funny last name?"

"Actually, I do. I started listening to her a couple of months ago. I don't agree with everything she says. But, when it comes to sex and relationships, I think she's dead-on. I don't think that one should have sex before marriage. I only wish I could have known about her 12 years ago. Things might be different right now."

Scarboro looked at Susan in disbelieve. Here was the biggest slut in the county. She somehow managed to contract the HIV virus, spread it around the whole county, and now she was preaching about not having sex before marriage. All of a sudden Scarboro jumped up from the couch.

"Oh my God!"

"What is it, Bryan?"

"Michelle! I was with Michelle this afternoon. Oh no, please tell me I didn't!"

"Michelle who? Did you have sex with her?"

Scarboro nodded yes. He started pacing the floor.

"Bryan, you need to tell her."

"Her father will kill me if I tell her. You don't know. He doesn't like me. He thinks I'm too old for her. He thinks I'm slime."

"Who is she?"

"Michelle Murphy, Allen Murphy's daughter."

Susan sat down on the couch. She knew Allen well. He was the most understanding person in the world as long as it did not involve his family. Once his family became involved, he was the most vengeful person in the world.

"Bryan, I know Allen. He will be upset. But he won't kill you, trust me! You need to tell Michelle. Tonight!"

"I know. I will."

Scarboro walked towards the door. As he opened the door, he turned around.

"We're not through, Susan. I will not suffer the rest of my life because of what you gave me! I will settle this, one way or the other!"

He walked out the door, slamming it behind him.

Susan took a deep breath. She felt relieved. She had told all but one who were in possible danger of having contracted the disease from her. They were the only one's that had never used protection. Her other lovers all were prepared and wore protection. Smart move, she thought. She could almost relax. She got up and went to the bedroom, locking her front door as she walked by. She needed to call one more person before she could go to sleep. She had no time to waste. She did not look forward to having to make the call, but it needed to be done. She sat down on the edge of the bed and picked up her phone. She dialed the number.

There was an answer on the other end.

"Hi, it's Susan."

18.

Julie Sutton dreaded going over to her parent's house. She did not want to see her father. Even at 34, she still did not feel comfortable being around him. She was still afraid, but she had a purpose in going tonight. Tom, she hoped, was getting his belongings together to move out of their house. She would stick to her promise. She would burn his belongings if she found them in the house. The other thing she wanted to do was to tell her mother about the upcoming trouble. She did not want her mother to the blind-sided. She deserved to know.

Julie's visit was a welcome break for Phyllis Knox. She loved her daughters dearly, and to the best of her ability, had given them a stable loving home, had taken them to church on Sunday, and sent them to the best private schools around. Julie had turned out to be as she had hoped. Susan on the other hand, she could not explain. She blamed herself for maybe pushing Susan too hard; pushing her to be more like Julie. She had failed. Phyllis Knox, at age 50, had beautiful gray hair that was draped to her shoulders. She had kept her youthful appearance despite many hardships. She was in excellent shape. She worked out three times a week, walked five miles every day, and kept a balanced diet. She was a sparkle of health.

She was glad that Julie had decided to come visit them. They talked about church mostly. The upcoming revival would be a success. They discussed the prayer's list they kept. There was always someone who needed a prayer. Julie and her mother decided to say some prayers for the people on the list. James Knox told them that he would retire and leave the women to their prayer session.

After a half hour of praying, Julie decided it was time to let her mother know about what was going to happen.

"Mom, I need to talk to you. It's very important. Please listen to me and try not to interrupt me until I'm through."

"Okay, Julie. What is it?"

"There's much to discuss, so just hear me out."

"All right, I'm listening."

"First, I'm going to divorce Tom."

"What? Why would you do that?"

"Just listen, mom. I've found out that he's been having an affair. He's had the affair since before we were married. The hard part about it is that the affair was with Susan."

Phyllis' face turned white.

Julie continued.

"Susan found out that she's infected with the HIV virus and that she possibly may have given it to Tom." Julie started to cry.

"It can't be true! Julie, tell me it's not true."

"I'm sorry, mom, but it is. Susan told me herself. She wouldn't be lying about this."

Julie cleared her throat.

"Anyway, we know Susan has her boyfriends and we know she wants to have sex all the time."

"Don't talk like that in this house!"

"Would you just listen to me, mother? This has something to do with you, too. Just listen!" Julie had lost her patience with her mother. She finally was going to stand up and say her peace.

"Susan is that way because of what happened to her when we were little. It happened to me too. I have the opposite effect of what Susan has. I hate sex."

Phyllis was clenching her hands together and was saying a silent prayer while her daughter carried on.

"The reason we are this way is because of what Daddy did to us."

Phyllis' head shot up. She looked at Julie in disbelieve.

"You look surprised, mother. I guess it is so unbelievable that you didn't know. You will hate yourself. Daddy molested us. He had sex with us, mama! He fondled us all the time, we had to masturbate him, he made us have oral sex with him, he forced us to be penetrated by him in every hole in our body. Mamma, I'm telling the truth."

"How can you say that about your father? He loves both of you so much. Why would he put Susan up above the garage if he didn't love her?"

"He's buying her silence, mother. He's supporting her to keep her quiet. It would ruin him if anyone outside of the family found out."

"You cannot prove any of this. No one will ever believe

83

you!"

"Well, according to Susan, she has evidence. She has videotapes that she secretly took. It shows daddy having sex with us."

Mother and daughter were so engrossed in their conversation, one being stunned and crying, the other talking and crying that they did not notice James Knox outside the living room door listening in on the conversation.

"Mamma, because of what daddy did, Susan has this terrible disease. And because of what Susan and Tom did for all these years, I may have it too!"

Phyllis was crying. Tears were running down her face. She looked older suddenly. She could not believe what her daughter was telling her, was the truth. It couldn't be true! Her husband could never do something like that. She had always trusted him, had the utmost respect for him. He was a deacon in the church for crying out loud.

"Mamma, what I'm going to tell you now is what will change your life forever. I've talked about this with Susan, and I'm going to help her with what she's doing. She's going to sue Daddy for what he's done to us. If she wins, Daddy will go to jail, maybe for the rest of his life. We've kept silent too long, mamma. It's time the truth be told."

"Sue him? Why would she do that?"

"He's the reason she's contracted the virus. His abuse branded her as it branded me. She's addicted to sex. That's the only way she can be happy. She's this way because of what he has done to her. He's responsible. He needs to be punished."

Julie's voice had dropped. She was no longer crying. Again she could feel the power of hate overtake her. She looked at her mother. Her face was white as snow. Her eyes had lost their sparkle and had turned dull. Tears were running down her cheeks. She had her hands together, clenching her skirt.

Phyllis looked up at Julie. She shook her head.

"I don't know if I can survive this, Julie. This is too much. I know I've been through a lot, but this is just too much. Don't go through with it. Think about me, Julie."

"No mother, I've thought about you; about the lie you've

84

been living. You are part of it too. You would never listen to us when we wanted to talk about it. Every time the subject of sex came up, you condemned us for even bringing up the subject. How did you ever get pregnant if sex is so bad? I will never be lucky enough to bear children. I will never now the joy that sex can bring. If you would have told us about sex, if you would have listened to Susan and me, maybe this would not have happened. Maybe you could have brought an end to this. But now, it's up to Susan and me to stop it. I'm sorry, mother, but we have to do this. I'm sorry if it will hurt you, if it will destroy you. But you could have stopped it a long time ago. If only you would've been more open-minded and not so stuck on your puritan believes and thoughts, it could have been different."

Julie kissed her mother on the forehead.

"I've got to go. Be strong, mamma. I love you."

"Don't leave me, Julie. Please don't leave me!"

"I've got to go, mamma. I'll see you tomorrow!"

Julie walked towards the living room door. James Knox quickly moved through the foyer, unseen by Julie. Julie made her way out the front door. Knox walked over to the window and watched her disappear. The headlights of a passing car made Julie turn her head to keep from being blinded. In the window of the foyer, she saw her father looking at her. A chill crept up her spine. Did he hear the conversation? She hoped not.

19.

After meeting with Susan Knox, Dimitri Van Acker went back to Kelly's to freshen up. It had been a hot summer day with temperatures nearing 100 degrees Fahrenheit. Every time he stepped out of his car, sweat beads started appearing on his forehead. His clothes had been soaked with sweat while looking at the house. When he arrived at Kelly's, he noticed that she was already home. Kelly told him that she quit her job at Tom Sutton's and was now 100% committed to Dimitri's business. She told him about how her mom and she had set up Tom Sutton. Van Acker found the story to be funny, although he hated that Helen had to go through the ordeal to find out what man her employer was. With the news that Kelly had quit and was now considered working for him, he in turn told Kelly about his meeting with Susan Knox. He gave her enough information to where she could start doing research. He told her that any information about any case he was working on was to be kept strictly confidential. Should he find out that she discussed cases with anyone except himself or his clients, he would terminate her instantly. Kelly understood the conditions and said she would start doing research on Monday morning.

Van Acker excused himself and took a cool shower. Feeling fresh again, he sat down at the kitchen table and did some preliminary paperwork on the Susan Knox case. He jotted down some notes and looked through his address book putting down a couple of numbers in his notes.

Kelly who had taken a shower while Van Acker was making his notes, walked back into the living room as Dimitri was finishing up.

"Dimitri, would you like to go over to my parent's house tonight?"

"I'd love to! I haven't seen your mom yet. I can't wait to see her."

"Let's go then."

"Okay, let's take my car."

Kelly had mentioned about wanting to ride in Van Acker's convertible. She was all admiration for it. While he had saved a lot of money, the one luxury Van Acker had spent considerable money on was his car. He had wanted a convertible, but could not decide which way to go. A colleague at the firm had let Dimitri test-drive his Mercedes 500. He immediately knew that was the car he wanted. Kelly was in love with it too.

"Here," Van Acker threw the keys to his car to her, "why don't you try it out?"

Kelly caught the keys and looked at them in disbelieve.

"Seriously?"

"Yeah, seriously."

Kelly hugged him and rushed out the door. She got behind the steering wheel and cranked the car. Van Acker got in on the passenger side and pushed a button on the dashboard. A compartment behind the seats opened and the top folded and disappeared inside the compartment. Kelly's eyes were all sparkle and she felt like a little girl in the candy shop.

Allen and Helen Murphy lived only about five minutes away from Kelly's. It was a short ride, but it was an exciting ride for Kelly. Van Acker told her to press down on the gas and test the car out. She did not have to be told twice and the five-minute ride under normal conditions lasted about half as long. Driving into the driveway, she honked the horn and was screaming at the top of her lungs. Allen, Helen and Michelle Murphy came rushing out to see what all the commotion was outside their home.

When Helen saw who it was, she rushed down the steps of the porch. Van Acker had barely enough time to get out of the car before she had her arms around his neck and was hugging him. They exchanged greetings and hugs. Allen Murphy decided that it was a perfect time for a little reunion celebration and told Michelle and Kelly to go get some steaks at the grocery store. Kelly looked at Van Acker to see if he would offer them to take his car. He smiled and told them to go for it. Both girls squealed and strapped themselves into Van Acker's car. Allen went down into the basement and got a couple of bottles of wine. It wasn't long before they all sat down, ate steaks, drank wine and talked about old times, politics and the future. There was laughter and happiness. Everybody had a good time. Then the phone rang.

Kelly answered the phone. It was for Michelle. Michelle told Kelly that she would take it in her room. Michelle hurried to her room and picked up the receiver. Kelly on the other end hung up.

"Hello?"

"Michelle?"

"Yes!"

"Hi, it's Bryan."

"Bryan, I thought you were supposed to be at some social?"

"I decided not to go. I had some thinking to do."

"You don't sound so good, Bryan. Is everything all right?"

Bryan Scarboro hesitated before answering. He did not know how to continue.

"Bryan, talk to me. What's going on?" Michelle insisted.

"Michelle, I received some bad news this evening."

"What Bryan, what is it?"

"I don't know how to tell you this."

Michelle was starting to get worried. It must have something to do with her, she thought.

"Bryan, does this have something to do with me?"

"Yes!"

Michelle turned pale.

"Tell me, Bryan. What is it?"

"Michelle, I found out that I...," Scarboro hesitated. He was looking for an easy way to break the news, but there wasn't. Michelle was insistent.

"Bryan, what did you find out that is so bad?"

"I may have contracted the HIV virus," he finally blurred out.

Michelle dropped the phone. She was staring at it, not knowing how it got on the floor and what she had just heard. She could feel her stomach contracting. She reached down and picked up the phone.

"Bryan, did I hear you right?" she said, hesitant and scared.

"Yes, you did."

"Bryan, you told me that I was the only woman in your life. You told me there was nobody else. Who is she? Some slut you slept with while in college? Tell me!"

Michelle was getting angry. Tears were starting to well up in her eyes. She felt weak.

"No. I... I lied to you, Michelle. I have been seeing someone else, for a while. I guess since I was still in High School."

"Who is she, Bryan? Do I know her?"

"I don't think it's relevant who she is."

"Like hell it's not! I want to know who!" Michelle raised her voice as she was clearly getting madder.

"All right, don't scream. I'll tell you. But you need to promise me that you will not confront her. Okay?"

"I can't promise that."

"You have to. I won't tell you unless you promise me not to confront her."

Michelle thought about it for a minute. If he was so backward to lie to her about having a relationship with someone else, then she was entitled to tell him a lie too.

"All right, Bryan, I promise not to confront her."

"It's Susan Knox."

Michelle's mouth dropped. Susan Knox!

"Are you sure?"

"Look, she told me tonight that she has AIDS. I've slept with her enough to know that I've been exposed. Yes, it's Susan."

"Listen, Bryan. I'm going to tell you once." Michelle was feeling her strength disappear and knew she had to get of the phone soon before she could no longer sound strong and angry.

"Do not, I repeat, do not ever come near me again. I never want to see you again. If you come near me again, I swear, you will regret it."

She pushed the power button on the phone. The phone slipped out of her hand and hit the floor. Tears were running down her cheeks. She collapsed on her bed. She had no strength left. Her mind quit working. She could feel her stomach contract. She had to get up. Get up off the bed and try to make it to the bathroom. She got up and staggered out the door to the bathroom. She barely made it before her stomach erupted.

Kelly, who had come in the house to get something to drink, heard her sister being sick in the bathroom. She went to check on her and found Michelle, white as a sheet, hugging he toilet.

"Michelle, are you alright?" Kelly asked worried.

Michelle did not answer. She just stared down in the toilet, her eyes fixated.

"Michelle, come on, honey, you need to get up."

Kelly tried to help Michelle up, but Michelle pushed her hands away.

"Don't touch me!" she screamed.

"Michelle, get up, now! Let's go in the living room, sit down and let's talk about what's wrong. Okay?"

Michelle turned her head to look at Kelly. Her eyes were empty. She nodded her head and managed to stand up. She was weak and almost fell. Kelly helped support her sister and guided her to the living room. She helped her sit down on the couch.

"I'll get mom and dad," Kelly told her.

"No!" Michelle exclaimed. "They can't know!"

"Know what, Michelle?"

Michelle started to cry again. She hid her face in her hands. Her body started to shake.

"Michelle, you need to tell me what's wrong. I can't help you if you don't tell me."

Michelle looked up at Kelly, her eyes red from crying.

"You can't help me. My whole life is over!"

"What are you talking about? Who was that on the phone?"

"Bryan. It was Bryan."

"Bryan Scarboro?"

Michelle nodded.

"We've been dating for a couple of weeks. This afternoon he took me to a motel room. We made love, my first time. It was wonderful. It felt so good."

"Michelle, you know Bryan's been sleeping around. I sure hope you used protection."

Michelle started to cry again. Kelly took this as a no for the use of protection.

"Michelle, honey, look at me. I gather you did not use protection. That was not smart. Why didn't you use protection? You know mom and dad have always preached to us that if we ever decided to have sex before we were married, we should insist on our lover to use protection. Why didn't you?"

"I don't know!" Michelle sobbed. "He seemed so sincere. He's been good to me. He told me he loved me, that I was the only girl in his life. I didn't know he's been sleeping around... I guess I didn't know him!"

"That's right. Now, if everything was so fine, why are you so sad right now? What did Bryan tell you that made you upset?"

"Please don't tell mom and dad! Promise?"

"I promise I won't tell if I think they don't need to know. Now, if I think that it's serious, then I will need to tell them. Do you understand that?"

Michelle nodded, hesitantly.

"Kelly," Michelle swallowed and again, tears were running down her cheeks. "Kelly, Bryan told me that he may have HIV. He found out tonight from one of the women he's been sleeping with."

Kelly felt her stomach hit bottom. She had never imagined that answer from Michelle. She scratched her head, trying to figure out what to do, what to say. This was serious. She had to tell her parents. But why worry them now. Could one time have given Michelle the virus? Bryan didn't even know if he had it. Michelle said he might.

"Michelle, I won't tell mom and dad yet."

"Now, there's something else I want to know. Did Bryan tell you whom he might have contracted it from?"

Michelle nodded.

"Can you tell me?"

Michelle had already made up her mind that she would not hold back that information. She would tell.

"Yes, it was Susan Knox."

Kelly whistled. She shook her head slightly, admitting that she was not surprised. She knew Susan's reputation.

"Listen, I need you to talk to Dimitri about his too. I can't tell you why; he'll have to tell you. But you need to tell him. It's important."

"Why? What does Dimitri have to do with this?"

"I'll let him tell you, okay? Now, when you go back out there, you just tell mom and dad that Bryan broke up with you and that you're heartbroken. Not a word about HIV till we know for sure. Deal?"

Michelle was agreeing with her sister. She did not want her mom and dad to find out. Kelly went back outside and told Dimitri that Michelle wanted to talk to him in private about something. Allen and Helen were curious. Kelly told them that Bryan had broken up with her and that she wanted to talk to Dimitri about it.

"You know the big brother thing!" Kelly explained.

Allen and Helen appeared to accept the big brother cover. Dimitri went inside and Michelle told him what she had told Kelly. After he heard Michelle out, he rushed outside.

"I need to go somewhere!" Dimitri looked at his watch. It was close to 10 o'clock. "I'll be back shortly to pick you up, Kelly."

"Is everything all right?" Allen asked, wondering why Dimitri rushed out the house so quickly after talking to Michelle.

"Yes, I just thought about something that I forgot to do earlier."

Dimitri got in his car and sped of, rocks and dust flying behind him. Allen Murphy was suspicious. He knew something was going on; something was wrong. Something was being kept from him and when it came to his family, he did not like things being kept from him. He would find out.

20.

Susan Knox jumped up out of bed. There was a load knocking on her door. She looked over at her alarm clock. 10:15. who could be knocking on her door this late in the evening. She grabbed a gown and put it over her naked body. She grabbed for her .380 sitting on her nightstand. Slowly she made her way to the front door. The knocking persisted. She could hear a voice on the other end of the door, a whispering but insistent voice.

"Susan! Open up! Susan?"

She looked out the window of her living room. She saw a man on her porch, dressed in shorts and a white shirt. She couldn't make out the face as it was hidden in the darkness.

"Susan? I know you're here. Open up! I've got to talk to you. Susan?"

Susan cocked her gun. She held it firmly in front of her as she unlocked the door as quietly as she could. She stepped away from the door.

"Who is it?" she demanded in a loud voice.

"Dimitri Van Acker. Let me in!"

Susan lowered her gun and opened the door.

"Dimitri? What are you doing here?"

"I need to know something for the case. I'm afraid if I don't ask you now, that I won't have the chance. Listen, I found out tonight that at least 2 people might already be infected with the HIV virus because of you. What's going on? Are you spreading the news?"

Susan looked surprised the news had traveled that fast and that Van Acker already knew about her telling possible victims.

"Yes. I've told a couple of people. Maybe I should have gotten in touch with you about it."

"Listen, there are innocent people out there getting hurt really fast. Do you know that Bryan Scarboro had unprotected sex this afternoon?"

"I know. He told me. Michelle Murphy, right?"

"Yes. He told her about the possibility of him having HIV and now she's scared to death. Let me tell you something. If you decide to tell anyone else about your AIDS diagnoses, you consult

93

me first. I'm your lawyer. There can be serious legal complications if you keep on telling people they might be infected. Do you understand?"

Susan nodded yes.

"I'm sorry. I've been so eager to get all this behind me. I wanted to go ahead and let everyone involved know why I can't have sex with them anymore. I guess I overstepped my boundaries."

"You sure did! Is there anything else I need to know before I leave? If there is, tell me now. If I'm going to represent you, you need to be honest with and up-front with me. No more behind the back stories to anyone. If you cannot follow these simple rules, then you need to find yourself another lawyer."

"Dimitri, I understand. I didn't mean to act behind your back. Besides, I needed to warn those people."

"All right, then. If there's anything else that you might think off that I need to know, call me on my cell phone. Here's the number." Dimitri gave Susan a piece of paper with his mobile number on it.

Outside, thunder was rolling and lightning was coloring the sky.

"I guess it's time for me to go. Remember, if you need anything, let me know."

"Okay, Dimitri, I will. Be careful out there."

"I will."

Van Acker walked out. When he started walking down the steps he heard a car speed off. He rushed down the steps and turned the corner of Susan's apartment. He could see the back of what looked to be a white Cadillac.

Could Tom Sutton have been outside, listening in? Van Acker shrugged it off. What were the chances that Tom would come back around Susan after she told him it was over? Van Acker got in his car and headed back towards the Murphy farm. When he passed the Sutton home, the curtains moved and a pair of eyes followed his car disappear in the distance.

21.

Tom Sutton had done what his wife had asked. He had gathered his belongings and loaded them in his car. He drove to Pinegrove, the next town to the north of Stuttgart and rented a room in the only motel in the little town. He bought a bottle of cheap whiskey and retreated to his room where he decided to watch television.

Flipping through the channels he found a murder mystery movie. It was a rerun from the Colombo series. Sutton watched, uninterested. He poured himself a glass of the whiskey and propped his back up against the backboard of the bed. As the movie progressed, he grew more and more interested in the way the murder was committed and how hard it was to find out who did it and how the murder had happened. Of course, the-ever-probing and questioning Colombo made the whole case seem easy. Sutton cut off the television. He thought about the way the murder was planned and how the evidence was either destroyed or distorted. He grabbed a writing tablet out of one of the drawers of the dresser in the room and jotted down some notes. A smile appeared on his face. It would work. It had to.

Sutton ran out to his car and got his suitcase. Back in the room he opened it and rooted through it trying to find what he was looking for. At the bottom of the suitcase, he finally spotted what he was looking for: a black pair of pants and a black T-shirt. He put them on. He put on his tennis shoes. They were white as snow and they stood out like a sore thumb. He put them on. Looking in the mirror, he seemed satisfied with what he saw. He walked out and locked the door behind him. He got in his car. He opened the glove compartment and took hold of a .380 revolver. A smile covered his face. Julie's gun he thought. He remembered giving Susan a replica copy for Christmas one year. Nobody thought anything about it. He just seemed to be the concerned brother-in-law. He had forgotten about the gun. Julie had put it in his car when they went to the mountains on vacation last year. She had failed to take it out when they came back home. It had been in his car since then. Sutton looked at the shiny metal. A thunderstorm was moving into the area. Lightning struck. The white flash lit up the gun. A cold shiver ran

95

down his spine. He put the gun down on the seat next to him. He grabbed in the glove compartment again. He found his flashlight. He put it next to the gun on the passenger seat. There was one more thing he needed. He got out of the car and walked around to the trunk. He opened it and among his gold clubs, he found a plastic trash bag. He picked up the trash bag, closed the trunk and climbed back in the driver's seat. It started to sprinkle and the thunder and lightning intensified. Sutton looked at his watch. Ten o'clock. He cranked his car and drove off towards Stuttgart.

The drive to Stuttgart was a difficult one. It had started to rain heavy and he could barely see 100 feet in front of him. Once or twice, he felt his car swaying as the tires caught a puddle of water. The 15-mile drive took about 30 minutes. Approaching the city limits, it stopped raining. He noticed a patrol car sitting on the left hand side of the road. He tried to see who the officer was. His windows were foggy and he could not make out a face. He wiped his windshield with his hand. Passing the patrol car, lightning hit and the road lit up. Sutton saw the officer's face. It was Hope Olson. Olson had seen the face of the driver of the white Cadillac too. She was wondering what Tom Sutton was up too this late in the evening, coming out of Pinegrove.

Sutton drove into town. He turned towards his house. He would see if Julie was still up. Maybe, just maybe, he could talk to her. Arriving at his house, he noticed that all the lights were out. He wasn't surprised. It was just past 10:30. Julie never stayed up late. He drove past the house and turned around. Passing back by his house, he did not see the curtains in the living room move to the side. Julie was still up. She had not, as Sutton had suspected, gone to sleep yet. She followed the car with her eyes as well as she could. The rain had picked up again. She saw the brake lights come on as the car neared her parent's house. She shook her head. Would he stop and go see Susan?

Tom Sutton neared Susan's place. He slowed down. He was ready to pull into the driveway next to Susan's car when he saw there was a car already sitting in that place. He noticed the tag. It was Dimitri Van Acker. What was he doing here? Sutton balled his fists. Maybe Susan was lying about having AIDS! She wanted to get rid of him. She had a new lover! Sutton turned his car away from the

96

house when Susan's door opened and Van Acker walked out. Pushing the accelerator, Sutton made a hasty departure. He did not want to be seen by Van Acker. Not now. He decided to go by his office and prepare for his plan. He had the tools he needed. All that was left to do was to find the perfect time to do it. Tonight would be perfect if the thunder and lightning stayed around a bit longer. He smiled as he pulled up into his parking spot at his office. He grabbed the gun, the flashlight and the plastic trash bag and ran the short distance to the backdoor of his office. Sutton disappeared inside and slammed the door behind him.

22.

After Michelle Murphy had cut their conversation short, Bryan Scarboro sat down with his head buried in his hands. What was he to do? Susan didn't want to have anything to do with him anymore, and now Michelle had told him never to come around her either. He shook his head. His life was over, as he knew it. From now on, everything would be different. A hell of a price to pay for having a little fun, he thought. There had to be something he could do. He had told Susan that kicking him out of her life would not be the end. Maybe he should follow up on his promise. But how? He could start talking to everybody she was associated with in town; tell them about her dirty little secret! He could haunt her, stalk her, and make life a living hell for her. His head shot up from out of his hands. His eyes lit up. Better yet..., he thought. He got up, quickly dressed himself and walking into his parent's living room. Both his parents were already asleep. He turned on the lights and walked over to his father's lazy chair. Next to it stood a table where his father kept his personal items: his billfold, his checkbook, his car keys, and his office keys. Scarboro grabbed the office keys. He turned the lights back off and slipped out the door. He got in his car and drove off towards his father's office.

Scarboro turned the key in the lock and he heard the spring release. He pushed open the door. A loud beep greeted him. The alarm was activating. He had 30 seconds to turn it off. Swiftly he walked over to the alarm pad and punched in the four numbers. The alarm went quiet. Without turning on any lights, he made his way to his father's office. As the office was in the back of the building, he wasn't worried about turning on the light. Quickly he moved to his father's desk and sat down. He opened the file drawer and scanned the contents. He found what he was looking for. Quickly he looked over the paperwork in the file. His eyes fell on the medication prescription, Coeurnechol. He closed the file and dropped it back into its proper place. Scarboro walked over to his father's medicine supply cabinet. He looked for the right key on his father's key chain and opened the cabinet. He found the medication. There were six vials in the closet. He grabbed two and deposited them into his pocket. He walked to the door, turned off the light and closed the door behind him. Quickly he moved back to the alarm pad, and reset the office alarm. He walked outside and pulled the door shut behind him. He could hear a car coming closer. He looked around. His car was parked several blocks away hidden in an alley between some of the older buildings in town. He would be seen by whoever was driving by. A risk he didn't want a take. He ran to the corner of the building and darted around it. He hurried to the end of his father's practice and hid in the back behind some thick bushes.

Hope Olson who had left her position on the North end of town was patrolling the streets. Passing through the business section of town, she thought she had seen somebody running down the street away from the doctor's office. She sped up and reached the corner of the building. She turned her search light towards the building and moved it to see if anybody was hiding. She didn't see anything. She turned the search light off and slowly advanced, looking in her rearview mirror. She was not dreaming. She knew she had seen someone. A little ways from the building she stopped her car. She would wait it out. See if whoever was hiding behind the building would come out.

Scarboro was watching the patrol car from around the corner of the building. It was Hope Olson. He knew that if she saw him, she would give him a hard time about sneaking around town at this hour. He decided to walk around the building the opposite way from her. Maybe he could make it to his car without being seen. Scarboro walked the length of the building complex. He turned the corner and walked towards his car. He had to cross one lit area. He was nervous. The thunderstorms that had been hanging around all night were still in the area and it started to rain. Scarboro knelt down and kept an eye towards the patrol car.

Olson waited a couple of minutes after it started raining. Maybe the rain would flush out whoever was hiding. But nothing stirred. She decided that she must have made a mistake. She would come back later in the night and make sure all the doors were locked. She had no desire right now to get wet from the rain. She drove off and headed back towards the South end of the county.

Bryan Scarboro was in the clear. He got in his car and drove home. He was soaking wet. On the short drive to his parent's house, he felt the hardness of the bottles against his body. He smiled as he walked into his house and walked upstairs to his room. He needed to change his cloths. Then he'd be ready.

23.

Hope Olson was 34 years old. She had been a deputy Sheriff for 4 years. She had enlisted in the Navy after graduating college and had worked in Navy intelligence. She had served during Desert Storm in the first Iraq war. After serving her term with the Navy, she declined to stay on and make a career out of the Armed Services, instead she returned to her hometown of Stuttgart and joining the Sheriff's department. She was well qualified for the job and her male colleagues treated her as on of their own. They all knew that when it came down to it, she could easily kick all of their combined butts without breaking a sweat. Hope Olson was physically active. She worked out four day a week at the local gym and was an expert in martial arts. She could take on anybody that would try to take her down.

The storms that had been pushing through the area were finally moving out. The sky cleared up and a full moon was illuminating Stuttgart. Hope Olson looked at her watch. It was close to eleven. Another hour and her second shift of the day would be over. She was tired and worn out after pulling a double shift. One of the other officers had called in, both his child and wife were sick in bed and he could not make it in. She had volunteered for the double shift. The Sheriff himself had offered to take the shift, but she insisted that she wanted to take it. It would mean double pay for the second shift. She could use the money. She had just bought a house and needed to do a lot of renovating to it.

Hope decided to check to locks at the local businesses before she returned to the station. It was a routine for the department to do frequent checks on the locks of the local businesses. Hope started on the south end of the business center and made her way crisscrossing the street to the north end. Everything looked fine. None of the doors seemed to be tampered with. She looked ahead. She had three businesses left to do. Dr. Scarboro's office was the last building on the street. It wasn't part of the row house complex of which most of the businesses were part off. It was sitting about 50 feet away from the other buildings. An alley that was unlit separated the office from the other buildings. Hope was always careful. She always walked down the alley on her way back to her patrol car. You never new if someone would be hiding in the alley and tried to jump you. She held her hand on her unlocked gun holster as she passed the alley. She had her flashlight in her hands. She turned it on and pointed the light beam into the alley. There was nothing there. Relieved, she continued and reached the entrance door to the doctor's office. Everything looked fine. It did not look as if it was tampered with. That done, Hope turned around and started her way back to her patrol car. She shone her flashlight into the alley before she entered it. Something caught her eyes. There was something shiny on the ground at the back corner of the doctor's office. Cautiously she moved down the alley to the place where the shiny object was. She reached the corner of the building. She pointed the flashlight to the ground. Hope saw a gold bracelet lying on the ground. She reached down and picked it up. The bracelet had a nameplate on it. Hope studied it more closely. It had an inscription on one side of the bracelet.

"Bryan S.," she read out loud.

Hope tried to recall her earlier patrol when she checked the locks. It had been before she thought she had seen movement around the doctor's office. The bracelet had not been there. She would have seen it for sure as she shone her light down the alley. So she had been right! She had seen someone. She wondered what Bryan had been doing sneaking around his father's office at this hour of the evening. She clinched her fist as she was furious with herself for not following her instincts. She had to find out what he was doing out here late at night, especially sneaking around, and hiding from anyone who might see him. Hope dropped the bracelet in her shirt pocket. She would go see him in the morning and ask him what he was doing here.

Hope left the alley and made her way back to her car. She had one last business to check on. Tom Sutton's office was not in the business section of town. It was located on a side street. Hope always made that her last stop. It was on her way back to the station. When she reached Sutton's practice, she pulled up into the back parking lot. She always checked the back door first and then walked to the front of the building. When she pulled up, she noticed that Sutton's car was sitting in the parking lot. Hope was feeling uneasy. Sutton never left his car parked at the office. As a matter of fact, she had seen him come from the direction of Pinegrove. She got out of her patrol car and walked over to the white Cadillac. She felt the door. It was locked. She shone her flashlight into the car. Empty! Hope was puzzled. She walked to the back door and felt the doorknob. Locked! Walking around the building to the street side she unlocked her holster and put her hand on the butt of her gun. She would be ready in case something was going on. At each window, Hope pointed her flashlight inside the building. She did not see anything or anybody suspicious. Still, she was not satisfied. She had a feeling that something was not right and this time she was going with her instinct. She walked back to her patrol car and called into the station.

"Charlie 1, this is Charlie 5, I need you to call over to the Sutton home and check on something for me, over."

"Go ahead, Charlie 5, what is the concern? Over."

"Check and see if Tom is at home, and if not, ask Julie if she knows where he is. Over."

"Any reason you are suspicious? Over."

"Yes, Sutton's car is parked at his office building. He's nowhere to be found. It's not like him to leave his car at the office. Over."

"Hold on. I'm placing the call now. Over."

"10-4"

Hope sat in here patrol car waiting for an answer. She scanned the area again. Not a sign of anybody around the building. Sure, Sutton lived only a mile from the office and could have walked home, but with it raining when he came back from Pinegrove, he would not have walked home in the rain. Hope went through a couple of possibilities. She analyzed each one and could not come up with a satisfying answer.

"Come back, Charlie 5."

"Go ahead, Charlie 1, I'm listening, over."

"I talked to Julie Sutton. She told me that she kicked Tom Sutton out of the house tonight. She suspects that he's spending the night at his office. Over."

"Thank you, Charlie 1. Over and out."

Hope stared at the office building. If Tom were spending the night in the office, why would he have come from Pinegrove that late

103

in the evening? There was a motel in Pinegrove. That would sure be more comfortable than sleeping on the couch in his office. She did not understand the reasoning for that. She shook her head and started the patrol car. It was almost midnight, time to head back to the station. Hope drove out of the parking lot. A black car with its lights dimmed drove by. Hope had not seen the car coming. The car was all but invisible in the night. Hope nearly hit the car coming out of the driveway. The car was speeding. As the car drove by, she noticed it was a coupe. She could not see the tag. She thought about pursuing the car but it was late and she was tired and after pulling a double shift, she did not feel like a car chase. She decided not to spoil the evening of the idiot in the black coupe and turned in the opposite direction of the speeding car and headed for the station.

24.

The person clad in black made its way closer to the house. The thunderstorms were out of the area and the moon was bright enough to provide the necessary light for the person to find the way to its destination effortlessly. The person blended into the shadows the moon provided. There was a small carrying pouch attached to the person's stomach.

The Knox' garage came into view. All the lights were out in the big house. Everybody was asleep. The apartment above the garage was dark as well. Susan Knox was asleep. The person stayed in the shadows of the trees and houses making its way to the Knox home. Reaching the steps to the apartment above the garage an object was retrieved from the pouch. A small beam of light protruded in front of the person. The flashlight was positioned in the person's mouth. Slowly and looking around, the person made its way up the stairs. Reaching the front door, the person reached in the pouch again. This time it took a little longer to find the wanted object. Hands were nervously moving around in the pouch trying to find what was needed for the next step. The moon lit up the porch and the intruder would be visible to anyone watching the apartment. Finally, the right object was found and the moonlight reflected from a flat piece of metal. The piece of metal was pushed into the lock of the door. A few quick moves and the spring released. Quickly the piece of metal disappeared back into the pouch. The door opened. A faint squeak sounded as the hinges turned. The intruder disappeared inside the house.

With the flashlight tightly pressed between its lips, the intruder scanned the area. The light beam of the flashlight shone into the living room, then the kitchen. The beam traveled across the walls. It froze when it lit up a wall outlet. The intruder grabbed into the pouch again. This time, a timing device was produced. It was a timing device used to let table lamps come on when one was not at home. The intruder looked at its watch. The timing device was pushed into sequence with the watch. Once the time on the timing device was the same as the watch, it was placed into the receptacle. The activation pin was pushed 40 minutes ahead of the current time.

The intruder got up. The beam of the flashlight was once

again moving through the apartment. The way to the bedroom was found. Slowly and carefully, the bedroom was entered. Susan Knox was asleep on top of the covers. The ceiling fan above the bed was moving at full speed. Susan was sleeping in the nude. The intruder smiled. The beam of the flashlight was moving through the room, scanning the contents of it. It stopped on a pillow. The pillow was picked up. Holding the pillow with the left hand, the intruder pulled a gun from its right pocket. The barrel of the gun was placed to the surface of the pillow. There was a second of hesitation, the arms of the intruder relaxed and the pillow and gun lowered. Then, the pillow was raised, the gun was pointed in the direction of Susan's chest and the trigger was pulled. The pillow muffled the sound of the gunpowder exploding inside the barrel. The pillow dropped to the ground and the gun disappeared back into the right pocket of the intruder's pants. The bullet had penetrated the body just underneath the left breast into the heart, and upward through the lungs. Susan's eyes shot open as the bullet hit her body. She opened her mouth but could not make a sound. The air in her lungs was not exiting from her mouth. She could not breathe. The bullet, slowed down by the friction against the pillow had not made it outside her body. It was lodged in the top of her spine just beneath her neck. Susan was grasping for air. She could not feel her body. She was paralyzed. Her head started to shake violently. Her brain was not receiving oxygen. Her heart was not sending blood to it anymore. Finally her body stopped shaking. Susan Knox was dead.

Little blood had flowed from the bullet wound. Most of the bleeding had been internally. The intruder had stood and watched the dying Susan. Now, she lay there, naked on the bed, eyes and mouth wide open. The small black hole in Susan's chest was barely visible as her left breast covered most of it.

"I hope you burn in Hell!" the killer said softly.

It was time to get out of the apartment. The killer made its way back into the living room, crossed into the kitchen and stopped in front of the stove. It was a gas stove. The killer turned the knobs of the burners on the stove to the on position. Soon the smell of gas filled the room. Quickly the killer crossed the living room to the door. Opening the door a little, the killer scanned the area. Nobody was around. The door opened and closed. The steps were taken two at a time. Just as quietly as the killer had appeared and completed its task, the killer disappeared. A few minutes later, a black coupe drove away from behind a building about 200 yards from Susan's apartment, a person dressed in black sitting behind the steering wheel. The clock on the dash read 11:35.

25.

Allen Murphy pulled Dimitri Van Acker to the side when he returned to pick up Kelly. He questioned Dimitri about rushing out in a hurry after talking to Michelle. He wanted to know what was going on. Michelle was upset. Did it have something to do with Dimitri?

The thundershowers were gone, and Murphy and Van Acker walked down the driveway, away from the house.

"Tell me Dimitri, what was so important that you had to rush out so fast? One moment, you're talking to my daughter, the next you're gone, and Michelle is crying. Tell me what's going on!"

Van Acker looked up at the sky. The clouds were clearing and the stars were starting to sparkle again. He wished the clouds would disappear for Michelle. He wished that her eyes would sparkle again like the stars. He didn't think they would.

He swallowed hard before he addressed Murphy.

"Allen, we go back a long time and I consider you one of my best friends. I don't know if you can handle why I had to leave so fast."

"What do you mean; don't know whether I can handle it?"

"The truth will be hard to take. However, before jumping to any conclusions, you need to understand that what I'm going to tell you may not be as bad as it may seem at first."

"Dimitri, my friend, quit talking in riddles. Tell me what it is!"

"All right, if you insist, I will tell you. But you need to promise me that you will not confront Michelle until I know that she'll be able to handle you talking to her about it. I made her a promise. I promised her that I would not tell you or Helen. The only reason I'm telling you, is because I don't want you to find out from someone else."

Murphy looked Van Acker in the eyes. A cold shiver ran down Van Acker's spine. He needed to be careful. He knew Allen Murphy. He needed to choose his words carefully. One word interpreted the wrong way could send him of the handle.

"Allen," Van Acker wrapped his arm around the older man's shoulders. "Michelle has been involved in something that may have put her in danger of contracting a disease. I cannot tell you whom with, but I don't hold you for a fool and I'm sure you will be able to find out for yourself whom I'm talking about."

"What disease?" Murphy asked his voice lower than normal.

"She may have been exposed to the HIV virus."

Allen Murphy's head dropped to his chest. He shook his head in disbelieve.

"Michelle? You mean Michelle may have been exposed to..." He couldn't go on. His emotions took over and he did not know how to continue. He was feeling guilt, anger, and helplessness all at the same time.

Van Acker put his hand on the man's shoulder. He squeezed his shoulder gently, letting Allen Murphy know that he understood what he was going through.

"Allen, listen, it has to do with one of my clients."

Murphy's head shot up.

"One of your clients? How many clients do you have already? You've been here a day! I can only think of one that you may have."

"I can't say anymore, Allen. I must say though that my client is not directly responsible for the actions of someone else. My client did not have sex with Michelle."

"I cannot believe Michelle would do something like that. She's a picture of morality. She's always talking about not having sex before she'll marry. I was convinced that I would not have to worry about her contracting anything. Kelly on the hand, that's a different story. But Michelle..."

"Look, I don't think that she was functioning in her full capacity at the time it happened. From what she told me, she had been lured into drinking. She's not into drinking either. But whomever she was with had enough power over her to get her to drink and then go to bed with him."

"It's Bryan Scarboro, isn't it?"

"Allen, I told you that I would not reveal the name. But you're a smart man. You know who it was."

"That little son of a..." Murphy was headed back to the house, his fists balled and his head shaking.

Van Acker ran after him and grabbed him by the arm.

109

Murphy tried to shake him off, but Van Acker was stronger.

"Allen, listen. You cannot do anything now that will make this right. If you go out there and find Bryan and do what I think you're gonna do, you will just make matters worse. The best thing to do is to stay calm and be rational. Michelle will need to be HIV test. If it comes back negative, then we'll go from there. She will have to be tested for a while, but if it stays negative, then she'll be fine. If she does show positive however, then I will tell you of what possible action you can take and whom you can take action against. Right now, everything needs to be taken one step at a time. Do you understand me?"

Murphy had stared at the ground while Van Acker lectured him. He now slowly raised his head. He eyes were glazed and Van Acker could see tears starting in the corners of his eyes.

"I understand, Dimitri. It's just so damn hard to spend all your life trying to raise your children the right way and then out of nothing you get hit in the head. All the work you do raising them is erased in a moment of deception by someone you don't have any control over."

Van Acker understood what Allen Murphy was saying. The Murphy's had done a good job with their two daughters. Both of them were decent young women. However, both of them made mistakes that were beyond what Allen and Helen could have foreseen while raising them. There was only so much you could teach them. You had to let them go and let them venture out on their own, let hem make their own decisions. Some worked through it without any problems; some have problems from day one. Van Acker didn't know how to convey that message to Murphy.

"Allen, you and Helen did the best you could with both your girls. All of us make mistakes. All of us fall victim to some slick talking guy or gal at some point in our lives. I've made mistakes that I wish I hadn't. But they were my mistakes. I couldn't blame my mom or dad. You cannot blame yourself. You raised them to the best of your ability. You gave them all the knowledge that you could and hoped that they would take that knowledge and apply it in their adult lives and expand on it as they go along."

Van Acker sighted. He didn't know whether he was making sense to Murphy whose eyes were still fixated and noncoherent.

110

"Com'on, Allen. It's getting late. Let's go in, sit down and drink us a beer."

Murphy looked Van Acker in the eyes.

"You know, I'm glad you're here to help me through this. If I had found out from someone else besides you, I'd probably be knocking that kid over the head by now. But you're right. I just need to wait it out and see what's going to happen. Thanks, Dimitri."

"Any time, my friend."

They headed back towards the house. As they came up to the house, Michelle rushed passed them, got in her mother's car and sped off.

"Wonder where she's going in such a hurry?" Van Acker questioned.

Helen Murphy walked out on the deck in tears.

"Allen, oh God, Allen. Something terrible has happened to Michelle."

"I know, honey, I know."

"Did she tell you?"

"No, she told Dimitri. He told me everything."

"What are we going to do? My baby, oh, my baby!"

Allen Murphy took his wife in his arms and held her close. She was beating her fists in his back. Kelly walked out on the deck. She wiped tears from her cheeks.

Van Acker made his way to her.

"Did she tell her?"

Kelly nodded her head.

"Do you know where she's going?"

"I have no idea. She just said that she couldn't stand it anymore, that she needed to get out. Then she ran out and took off."

Allen and Helen walked in the house. Van Acker looked at Murphy and motioned that he would take Kelly home.

"I'll see you tomorrow, Allen."

Van Acker and Kelly drove off. The ride was quiet. Neither said a word. They arrived at Kelly's house just after eleven. Van Acker excused himself and went straight to bed. Kelly sat down at the kitchen table. She was upset, more so than she admitted. Her mind was racing. What could she do? What could make the situation easier? She exhausted herself thinking about the situation.

She finally got up and walked into her bedroom. She collapsed on the bed. The clock on the nightstand read 11:45.

26.

The pin on the timing device in Susan's apartment was ready to activate the unit. This would create a little spark. The apartment by now was filled with gas escaping from the stove.

The combination of the AC and the ceiling fan above the bed, had cooled Susan's body at a hastened pace. If the oncoming inferno did not destroy the evidence of murder, then for sure, the time of death would be placed earlier than it had taken place.

The activation pin pushed the mechanism inside the timing device to the on position. A small spark was created. The spark came in contact with the gas in the apartment causing the gas to ignite, causing an explosion. The pressure from the explosion shattered the windows and glass was projected away from the apartment. As the fireball spread through the apartment, everything that came in contact with it was scorched within seconds of the explosion. All flammable materials caught fire and set the apartment into a blaze.

The explosion was heard throughout the small town of Stuttgart. Everywhere, people shot up out of bed, wondering what the bang they had heard was and where it came from. Looking out their windows, the citizens saw a bright glare coming from the direction of the Knox home.

***

James Knox had just lain down in the guest bedroom when the explosion occurred. The guestroom faced the apartment and the pressure from the blast shattered the windows of the guestroom and propelled the broken glass inside. Pieces of the glass hit Knox and he was cut in several places. He got up and wiped his hand over his face. Blood from the cuts were on his hand. He walked over to the window. He looked at his garage and Susan's apartment. They were engulfed in flames. He hurried to his own bedroom to wake his wife. Phyllis was already up out of bed and into the hallway. She could not see Susan's apartment. Knox told his wife of what had happened. Phyllis started to cry and beat Knox on the chest. Then she fainted.

113

***

Allen Murphy had just gone to bed when he heard the explosion. He got up out of bed and walked outside on the porch to see if he could see anything. He saw an orange-yellow light illuminating the sky. Instinctively, Murphy knew there was a fire. He was a volunteer fire fighter and fire chief of his station. He gave lectures and instructional courses at the local schools and at the other fire stations. Murphy ran back in the house and put his clothes on. He grabbed his alert radio and headed out the door. As he got into his truck, the alert radio started chirping. The message that Murphy received confirmed his suspicious. There was a fire. He listened to the dispatcher to make sure that he would have the exact location. When he heard the location, his mind went blank for a second. The Knox apartment! That's were Susan Knox lived. For a second he hesitated and deliberated whether to go to the fire or not. His conscience would not allow him not to go. He had a duty to fulfill no matter who was in trouble. He pressed down on the gas pedal a little bit harder. As he was driving towards the fire station, he grabbed his cell phone and dialed Kelly's number. It only rang once before there was an answer.

"Kelly?"

"No, this is Dimitri. Allen is that you?"

"Yes, listen, there's a fire at Susan Knox' apartment. From the sound of it, there was an explosion. I think you need to be in on this one."

"Thanks for calling Allen. I'll see you there."

Both Kelly and Van Acker had heard the explosion. Van Acker had been asleep. The noise from the explosion was so intense that he woke up instantly. It reminded him of the explosion in an apartment building across the road from his apartment when he was in school in Belgium. He had never forgotten that event. The destruction to the building, the surrounding buildings and the cars parked in the street had stuck with him. He rushed out the bedroom door the same time Kelly did. Both looked at each other with frightened eyes. Walking outside they could see the orange glow of the fire. They were both wondering what had happened. As soon as

114

Van Acker got the call from Murphy, he told Kelly of what her father had told him. He put on his clothes and made his way to Susan's apartment. Kelly got dressed too. She was not going to miss the excitement.

***

Hope Olson had just clocked out when the explosion happened. The Knox' residence was only a few blocks away from the station and both Hope and the dispatcher dropped to the floor when the explosion occurred. Hope was the first to get up off the floor. She looked out the window. The blaze from the fire extended above the buildings between the station and the Knox home. She told the dispatcher to sound the alarm to all volunteer firefighters. She would find out where the fire was and call back to give specific instructions. Hope rushed out the station, got in her patrol car and headed towards the fire. When she reached the Knox' house, the garage and apartment above the garage were in full blaze. She called the dispatcher and told her that it was the Knox' garage and Susan Knox' apartment that were on fire.

***

Within 7 minutes from the call, Allen Murphy arrived at the scene with the first fire truck. Two volunteers, one of whom was Phil Langston, with his station arrived at the same time. They started unrolling the hoses and made the connection to the fire hydrant across the street from the apartment. Murphy was glad the fire was within the city limits and not outside in the county. At least now, with access to a fire hydrant they had all the water supply they needed. If the fire would have occurred outside the city limits, they would have to result to the water stored in the tanks of the fire trucks. This could mean having to leave the scene of the fire to go refill the trucks. Within a few minutes, Murphy and Langston hooked up the hose to the hydrant and turned the water on. The third firefighter was struggling to keep the pressurized hose steady while shooting water on the burning building. The other fire stations had their trucks on the scene shortly after that. It wasn't long before all stations had their hoses out and were suppressing the fire.

**

When Van Acker arrived at the scene of the fire, he stopped his car a good distance away from all the commotion. He got out of his car and looked at the scene playing out in front of him. Firefighters were everywhere running around with hoses spraying water on the building. Others where trying to enter the building. The only way into Susan's apartment was to use the wooden steps to the front door. Water was sprayed onto the steps to keep them from catching fire. Dimitri walked closer to the burning building. He was looking around, trying to find a familiar face. He spotted Murphy and pushed his way through the crowd to him.

"Allen! Allen!" Van Acker shouted as loud as he could to overpower the noise from the fire, the fire trucks and the crowd of thrill seekers that had gathered around the burning apartment. Van Acker finally got Murphy's attention and he motioned for Van Acker to come closer.

"I don't see Susan anywhere, Allen. Have you seen her yet?"

"No. I'm afraid that she didn't make it out in time. I'm ready to go into the building now to see if I can find her."

"All right! Let me know if you find her, okay?"

"Will do!"

The intensity of the fire had decreased with the gallons of water being poured onto the building. Murphy saw his change to enter the building. He put on his helmet and pushed the visor down over his eyes. With care he started up the steps. He made it to the top without incident. The door to the apartment was no longer there. The force of the explosion had catapulted it towards the Knox' house and had hit the house, knocking a hole in the wall. The door was sticking halfway out the wall. Murphy entered the apartment building one step at a time. He did not want to take any chances. The flooring was still burning in some places and he did not know to what extent the floor had weakened. He knew not to call out Susan's name. The answer would be silence. He looked around, pointing his flashlight around the apartment. He noticed the roof over the living room area was gone while over the rest of the apartment the roof was still in place, however burning severely. He made a mental not the explosion must have happened in the living room. Murphy eased his way into the hallway and found his way to Susan's bedroom. Even though the fire had been intense, the bedroom portion of the house had not burned as bad as the rest of the house. Still, flames were shooting from the floor along the walls and onto the ceiling. The firefighters below followed Murphy's movements and made sure that they were applying water in the right places. Murphy pointed his flashlight on the bed and felt his stomach drop. On the bed, he could see the charred remains of a woman. Susan must have been sleeping when the explosion happened. The fire must have spread through the house fast and had caught her of guard, burning her in the process. Murphy grabbed his radio and announced to the EMT's that he had an expired body. The EMT's in turn got their cart out of the ambulance and positioned it at the bottom of the steps. Murphy reached over and lifted Susan's body from the bed. Her petite figure was no challenge to him. He lifted her over his left shoulder and eased his way back to the door opening. He walked down the stairs. The gathered crowd grew silent. Murphy laid the body on the cart and the EMT's immediately covered the body with a white blanket. Murphy tried to find Van Acker. He had no trouble finding him.

Van Acker rushed through the crowd at Murphy. In the light of the fire trucks, Murphy could see that Dimitri Van Acker was red in the face and obviously upset.

"What the hell do you think you're doing? You can't just take a body out of a burned up house. What if there was foul play? What if there was evidence on the body? You could have destroyed the evidence!"

Murphy was surprised by the sudden outburst from his friend. Dimitri Van Acker had never raised his voice at him. They had their differences, but it had never come to any shouting.

"Look, Dimitri," Murphy said in a calm voice. "There was no foul play in her death. She burned. More than likely, she suffocated before she died, but she died because of the fire."

Van Acker shook his head.

"I can't believe this. This place really is backwards. I didn't want to listen to my friends in DC when they told me I was moving back to where the clock stopped 100 years ago. I'm starting to think

117

they were right." He pointed his finger at Allen Murphy.

"Let me tell you something, my friend. Never, ever, assume there is no foul play when you deal with a fire. I know that you're the expert when it comes to dealing with fires. Well, I'm here to tell you that you may not be the expert you think you are. I've dealt with cases where people burned up, drug dealers found dead in their burned homes. I've been in those houses. I've seen the destruction of fire, and I've seen what the forensic scientists look for when investigating a burned-out house. I can tell you whether this was intentional or not. I can tell you right now," Van Acker looked around. He had gathered a crowd. He needed to be careful about what he said. Not only did he need to protect Susan's name at this time; he also needed to think about his future.

Murphy, who had taken the verbal onslaught as calmly as he could, pulled Van Acker to the side.

"Listen, Dimitri. I'm not going to stand here and listen to you telling me that I don't know how to do my job! You got that? You're my friend and I want to keep it that way. Now get your ass back behind that line and let me do my job!" Murphy pointed to the yellow caution tape the Sheriff's department had placed around the apartment perimeter.

Van Acker looked at the ground. He shook his head and finally walked back towards the yellow line. He turned around and looked at Murphy.

"I'm telling you. Investigate this fire. It's foul play!"

***

Hope Olson who had stayed at the scene of the fire had watched Van Acker and Murphy argue. She couldn't make out what about, but she suspected it had something to do with the fire. Van Acker had to walk near her car to get to his car. She would approach him and find out what was going on.

Before Dimitri Van Acker could make it to Hope's car, he was pulled aside. Van Acker looked at the woman who was pulling his arm. It was Phyllis Knox, Susan's mother. She had tears running down her cheeks and she looked pale.

"Young man, I overheard you talking with Allen Murphy. I

want to know why you think my daughter was murdered."

Van Acker was caught of guard by the word murdered. He had referred to the fire being foul play; not that Susan had been murdered.

"Ma'am, I didn't say that your daughter was murdered. I said that I think the fire is foul play."

"Why would anyone even think about hurting Susan? Much less murder her!"

"Ma'am, I can't answer those questions. I don't know if you remember me."

"I know who you are. Dimitri Van Acker. You used to date Susan. She let you go. God knows why, but she did. I understand that you're a lawyer now."

"Yes, ma'am, I am. Susan had asked me to help her with some legal matters."

"You came all the way back from up North just to help out Susan? It must be a legal problem!"

"No, ma'am, I was planning on moving back anyway. It just happened to fall in place with Susan's needs."

Phyllis looked around and pulled Van Acker's shoulders down so she could whisper in his ear.

"Wouldn't have anything to do with sexual abuse, would it?"

"I'm afraid that at this point I'm not at liberty to discuss that with anyone."

"Wouldn't have something to do with her having the AIDS virus, would it?" Phyllis kept probing.

"With all due respect, ma'am, like I said, I cannot discuss the matter at this time."

Van Acker excused himself and started his way to his car again. When he reached Hope's patrol car, she called out his name.

"Dimitri!"

Van Acker looked at Hope. She was a sight for sore eyes.

"Hi, Hope. Hell of a mess, ain't it."

"Sure is. Wonder what happened?"

"I don't know. But I don't think it was an accident."

Hope looked at Van Acker with questioning eyes.

"Why don't you?"

"I'd rather not discuss it here." Van Acker looked around. It

119

seemed that every citizen in Stuttgart was in the street, watching the fire, the excitement and the devastation. He didn't understand it.

"Listen, I'm off duty. We can go to my place. We can talk there."

Van Acker looked at Hope. She was smiling at him. He sighted.

"Okay. That sounds good."

"Follow me. It's a couple of miles outside the city limits."

Van Acker got in his car. Hope turned away from the Knox home, Van Acker right behind her.

***

From a distance, two people had watched the commotion around the Knox house with great intensity. Julie Sutton had still been up when the explosion occurred. She had sat in a chair near the window and watched the ordeal. She had cried. She knew Susan would not survive the fire. There was nothing she could do. She made up her mind that she would continue her sister's cause. She would talk to Dimitri Van Acker. She would go after her father.

***

Bryan Scarboro was parked on the side of the road, two houses up from the Sutton home. He had witnessed the explosion. Sitting in his car, he had seen the glass being thrown from the windows; had seen the front door being catapulted into the Knox' house. He had witnesses the fire trucks pulling up, Allen Murphy entering the apartment and bringing out a body over his shoulder. He knew the body was Susan Knox. Bryan smiled.

27.

Patricia Langston looked over at the sleeping woman next to her in the bed. Michelle Murphy had shown up just around 1:00 am. Patricia and Michelle had been friends for years and Michelle knew she could always find shelter at Patricia's. Patricia had eagerly agreed to let Michelle sleep in the bed with her.

Patricia Langston was 21 years old and a last year student in nursing. She had dark brown hair, brown eyes and chubby cheeks. She was short with a slender, medium built body. She was the daughter of Phil and Pam Langston and had moved out of her parents' house shortly after graduating high school. She had saved money from her part-time job and could make the down payment for a single wide mobile home. She had enrolled in the local junior college with a state sponsored scholarship and kept her part-time job as long as she needed. As soon as she was able to work in the hospital, she found a position in the emergency room at the Medical Center. She had not dated for a long time and had just recently started a relationship. The man she was seeing was much older then she was and they had kept their relationship a secret for now. She had feelings for women also, and she figured that she could be described as bisexual. She had had a few relationships with other women, but nothing had ever turned out the way she imagined. She had a secret crush on Michelle Murphy, but she knew that there could never be a sexual relationship between the two of them. Even if it could lead to that, she knew that if anything went wrong, she would loose her best friend. Besides, she was happy in her current relationship and she did not want to risk that. Of the men who had chased her, one of them was Bryan Scarboro, but she had continuously turned him down. She had no desire to start anything with him. She had warned Michelle about Bryan, but the poor girl had not listened.

Now, in the middle of the night, Patricia was looking at a devastated Michelle Murphy, remembering their conversation and the fear and anger that she had seen in Michelle's eyes.

Michelle had been crying when she knocked on Patricia's door. Patricia, who was still up when the explosion at Susan's apartment happened, was sitting at the kitchen table. She had let

121

Michelle in. Michelle had slumped down on the couch and cried. Patricia had sat next to her and put her arms around her friend's shoulders.

"Michelle, what's wrong?" she had asked.

Michelle had looked at Patricia with red, teary eyes when she started her story.

"Patricia, I should have listened to you! I never should have fallen for Bryan. He is nothing but a smooth talking, no-good bastard!"

Patricia had not responded. She was the listening party and she let Michelle spill her guts.

"I thought he loved me. But instead the only thing he wanted was to get me in bed and violate my body!" Michelle started crying harder.

"Did he rape you?" Patricia managed to ask.

Michelle nodded no.

"No, the bastard sweet-talked his way into my panties and then calls me the same evening telling me that he may be infected with the HIV virus."

Patricia had turned white. She had hugged Michelle, held her close, and made her feel comfortable and safe.

"I don't know if I should ask you this, but did you ask whom he may have contracted it from?" Patricia had ventured to ask. She had a good idea, but she wanted to know if Michelle knew.

"Yes, I demanded to know. It was Susan Knox, the town whore!"

"Listen, Michelle, you need to stay calm right now. First, you need to think about yourself. You need to get tested for the virus in about three to four weeks. That's the earliest that any signs of the virus could show up."

"I know. I'm going to take care of that as much as I don't want to."

"That's good."

"I guess Susan got what she deserved this evening. I hope she burns in Hell!"

Patricia looked at Michelle with questioning eyes.

"Did you go look at the carnage?"

"No, but I drove by on my way here and saw all the

commotion. It's funny how justice can be served sometimes." A smile spread across Michelle tear streaked face. "Do you think it is God punishing her, Patricia?"

Patricia averted her eyes for a second. She did indeed believe in justice. Whether it was God doing the punishing or not, she had her own opinions on that.

"I don't know. I think it is just a coincidence."

Michelle lost the smile on her face.

"Yeah, just a coincidence."

There was a long silence between the two women. They stayed sitting on the couch for a while, hugging one another. Finally, Patricia realized the time and told Michelle they should get some sleep. Michelle had asked if she could sleep in the room with Patricia. Patricia was thrilled with the idea, but she pretended that under the circumstances she wouldn't want it any other way. Patricia had given Michelle some night clothes and a spare tooth brush and it wasn't long before Michelle was sound asleep.

Patricia had a hard time going to sleep. She had a lot on her mind. Not only was she concerned about her friend Michelle, but there was something else weighing on her mind. She was glad that Michelle had been too devastated to notice her eyes being red from crying. For now, Patricia would keep her problems to herself and worry about her friend first. There would be plenty of time to tell her everything she not only wanted, but needed to tell her.

28.

Dimitri Van Acker followed Hope Olson to her house. Just as she had told him, she lived a couple of miles outside Stuttgart. The house was a one-story ranch with three bedrooms, a living room, a kitchen, a dining room and two bathrooms. The house was nicely decorated. Obviously Hope took pride in her home. Nothing was out of place and it showed that there was not a man living in the house.

Even though it was nearly 2 a.m., Hope was still perky and was bouncing through the house. Van Acker felt exhausted. He had had a full day and was ready to get back to bed. However, he knew that Hope was still interested in him and that made him forget a little about being tired. He enjoyed being in her company. Hope showed Van Acker around the house. Everything looked spotless. Back in the living room, Hope motioned for him to sit down on the couch.

"Please sit down. Make yourself at home."

"Don't make it too comfortable for me. I may be falling asleep."

"Here," she grabbed the remote control to the television and threw it in Dimitri's lap. "Find something interesting to watch, something that'll keep you awake. I'm going to take off my uniform and put on something more comfortable."

"Okay. Just poke me in the side if I'm snoring too loud!" Van Acker joked.

"You better not! I've been dying to talk to you."

Hope disappeared into her bedroom. Van Acker followed her with his eyes as she walked down the hall. He liked what he saw. He focused his attention to the remote in his lap. He turned the television on and flipped through the channels. He stopped at a movie channel, showing a movie about computer hacking using the Internet. Dimitri had always liked the movie. He was fascinated with computer technology and the way the Internet could be used to commit crimes. Van Acker was engrossed in the movie when Hope returned. She was barefooted and had on a pair of baggy gym shorts and a loose fitting T-shirt. Van Acker looked up at her, his eyes full of admiration. He didn't know what it was, but he felt attracted to her. Hope noticed it and felt a little blush appear on her cheeks. She too, was attracted to Van Acker.

"Don't stare too hard. You may strain your eyes!" Hope joked, breaking the silence.

"I'm sorry. I don't know what's come over me. I guess it feels good to be around somebody who makes me feel at ease."

"I know what you mean. Most guys around here think that I'm desperate to find somebody. Truth is, I just haven't found a guy that I can talk to without having to wonder whether he's planning on taking me to bed as soon as he sees his chance. I guess since I'm in my thirty's and still single has something to do with that."

"That's right. Why are you still single, Hope?" Van Acker asked.

Hope could tell by the sound in his voice that he was kidding with her.

"I don't know. Maybe I should have become a nun, locked away in some faraway convent."

"Now that would be a waste! A beautiful woman like you, locked away in a convent. I don't think so!"

"Dimitri, let's get serious." Hope said. She sounded subtle but her voice sounded pressing.

"Right," Van Acker agreed. He grabbed the remote and turned the television off.

"Why are you back in town?" Hope shot her first question.

"Gee, you don't hold back any punches do you?"

"Dimitri, I cannot afford to hold back any punches. To tell you the truth, I've been waiting for this day for a long time. I didn't know whether you'd come back or not. Most women would not have waited, would not have been so patient with you. And here you are, coming back out of nowhere. I don't know whether you're going to stay this time or if you will disappear on me again. If you leave again, I will not wait this time."

"Hope, I never meant to leave you hanging. I didn't expect you to wait for me. I didn't even know that you felt this way for me. If I had known, I might have stayed or would have come for you. But you never let on that you liked me that much. Besides, you were in the Navy. The only times that I did see you was when you were on leave, and that wasn't too often, remember?"

"I tell you what. Why don't we forget what happened in the

past. Both of us may have some blame in not getting our feelings for each other across. Let's start over, make this a new beginning."

"That sounds good to me."

"Did you mean what you said yesterday, that you liked me when I was still in the Navy?"

"I did. And maybe I should have let you know that, but, like you said, that's in the past now."

"So tell me, Dimitri, are you going to stay this time? I know you mentioned finding a house and all."

"I'm here to stay, Hope. I'm not going to pick up in the middle of the night and disappear."

"Good! Now that we've got that cleared up, what was going on between you and Allen Murphy? It seemed that you two were arguing about something."

Van Acker looked down and thought long before he answered the questions. He could trust Hope. She would not step outside her boundaries. Besides, she was a deputy Sheriff and would uphold the law.

"Yes, we were arguing. I don't think that Susan's body should have been removed from the apartment until a formal investigation took place. There needed to be a forensic scientist at the scene to analyze the apartment once the fire was put out. I don't believe the fire was an accident."

"Why not? Do you know someone who would want her dead?"

Van Acker smiled.

"I know several people who would want her dead." Van Acker hesitated. "What I'm about to tell you needs to stay in this room. You need to promise me that you will not mention this to anyone. Promise?"

Hope looked at Van Acker with questioning eyes.

"All right, I promise."

"Susan tested positive for HIV. She is at the point where she had full blown AIDS."

Hope whistled through her teeth.

"I guess you know that she was never lacking for companionship. Well, she started telling some of her companions about the AIDS. At least three of them know. One told his girlfriend that he may have it, and Susan told one lover's wife that he's been sleeping around with her."

Hope looked at Van Acker in disbelieve.

"Here's the kicker. Susan's brother-in-law, Tom Sutton is, I should say was, one of her lovers. She told Tom and then told her sister too. It seems that Susan and Tom were fresh with each other since before Tom and Julie got married."

Hope was speechless. She stared at Van Acker, her mouth partially opened and her eyes got as big as saucers.

Dimitri continued.

"Gerald Radcliff and Bryan Scarboro are the others that I know she told. It happens that both of them visited her apartment too. Now, Bryan was seeing Michelle Murphy. They consummated their relationship yesterday in a motel room. Bryan found out that Susan had AIDS. Susan told him that he needs to tell Michelle. He did, and she got all upset and flew of the handle. I rushed over to Susan's and told her not to talk to anyone else unless she talks to me first. When I got back to the Murphy house, Allen was suspicious. Since he is my friend, I told him that Michelle and Bryan got it on with each other and that Bryan has been seeing one of my clients, and that my client has AIDS. Allen is not stupid. He knows I only have one client now. So there it is. There are several people that have a motive to get rid of Susan."

Hope had listened to Van Acker rattle of the names of all the parties involved. Before she could respond, he continued.

"There's more. The reason Susan wanted to use my services is to start a lawsuit against her father. She revealed to me that he sexually abused her and her sister Julie when they were children. She has evidence of it, she told me. It seems that she was making videotapes of the abuse. The abuse is why she started sleeping around with everyone. It must have been a psychological reaction. So her father, if he got wind of the fact that she was going to expose him, could in fact be a possible suspect too. Especially since there is supposed to be evidence of his abuse."

Hope had leaned back in the chair and looked at Van Acker.

"You could possibly have six or seven suspects."

"Yeah, you're right. That's a lot of people whose whereabouts need to be investigated."

127

Hope turned her eyes away from Van Acker and stared at the black screen of the television set.

"You know, Tom Sutton was kicked out by his wife last night. She suspected that he was staying in his office for the night. But I saw him come in from Pinegrove around 10:30. Why would he come back to Stuttgart to sleep in his office when there is a motel in Pinegrove? And then when I went to check the locks on the businesses in town, his car was parked at his office but he was nowhere to be found. There were no lights on in the office and I could not see anything when I shone my flashlight inside. I personally don't think that he was there."

"What time was it when you patrolled that area?"

"It was right before the end of my shift. I guess around 11:45 or so. I know that I returned to the station a little early."

"If he was not in his office, where was he?" Van Acker mesmerized.

"I don't know." Hope answered more to herself than to Van Acker.

There was a silence between them. Both were engrossed in their own thoughts. All of a sudden Hope jumped up. She rushed into her bedroom. Dimitri got up and followed her.

"What's wrong?"

"I just remembered something. It didn't really bother me until you told me Bryan Scarboro was one of Susan's lovers and a possible suspect."

"What is it?"

Hope grabbed in the shirt pocket of her uniform. She found the metal object and showed it to Van Acker.

"A bracelet? What does this have to do with Bryan?"

"The bracelet belongs to Bryan Scarboro. I found it in the alley next to his father's office. When I patrolled the area earlier in the evening, I thought I saw somebody sneaking around the building. I couldn't be sure. I waited awhile to see if anyone would come out. Nobody did. When I checked the locks, I found the bracelet in the alley."

"So, he could have lost it earlier in the day."

"No! The bracelet was no there when I did my first patrol. I always walk the alley and would have seen it. Bryan was in the alley

128

and lost the bracelet trying to hide from me. He was sneaking around his father's office. But why?"

"If he did not want to be seen by anyone, he surely didn't want his father to know he was there. What could Bryan need from the office that late at night? And why wouldn't he want anyone to know that he got it?"

"Drugs?"

"That's a possibility."

They returned to the living room. Hope realized that she had not offered her guest anything to drink yet.

"Dimitri, I'm so sorry. You can tell I don't have many people over. I've lost all my class. Would you like something to drink?"

"I'd like that very much."

"A beer?"

"Sure, sounds good."

Hope grabbed two beers out of the refrigerator. She gave one to Van Acker and sat down on the couch next to him. Both took a couple of swallows from the beer before they started reasoning again. Hope started.

"You know, a black coupe almost ran into me when I came out of Sutton's parking lot. It came from the direction of Susan's apartment."

"Did you get a look at what type coupe it was?"

"No, I wanted to get off so bad, I didn't go after the car."

Van Acker got up and walked to the window.

"Come here, Hope. Did the car look like this one?" He pointed towards his car.

"I can't tell. It looked similar though."

"Do you know if any of our suspects drives a black coupe?"

"Let' see. Tom Sutton drives a white Cadillac. Gerald Radcliff drives a black car. I do believe it's a coupe. Bryan Scarboro drives a red BMW."

"How about Julie Sutton, does she have her own car?"

"She does. It's an SUV that's bigger than a boat."

"How about James Knox?"

"He drives a pick-up. And Phyllis drives a white Town Car.""Well, I know that Allen Murphy drives a red and white pick-up. Besides, I was with him all evening except for about thirty minutes when I was with Susan at her apartment."

"What about Michelle, what does she drives?"

"She drives a white coupe, but Helen drives a black one."

"I don't know, Dimitri. We might be chasing our own tails going the car route."

"Yeah, I know what you mean, besides, it's getting mighty early in the morning. I need to be going."

Hope put her hand on Van Acker's knee.

"Please don't go. You can stay the night. I've got a spare bedroom. You can stay in there."

"Are you sure you don't mind? People will be talking if they see my car parked in our drive way."

"They won't necessary know it's you."

"How many black Mercedes SL 500 Convertibles are driving around Stuttgart with a Virginia license plate?"

"You're right. I only know of one, and I don't care! I'm 34 years old and I'll do as I please with whomever I please! I'll be the first to tell them too!"

"You know, I like you. I like the way you think."

"Well, you're not so bad yourself, you know."

They both smiled.

"Com'on, let me show you to the guestroom."

Van Acker followed Hope to the guestroom. The room looked clean and neat, just like the rest of the house. Hope lingered by the bedroom door. Van Acker who had walked into the room turned around and looked at her.

"You sure you want me to stay?"

Hope just nodded her head. She had a big smile on her face. Van Acker walked over, took her head in his hands and drew her lips to his. They kissed tenderly, Hope standing on her toes, her arms around Van Acker's neck. They finally let go. Hope turned around and went into her own bedroom. As she closed the door, she watched as Van Acker stood in the doorway of the guestroom, motionless, speechless. She smiled and closed her door. It wasn't long before both of them were asleep and dreaming of one another.

29.

It was close to 3 a.m. when the fire at Susan Knox's apartment was finally under control. The entire apartment was destroyed. The explosion had blown away over half of the roof, and the consequent fire had destroyed both the garage and the apartment. The cars in the garage were completely burned out. The burned wood and the water dripping down from it portrayed a gloomy picture in the summer moonlight.

James and Phyllis Knox had been seen by the EMT's. The cuts on James' face were treated and Phyllis was given a sedative to calm her down. After her conversation with Van Acker, she had become very anxious and upset about the death of her daughter and that someone may have murdered her. After the fire had been subdued, and the curious had finally gone home; Julie Sutton had gone over to her parent's house. She would stay the night with them, just in case they needed anything. Susan's body had been taken to the funeral home. There was nothing that could be done now. They would have to wait until Monday. After everybody had gone inside, the topic of conversation was the funeral. Susan's body had to be put to rest. It was agree that they would see to hold a funeral service on Tuesday. The quicker they could get Susan's death behind them, the better. All were in agreement.

James Knox sat down in his chair by the window, looking out at the remains of his daughter's apartment. He started to cry. He balled his fists and slammed them down on the chair rail. He was mad with himself. Why did he ever do to Susan and Julie what he had done? Why could he not have had more self-control? He knew he was the reason why Susan lead the life she did. The years of sexual abuse had driven her away from him and into the arms of many lovers and into the use of drugs. Maybe this Van Acker guy was right after all. Maybe somebody had murdered his daughter. He wished he could turn back the clock and start over; bring back the days when his daughters were still children, before he started his abuse. He would love them better. He would keep his hands-off them. But there was nothing he could do about it at this point. The damage had been done a long time ago. In a way, he felt responsibly for Susan's death. He was sure it had not been an accident. From

131

the conversation between his wife and Julie, he knew that Susan had been infected with the AIDS virus. He also knew that Tom Sutton had been involved with her. Sutton would be capable of murder. That much he knew. He would confront Sutton in the morning. But how many of the other men, and some women, Susan had been involved with knew about the AIDS? If she had told Sutton about her condition, then how many others would she have told? Knox got up and wished his wife and daughter a good night. He went to bed, saying that he needed to get rest. He disappeared up the stairs.

Phyllis was finally calm and lay down on the couch. Julie gently rubbed her hair. She felt like a mother taking care of her little one. She had told her mother that the death of Susan was an accident, to forget the idea that someone would have wanted Susan dead. Tom? She had told her mother that Tom could not commit murder, that he was too much of a coward to do that. He would be too scared to be found out and have to spend the rest of his life in prison, not to mention the thought of the electric chair. No! Tom was a lot of things, but a murderer he was not. Julie wondered how many people in Stuttgart stood to lose their reputation and good name because of their relationship with Susan. Some of those people might actually be capable of murder. She shook her head. She needed to find some rest herself. The next couple of days would be hard. She covered her mother with a blanket and sat down on the recliner opposite the couch. She pushed the recliner out and pulled a knit blanket over herself. It wasn't long before she too was asleep.

30.

Allen and Helen Murphy were up late. Murphy had returned from fighting the fire. Helen had been up most of the night pacing the bedroom, thinking about Michelle and how she could have made such poor decisions. It was beyond comprehension. Murphy had begged his wife to come to bed, but she had refused, telling him that she was not ready yet, that she needed more time to think about the situation with Michelle. Murphy had finally given up on waiting on her to lie down and had fallen asleep. When he woke, Helen was laying in bed asleep. She was making subtle snoring sounds. Murphy smiled. She had finally given up and found some rest.

He got up and took a shower. It was still early for a Sunday morning. After showering and shaving, he found some Pop Tarts and a glass of milk and called it breakfast. By 6 o'clock he was out the door.

Murphy had thought hard about what Van Acker had told him earlier at the fire. The words "foul play" had stuck with him. It was hard to believe that someone would try to murder Susan Knox. Van Acker had to know something to make the accusation, he thought as he climbed into his pick-up and drove away from the house. He would find out soon. He would go talk to Van Acker and push him until he told him where his ideas of murder came from.

On the way to Kelly's house, Murphy's mind lingered back to the conversation he had with Van Acker. He had never known Van Acker to lose his temper with him. It had surprised him. Whatever was bothering Van Acker, had something to do with Susan. Then, he couldn't help but think back at his youngest daughter running out of the house and speeding away in her mother's car. Michelle had not come back during the night. He wondered where she was and if she was alright. He hoped she hadn't done anything drastic. A cold shiver ran down his spine as he imagined his daughter going to Susan's apartment and setting the place on fire. He shook his head. No, Michelle wasn't capable of such drastic measures. She had probably gone over to Patricia's or another friend to spend the night.

As he reached Kelly's driveway, he noticed that only Kelly's car was in the driveway. He pulled up into the drive way, intend on turning around, not disturbing Kelly. As he put his pick-up truck in reverse, the front door to Kelly house opening and Kelly, dressed in a long T-shirt stood in the doorway, motioning her father to come in.

Murphy pulled up close to the house.

"Good morning, honey. You're up early!"

"Couldn't sleep. I've been worried about so much!"

"I know the feeling. Your mother was up all night pacing the bedroom worrying about your sister. I have a lot on my mind too. There's something Dimitri said at the fire that has been bothering me."

"What is that?"

"He got mad with me for removing Susan's body from the apartment before someone went in and investigated the apartment. He was talking about the need for a forensic team to come in and investigate. He seems to think that the fire was deliberately set to murder Susan."

Kelly looked away from her father. She knew exactly where Van Acker was coming from. He had shared enough information for her to know there were people in town that would appreciate Susan being dead.

"Dad, I know where Dimitri is coming from. I cannot tell you who all is involved. I do know that Susan hired Dimitri to represent her in a lawsuit. You know that she was infected with the AIDS virus. Well, there are some people in town that have been with her that stand to lose a lot if ever they were linked to having an affair with Susan or end up having the HIV virus or get AIDS. The fact that they might have contracted the virus could mean the end of their careers. So, yes, I think Dimitri knew what he was talking about."

"Who are you talking about?"

"I'm not at liberty to discuss that with you at this point, dad. I'm working for Dimitri. He made it clear that if I spill the beans on any case he's working on, I'm going to be out on the street looking for another job."

"Alright,j I can appreciate that."

Murphy looked away from Kelly for a minute. He looked at the driveway. He needed to find Van Acker.

"Kelly? Do you know where Dimitri went to this early in the morning?"

"The fact is, dad, he's not been here all night. I saw him

talking to Hope Olson at Susan's apartment. Kelly looked sad suddenly. "I suspect he went over to her house and spent the night there. I think that they will get together."

"I don't know about that. I do know that it didn't take him long to hook up with someone."

"They used to go out. I don't think this is a case of love at first sight; let's jump in the bed together."

"Well, even if it is, I guess it's none of our concern. I'll drive over there and see if our lover boy is at Hope's."

"Or you can wait here. He'll come back to change his clothes, I'm sure. I doubt Hope has anything that will fit him." she said sarcastically.

"I can't wait that long," Murphy said, missing the sarcasm in his daughter's voice. "If Dimitri is right about it being foul play, I need to talk to him and see if he'll let me in on what he knows. I need to do an investigation into the source of the fire at Susan's apartment anyways."

Murphy kissed his daughter on the forehead and told her he loved her. He climbed back into his truck and took off towards Hope Olson's house.

Murphy knew where Hope lived. It was only about a mile from Kelly's place. It would take him all of two minutes to get there. When he drove into the driveway, he saw Hope's patrol car and Van Acker's convertible in the driveway. He smiled. Kelly had been right. Van Acker had indeed spent the night at Hope's.

He knocked on the door. No answer. These two must have had some night, Allen thought. He knocked again, this time more persistent. He finally heard a voice on the other end of the door.

"All right, all right! Hold you're horses! I'm coming!"

It was Hope's voice. Murphy could hear her stumble through the house, making her way to the door. The door opened and Hope Olson stood in the doorway, her hair out of place, and sleep still in her eyes, wearing a light white cotton nightgown. She looked surprised to see Murphy at her front door this early on a Sunday morning.

"Allen? Hi. Everything okay?"

"Hi Hope. I'm sorry to disturb you this early, but I need to talk to Dimitri."

135

"Oh? Okay!" She rubbed some sleep out of her eyes and motioned towards the spare room. "He's in there, the spare room."

She saw the surprise on Murphy's face when she mentioned the spare room. She smiled.

"What? You think he would be in my bed?"

Murphy flushed. That was exactly what he'd been thinking.

"You caught me! I was sure that was what was going on. My apologies."

"No need. Anyone driving by here that sees his car in my driveway will have that exact same thought."

Murphy smiled and padded Hope on the shoulder.

"One of the drawbacks of living in a small town, isn't it?"

Hope nodded. Murphy walked in and followed Hope to the spare room. Hope opened the door. Van Acker was still asleep.

"He's all yours, Allen. I hope you know what you're doing waking him up."

"I don't know. I'll just have to take my chances."

"I'll be in the kitchen making some coffee, just in case you need me to help out or something."

"Thanks," he smiled, winking at her.

Murphy walked over to the bed. Van Acker was sound asleep. Murphy tapped him on the shoulder. Van Acker turned onto his other side. Again, Murphy tapped him. This time Van Acker opened his eyes.

"What? Hope? What is it?"

"Wake up Sleeping Beauty!"

"What? Allen? Is that you? What time is it?"

"Yes it's me. Get up! I need to talk to you. It's important."

"Alright! Give me a couple of minutes to splash some water on my face and get dressed."

"Hurry up! I've got a busy schedule."

Van Acker gave him a grump.

It took Van Acker a couple of minutes to get dressed and freshen up. When he walked into the living room, Murphy and Hope were sitting on the couch, drinking coffee and carrying on a conversation.

"I hope you're not talking about me!" Van Acker said, smiling, as he walked over to a recliner.

"We wouldn't dare do that, would we, Allen?" Hope winked at Murphy, making sure that Dimitri saw.

"I was filling Hope in a little bit from when you used to live with us. I've got some interesting stories to tell."

"Just make sure you tell her the stories that make me look good. I don't want her to get the wrong impression of me."

All three smiled and joked around a little longer. Van Acker made himself a cup of coffee.

"So, Allen, what is so damn important that you had to wake me up this early in the morning?"

"Our little disagreement last night." Murphy said, looking at Hope.

Van Acker noticed the sideways glance.

"Don't worry about it, Allen. I've already filled her in on what it was about."

"Dimitri, I need to know more. I need to know why you think that someone might have done Susan Knox in."

"Well," Van Acker rubbed his hand through his hair. He thought for a moment before he continued. "I guess I can tell you. Just make sure you don't tell anyone else."

"All right, I promise to keep quiet. I'm listening."

"Susan Knox was sleeping around with some prominent people. She was involved with Tom Sutton and with Gerald Ratcliff, just to name two. You already know about Bryan. If Susan would start talking about having AIDS and who she's been sleeping with, you can imagine what uproar we would cause here in Stuttgart."

Murphy studied the carpet in the living room as Van Acker was telling him about Susan.

"What I cannot tell you is why she came to me to get legal advise. It has nothing to do with her lovers; but it is related to her AIDS though. I cannot tell you anything else."

"Let me guess. She found out who gave her the virus and is going to sue him?"

"I can't tell you, Allen. Now that Susan is dead, I don't know if what she started will be carried through. That's all I can tell you about that."

"I understand. I have some insight now and I understand why you got so upset with me last night."

Silence fell in the living room. Hope got up and brought the coffeepot around. Both Murphy and Van Acker were glad to get a second cup. Murphy broke the silence.

"I'm going over to Susan's apartment to do my investigation into the source of the fire. It comes with being the fire chief. Do you want to come and help me look around and see if we can find anything?"

Van Acker's eyes lit up.

"I'd love too. I'm curious to see how you will find out how that fire started."

"Would you two gentlemen mind if I tagged along?" Hope asked, full of anticipation.

"That would be great, Hope." Van Acker said.

Hope got dressed in a hurry and rode with Van Acker to the apartment where they met Allen Murphy.

31.

The church bells were ringing. The morning sun was shining on Stuttgart. It promised to be another hot day. It was just 10 o'clock and already the temperature was at 85 degrees. The Sunday worshipers were starting to gather around the church for Sunday school. They were standing in little groups, talking softly. Once and a while, one of them would motion towards Susan's apartment. Then one would point towards the Sutton home. Either way, the Knox and Sutton families were the focus of attention. Matthew 7, 1 "Judge not, that ye be not judged", was far from the worshipers' minds. Most of the worshipers were out the previous night to see the fire and to keep their ears sharp just in case they could pick up any gossip. And there was a lot of it going on. Some had seen Julie Sutton throw out her husband Tom, others had overhead that Tom had been fooling around with Susan. Still others had picked up bits and pieces about AIDS. As usual, when different stories came together, the gossip machine was working at full speed.

Julie Sutton and her mother Phyllis arrived at church right before the beginning of Sunday school. Phyllis taught the young adult Sunday school class and Julie was involved with the toddlers during that time. Phyllis, holding on to Julie's arm, walked straight past her friends. At least until last night, she thought they were her friends. When it was time to give her support, they were not to be found. They were in the street watching the fire, but they never came close to Phyllis to give the support she needed in her time of need. Only a few had come and offered her a shoulder to cry on. Those were already inside, waiting for Phyllis. They were not part of the group who pretended to be friends with you and then when you needed them were not there to help. Phyllis did not even look towards the gathered crowd outside the church. She walked up the steps into the sanctuary, walked down the aisle, up onto the stage and disappeared inside a room that was located in the back of the sanctuary. Julie went to the toddler's classroom and got ready for her Sunday school class. She had wanted to go to the funeral home, but the funeral director Joshua Underwood had told her that Susan's body would not be prepared for burial until Monday. She was informed that Monday morning would be a better time to come by

139

and start preparations for the visitors. She had told her mother that she would attend church in the morning. It would be a perfect time to find peace with herself and with God for what had happened. Phyllis had agreed. James Knox had informed his wife and daughter that he would not be attending church. He wanted some time alone to reflect on the events. Julie had been suspicious of the reason he did not want to attend church. She doubted that reflecting on the events would be what her father had in mind. She had a faint idea what he would be doing.

Dr. David Brubaker was sitting behind his desk in his pastoral office going over his sermon when Phyllis Knox knocked on the door. He straightened out his papers and adjusted his tie. He walked over to the door and opened it.

"Phyllis, how good to see you. Come in. I want to express my deepest sympathy for the loss of Susan."

Phyllis shook Dr. Brubaker's hand and thanked him for the condolences.

"Reverend, I don't know where I stand anymore. I have seen and heard so much since yesterday that I am confused about what is truth and was is not. What I am most confused about is that my husband is being accused of having sexually abused both Julie and Susan when they were children." Phyllis felt weak and held on to the chair sitting in front of Dr. Brubaker's desk.

"Phyllis, please, sit down." Dr. Brubaker looked into the hallway before closing the door to his office. He wanted to make sure that no one was overhearing the conversation.

"Tell me, Phyllis, who told you that James abused your girls."

Phyllis told Dr. Brubaker about Susan, about her experience in the army, her stay in New York, the drugs, the sex. She told him that Susan had been diagnosed with AIDS. She told Dr. Brubaker about the lawsuit that Susan and Julie were planning to file against their father. Finally, she told him about Tom Sutton having an affair with Susan and the possibility that both Tom and Julie could be infected with the virus also.

Dr. Brubaker had listened closely to all the details that Phyllis Knox was throwing in his direction. He had a hard time believing the entire story. He took off his glasses and laid them down on his desk. He rubbed his finger over his eyes and temples. Then, his hands moved down to his chin were he rubbed back and forth over his smooth shaven skin.

"Phyllis, how much of this story do you believe to be truthful?"

"Julie told me the story. She is not the one that would lie to me; however, she got her information from both Susan and Tom. I know, now, that their word might possibly not mean a whole lot since they were having an affair with one another. But why would Susan tell someone that she was infected with the AIDS virus if it wasn't true?"

"You're right. That would give her a bad reputation in town. She was well liked by everyone, even though we did not always agree or approve of her behavior and actions. No disrespect Phyllis, but it doesn't surprise me that Susan contracted the disease. We know she had several male companions. It would be ignorant of us not to think that she was sexually active with them."

"You know, that reminds me of something that Julie told me last night. She said, and I guess that she was right, that we never wanted to talk about sex. The girls tried to tell me many times that something was going on between them and their father. Every time they brought up the subject of sex, I told them no to talk about it, that it was not a subject that you talked about. I guess I didn't know how to approach the subject. I wish now, I would have been more open-minded about sex."

"Phyllis, sex is not bad. Without it, we would not be around. It's all right to talk about sex with your children. It's not a subject that needs to be discussed in church or school. I believe the subject needs to be approached at home. It's the parents' responsibility to make sure that their children know what sex is, how it is done and what the results are. Keeping children in the dark about sex is like keeping them in the dark about guns. Children are naturally curious. There comes a time in their life that when they no longer get the answers they're looking for from their parents, they start experimenting and getting answers elsewhere. That's why we have accidental shootings with children and that's why we have such a high rate of teen pregnancy. If parents would just talk to their young teenagers about what sex can do, I believe we would be better off. Not only do we have the danger of teenage pregnancy, but this day

141

and age, we have to worry more about sexual transmitted diseases like AIDS."

Phyllis could only listen and agree with Dr. Brubaker. She wished she could have had this conversation 25 years ago, when her children were still little. A lot would be different now. Phyllis stood up and walked towards the door.

"Reverend, I'm glad I had an opportunity to talk to you. It may seem futile to talk about his subject now; however, this event in my life has made me think differently. I think I will get involved in giving the local children some advice and answers to those questions they have on the subject."

Before she walked out, she turned around one more time to address the Reverend.

"Reverend, we were thinking about holding the funeral on Tuesday. Would that work out with your schedule?"

Mentioning the funeral made her start crying. She had avoided the subject, did not want to talk about it, but reality made it unavoidable not to talk about it. Susan's body had to be put to rest. She would finally find peace.

"Tuesday would be fine. Just give me a call about what time and I'll be glad to rearrange my schedule should it interfere with other plans I might have."

"Thank you, David." Phyllis grabbed Dr. Brubaker's hands and held them tightly in hers.

"My prayers are with you. Everything will turn out right. God has a purpose for all of us. He gives and takes when he is ready and we should be happy that he takes us. Susan is in a better place. She is no longer tormented. She is at peace."

Phyllis wiped tears from her cheeks. She managed a smile. She fumbled with her pocketbook as she found her way to her Sunday school classroom. She dreaded it. Going in there meant that she would have to answer a million questions. She was not up to it. She would stand firm and give her prepared Sunday school class and tell them she did not want to talk about Susan's death or any related subject matter. She reached the door to her classroom. She paused, straightened her skirt, pushed a couple of hairs back in place and entered the classroom.

32.

Tom Sutton woke up around 9:30. He was back in his hotel room in Pinegrove. He had enjoyed a good nights rest. After watching the fire destroy Susan Knox' apartment the night before and watching Allen Murphy carry her charred body out of the apartment, he felt good. It wasn't looking as bad as it had been the night before. Susan's death was a blessing. Not that he cared much about her at this point anyways. He wouldn't be able to have sex with her anymore, so what was the point in having her around. He would need to check himself for the HIV virus, but even if he showed positive for the virus, that didn't mean that he couldn't go on and have sex anymore. He would just have to be more careful.

He showered and shaved and got ready for the day. Picking through his suitcase he selected some clothes which weren't too wrinkled. He looked in the mirror, fixed his hair and walked out the door. He wanted to go by his house while Julie was in church. He knew that no matter how shaken Julie would be about Susan's death, that she would not miss church. He wanted to get the rest of his clothes and personal items, including some work he had taken home. At all cost he wanted to avoid another confrontation with Julie. She might burst into another rage. With the church right across the road, the last thing he needed was a group of witnesses seeing the two of them argue and overhearing what they were talking about. There had been enough witnesses to their argument the day before. His political life could not take another hit. Too much had already been said in front of to many ears.

When Sutton arrived in Stuttgart, the members of his church had already disappeared inside. He sighed in relief. Passing by Susan's apartment, he could see the charred remains of what had once been the garage and apartment.

"I won't have to worry about you spilling the beans anymore!" he said out load as he looked at the caution tape and burned out building.

He pulled into his driveway, quickly got out, looked around and made his way to the front door. He turned the lock and entered the house. The familiar smell of Julie's perfume entered his nose. He coughed and made a face. He was glad he wouldn't have to smell

143

her any longer. He ran upstairs into the bedroom. He was glad to see that Julie had not kept her word about burning his clothes. He grabbed a garment bag and started putting the rest of his clothes in it. Making sure that he had all his belongings, he made his way back downstairs. Tossing the garment bag by the front door, he walked into his study. He grabbed a brief case sitting by the desk and loaded several files and paperwork into it. He decided to take the stack of bills laying on the desk with him. That would at least make a good impression with the judge when Julie was going after alimony. Sutton closed the briefcase and made his way to the front door. As he passed the living room, he noticed a chair sitting by the window. Curious, he walked to the chair and sat in it. Slowly he pushed the curtain aside. He had a perfect view of Susan's apartment. He got a little frightened and his stomach felt ready to erupt. Julie! She had sat here and watched the entire ordeal! How long had she been watching? Had she seen him pass by? Had she seen him sit at a distance and watch the fire? A cold chill ran down his spine. He shook his head.

Sutton got up and started towards the door when his eyes fell on a little notebook on the coffee table. He had never seen it there before. Curious, he grabbed it and opened it. He could barely make out the writing. It looked like it had been written in a hurry or by a shaking hand. He tried to read the notes.

"Dimitri... twice... Bryan Scarboro... left mad... TOM... drive by late... somebody in black, short stay... FIRE!!!!... SUSAN!.. Dead!!! REVENGE... Help Me GOD... TOM? Black car."

Sutton turned white as he read the notes. Susan had seen everything that went on at her sister's apartment. She knew he had driven by. Some of the notes did not make any sense. What else did she know? What else had she seen?

"I underestimated you, Julie, you little bitch. I need to know how much you have seen, what you have seen and how much you know. We'll see how far your little James Bond routine is going to get you!"

Sutton put the notebook back on the coffee table. He decided to leave it there, letting Julie think that no one but her knew about the contents of the notes. He grabbed his garment bag and opened the door. He looked around making sure nobody was outside walking around. The coast was clear. He walked the short distance to his car, opened the door and threw the bag inside, put the briefcase in the backseat and left. He drove past Susan's apartment one last time. As he passed, he noticed someone walking around the apartment. He couldn't make out who it was. He didn't care. The damage was done and he didn't want to be seen near there. He sped up his car and made his way back to Pinegrove. He would wait till morning to come back to his office. He would relax the rest of the day. Tomorrow there would be plenty of time to look for an apartment or house for rent, make his appointments and try to act upset by the loss of his sister-in-law. A broad grin spread over his face.

33.

James Knox waited until everybody was inside the church to make his move. He had to know if it was true what he had heard. If Susan had videotapes of him having sex with her and Julie, he needed to find them. He could not let those be exposed, ever. If no tapes were found, it would be shrugged off as the tail of a half-crazed oversexed woman. He walked across the driveway to the burned-out remains of the apartment. Hesitantly he looked around to make sure that no one was watching. He felt the hand railing of the stairs. It was lose but would probably hold. The treads to the stairs were black with ashes. He stopped up on the steps, one by one. The first time since Susan moved in, he thought. Never before had he set foot in her apartment. After coming back from New York, Susan had made it clear to him that he was not welcome in her home. He had not pushed the issue. He knew why she didn't want him to visit her. He just didn't want to admit and face the truth about what he had done when his daughters were younger. Now, he stood at the top of the steps, looking into the apartment. He could not recognize anything. Everything inside the apartment was burned and charred. Uneasy, he stepped into the apartment. He felt his feet, making sure the floor underneath them would hold up his weight. He decided to try the bedroom first. Slowly he walked down the hall to the bedroom. When he walked in and saw the burned bed, he started to cry. In the middle of the bed, he could see an area that was lighter than the rest of the bed. It was shaped in the form of a body, Susan's body. The shape in the middle of the bed was Susan's outline, the place where she lay when she burned to death. Knox started crying harder. Tears were running down his cheeks as he stood and looked at the bed. He took a deep breath and tried to compose himself. He was here for a purpose, he reminded himself. Those tapes needed to be found.

Knox started with the closet. He opened the door. Susan's clothes were hanging in the closet. Some were burned, some looked like they had melted, but most of them had been saved from the inferno. Knox looked around in the closet. A shelf in the closet had boxes stacked on them. He looked in the boxes, one by one, making sure he put them back in the exact place he found them. None of the

146

boxes contained what he was looking for. More boxes were sitting on the floor in the closet. He looked through them, nothing recognizable. Most of the items in the boxes were waterlogged and covered with soot. In disgust, he started to walk back towards the living room He looked around. His eyes focused on what once used to be a television. It had sat on a microwave cart. On a shelf underneath, he saw what looked like melted plastic. If those had been tapes, they were destroyed and he would not have to worry about them. Knox walked into the kitchen part of the apartment and looked through what was left of the cabinets. He could not find anything that remotely looked like a videotape or what had once been a videotape. He felt relieved. If Susan had them at the apartment, they had been destroyed.

Knox made his way back to where the front door had been. He walked down the steps. He looked into the garage. Both cars where destroyed. The heat from the fire had melted the tires. The windshields had also melted away. The plastic from the bumpers was no longer there. The metal frames of the cars were all that was left. James shook his head. He wondered what had happened. Was it a gas leak? Did Susan have a chance to get out? Did Susan deliberately let the gas escape and committed suicide? Or could it have been foul play? Did one of Susan's former lovers decide to kill her before she ruined his life? Several questions raced through James Knox' head. He did not have an answer to any of them. He started crying again. He walked back towards his house, his chin on his chest, a beaten man. He blamed himself. But it was too late now. He could not change what he had done. Before he walked into his house, he turned around one last time to take a look at what had caused his daughter's death.

As he turned around, he could see a white Cadillac drive by, the driver looking all too familiar. Tom Sutton! James wondered what Sutton was up too. He was one of Susan's lovers. James had known about it. More than once he had stood by the window and watched Sutton walk up the stairs of Susan's apartment. It would never be long before he could make out two shadows in the bedroom, moving the way lovers do. Several times, he had tried to tell Julie. He never could. He didn't want to hurt his oldest daughter any more than he already had. She was so frail, so insecure. Thanks to me, he

147

thought. Telling Julie that Sutton was having an affair with her sister would tear the family apart. It would mean that Julie could loose all she had wanted. She was under the impression that she had a patient, understanding husband who did not seem to be bothered with her sexual problems. Why would he? He found his sexual pleasures in the arms of her sister. Knox shook his head. He should have put a stop to this a long time ago. But now it was too late. Susan was dead and Julie had kicked Sutton out. He wished it had happened differently, then maybe, just maybe Susan might still be alive. Again, tears were running down James Knox' cheeks. He turned and walked into the house. He needed a drink.

34.

Michelle Murphy woke up early. She looked over at Patricia Langston who was still asleep. Quietly, Michelle slipped out of bed and exited the bedroom. In the kitchen, she looked in the refrigerator and found a jug of milk. She grabbed a glass from the cupboard and poured herself a tall glass of milk. She sat down on the couch and sipped her milk, savoring the cool liquid flowing down to her stomach. She reflected on the events of the previous night. She had been stupid. Then again, she had not been thinking clearly. She shook her head. She needed to forget about what happened. She needed to grab the bull by the horns and push herself back into her regular life. Sure, she needed to get tested for the AIDS virus. She should have made Scarboro wear a condom. She felt sick to her stomach knowing that she had let him spill his semen inside of her. She prayed that she would test negative. She didn't think that she could handle having to know that she was slowly dying of AIDS.

Michelle finished her milk and put her glass in the sink. She gathered her clothes and got dressed. She had to take her mother's car back. For sure her mother would be worried about her by now. Before walking out the door, she wrote a quick note to Patricia, thanking her for letting her spend the night and for being a friend. She'd be back later. Maybe they could do something together; go to the mall or catch a movie.

Michelle drove slowly on the way home. She thought about what she would tell her mother. Besides the fact that she might have AIDS, nothing much had been said about how she might have contracted it. She knew the question would come up. And how would she face her father? He had always been proud of her. She brought home good grades, went to church, was involved in the community and never had caused him any headaches. Now this had happened. All the trust he had in her would be gone. She hoped he wouldn't be home when she got there.

Driving up into her driveway, she let out a sigh of relieve. Her father's truck was not in the driveway. That would make her arrival a bit easier. She parked her mother's car back in the place where she got it from. Entering the house, everything was still quiet. It was too early for her mother to have left for church yet, but usually by this time, she would be getting ready to go. It was unlike her mother to miss church. Michelle walked towards her parent's bedroom and peaked around the corner. Her mother was still asleep. She probably had a hard time falling asleep, worrying about her and where she might have been. She decided to make her mother breakfast. Having coffee, bacon, scrambled eggs and toast might put her mother in a good mood.

The scent of brewing coffee reached Helen Murphy's bedroom. She opened her eyes and looked at the clock. It was after nine. She sighted. At least she had been able to get some sleep. She realized that church was going to be out today, but who cared. She had to take care of her family. There would be lots more time for church later. The smell of coffee registered in her conscious mind. Allen must have made her breakfast, she thought. She got up and put on a robe. She walked into the living room and followed her nose into the kitchen; on the table stood a full spread of breakfast. She looked around to see if she could find her husband. He was not in the house. Then she walked outside on the porch and found his truck to be gone. She noticed that her car was back in the yard. Michelle!

Helen walked back into the house and went straight to Michelle's bedroom. Passing the bathroom, she heard the shower running. Helen took hold of the door handle and was ready to open it. She hesitated. She let go of the handle and walked back into the kitchen. It would be better to give Michelle the privacy and time alone that she needed. She would have some hard times ahead of her. Helen sat down at the kitchen table. The food on her place smelled great. She decided to wait for Michelle. Helen picked up the newspaper. Her husband always got the newspaper out of the mailbox and brought it in the house before he left on Sunday mornings. She looked over the front page of the paper. Nothing was mentioned about the explosion. The event had obviously not reached the big city yet. It wouldn't take long though. If Van Acker was right and the fire was foul play, big city investigators would be swarming all over the town of Stuttgart. She hoped Dimitri was wrong. She turned the pages of the newspaper and scanned the stories. It was the regular news. Politics on a national and local level were discussed. Helen flipped through the sections and found the coupon pages. She carefully studies the coupons. Every time she found one that she could use, she tore it out of the paper and put it aside. She was finishing up when Michelle emerged from the bathroom.

Helen got up and gave her daughter a hug and a kiss. Michelle returned them and squeezed her mother tightly, feeling the comfort that she had expected from the encounter.

"I'm sorry I left out of here in such a hurry last night," Michelle started.

"I wish you wouldn't have. I was worried about you. I didn't know what you were going to do. You didn't do anything crazy, right?"

"No..., I just drove around. I tried to clear my head and I ended up going over to Patricia's. I spent the night over there."

Helen looked at her daughter. She instinctively felt that Michelle was not telling the whole story.

"Are you sure that nothing else happened after you left the house?"

Michelle flustered a bit, but was able to keep her composure.

"No, I drove around, stopped by the side of the road for a while and then went to Patricia's."

Helen was not convinced. She decided not to push the issue now, but she would come back and pry some more, see if she could get some more information out of Michelle.

"Thank you for fixing me breakfast."

"You're welcome. I figured you could use it after what I put you through last night."

"I must say that you had me worried. First finding out about the possibility that you may have...," Helen hesitated. She didn't know how to bring the words across her lips.

"That I may have HIV?"

"Yes! God, it's hard for me to say that. I never thought one of my girls would be exposed to it."

"It's not like I tried to get it, mamma," Michelle fired back, unaware that she was steadily raising her voice.

"Michelle, I didn't say that you were trying to contract it! I'm simply saying that I never thought I would have to face something like this. I guess I had no idea that you were involved with anybody at this level."

151

"Mom, I didn't want to have sex with Bryan. He got me tipsy and I lost all control. I know that I shouldn't have taken the alcohol from him but he's such a smooth talker. I should have seen through him. God knows how many times he's talked himself in some young, innocent college girl's panties. I thought he liked me for the person that I am. I guess the only reason he went out with me was to get a young, high school graduate in the bed and add another notch to his stick. I guess I was just another mark on his long list of successfully delivered date rapes."

Michelle paused. Helen was listening to her daughter vent her anger. She put her hands over Michelle's hands.

"I guess your dad and I should have warned you that not all men are gentlemen. Sometimes the smooth talkers are the one's that wear the sheepskin suit to hide their devilish self."

"Mom, don't blame yourself. I'm the one that drank the alcohol and lost control of what I was doing. My actions made it to where I was exposed to being infected with the virus. I should have made Bryan use protection. I wasn't thinking straight. I was overtaken by emotions that I had never felt before. He made me feel like a million bucks. I felt so beautiful, so sexy, so much wanted. He had me convinced that no other woman in the world would be able to give him the sexual satisfaction that I gave him."

Michelle paused and swallowed hard. Helen was listening to her daughter. She had a smart girl in front of her. Too bad that one doesn't think about the effects of their actions in the heat of the moment, no matter how smart they are.

"Michelle, if he was not wearing protection, it could mean that you may be pregnant too. You do realize that don't you?"

"I don't think that I can be pregnant. I've been on the pill for a while."

Michelle blushed at the turn the conversation had taken. Her parents had always been open about sex and she had always been able to bring up the subject. Still, talking about her own experience, telling her mother about what she and Bryan had done the night before made her feel uncomfortable.

Helen cut in.

"Honey, the pill isn't 100% effective. You could still be pregnant."

152

Michelle's head dropped to the table. She started crying. Helen continued.

"You will need to have a pregnancy test done in a couple of weeks. We can do this at home. Nobody needs to know, not even your dad."

Michelle looked up at her mother. A slight smile appeared on her face.

"You won't tell daddy?"

"I won't tell him that we're going to do a pregnancy test. But remember you father is not stupid. If there is a chance for you to have contracted the HIV virus, then there is also the chance that you could be pregnant. He won't mention it, but I guarantee you, it will be on his mind."

"I'm so afraid that he'll think less of me for doing this!"

"Honey, your dad loves you very much. I'm sure he feels disappointed, but I don't think that he'll think less of you. You will need to show him that you can still be trusted."

Michelle just nodded. She straightened herself in her chair and poured herself a cup of coffee. She grabbed a plate and put her share of the breakfast on it. Silently, mother and daughter sat and ate their breakfast, both reflecting on their conversation, each having their own doubts and worries.

35.

Hope Olson and Dimitri Van Acker arrived at Susan Knox's apartment around 11 o'clock. Allen Murphy was not there yet. Across the street they could see the Baptist church. The parking lot was full of cars and music filtered through the walls to the outside.

"I'm glad that everybody is in there and not out here," Hope said

"I know what you mean. It's sad that of all people those attending church are the worst gossipers of all. I don't get it. They should be the one's setting the example for the rest of us. But they're the first to get to the scene of an accident and they're the first to speculate about what happened, who was involved and why it happened."

Hope shook her head in agreement. She felt guilty about not having been to church in a while but she did not feel comfortable going. It seemed to her that church consisted of a group of hypocrites who kept their image holy as long as they were in the presence of their churchgoing friends, but after they got home they lived their lives opposite of what they preached. Sure not everyone attending the church was like that, but to Hope it seemed like they were all the same.

Van Acker saw Hope staring in the direction of the church. He tapped her on the arm and Hope returned to reality.

"Everything alright?"

"Oh, yeah, I was just thinking about what you said. You know, people in the church gossiping and such."

"Well, I don't like it. But it's something we have to live with. If you compared the lives of the churchgoing people with the church they go to, I guess it would be hard not to find any hypocrites. I guess you don't feel comfortable being around a group of hypocrites like that, right?"

Hope just nodded. It was scary how well Van Acker read her mind. She felt butterflies in her stomach.

Van Acker responded to her nod.

"You know, I used to feel the same way. I quit going to church. The preacher would be preaching about not drinking and smoking. Everybody in the church would call out AMEN. Then as soon as they walked out of church half the congregation would light up. The other half would go home and get a beer out of the refrigerator while watching the football game. That used to bug me. I don't smoke but I do drink. It was hard for me to go to church and listen to the preacher talk about how bad alcohol is and how it's destroying families and society. I quit going to church because of that. Then, talking to a friend of mine in DC, he explained that even though you may not exactly live the way the church tells you to, it is better to look the other way and take the chance to be able to worship God as close as possible to the way you believe. There are some parts of every dogma, and I think of religion as a basic dogma, that we don't always agree with. We just need to find the dogma that most closely mirrors our own believes and way of life. So I found a church where I felt as comfortable as I could and started worshiping again."

Hope looked at Van Acker with admiration. He had such a strong character. At this point she could not keep her eyes and focus away from him. She managed to respond.

"I guess you're right. Even if we don't agree with it all, if we can live a little better by going to church, then I guess it would be worthwhile."

"That's right."

Their theological discussion came to and end as Allen Murphy drove up. He pulled his truck as close to the burned-out apartment as possible. He opened his toolbox and took out a video camera as he greeted Hope and Van Acker.

"Hi, you two. Sorry I'm late. I had an emergency at the farm. We had two fans shut down in one of the chicken houses. The poor girls were about to perish."

"Poor 'Girls'?," Hope asked, wondering if Murphy was indeed talking about the chickens.

"Yeah, I've got to take care of those girls. They are my livelihood after all."

Van Acker was amused by the way Murphy referred to his chickens. He once had the same reaction Hope did. He had learned to deal with Murphy and the way he treated and talked about his chickens.

"Are you two ready to go on an adventure?" Allen Murphy

155

asked.

"I don't think I would call this an adventure," Van Acker responded. "I've been in too many of these already. Let's just hope we don't find what I think we're gonna find."

Allen Murphy headed up the steps. Van Acker hesitated. He remembered an investigation in an Alexandria, VA suburb. The fire marshal investigating a house fire had brought a gas-stove knob with him. He determined that way whether the gas stove had been on or not.

"Allen?" Van Acker asked, "do you have a spare stove knob in your truck?"

"I don't know. If I do it'll be in the toolbox or the cabin on the dash. I replaced some on our stove not too long ago. I may still have an old one in the truck. Why?"

"I'll show you." Van Acker looked in Murphy's truck and found the needed object.

The three of them entered the apartment.

"Dimitri, I can tell you the source of the explosion was in the living room. You can see there is not much left of the ceiling."

Indeed, the blue summer sky was visible through a large hole in the ceiling. Van Acker walked into the kitchen area.

"Allen, let me show you why I wanted the spare knob."

Murphy and Hope both gathered around Van Acker, curious to see what he had up his sleeve. Van Acker wiped the ashes from the stove. The plastic knobs had melted. The metal stubs from the regulators stood out. Van Acker cleaned up the area around where the knobs where supposed to be. It was an older stove and the HI and OFF marks had been molded in the steel panel of the stove. This would help make a quick determination. Van Acker pushed the spare knob over one of the controls. It showed the control knob had been turned to HI. Hope turned white. She knew what it meant. Van Acker performed the same procedure on the other three control stems. All of them showed the same finding. All four controls knobs had been turned to HI. Murphy showed admiration for Van Acker.

"That was a quick way to find out if the gas stove was turned on. I would have checked it by turning the gas back on."

"I saw someone perform this test up North. I thought it was

156

clever. Unfortunately, it does make my presumption come closer to the truth. Unless Susan was cooking on all four burners, Susan or someone else had the stove turned on."

Hope agreed. She added:

"We have our fuel source for the explosion. Now we need to find what the fuse was."

Murphy looked at the light switch on the wall. It had burned, but there was no sign of an explosion occurring near the switch. Hope and Van Acker both were searching around the living room to find a possible ignition source. Hope almost screamed when she found what they were looking for.

"There!" She pointed at the wall behind a burned up couch.

A black hole was visible in the wall. Wiring was hanging from it. It had clearly been a receptacle. Murphy took a closer look at the wall. The sheet rock had been blasted backwards into the hole. He put his hand inside the wall cavity. He pulled out insulation and sheet rock, two items that do not burn all that well. He grabbed in the hole again. He felt something that did not belong. He was able to take hold of it with his fingers and slowly pulled it up. He presented a burned box looking object. Murphy cleaned a spot on the kitchen counter and placed the object on it. Hope and Van Acker huddled around to see if they could identify the object.

"Look here, it looked like something was stuck in the receptacle. It has two prongs on it," Hope remarked.

"You're right," Van Acker agreed.

Murphy pointed at the round part of what looked like the front of the object.

"I guarantee this is a timer. You know one of those you use to make a light turn on and off when you're on vacation."

"OK, so what is the possibility of someone trying to blow up the apartment depending on Susan having a timer like that?" Hope asked.

Van Acker scratched his chin, leaving soot marks on his face.

"You know what?" he asked, more to himself then to Murphy and Hope. "Let's assume that Susan had a light on the timer. Where is the lamp?"

Van Acker pointed towards the hole in the wall. Nowhere on the floor were there signs of a lamp or charred remains of one. Van

157

Acker continued.

"Even so, why would Susan want a lamp to turn on in the middle of the night?"

Murphy was starting to follow Van Acker's reasoning. Hope looked puzzled. Van Acker noticed the blank look on Hope's face.

"You would want a lamp to turn OFF in the middle of the night, right?"

Hope nodded.

"So, why did the timer activate instead of deactivate? The deactivating process in one of these timers does not create a spark necessary to ignite the gas. So, the timer was activated. The spark on the timer is small. There would have to be a lot of gas in the room before the gas would ignite from the spark in the timer."

Murphy nodded his head and broke in.

"Whoever turned the gas stove on, knew that activating the timer would create a spark and ignite the gas. They also knew it would take a large amount of gas to ignite it. Setting the timer to go off after a large amount of gas had been able to fill the room would be the logical thing to do, especially if one does not expect for a light switch to be turned on."

Van Acker felt uneasy. He again took over the reasoning.

"There are two possibilities here. Someone besides Susan turned on the gas. Susan woke up, smelled the gas and went into the kitchen to turn it off. More than likely in this case, she would turn on the light. That would ignite the gas. Susan would be thrown from the explosion. She would not be found lying on the bed. The second reasoning, and the most likely one is that someone entered the apartment, turned on the gas, planted the timer and left. Susan was sound asleep and became unconscious by the presence of the gas. The timer went off and the explosion happened. Susan was till lying on the bed and burned to death."

Murphy had to agree.

"I'm afraid you're right, Dimitri. I don't think that Susan turned on the gas herself and set the timer to off and blow herself into oblivion."

"I know that she didn't! She was too set on pursuing the lawsuit she had hired me for."

Hope had listened and everything was starting to make sense

158

to her. There was one thing that she was not sure off. She said her peace:

"What if Susan was already dead before the explosion occurred? Would whoever turned on the gas and planted the timer take the risk that she might wake up? Can we be sure Susan was unaware that turning on the light switch would blow up the apartment with that much gas inside? If it was I, I would not take that chance. I would make sure that she's dead first and then I would make it look like an accident; make it look like an accidental explosion."

Van Acker whistled.

"You know, Allen, I think our deputy Sheriff here has a point. If you went through the trouble to break in, turn on the gas and plant a timer, you wouldn't want your plan to be ruined because the person you're trying to blow up is smart enough not to turn on the light switch. Killing them first and then burning the evidence would be the way to go. I think we need to have an autopsy done on Susan's body."

Hope and Murphy both agreed.

All three walked back down the stairs. The fire investigation had not taken too long. The criminal investigation would more than likely take a whole lot longer. Hope decided that she would go ahead and get an investigation started by calling in a medical examiner from Macon. Murphy would write his report and put a final edited tape together of their findings and turn it into the Sheriff's office. Hope insisted that he make it to her attention. She was ready to lead the investigation. Van Acker decided that he would talk to the Knox' and explain to them about the upcoming autopsy. They left the scene. Murphy headed back to his farm while Hope and Van Acker went over to Kelly Murphy's. Van Acker was in desperate need of a shower and a change of clothes.

36.

Bryan Scarboro woke up late. Like most people in Stuttgart, he had watched the commotion at Susan Knox's apartment. He had stayed till just about everybody had left the site. He had felt full of energy as adrenaline rushed through his body. He felt happy and relieved. Susan was dead. The fire destroyed any evidence of him ever setting foot into her apartment. He didn't know if there even would be an investigation into the fire. He hoped not. Should they hold an investigation, he was sure that they would do an autopsy on Susan's body. He knew that they would find out that Susan was an AIDS carrier. Would anybody question who she'd been sleeping with? He hoped it would never come to that. The less attention Susan's death received the better. That way, the trail to him would not be traveled.

Scarboro rubbed his eyes as he got up out of bed. He made his way to the bathroom. Reaching the bathroom door, he looked into the living room and saw his father sitting in his chair by the window. As Bryan entered the bathroom, his father called him.

"Bryan, I need to talk to you." Earl Scarboro said with a demanding voice.

"Okay, Dad, let me use the bathroom first."

Earl Scarboro was sitting in his lazy chair, looking out the window into his flower garden. His face looked gray and he had a worried look in his eyes. Scarboro sat down opposite his father. Dr. Scarboro slowly looked up and into his son's eyes. A cold chill ran down Scarboro's spine. He had not seen his dad look at him this way since he accidentally set the kitchen on fire cooking eggs when he was 10 years old. Scarboro wondered what his father knew.

"I want to ask you something, son, and I want you to tell me the truth."

Scarboro swallowed.

"What is it, Dad?" Scarboro asked.

"Did you for any reason go to the office last night after your mother and I went to bed?"

Scarboro's eyes turned towards the side table next to his father's chair. He thought he had put the keys back in the exact spot that he had taken them from.

"No, I sure didn't," Scarboro lied.

"I'm going to ask you again, Bryan. Did you take my keys and go back to the office?"

"Dad, I told you, I didn't! Why would I lie to you about that?" Scarboro didn't know whether his face was starting to blush or not, but he could feel beads of sweat forming on his forehead.

Earl Scarboro leaned back into his chair.

"Bryan, these keys are not in the same place that I left them in last night. You see, I have a specific way that I leave them. I do this on purpose. I want to know when someone touches them, or, takes them. You see, your mother knows not to touch my office keys. When I looked at them this morning, I noticed the tag on the key chain was not lying in the same position I left it in last night. Now, let me ask you one last time, did you or did you not take my keys last night?"

Scarboro rubbed his chin and felt like a fool. He should have paid more attention to the way the keys were laying. He knew his father was a nut for details. He had been too excited about his actions to pay attention to the smaller details. Scarboro brainstormed while he was rubbing his chin. He needed to find an explanation why the keys were not in the same position as they were before he picked them up.

"Dad, I swear to you, I did not take the keys and go back to the office. I did however move them. You see, I had a little too much fun last night and was drunk when I got home. I decided to sit down in your chair and watch some TV before going to bed. Well, you see, I grabbed for the remote control and knocked the keys on the floor. I put them back where I found them. I'm sorry you thought I tried to sneak behind your back." Scarboro looked at his father with wondering eyes. He wondered if his father would buy his story.

Dr. Scarboro shook his head and smiled.

"Bryan, I tell you, one of these days you may not make it home. You should watch your drinking when you're driving. I don't want to get a phone call in the middle of the night telling me that you were in a wreck and killed some innocent folks or even worse, killed yourself."

"I'm sorry Dad, but I was right here in town. Michelle broke

161

up with me last night and I was down in the gutter. I guess finding a friend in a bottle of whiskey wasn't the smart thing to do."

"The Murphy girl broke up with you?"

"Yeah, everything was going great between us. I don't know why she decided to break it off. We had something going."

"To tell you the truth, Bryan, I thought she was a little too young for you anyways. I thought you might be interested in someone a little bit older."

"Dad, I think that I can make my own decision on who I date and how old I choose them to be. I like the younger girls. Is there something wrong with that?"

"It was just a suggestion!"

Scarboro was about to get up when his father motioned him to set down again.

"Bryan, there's something else I would like to talk to you about. I don't know if you heard last night, but there was a fire at Susan Knox's apartment. She didn't make it."

Scarboro looked as surprised as he could. He dropped his mouth open and played the role of the surprised co-worker as good as he could.

"Susan is dead?" he asked.

"I'm afraid so. There is one thing we do need to do as soon as possible" Dr. Scarboro continued the conversation. "We need to find a replacement for Susan. We cannot run the office without a secretary. Do you know of anyone that would be qualified to do the job?"

Scarboro had no idea whom to recommend for the job. Michelle Murphy would have been perfect, but since she'd rather see him dead than alive, he didn't even dare approach her.

"I'm sorry, Dad, I can't think of anyone right of hand. It may not be a bad idea to run an ad in the paper. I'm sure there's somebody out there that needs a job."

"There are plenty of people out there that need a job, Bryan. But you need to be careful whom you choose. Not everybody is qualified for this type work. It involves more than just answering the telephone and writing down a few notes. I need somebody that has secretarial skills and also knows how to be nice to people, no matter how rotten they treat her."

162

"I take it that you're looking for a woman?" Scarboro asked.

"At the risk of sounding discriminatory, yes I am. When it comes to people that are not feeling well, people who are sick, seeing a woman with a soft friendly voice can make them feel better spiritually. Just think about yourself. You always wanted your mother before me when you were feeling bad. Even though I am a doctor, you still wanted the warm soft voice and touch of your mother. Therefore, I believe that a friendly, soft-spoken woman is the perfect choice to be a doctor's receptionist."

"You know, that makes sense. I'll tell you what; I'll make up an ad and have Gail at the Gazette run it. I guarantee you that we will have us a secretary by the end of the week."

Scarboro got up. He squeezed his father's shoulder as he walked by him.

37.

Joshua Underwood was reading the newspaper when the phone rang. Surprised he looked towards the telephone hanging on the wall in the kitchen. It had been years since his phone had rung on a Sunday. Ever since a drunk driver had killed his wife and his two daughters in a car wreck, he had reframed from socializing outside his business, and unless there was an emergency, he did not expect any phone calls.

Joshua Underwood had been happy and full of life once. But that happiness seized to exist 30 years ago when his wife and daughters were hit head on coming back from church on Sunday afternoon. His wife had been killed instantly while his two daughters were hospitalized. His youngest, who was two years old, died a few hours after being admitted to the hospital. His eldest remained in a coma for three weeks. She passed away on her fifth birthday. The driver of the pick -up truck that had hit his wife's car had walked away from the wreck with only minor scrapes. The man had been drunk. Even though he was charged with three counts of vehicular homicide and spent time in prison, he was released on good behavior after just five short years. To Underwood that was not justice. The incident had marked him. Underwood had turned bitter. Nobody remembered him smiling since the accident. He had turned to a life of solitude, living like a hermit. The only time he made a public appearance was on Sunday mornings when he attended church. He had not missed a service in 30 years. He always sat in the back of the church and was the first to leave.

It seemed to everyone that his profession somehow suited his mood, attitude and lifestyle. Joshua Underwood was the owner of Underwood's Mortuary. He had established the mortuary just two years before his wife's accident. He had decided to continue running the mortuary even though dealing with the dead constantly reminded him of his wife and daughters. The last couple of years, his health had started to dwindle and Underwood had hired an assistant to help him run the mortuary. Any calls that came after hours or on Sunday went to his assistant; therefore, Joshua was surprised to hear the phone ring.

Slowly, he got up and walked over to the telephone. He

looked at the clock. Just after two o'clock in the afternoon. He answered the phone.

"Joshua Underwood here, how can I help you?"

"Mr. Underwood, this is Dimitri Van Acker. I am the lawyer of the deceased Susan Knox. I understand that Susan's body was brought to you mortuary last night."

"Yes she was. Tragic what happened to the woman. And so young! I couldn't believe it when I heard about her death in church this morning."

"Yes, it was tragic. Actually, the reason I'm calling is to check and see when you were planning on preparing the body."

"I don't know. I think my associated might be able to fill you in on that a little bit better. He does the embalming."

"Well, I have tried to get a hold of him, but I'm not getting an answer."

"That damned man! One of these days, his partying is going to be his demise!"

"Mr. Underwood, let me explain to you why I'm bothering you. You see, we ran an investigation on the fire this morning. That is, the fire Marshall, a Sheriff Deputy and myself. We came to the conclusion that the fire in Susan's apartment was foul play. We are requesting an extensive autopsy on the body. It may be a couple of days before we can schedule the autopsy. Therefore, the body cannot be embalmed prior to the autopsy."

"I see. The only way that I can wait with embalming the body is by either a written consent from the next of kin or by court order."

"I understand that. I will have a court order to you tomorrow. I just need to make sure the embalming will not take place today."

"Oh no! We never do embalming on Sunday. Personally I don't think that it is right... I tell you what I'll make sure to talk to my associate and tell him to hold off a couple of hours in the morning before starting the embalming. That should give you plenty of time to produce the necessary paperwork."

"Mr. Underwood, I thank you. Let me give you a number where you can reach me at, should you have any questions."

Van Acker gave Joshua Underwood his cell number. That way, he would be able to get in touch with him.

165

Joshua Underwood put the receiver on the base unit. He shook his head in disbelieve. Would somebody have killed the Knox woman like that lawyer said. To his recollection, nobody had ever been murdered in Stuttgart. This would be a first.

"The small towns of America are no longer safe from the big city crimes," he said half aloud.

Underwood did not go back to his chair to continue reading the paper. Instead, he grabbed his car keys and headed out the door. He was curious. He needed to see for himself before anybody else got a hold of the body. He would examine the body and see if he could find anything. For the first time in 30 years he felt alive. He wanted to be part of this. He wanted to get involved. If it was indeed murder, he wanted justice. He would help any way he could to see the murderer punished.

38.

    After her father had come by looking for Dimitri Van Acker, Kelly Murphy had stayed up. She needed some time to reflect on what had happened in the past 2 days. Since Van Acker showed up, everything started happening. She shook her head. It had to be purely coincidental. Sure, Susan Knox had wanted his legal advice and help, but what if Van Acker would not have been able to come down? Would she still have told everybody that she had AIDS, or did she specifically wait until she knew she would get legal counsel? Was Susan Knox murdered as Van Acker had insinuated or was it an accident? Kelly knew for sure that Susan's death was not suicide. Why would she hire a lawyer to help her with a legal problem if she were going to kill herself? No, it had to be murder or an accident. She hoped that her father would be able to shine some light on that when he investigated the fire. Susan's confession to Bryan Scarboro about her having AIDS directly affected her sister's life. That was the good part that came from it. At least now, Michelle knew what the possibilities were. If Susan hadn't talked, and Michelle had contracted the disease, she would not have known. She hoped everything would be alright with her sister.

    Kelly snapped out of her thoughts when there was a knock on the door. She got up from the couch and pulled her robe tighter around her waist. She looked through the window of the door. Kelly recognized the woman at the door. She let her in.

    "Patricia, hi! What's going on?"

    "Hey Kel, I'm sorry for barging in like this. I'm coming by to make sure that everything is alright with Michelle."

    "I hope she's alright. She took off last night from mom and dad's, took mom's car and disappeared. I haven't heard from her since."

    Patricia looked at the floor and blushed.

    "She spent the night with me last night. She was very upset. This morning when I woke up, she was gone. She's not answering her phone."

    "Did you two talk last night?"

    "Yeah we did. She told me about what happened between Bryan and her. She told me that he might have the HIV virus from sleeping around with Susan Knox."

"I know. We were all at home when she got the call. Everybody in my family knows by now. It's been a crazy night for us."

"I can imagine." Patricia paused.

She turned her eyes away from Kelly before she continued.

"You know, Kel, things are gonna be crazy around town for a while. Susan's death is going to be the talk and I'm sure there will be some investigations in the explosion and fire." She swallowed and looked at Kelly.

"You know there will be questions to whether the explosion was an accident or not. If Susan told Bryan, there's a good chance that she's told some of her other lovers. There might be several people in town who are extremely happy this morning that Susan is no longer among the living so she cannot tell her stories about her bedside manners."

"I'm well aware of that. What you're trying to tell me?"

"I'm sure that whoever is running the investigation, will look at Bryan Scarboro and Tom Sutton to name just two. If they look at Bryan, they will also be looking at Michelle. She might be in for some difficult times. She'll need all the help she can get from all of us. I know that Michelle would never be able to do something as rash as killing Susan Knox. She might have thought about it, but I don't think she'd be able to do it. Nevertheless, there will be questions and they will look at her alibi. I just want you to know that I will help her as much as I can."

Kelly looked at Patricia with suspicious eyes.

"Is there something you know about what happened last night that you're not telling me? Is Michelle in trouble and you're trying to protect her?"

Patricia looked Kelly straight in the eye.

"Like I said, I know she had nothing to do with it."

"If you know she didn't have anything to do with what happened last night; are you telling me that you know that Susan was murdered? And if that's what you're saying, do you know who murdered her?"

"I'm not stupid, Kel. I know all about Susan Knox and what she did and who she did it with. Hell, everybody in town knew.

There are no secrets around here. Everybody knows about Susan's lifestyle. How many people have slept with her and how many could be infected with the HIV virus who stand to lose a lot more than Michelle? If whoever did this is in a power position in Stuttgart and wants to protect his or her position, there's no doubt in my mind they will try to pin it on Michelle. That's all I'm saying. I'm here to warn you that it might get ugly." She paused for a second then continued. "I don't know what time Michelle left home last night, but I knew when she got to my house. She got there way late. If someone is investigating and they track down her times, they will be suspicious."

"I understand. Thanks for coming by and giving me a fair warning. I'll make sure that I talk with mom and dad and Michelle about your concerns."

Kelly walked over to Patricia and gave her a hug.

"It's always good to see you. I wish it could have been different between us."

Patricia looked down at the floor.

"I know. But I understand. You were confused at the time. I must say that I never forgot our time together. I will always remember that night."

Kelly blushed at the memory. She thought she had been able to push the memory to the back of her mind, but at times like this, when Patricia was close to her, the memories flooded back. The one-night stand she had with Patricia had meant a lot to her. She had wanted to know what it would be like to be with another woman. She had enjoyed herself, but it had not done much for her. She decided that night she was straight and that she would only be with a man.

"Thank, Patricia. We'll keep Michelle safe."

Patricia walked towards the door and without saying anything else, walked out and left Kelly standing with her own tormenting thoughts.

It wasn't until Kelly heard the door open that she returned back to reality. She screamed out loud. In an instant, she crossed her living room and pushed the door back shut, pushing the person trying to walk into her house of the steps and onto the ground. Kelly locked the padlock of the door and ran to the phone. When she reached the phone, there was a wild knocking on the door and Kelly could hear someone yelling. She though she recognized the voice. It was a female voice that had a clear distinction to it. She held the phone ready to dial 911 as she walked to the kitchen window. She took a look outside and recognized the people outside her door. She breathe a sight of relieve and felt stupid as she saw Hope Olson and Dimitri Van Acker standing on the steps.

Kelly opened the door. Van Acker stood at the bottom of the steps brushing off his clothes. Kelly started laughing out loud; more so because she was relieved it was only them rather than that she thought the situation was comical.

"So you think it's funny, don't you?" Van Acker asked a little agitated with the situation.

"I'm sorry, Dimitri," Kelly giggled. "I didn't know who it was opening my door."

"Gee girl, you must have been asleep or in a daze. Hope and I were talking as loud as we could so you would know we were in the yard."

"Look, I said I was sorry! I had a visitor and our conversation had me a little upset. I guess I must have been in a daze because I sure did not hear you guys talk or come up the steps."

Hope and Van Acker walked into the house. Once inside, Van Acker introduced Hope to Kelly.

"Kelly, this is Hope Olson, but I'm sure that you two already know each other, right?"

The two girls nodded their head and eyed each other closely. For a couple of seconds nobody said a word.

"So Kelly, who was the mystery visitor and what was said to make you go into a trance," Van Acker asked, breaking the silence.

Kelly sat down on a kitchen chair and nervously pushed a couple of hairs back. She looked towards Hope then flashed her eyes back at Dimitri. Dimitri saw the hesitation in Kelly's eyes, wondering if Hope was safe to be talking around.

"Kelly, if it's private and you don't want Hope to know, just tell us. She'll understand."

"Yeah Kelly, if you don't want me to be in on the conversation, I'll be glad to step outside for a couple of minutes," Hope added.

"Dimitri, I don't know. It's got something to do with what

170

happened last night."

"Last night?" Van Acker asked. "Are you talking about at your parent's house or at Susan Knox' house?"

Again, Kelly eyed Hope with questioning eyes.

"Kelly, you can trust Hope," Van Acker said. "I know that she's a deputy Sheriff, but right now, she's off duty. Anything you say right now will be off the record if you want it to be."

Kelly still felt uneasy about Hope being in the room.

"I don't know Dimitri..."

Before Kelly could finish her sentence, Hope padded Van Acker on the arm and motioned that she was going outside. She winked towards Kelly, trying to make her feel that she was not trying to intrude on whatever she and Dimitri had to discuss.

"Alright now, Hope is outside, what's going on?"

"Patricia Langston came by right before you guys came up."

"I thought I recognized that girl. We passed her about a half mile from here."

"That was her. Anyway, Michelle spent the night with her last night."

"Good! At least now we know she wasn't doing anything crazy..."

Kelly broke in.

"Would you just hear me out," she said, getting mad.

Van Acker raised his hands in mock surrender, extending his palms to Kelly, letting her have the word.

"Anyways, Patricia said that she's worried about Michelle, especially with Susan more than likely being killed and that certain people will try to blame her, especially people of power. People like Tom Sutton and Bryan Scarboro, just to name those. Patricia warned me about something else too. She said that Michelle didn't get to her house till late, well after the fire and stuff. She's worried that this will not look good at all either..." Kelly started crying.

"It's okay, Kelly."

Van Acker pushed a hand through his hair. He needed Hope in on this one, but he couldn't let Kelly know. He would have to be careful. He could tell that for whatever reason Kelly did not trust Hope. It almost felt is if Kelly felt threatened by Hope. He realized of course that he was not directly involved with the investigation. He

171

still served as Susan's lawyer and first and foremost needed to protect Susan's rights. Still, he could not help but feel the need to help with the investigation. He enjoyed detective work. Since he'd been a little boy, he had always enjoyed detective stories and how they solved the mysteries. This was the first real chance he had to be involved so closely. He would have to be careful. And there was the time frame problem of which Kelly had spoken. Though nobody thought Michelle was capable of blowing up Susan's apartment, the stress she was under after finding out she might be infected with HIV could easily have made her snap. He reached out and grabbed Kelly's cheeks and locked his eyes with hers.

"Listen, we know for sure the fire was foul play. Susan was killed. Next we need to know if she was dead before the explosion or if the fire killed her. That's for the medical examiner to figure out. Until we know how Susan died, I will not tell anyone about the time frame between Michelle leaving home and arriving at Patricia's. I won't even tell Hope. But if we find out how Susan died and if evidence start to point in Michelle's direction, I will have to take the side of the law. You do understand this, right?"

Kelly nodded her head.

"Now, can I call Hope back in here? It's hot out there!"

"Sure, I'm sorry. But you do understand why I didn't want to tell you in front of her, right?"

Van Acker didn't say anything but shook his head. He motioned Hope to come back in.

"I'll grab a shower and change my clothes real quick. Hope and I are going on a picnic this afternoon. If you two ladies would excuse me." Van Acker grabbed some clothes out of his suitcase and disappeared into the bathroom, smiling ear to ear.

Hope and Kelly sat next to each other on the couch. The outgoing nature of Kelly soon had them engrossed in a conversation and they seemed like old friends when Van Acker emerged from the bathroom. Everybody said good-bye and Hope and Van Acker took off.

Kelly looked at them leave from the window. She secretly wished it were her Dimitri was taking on a picnic. She was so in love with him. All she'd ever be to him was a little sister. A tear flowed down her cheek as she stepped away from the window.

39.

After church, Julie Sutton stayed with her parents and had dinner with them. Not much was said during the meal. Each had their own thoughts and concerns. Even though it was a hot summer day, the house felt cold to Julie. Each time she looked out the window at the ruins of Susan's apartment, she felt a cold shiver running down her spine. Could she have prevented her sister's death? She didn't know. She felt sad for her mother. She deserved better. But what could she do?

Julie returned home shortly after she helped her mother clean the kitchen and straightened up the house. It would be crazy the next couple of days. Trips to the funeral home, the burial, the curious trying to poke their nose into something it didn't belong in. She didn't look forward to it. At home, she went upstairs and changed her clothes. For the longest time she stood in front of the mirror, naked, looking at her body. She had never been able to do this. Now, she forced herself to look at her own body, its shape, its beauty and its flaws. Why could she not appreciate the beauty that God had given her? Her nakedness was like a curse. A curse her father had brought upon her, a curse that could not be broken unless the painful truth is told. She took one last look at her heaving breasts and dark patch of hair at the cross of her legs before she put on her underwear, a pair of shorts and a T-shirt.

Coming downstairs she looked through Saturday's mail. She noticed that someone had gone through the mail. Tom! He had been back! He must have collected his last few remaining items before she would set fire to them. She'd have the locks to the house changed. Flipping through the mail, she noticed a letter addressed to 'Julie Knox'. Julie laid the rest of the mail back on the desk and took the letter with her to the living room. She tore one side of the envelope and pulled the letter from it. Julie turned white when she saw the signature. She began reading the letter.

Dear Julie,

I'm writing you this letter because I don't knowhow much more time I have in this world.

By now, you will know about my condition. You will also know about my affair with Tom.

For that I am deeply sorry. I hope you can find it in your heart to forgive me.

In case I am no longer among the living when this letter reaches you, it will mean that either my disease or a person from my past has caught up with me.

Either way, I need for you to do me a favor. Our father has done both of us great injustice, and I have evidence of his doings. Before you get the evidence, please contact Dimitri Van Acker, my lawyer and have him escort you to the bank. The evidence is in a safety deposit box. Without Dimitri you will not be able to get the contents of the box because he is the administrator of my estate after my death. I talked to Jackie at the bank and she is aware of everything.

Please continue what I started if I don't have a chance to see it through.

If I am still among the living when this letter reaches you, please put it in a safe place. I don't know if you'll ever need it. I hope you don't. But if you do, please remember that I've always loved you and I never intended to hurt you.

Love always,

Susan.

Julie Sutton dropped the letter in her lap and wiped tears from her face. Susan knew she was going to die soon. Her disease was not in the critical stage yet. She must have known that confessing her disease to her lovers would force one of them to end her life. She wondered if Tom would be able to commit murder to keep his affair with her sister a secret. The newly revealed side of Tom convinced her that he would be able to commit a crime like that. She wondered whom he would have gotten the black coupe from if he was the one who had done it. Surely, whoever was driving the black coupe was the one that caused Susan's death. But the person running in the black outfit seemed smaller than Tom. Then again, it was hard to guess the size of a person running in nearly dark conditions and wearing a black outfit.

Julie shook her head. How was it that her life could be so messed up even though she worshiped the Lord with all her might? She prayed day after day that she would be able to live a normal life, a life free from her inhibitions and problems. A life filled with joy

174

and happiness. She thought the good Lord had provided her with a patient husband who was willing to wait for his wife to feel comfortable in performing her marital duties. She had been wrong. The good Lord had denied her that request.

Julie started crying again. Heavy sobs made her body shake violently. Suddenly she looked up as if she heard something. She got up out of her chair and walked upstairs. In her bedroom she looked in the mirror. Her eyes were puffy red and showed signs of distress. She opened her closet and looked in it. Everything she owned looked so conservative! Pushing aside dresses, blouses and skirts, she finally was able to put together something less conservative. She laid everything out on the bed: a white lacy silk blouse and a black skirt underneath it. Before she laid the skirt down on the bed, she held it in front of her and looked in the mirror. It reached just underneath her knees. Julie walked into the sewing room, reached in her sewing box and took hold of the scissors. She cut off 8" from the bottom of the skirt. Again she held it in front of her and looked in the mirror. That was better. She sat down behind her sewing machine and had the bottom of the skirt hemmed in no time. She returned to her bedroom and laid the skirt underneath the blouse. Julie looked satisfied with what she saw. Next, she went through her nightstand drawer and pulled out a pair of black panty hose. She had bought them for a party that Tom had taken her to. She had worn a long evening gown and the black panty hose were barely visible underneath the long gown. She had not worn them since that party. She believed that any type of black underwear was not pure and reflected someone's thoughts. Today, she would put a stop to those thoughts. Julie reached inside her panty drawer and pulled out a white, lacy pair of panties. Tom had bought them for her and wanted her to wear them around the house. She had worn them once and had hidden them in the bottom of the drawer. They did feel good but she felt as if she wasn't wearing anything. She took hold of a lacy bra and put it next to her panties. Taking a step back she looked at the composition. A smile appeared on her face. It was time to take a step towards change.

In front of the mirror, she slowly took of her shorts and T-shirt. She removed her bra and panties and once again looked at herself in the mirror. She started to like what she saw. Walking

175

away from the mirror towards the bathroom, she looked around and watched her backside in the mirror. Smiling, she slapped her butt. It was still firm.

40.

Joshua Underwood entered the funeral home through the back door and turned off the alarm. He had parked his truck away from the building, out of sight from any passerby on the street. He did not want to be found examining Susan's body. Turning on the light in the hallway, he forgot to lock the door behind him. He moved quickly to the embalming room. He looked over the five cooler compartments and found the one with Susan's name on it. He opened the door and slit out the table. A white sheet was spread over the body.

Slowly Underwood moved the sheet back, revealing the unrecognizable body. Even though Underwood had seen countless dead people in various stages of decomposition and deformation, he had to lean up against the wall when he saw Susan's charred body. The skin looked as if it had huge craters on it where the burn blisters had popped. The evenness of the blisters over her body made him believe that she had not been wearing any clothing when she burned. He grabbed a pair of vinyl gloves and put them on his hands. He also reached in a drawer and pulled out a surgical face mask. He swiveled an examination light towards his general direction and lit up the body. With great care he started feeling the body for unusual skin conditions. The head was the first part of the body that got examined. Underwood felt over the skull down around the temples and then over the face. He felt nothing out of the ordinary. He then lowered his hands towards the throat and the neck area. No lacerations or puncture wounds were found.

Next was the main body. Slowly, Underwood moved his fingers over Susan's chest, down to her breasts. He felt the right breast, moved it around and felt the breast on the underside where it met the rib cage. He moved over to the left breast and followed the same procedure. There was a slight hesitation in his hand movements when he felt the bottom of her left breast. He repeated his hand movements on the breast. Again, when he reached the bottom of the breast there was hesitation. He moved closer to the body and visually inspected the area up close. He moved back to the right side of the table. He felt under the breast. His eyes lit up. With his right hand he pushed Susan's breast up and brought his face closer to the body. With his left hand he moved the skin around.

"BINGO!" he shouted, his face filled with joy.

Joshua Underwood ran to the desk in the corner of the embalming room and grabbed a pencil from a drawer. Quickly he positioned himself back at the left side of the table, pushed the breast up and found the area he was looking for. He put the tip of the pencil against the skin and started gently pushing against the pencil. As he expected, the tip of the pencil disappeared inside the skin. He pulled the pencil out and discarded it in the trash can with his gloves and face mask. Joshua walked over to the desk and pulled a piece of paper from his shirt pocket. He reached for the phone and dialed a number. No answer. He was asked to leave a numeric message and punched in the phone number to the funeral home.

Joshua Underwood was nervous. He had just discovered that Susan had been shot. Boy, would they look up to him now! He couldn't wait to tell that lawyer. Wait with the embalming of the body? Damn right, he'd wait!

Underwood sat down at his desk. His right leg was jumping up and down, uncontrollably. He got up, paced the room and walked back over to Susan's body. He pulled the cover back over the corps and pushed the table back into the wall. He closed the door and walked back to the desk. He sat down, waiting. Waiting for the call in which he'd explain that he found the cause of Susan's death. He could hardly wait!

In all his excitement, Underwood had not heard the back door open and shut. The intruder made the short trip to the embalming room without making a sound. Underwood had been observed finding the bullet hole in Susan's body. The intruder had silently stood back and enjoyed watching Underwood moving about the room, nervous and obviously excited. When Underwood sat back down after returning Susan's body into the wall cooler, the intruder had entered the embalming room. His back towards the door, Underwood had not seen or heard the person entering the room until he heard his name being called out.

"Joshua, Joshua. You just couldn't resist, could you?"

Joshua Underwood turned around, frightened. The blood drained from his face as he looked at the person in the room with him. He tried to speak, but couldn't

"Joshua my dear man, you should have stayed home this afternoon, just like you always have done. Now, you won't ever get to do that again. And, you will also never tell anyone what you found here today. Guess the bright little lawyer from Washington is going to have to wait a little longer to find out what happened!"

Underwood swallowed hard when the person in front of him produced a revolver. He tried to speak but couldn't get any air to flow past his vocal cords.

"Don't worry, old man, it won't hurt too much. It'll be like a needle breaking your skin, and then... Well, then no more pain! Ever!"

The bullet hit Joshua Underwood in the middle of the chest, pushing him back into the chair, a crimson stain forming on his white shirt. Frantically he reached for the phone, his fingers crawling across the desk, trying hard to make it to the receiver. His hand never reached the receiver. A second shot hit him between the eyes and left him leaning back in the chair, his eyes wide open. The back of his head was no longer there. Blood, skull fragments and pieces of brain tissue covered the wall behind the chair.

The shooter quickly reached inside Underwood's pant pockets. A wallet and checkbook were all the shooter found. Flipping through the wallet, a stack of bills was removed. Leaving the embalming room, the killer tossed the wallet into the embalming room. Inside the room the phone rang. Quietly, the intruder left the funeral home, looking towards each side of the door before darting into the open. About a hundred feet away, a car was waiting. No one paid any attention to the black coupe driving off.

41.

Hope Olson and Dimitri Van Acker had gone back by Hope's house to pick up some items for the picnic. Hope made sandwiches, while Van Acker cleaned out a cooler and collected ice. It wasn't long before they were ready to go on their idyllic trip. Hope knew a place a little ways out of town that was quiet and hidden from the main road. No one would find them. She was feeling giddy as she gave Van Acker directions on how to get there. Without too much trouble, Dimitri pulled up to an open spot in the middle of some woods. It had been a bumpy ride from the road through the woods before they reach the open spot and a few times Dimitri had been worried if his car was going to make it.

The sun was blocked by some of the trees and Hope spread a blanket on the grass. Both were quiet as they ate their sandwiches. Hope finally broke the silence.

"Dimitri, tell me, how do you feel about Kelly?"

Looking at Hope with questioning eyes, he responded.

"Kelly? I don't readily know how to answer that question. I've always looked at her as a little sister. I guess that's how I still feel about her. Why?"

"Have you ever felt attracted to her beyond her being a "little sister"," she prodded.

"No, I don't think so."

"Come on don't tell me you couldn't feel attracted to a beautiful woman like that!"

"Oh, sure, I can feel attracted to a beautiful woman like that, but I don't feel that way about Kelly. I think my mother is beautiful too, but I don't feel attracted to her!"

Hope slapped him on the arm.

"You know what I mean! You don't have any blood relationship at all with her. You may say you look at her as a sister, but when it comes down to it, you could and can become involved with her."

"You're right. I could. But I won't. Besides, do you feel threatened by her?"

Hope thought about that for a moment.

"Yes I do! I don't think you should spend another night over there."

"Then where do you propose I should spend the night?"

"At my house," Hope said nonchalantly.

Dimitri smiled.

"I believe that you're trying to hook up with me."

"No, I'm not trying to hook up with you. I'm just trying to make up for lost time. I missed you, you know."

"So if I stay with you till I have all the paperwork on the house finished up, what will the good folks of Stuttgart think about one of their unmarried deputies having a man living with her?"

"Screw the good folks of Stuttgart. I don't care what they think. As long as I do my job as a deputy to the full extent of my abilities, they should not judge me. I can probably dig up plenty of dirt on every single one of those who would be talking."

"I'm sure you could."

"So what is it going to be? Are you gonna move in with me or not?"

Van Acker scratched his head. He was faced with a dilemma. Not staying at Kelly's would make Kelly mad with him. He could bring up the argument that an employer and his employee should not live under the same roof if they were not married. On the other hand, not staying with Hope might jeopardize how she felt about him. He did not want to risk losing her.

"I don't know yet. I'll tell you later this evening who I'll stay with. Besides, it'll only be for a short while anyway. I should be able to move into my house by the end of next week."

Hope did not answer him. She moved some of the items on the blanket to the side and leaned over towards Van Acker and kissed him.

Van Acker returned the kiss, cherishing the soft feel of Hope's lips against his. He slowly opened his mouth and slid his tongue up against her lips. Hope parted her lips and let Van Acker slip his tongue inside her mouth. It wasn't long before the two of them were sprawled out on the blanket, loving and caressing each other. Both longed for the tender, gentle touches they were giving each other. Their hands explored each other's body. Van Acker pushed Hope's shirt up and uncovered her breasts. Hope pulled her shirt up over her head and threw it to the side. She reached behind

181

her back and unhooked her bra. Slowly she let the straps to her bra slide down her arms, exposing her breasts to Van Acker. He stared at Hope and felt himself get hard. His face was starting to turn a couple of shades darker. Hope reached for Van Acker's hands and put them on her breasts. He could feel the hardness of her nipples against the palms of his hands. Hope closed her eyes and arched her back as Van Acker softly started to massage her breasts. He took them in his hands, felt of them, felt the hardness of her nipples. As he was about to bend down to kiss her nipples, Hope pushed him back up and started to pull his shirt off. She ran her fingers through the hair on his chest. She pushed him down on the blanket and cradled herself next to him, tenderly rubbing his chest while Van Acker rubber her back. Both closed their eyes enjoying the closeness they felt and needed.

The ringing sound of Van Acker's cell phone startled both of them. Dimitri's eyes shot open and he looked a little bewildered. Hope was still cradled in his arms, asleep. He looked over towards their basket. His cell phone! He slid away from Hope and grabbed his cell phone. When he reached it, it stopped ringing. He checked the number. It did not look familiar to him. Gently he nudged Hope in the side. She opened her eyes.

"What's wrong?"

"My cell phone just rang. I was to late getting to it. Do you recognize this number?"

Hope looked at the number.

"If I'm not mistaken, that's the number to the funeral home. Why would anyone call you from there on a Sunday afternoon?"

"I don't know." Van Acker answered, looking a little worried. "You don't think Mr. Underwood took it upon himself to go and take a look at Susan's body, do you?"

Hope sat up and reached for her bra.

"That would surprise me. He never goes anywhere."

"Let me call the number back and see who it is."

Van Acker got up and dialed the number while Hope put on her bra and shirt.

"I'm not getting answer," he told Hope who lifted herself on the hood of the car.

"Something is not right," Hope said, sliding to the ground.

"This doesn't look good, does it?" Van Acker asked, noting the worried look on Hope's face.

"I don't know. We may be jumping the gun, but I have a feeling that something bad has happened to Joshua Underwood. What time is it?"

Van Acker looked at his watch.

"Quarter till five."

"You want to drive out to the funeral home and check it out?"

"If it'll make you feel better, yeah, let's go."

Without saying a word, Hope started collecting their picnic items and put them in the car. They'd be at the funeral home in just a matter of minutes.

42.

Allen Murphy spent a good part of the day at the farm. He made sure that all the ventilators in the chicken houses were working properly and opened the large louvers to let as much air as possible flow through them. The recent heat wave had cost him more chickens than usual. He blamed himself. With an increase in production came an increase in income. At least, that's what Allen had assumed when he increased the capacity of his houses. The cramped chickens suffered with the increased number of fowl in the houses and thus more of them died. Allen tried hard to keep the inside of the houses as cool as possible, but with days of over 100 degrees, it was hard. The metal houses served as an oven. On days without any wind it was especially hot. Besides taking care of the ventilation, one of the harvesters wasn't working. At took Allen over 2 hours to get the feed motor to start working again. Luckily, he knew how to fix most anything on the farm, a luxury most farmers these days didn't have. Having to depend on mechanics and service personnel would have cost him thousands of dollars over the past year. Fortunately, he had been able to keep his downtime to a minimum.

Allen Murphy was tired when he came home around 5 o'clock. Fighting the fire at Susan Knox' apartment, getting up early to find Dimitri Van Acker, investigate the fire, and work at the farm for the rest of the day had worn him out. Yet the day was not over yet. He still needed to sit down and write a report about his findings at Susan Knox apartment. Helen greeted him with a kiss when he walked into the kitchen. It had been a daily ritual when she stayed home with the girls. Murphy had grown used to it. These days, with Helen working, he only received these kinds of greetings on the weekend.

"Hi honey, how are you?" Helen asked.

"Worn out, how about yourself?"

"I'm alright."

"Have you seen Michelle?"

"Yeah, she was here this morning when I woke up. She had me breakfast cooked and everything."

"Where did she spend the night? Did she say?"

"She was over at Patricia's. I confirmed it with Patricia. She was there."

"Is she at home?"

"No, she went over to Kelly's. Bryan's been trying to call her here. He doesn't know Kelly's number so he won't bother her there."

"I'm telling you, Helen, I see that boy bother her again, he better watch out!"

"Don't do anything crazy, okay? There's been enough harm done already in this town in the past couple of days. We don't need anymore foolishness!"

Murphy didn't say anything. He opened the refrigerator and grabbed a beer.

"You know, Helen, someone blew up Susan's apartment last night."

Helen looked at her husband with frightened eyes.

"You mean it was foul play?"

Murphy just shook his head and took a swallow of beer.

"Whoever did it might have possibly killed Susan before they made the apartment go up in flames."

"Are you for real?" Helen asked in disbelieve.

"You know, I should have listened to Dimitri last night. He told me all along that it might be foul play. I didn't believe him, got upset with him!"

"Did you two get into an argument?"

"Well, it wasn't much of an argument. I told him to get his butt behind the caution line and stay out of something he didn't know anything about. I guess he knows more than I thought!"

"Have you spoken to him since?"

"I went to find him this morning. I thought about what he said and it made sense. Besides, if it is foul play, there needs to be a further investigation. I don't know Helen, but if Dimitri hadn't been here, I guess we would have buried Susan and forgotten about what happened. A killer would have been of the hook."

"Do you know who might have done it?"

"I don't know. Susan was liked, especially with the men around town." Murphy hesitated. He promised Van Acker he wouldn't tell anyone. He could not break that promise. He decided

185

not to tell Helen about Susan's confession to her lovers.

"You know, I bet some jealous wife got a hold of her!" Helen remarked.

Murphy took another swallow of beer and shook his head.

"I don't think we need to jump to any conclusions. We need to let the Sheriff's department worry about whom might have done it."

Murphy finished his beer and deposited the empty can in the trash.

"I'm gonna go take a shower. I've got to sit down and write up my report about my findings. I want to give it to the Sheriff in the morning."

"Okay honey. I'll have supper ready in about an hour."

Murphy kissed Helen tenderly and pinched her gently on the buttocks. Helen squirmed and slapped him on the hand. He walked towards the bedroom, smiling.

After he finished taken a shower, Murphy watched the evening news and caught the highlights. After supper he sat down in front of the computer and started writing his report. He was a slow typist. He had never had any lessons in typing and taught himself. He had improved from the two-finger method to at least using most of his fingers. It took him a little over two hours to write the report. He printed it out and looked it over. Everything was there. Satisfied, he grabbed an envelope and put the report in it. Helen had retreated to the bathroom to take a bath and Murphy decided to take a quick look on the Internet. He enjoyed getting in the chat rooms and chat with people about the current events in the world.

When he got online, he first checked to see what website had been called up since he last got on. He did this to keep track of what Michelle was watching while on the Internet. Even though she was 18, he still felt like he needed to protect her. He pressed a couple of buttons on the screen and about 10 websites showed up. He scanned them carefully. All of them except the one on top of the list were websites that he had called up. The top one he did not recognize. WWW.PERFECTCRIMES.COM. Murphy was curious. He clicked on the website. Less than a minute later, he was facing a screen that gave him various choices. The choices ranged from 'Bloody and Gruesome' to 'Clean and Neat But Deadly'. His heart started beating faster. One of the choices listed was 'How to destroy evidence at the murder scene'. Murphy clicked on that choice. On the screen appeared an elaborate list of ways to destroy evidence at a murder scene. Since the computer remembered which sites or selections were made, he noticed the word 'Fire' was highlighted. He started to feel uneasy. With a shaking hand, he moved the cursor to the word 'Fire' and clicked. An article appeared on the screen. Murphy started reading. It described different ways on how to set a building on fire. There was one section that addressed the use of explosions to start fires. Murphy paid close attention to it. He read almost literally what Van Acker, Hope and he had discussed at Susan's apartment. It described placing a timer in a room near a source of escaping gas. Gas stoves and older model gas bottles used for grills were recommended for the job.

Murphy was so engrossed in reading the article that he had not noticed Helen coming in the room. When she touched his shoulders, he jumped. When he realized it was Helen he relaxed.

"Sorry honey. I've been reading this article and I'm getter worried and scared."

"Why, what's it about?"

"It's about how to set fire to a building to destroy criminal evidence."

"What? How did you find that website?"

"It was the last one opened on the computer."

Helen looked at Murphy in disbelieve.

"Trust me, it wasn't me!" Murphy explained.

"And I haven't been online since you were last on."

Both looked at each other. Simultaneously they said the same word:

"Michelle!"

43.

Tom Sutton was sitting behind his secretary's desk in his office. He had decided not to return to his hotel room. Instead, he went to his office and tried to finish some work. He needed some reports typed up, and with the prospect of both Helen and Kelly not returning, he was forced to type them up himself. It had been a while since he had used a word processor. Struggling, he started typing the reports. Amid outburst of rage and disgust, he had not noticed the door to his office opening. It wasn't until the person in the doorway spoke out that Sutton realized he was not alone. He jumped and scrambled up.

"Relax, Tom! It's only me!"

Sutton looked at the person standing in the doorway.

"Andy! You scared the shit out of me!"

"I didn't think that you scared so easily." Andrew Hinson joked.

"Well, I do when someone sneaks up on me while I'm in the middle of something!"

"I thought you had two secretaries helping you out to do all of your typing?"

"I did! They both decided to leave me at the same time, left me holding the bag!"

"They both quit, huh?"

"Yeah." Sutton stroked his hair. "Kelly's started working with that Van Acker fellow. Figure that one out!"

"I'm not surprised. I think those two have something going anyways. He's staying with her, you know."

Sutton nodded affirmatively.

"So what can I help you with, Andy?"

"Let's go in your office, okay?"

Sutton showed him the way.

Andrew Hinson was the Sheriff of Dawson County. Andrew had moved to Stuttgart when he retired from the Air Force. He had served two tours of duty in Vietnam and was highly decorated. He had stayed on with the Air Force long enough to receive his full benefits and had quickly retired. He and his wife had wanted to live in a quiet country setting. That's when they stumbled across

188

Stuttgart. They both fell in love with the little town. They bought a nice little house on the edge of town with a couple of acres attached to it. They got a couple of goats and a few pigs and were happy raising their little livestock. Unfortunately their happiness was cut short when Andrew's wife developed cancer and died within six months of her diagnosis. Hinson was devastated. He mourned for over a year before he finally realized that mourning and blaming himself for his wife's death was not what she would have wanted him to do. She would have wanted him to go on with his life. So finally, after a year he did. He decided to run for the office of Sheriff. He would make himself useful in the community. In the short time that he had lived in Stuttgart, he had become well liked and he felt that he could win the office. He won and was now in his second term as Sheriff. Andrew ran the force as if it were the military. Besides the secretary and the dispatcher, everyone on the Sheriff's department was former military. The department was efficient and had budget money left over at the end of every year that Andrew had been Sheriff. The department had been able to buy new patrol cars and every one of the deputies had their own car assigned to them. Hinson had been criticized by the County Commissioners for purchasing new vehicles but he promised them that he would have better result with new vehicles than with older, worn out vehicles. Crime in the county had dwindled down as he was not afraid to fill the small county jail. When it came to speeding, Dawson County soon became know as a speed trap. But the revenue to the county coffers was considerably and the citizens didn't complain. They adjusted their driving speed and supported their Sheriff. He was headed for his second reelection.

Tom Sutton and Andrew Hinson walked into Sutton's office. Hinson sat down in the chair in front of Sutton's desk. Sutton walked around behind his desk and sat down himself.

"So what's up, Andy?"

Hinson looked Sutton in the eyes, a deep penetrating look that made a chill run up Sutton's spine.

"I want to know what you think about that Van Acker fellow. Seems to me he's gonna try to mess with the peace in Stuttgart."

"I can honestly tell you that I don't care for the man. However, I don't understand where you're coming from with him breaking up the peace around here."

Hinson stroked his chin.

"You know, Tom, it's funny, the day after he comes to town, a house blows up and one of Stuttgart's well known citizens dies. This town hasn't known this much havoc in all of its existence." Hinson paused to let his words sink in. He continued.

"You know, Tom, I don't think Van Acker belongs in this town. He's a big city lawyer. He doesn't know anything about how things are run around here. I personally think we need to get rid of him. Boot him out of town. Find something on him that will force him to leave. Hell, maybe even get him arrested and send him to jail!"

Sutton looked at his friend in disbelieve. His mouth had dropped open while listening to Hinson.

"Andy, I... I said I didn't like him. I didn't say that I wanted to get rid of him."

"Let me ask you this, Tom. Will his being here affect your business?"

Sutton nodded his head affirmative.

"Will his being here affect the way I run my business?" Hinson asked.

Sutton didn't know how to answer that question right away. He looked at Hinson with questioning eyes. Hinson saw the troubled look on Sutton's face.

"Let me explain, Tom. I have run this county for six years now. I have my deputies trained the way I want them. I also have the citizens of this county trained. You're the lawyer of the town, hell, say the county. Between the two of us, we are the law around here. There's nothing that anyone can do about it. If the people don't do as I please, I fine them and lock them up if I can. It's worked great for the past six years. The people fear me and the office I represent. Plus, I keep you busy! All of these fine upstanding citizens who end up in my jail pay you to represent them. You make money because of the way I run this county. Now, if we get this big city lawyer in here, he will make it hard on you, but he will also make me look like a fool. He's not an insider. He'll poison the minds of the citizens by telling them that they're not being treated right by their Sheriff, while all I'm trying to do is keep them in line.

190

I'm telling you, Tom, he's bad news!"

Sutton listened to Hinson and couldn't help but agree. He had never been faced with a situation like this. He had never thought about the way things were really being run in Stuttgart. Hinson was right. They were the law in the county. No matter what anyone thought, Hinson and he, not the commissioners, were running Dawson County.

"What are you thinking about doing, Andy?"

"I've got a few ideas about what I can do. You'll know about it when it happens."

Hinson got up and started walking towards the door. He turned around and looked at Sutton.

"We need to keep the power in this county, Tom. At all cost!"

Andrew Hinson disappeared from Sutton's office. Tom Sutton put his hands on his desk and took a deep breath. He shook his head as he recalled his conversation with Hinson. He wondered what Hinson was up to.

44.

Hope Olson and Dimitri Van Acker arrived at the funeral home a little after five o'clock. They drove into the parking lot. Van Acker noticed a truck sitting a little distance away from the building, half hidden by the shrubbery bordering the parking lot. He pointed at the truck. Hope nodded her head.

"That's Joshua's truck."

Van Acker pulled up to the back door as close as possible.

"Dimitri, the door is not closed!"

Van Acker nodded his head, grabbed under the seat and took his revolver out of the scabbard. Hope's eye grew big when she saw Van Acker reveal his .44 Magnum.

"You honestly think that will be necessary?"

"I don't like to take any chances. If anyone is in there besides Underwood, I want to be prepared."

They exited the car and slowly walked towards the back door. Van Acker pushed against the door and swung it open. He cocked the revolver. They entered the building. Hope positioned herself up against the wall on one side of the hallway, while Van Acker took position along the opposite wall. Slowly they walked the hallway towards the first door. The door was on Van Acker's side of the hall. When he reached it, he tried to turn the doorknob. It was locked. They continued to the next door. This one was on Hope's side of the hall. It was locked too. Next was a room on Van Acker's side of the hall from which light was emitting. Quietly, Van Acker positioned himself as close to the door as possible. Hope looked at him with anxious eyes. Van Acker returned the look. Without warning, he turned into the doorway and took a quick look at the part of the room that he could see. He returned back to his original standing position as quickly as he had taken a look into the room. He shook his head, signaling to Hope that he did not see anyone in the room. Hope moved further up in the hall until she had a look at the part of the room Van Acker could not have seen. She positioned herself and darted across the hallway to the opposite side of the door from where Van Acker was standing. She continued her movement and looked into the room. She darted back up against the wall, away from the door opening. Van Acker looked at her for a reaction. He got one he was not expecting. Hope's face had turned white as snow. Van Acker took another look into the room, this time viewing the right side of the room. Immediately he saw what had Hope's face turn white. In the chair in front of the desk, slumped over, was the body of a man, a hole in the back of his head; blood, brain and skull fragments scattered on the wall. Van Acker fought the sickness that was forming in his stomach. He motioned Hope to come in. She slowly set foot into the room.

"Is this Joshua?" he asked.

"I can't tell. I need to see his face."

Van Acker looked around and found a box of rubber gloves. Carefully, making sure he did not touch anything, he grabbed two gloves and slipped them on. He then took the victim by the head and leaned it back.

"Oh God! It's Joshua!" Hope exclaimed. Tears were forming in her eyes. She leaned up against the wall and had a sickening sensation in her stomach. She had seen blood and gore while enlisted in the Navy, but this was different. She had softened up since she left the service.

Van Acker returned Joshua's head to the position he had found it in. He then walked over to Hope.

"You gonna be alright?"

Hope nodded that she would be fine. She took a couple of deep breaths and grabbed her cell phone. Without saying a word, she dialed a number.

"Jesse? Hi it's Hope. I'm over at the mortuary. You need to call an ambulance and send Frank over here right away. Also, call Andy and tell him to come over here. Joshua Underwood has been killed. No, I can't."

Van Acker, who still had his revolver in his hand, realized that fact, and pushed it in the back of his shorts. Hope noticed the action.

"Dimitri, you need to go put that thing back where you got it before Andy gets here. Don't ask me why, just do it." Hope said, sounding like a deputy more than like a friend. Van Acker walked out the room and headed back to the door without saying a word. He didn't know how to approach Hope. She would have to do her job as a deputy, even if she was off duty. As he reached the door, he noticed a small piece of black fabric hanging on the door lock. Looking over his shoulder to make sure that Hope did not see him, he carefully removed the piece of fabric. He opened the trunk of his car and deposited the piece of fabric in a film canister and put it in a secret compartment in the side of the trunk. He put his revolver back in the scabbard and returned to the embaling room in the mortuary.

"Find anything?" he asked Hope.

"I found Joshua's wallet. All the money is missing. This looks like a robbery."

"Or whomever shot the old man wanted it to look like robbery," Van Acker said, talking more to himself than to Hope.

"You think this is what happened?" Hope asked with disbelief in her voice.

"Think about it! Why was Joshua here? I told him not to mess with Susan's body. And you said so yourself, he never goes anywhere! He was here because he was curious! He decided to check out Susan's body on his own, see if he could find anything. So he comes out here and examines the body. Whoever killed Susan passes by and sees Joshua's truck in the back. Wondering what the man is doing here, the killer investigates what Joshua is doing. I bet Joshua was so excited about the prospect of finding something that he forgot to lock the door behind him. Susan's killer makes an easy entrance and BOOM: Joshua is dead and he cannot tell anyone what he found. I bet he called me to tell me what he found!"

"Dimitri, in all honesty, don't you think that's a little farfetched? That's just too perfect. Let's say Susan's killer did this, how would that person know that Joshua is examining Susan's body?"

"Okay, who in town besides you knows that Joshua stays to himself and never works on Sunday? Whoever killed Susan is local and knows Joshua Underwood's story. I'm telling you, we're looking at the same person."

Hope looked at Van Acker and didn't answer. The room was quiet as she thought about his reasoning. A couple of minutes went by before she answered.

"I don't think so. I think that whoever killed Joshua stumbled on him by accident. You know, a mortuary has some interesting chemicals that drug users would love to get their hands on."

Van Acker started to respond but was cut sort by the person standing in the doorway of the embalming room.

"Hope," the man addressed Hope with an authoritative voice, "can I ask you what let you to come out here?"

Van Acker slowly moved his eyes from side to side signaling to Hope not to tell him the entire story. She looked back at him, her eyes showing signs of madness. Van Acker didn't know what to think. Mostly he did not know who the man in the doorway was. As if on cue, Hope said:

"Andy, first let me introduce you to a good friend of mine, Dimitri Van Acker."

Van Acker stuck his hand out to the person in the doorway. Andy returned the favor.

"Nice to meet you, Dimitri, I am Andrew Hinson, Sheriff of Dawson County. How are you?"

"Nice to meet you too, Andrew. I'm doing alright. I wish I could say the same about old Joshua over there." Van Acker pointed towards the body.

"Hope, what were you two doing here?" Hinson asked again, this time a little bit more insistent.

"Well, I've been a friend of Joshua's for a long time. I wanted him to meet Dimitri. We drove by his house and found he wasn't there. That was unusual. So, I decided to see if he was here by chance. When we got here, we found the door ajar. That's when we found the body."

"Have you found anything of interest?" Hinson asked.

"I've found Joshua's wallet. It's empty. It looks like this was a robbery."

"We'll have the place dusted for prints. I don't think we'll find a lot though."

Hinson walked over to the victim and pushed the head back. He brought his face closer to that of Underwood. He moved his head, noting every detail on the dead man's face. He put the head back in its original position.

"Looks like a .44, close distance. Whoever did this knew what he was doing. I suspect the first shot was in the stomach. Painful! From the way the body is positioned, I'd say old Joshua was grabbing for the phone."

Van Acker felt he needed to add something. Hesitantly he started.

"If I may interrupt..."

He looked at Hinson with anticipation, who nodded for Van Acker to continue.

"More than likely, the second shot entered the forehead at an angle. Looking at the hole in the back of the head, you can see that it's not positioned in line with the hole in the front of the head. Either the bullet went in at an angle or it changed direction after entry. I would safely say the latter is an impossibility figuring the speed of the bullet at this close range."

Hinson nodded his head affirmatively.

"You make a good point, Van Acker. Where did you learn about ballistics and murder scene investigations?"

"I've been a layer in Washington, DC. I represented the scum of the city. More than once I was called to identify one of my clients. You hang around crime scenes long enough; you learn quickly what to look for."

"You're pretty bright, for a lawyer." Hinson remarked, looking Van Acker dead serious in the face. "I bet you could just about commit the perfect murder, couldn't you?"

"I don't know what you're suggesting, but I believe there is no such thing as a perfect murder. One may only think there is a perfect murder." Van Acker shook his head. "Nobody is perfect, therefore no crime is perfect. One will always leave some evidence behind."

Hinson didn't say anything but studied Van Acker more closely. He knew he had a tough opponent on his hands. If he wanted to get rid of Van Acker, he would have to play it smart. Hinson turned away from Van Acker and addressed Hope.

"Hope, I need to talk to you about another matter, do you mind if we go into the hallway and talk privately?"

"No, not at all," Hope answered, looking towards Van Acker.

Hinson led the way into the hallway. Hope followed closely behind him. They left Van Acker alone in the embalming room.

Van Acker looked around. For the first time since they discovered the body, he had a chance to look around. He looked over the contents of Joshua's desk. Nothing stood out, a phone, a couple of pencils, a picture of what probably were Joshua's wife and kids and a notepad. Dimitri focused his sights on the notepad. Bringing his face closer to the notepad, he noticed that a note on the previous page had been jotted down rather hard and had left an impression in the page below it. The page that had been written on was missing. Van Acker looked towards the door. Hope and Hinson were not to be seen. He moved his hand towards the notepad and pulled the top piece of paper away from the glued backing and stuck the blank page in his pocket. He would analyze that later. He moved away from the desk, towards the storage drawers. There was only one drawer that had a tag on it. Van Acker read the tag.

"Susan Knox, burn victim."

He was tempted to open the door but rejected the idea. He did not want to disturb any prints that might be on the pull handle. He looked around some more. The preparation table was made from stainless steel and gave a cold atmosphere to the already gloomy looking room. A trash can was positioned underneath the table. Van Acker noticed a pair of gloves. A round pink object drew his eyes. He bent down and examined the pink object. It was the eraser part of a pencil. He grabbed inside his right pocket and grabbed his keys. With them he moved the rubber gloves to the side. Sure enough, it was a pencil. Van Acker wondered what a pencil was doing in the trash can. He moved the gloves back over the pencil, covering up the eraser, making the pencil unnoticeable. He straightened up and moved back towards where he had been standing before Hope and Hinson left the room. He had seen plenty and had some research to do on the paper he had in his pocket.

Hinson walked towards the far end of the hallway and turned around. Hope was right behind him.

"What's up, Andy?" she asked curiously.

"I understand that you were the officer on duty last night when the explosion at the Knox apartment happened."

"That's right. I was about to go off when I heard the explosion. Why?"

"Well, I know about how you do your rounds through town. Sutton's place is the last you go by. That's not too far from the apartment. Did you see anything suspicious?"

Hope's eyes turned to slits. She wondered why Hinson was

questioning her. She decided to test the waters. She pretended she was thinking hard about the question.

"No. The only thing that I think might have been out of place was a car speeding by Sutton's place right about the time I was pulling out. I nearly hit it. I don't think that it is related to the explosion though. Why? Do you think that the explosion wasn't an accident?"

"I'm playing it safe, Hope. I don't want to leave any stone unturned."

"I understand. As a matter of fact, I met with Allen Murphy this morning to help with his investigation as to the source of the fire and the explosion. Allen has some ideas about the explosion. You should have his report in the morning..." Hope hesitated. She wanted to be the investigating officer on the Knox case. This was her chance to ask Hinson if she could run it.

"Andy..." she stopped and looked for a reaction.

"Yes Hope, go ahead."

"Andy, I was wondering if I could lead the Knox investigation. I mean, I was the officer on the scene and am familiar with what happened last night. Besides, I was part of the investigation with Allen. What do you think?"

Hinson was surprised by the question. It was not usual for a deputy to ask to be in charge of an investigation. He needed to get some more information.

"Let me ask you something. Did you and Murphy investigate the apartment by yourselves or were there some other people there?"

Hope knew where the question was leading. She had heard the resentment in Hinson's voice for Van Acker being with her. She decided that she would not tell Hinson about Van Acker joining them in the investigation.

"No, it was just the two of us. He came by my house to get me. He knew I was the deputy on the scene. He wanted me to be part of it. Why?"

"I was just wondering. I don't want anybody nosing around that doesn't have any business nosing around, if you know what I mean."

The last part was said with definite intonation. Hope understood perfectly well the remark pointed in Van Acker's direction. She didn't understand what Hinson's problem with Van Acker was. Whatever it was, she would warn Dimitri about it.

"I understand, Andy. I'll keep Dimitri a safe distance away from my investigation." She paused. Hinson just looked at her with questioning eyes. "Does that mean that I can lead the investigation then?"

Hinson produced a smile.

"Yeah, you can lead the investigation. But remember. If I so much as see that foreign dude around you when you're working, I'll pull your ass from the investigation on put you on probation. Do I make myself clear?"

Hope nodded her head. It wouldn't be easy to keep Dimitri away from her. Or rather, it wouldn't be easy for her to stay away from Dimitri. She would tell him that he'd have to stay with Kelly.

Hinson excused Hope. Two more deputies had arrived on the scene and they brought in the fingerprint kit. Without saying too much, they went to work.

Van Acker saw Hope walk by and left the embalming room. Outside, he met her by his car. He could see a worried look on her face.

"What's wrong?" he asked.

Hope looked at him. Without saying a word, she opened the door and got in the car. Van Acker followed her example.

"Like to tell me what's going on?" he asked as he got in.

"It's nothing, sweetheart. Let's just get out of here, okay?"

He started the car and drove away from the funeral home. He headed towards Hope's place.

In the doorway of the funeral home, Andrew Hinson watched as the car disappeared. He looked troubled. His fists were balled and he bit his teeth together. There was more to Van Acker than he'd thought. It wouldn't be as easy to get rid of him as he had expected.

45.

The neon lights in the window blinked on and off. Inside, heavy smoke from cigarettes filled the room. Peanut shells covered the floor. The waitresses dressed in short skirts and tank tops that barely covered the essentials, paraded through the bar, making their customers happy with beer refills and an occasional flash of their cleavage. Larry's Lounge was busy. The bar was filled near capacity. An important baseball game had drawn the local team's fans. Two big-screen TV's provided everybody with a good view. Most of the customers were more interested in drinking beer, eating peanuts and sneaking the occasional peek inside the waitresses' tank tops. There were some that had brought their wives. Most of the customers, however, had left their better halves at home or were not married and hoped a single good-looking lady would enter the bar at any given moment. Larry was positioned behind the bar and had a big smile on his face. Business was good and the cash was flowing. Throughout the bar, a couple of bouncers walked the floor. Should any of the customers become rowdy or start to harass the waitresses, they made sure the troublemakers were escorted out.

The door opened quietly. A woman entered the bar. As if by command, the bar became less noisy as the male customers noticed the woman. Here and there, a few whistles could be heard. All eyes followed the woman to the bar. The white silk blouse she wore was transparent and showed off the lacy bra she wore. Her black skirt came to halfway up her thighs. Black seamed stockings lead all the guys' eyes straight up the back of her legs to the hem of her skirt. The black high heel pumps tightened the muscles in her calves. As she sat down on the bar stool, she made a special effort to cross her legs as slow as possible, giving a few of the customer's opposite her a view underneath her skirt. She motioned to Larry.

"Give me a scotch, straight up."

"Coming right up, darling!" Larry said, admiring the beautiful woman in front of him.

Waiting for her drink to arrive, she grabbed inside her purse and produced a cigarette. Hesitantly she lit the cigarette. She took a small draw on the cigarette. Surprised by the stinging feeling in her throat, she coughed. Tears jumped in her eyes. With great effort, she gained control of the situation. Once again, she was calm and collected.

She gazed around the bar, searching for a familiar face. She could not see one. What a relief. She turned back to the bar and sipped on her drink. Julie Sutton wondered how long it would be before one of the animals would make a pass at her.

A middle-aged man entered the bar shortly after Julie did. He scanned the room. He noticed Julie sitting at the bar. Nonchalantly he walked the short distance to the bar. He positioned himself on the stool next to her. He looked her over, starting with her face and letting his eyes move over her body, pausing at her breasts and legs.

"Hi, my name is Lester. How are you?"

Julie froze for a second. She had not thought someone would make a move at her so easily. She managed to respond.

"Nice to meet you, Lester, I'm Julie."

"New to the bar scene?"

Julie blushed.

"Yes!" she admitted. "How did you know?"

"You look nervous. My guess is that you don't wanna be here. What happened? You found out your husband is cheating on you?"

"You must have psychic powers. That's exactly what happened. On top of that, I lost my sister in a fire last night."

"My condolences for the loss of your sister."

"Thanks."

Lester looked at the drink sitting in front of Julie. She had barely touched it.

"You don't like Scotch, do you?" Lester said, changing the subject.

"No," Julie sighted, "I'm not used to drinking at all. I just thought that it might ease the nerves a little bit."

Lester motioned to Larry.

"Let me get you something that you will like."

Julie looked surprised. Lester was not a bad looking man. He was tall, had short dark hair and looked muscular. His skin was bronzed; a sign that whatever he did involved being outside in the sun. He had big hands with thick fingers. Julie noticed that he was not wearing a wedding band. She felt safe just sitting next to the

201

man. Larry came back and presented Julie a drink. She looked at it with questioning eyes.

"That's a Mudslide," Lester told her.

"What is in it?"

"I don't readily know. I just know that Larry, here, makes the best Mudslides in the state. Go ahead, try it."

Julie took the straw in her mouth and sucked the brown liquid into her mouth. It was sweet and she couldn't tell if there was alcohol in the mixture or not.

"Is there any alcohol in this?" she asked Lester.

"Yeah, but not too much, just enough to relax you."

"Thank you Lester, that was sweet of you!"

"Don't mention it. So what do you do besides being married?"

Julie produced a smile.

"Nothing! I'm a housewife. I'm involved with my church. That's about it!"

"Do you have any kids?"

"No, I don't," Julie said, nodding her head.

A silence fell between them. Julie felt uneasy with the conversation. She did not mind talking to the man, but she did not know how to carry on the conversation. She decided to try her luck.

"So, Lester, what do you do for a living?"

Lester hesitated for a minute.

"I'm a superintendent for a large construction company here in Macon."

"That sounds interesting."

"I don't know about that. It's a lot of headache, if you ask me."

Julie sipped some more of her drink. She looked at her watch. It was almost 6 o'clock. She would miss her prayer meeting at the church. She wondered if her mother would be worried about her not showing up. It was the first time that she would miss the meeting. She felt guilty. Here she was sitting in a bar talking to a man she had just met, while she should be getting ready to go to her prayer meeting.

"Are you okay?" Lester asked, seeing the absentminded look on Julie's face.

"Oh yeah. I was just thinking about something."

"Listen, I don't know if I'm coming on too strong, but would you like to go somewhere else?"

Julie felt an uneasy feeling in her stomach. This stranger was coming on to her. Her! Julie Sutton! The temptation of going somewhere with the stranger felt wonderful to her. She was not used to getting this much attention.

"What do you have in mind," she said, her voice trembling a little.

"If you didn't mind, we could go to my place. I only live a couple of miles from here."

Julie could not believe the words that came out of her mouth next.

"Alright, that sounds good."

Julie Sutton and Lester left the bar. She followed Lester the short distance to his house. He lived in a quiet middle class neighborhood, in a small ranch style house with a carport next to it. The yard was small. The grass was neatly cut and an array of different flowers lined the driveway. Julie pulled in behind Lester. Nervously looking around, she got out of the car. Right behind Lester, she entered the house. The inside of the house looked impeccable. It was modestly decorated, not fancy, but reflecting a lot of class. Julie stood in the middle of the living room, feeling uneasy, like a high school girl going over to her boyfriend's parent's house. Lester noticed it.

"Why don't you take a seat on the sofa, Julie? Make yourself at home."

Julie didn't say anything. She nodded her head and took a seat at the edge of the sofa, her back straight and her hands in her lap. Lester asked her if she wanted something to drink.

"I'll take some soda if you have it," she responded.

"Coming right up!"

Lester gave her a glass of coke and took the seat next to her, holding a bottle of beer in his hands.

"Why don't you lean back and make yourself comfortable, Julie. There's nothing to be nervous about."

Julie sat back and let her back find the soft cushion of the sofa. It did feel good. She took a long sip of her coke.

"Julie, you know, I just don't invite any woman into my house. I think that you're really nice. I would like to get to know you better."

"Thanks," was all Julie could say. She felt guilty. Even though Tom was the one that had been cheating on her, she did not feel right about being in another man's house.

Lester moved a little closer to her. Julie felt uneasy. She didn't know what to think. On the one hand, she was flattered that this man was obviously attracted to her, on the other hand she was scared of what she knew was sure to come. When a man takes a woman home from a bar, it could only mean the man wanted to have sex with her. Julie started to break out in a sweat. Her hands were shaking a little. Lester noticed.

"Relax, Julie. There's nothing to be worried about."

"I'm sorry, Lester. I just don't know if this is the right thing for me to do."

"Why not? From the way you talk, you're not used to getting a lot of attention. Let me show you how a real man treats a lady, okay?"

Julie didn't say anything. Lester started rubbing her back. Gently, his big fingers stroked her across her back. Julie started to relax. The muscles in her neck and back felt less tense. She turned her back towards Lester so he could massage her back better. She was starting to feel relaxed. What Julie didn't know, was that the coke she had been sipping on was drugged. It wouldn't be long before Julie would surrender to Lester's every demand. Lester whispered into Julie's ear.

"Why don't you unbutton your blouse?"

The drug was working. Without much hesitation, Julie started unbuttoning her blouse. When it was completely undone, Lester slipped it over her shoulders and down her arms. The blouse ended up on the floor. Lester unhooked her bra and removed it. Julie didn't resist. He told her to remove her panty hose. Julie stood up, hiked up her skirt and pushed down her panty hose. Lester was getting aroused. He ordered Julie to take off her panties. Hiking up her skirt again, Julie started to slide down her panties. Lester watched the action with great intensity. He licked his lips. Julie gave her panties to Lester. Without moving his eyes away from

Julie's body, he stuck her panties into his pocket.

"Let's go into the bedroom," Lester ordered.

Julie obeyed without saying a word. She was like a robot, completing the orders she received. She followed Lester into the bedroom.

"Lay down on the bed."

Julie followed the order.

Lester took off his clothes. He walked over to the closet and opened it. Inside the closet he turned on a video camera. He looked through the viewfinder to make sure that he had the right angle and zoom. Once he was satisfied with the setting, he moved back into the bedroom. He climbed on top of the bed next to Julie.

***

The drug that effected Julie's rational thinking started to wear off. She regained her senses. She looked around. She was lying on a bed in a strange room. She did not recognize anything. She pushed the covers away. She was completely naked and the smell of sex filled the room. She pulled the covers back over her naked body. The house she was in was silent. She got up, wrapping her naked body in the bed sheet. She walked into the living room. She saw her blouse on the floor, her bra lying on top of it. She couldn't find her skirt. She searched the living room. Nothing! Julie walked back into the bedroom. She walked around the bed. Nothing! Julie began crying. She sat down on the bed, her body shaking as she sobbed. She looked at her watch. It was almost 9 o'clock. Julie got up and kneeled down to look under the bed. A sigh of relieve swept over her face. Her skirt had somehow been pushed under the bed. She extended her arm and grabbed her skirt. Julie put on her skirt, walked back into the living room and recovered her bra and blouse. She got dressed. She was still missing her panties and panty hose. Julie searched the entire house but could not find them. She decided to leave the house without them on. She felt cheap. She had been manipulated. The man she had met in the bar had taken advantage of her. Ashamed and feeling dirty, Julie left the house and returned to Stuttgart. The hatred she had felt before returned. She hated men!

A few houses away, a man in a white sedan watched Julie

leave. He grabbed his cell phone and dialed a number. After a few rings, there was an answer.

"Yeah, this is Eddie."

"Did you do it?"

"Yeah man. It was a piece of cake. She was totally nonresistant."

"I told you the drug would work. Do you have the tape?"

"Yeah, I've got it. When do I get the rest of my money?"

"When you deliver the tape, you'll get it."

"Where do you want to meet?"

"Meet me in 30 minutes at Larry's. Make sure you're there, and make sure the house is clean, understand?"

"You got it, Mr. Sutton. I'll take care of everything!"

The phone went dead.

Eddie Jovanovich, alias, Lester, returned to the house, cleaned it up the way he found it. He left the neighborhood to return to Larry's. There he would wait for Tom Sutton to arrive. He would receive the rest of the money he was promised. $1,000.00 for drugging the guy's wife and having sex with her while he taped it. He didn't pass up that opportunity. He smiled as he drove away from the house. By the time the little bitch found out what happed, 'Lester' would be long gone, and the poor owners of the house would look confused if she ever went back there to find him. He grabbed Julie's panties from his pocket. A smile appeared on his face as he moved the panties and panty hose through his fingers. He could feel a hard on forming in his pants. Another pair added to his collection. He opened the glove compartment and put the panties in it while he lowered the window and dropped the panty hose on the street. He pushed the gas pedal a little harder. He wanted to take in a few drinks before Tom Sutton arrived at Larry's.

46.

The phone rang at Kelly Murphy's.

"Hello?"

"Hi Kelly, it's mom."

"Hi mom, how are you?"

"I'm fine. Listen, is Michelle there?"

"Yeah, she's here. You wanna talk to her?"

"No! I need you to do me a favor though."

"Okay, I'm listening."

"You need to find out if she was on the Internet last night on our computer. We found that someone accessed an Internet site. The name of it scared us. Your dad didn't look it up and neither did I. The only one we can think of that might have, is Michelle."

"What was it?"

"PERFECTCRIMES.COM"

"I see. And you think that it has something to do with Susan Knox, right?"

"Well, according to your dad, the description of the murder on the Internet matches with what happened to Susan. I hope it is a coincidence. I need you to peel Michelle's tongue and see if she's the one who looked it up and if she possibly might have killed Susan."

Kelly looked annoyed. She did not feel like interrogating her sister. She didn't know if she could treat her sister in that fashion.

"Alright, I'll try. Anything else?"

"That's all. I love you sweetie."

"I love you too, mom."

Kelly disconnected the call. With weary eyes she looked at her sister. Michelle had questioning eyes.

"What was all that about?" she asked.

Kelly glanced at Michelle. She didn't know if she could question Michelle about what her mother had informed her off. She walked to the kitchen table and sat down. She brought her hands to her chin and propped her head looking Michelle straight in the eye. Michelle knew something was bothering her sister and that it had something to do with her.

"Kelly?" Michelle asked insistent.

Kelly took a deep breath as she looked at her sister and started to speak.

"Michelle, I want you to be honest with me. Okay?"

Michelle nodded her head affirmatively, not saying a word.

"Last night, did you go to Susan's apartment?"

Michelle's face turned white at first then a deep crimson color marked her cheeks. She looked down at her feet.

"Kelly, you've got to believe me when I tell you that I had nothing to do with Susan's death."

"So you were there last night?"

Michelle got up from the couch and started pacing the room "Yes, I was."

"Why?"

"I don't know. I thought that if I could face her; tell her what a bitch I thought she was that I might feel better."

"Did you talk to her?"

"No. I didn't have the nerve to walk up to her door and confront her. I started thinking about it when I was sitting in the car waiting to go tell her off. It's not her fault that Bryan slept with me. Sure, she's nothing but a little whore slut, but she's not the one who made love to me. If I should be mad at anyone, it should be Bryan, not Susan."

"So you didn't go into her apartment?"

"No! I told you! I did not see her and I did not go into the apartment!"

Kelly looked out the window. It was getting dark outside. She didn't know if she could believe her sister. She felt bad for feeling that way, but she was sure that Michelle wasn't telling her everything.

"Did you go online last night before you went over to Susan's apartment?"

"What?"

"I asked you if you were on the Internet last night before you went over to Susan's apartment!"

Michelle thought for a moment.

"No, I didn't."

"Don't lie about this, Michelle! You could be in enough trouble as it is. Now tell me, did you go online last night or not?"

208

Kelly's voice was reaching higher and higher pitches and she was trying hard not to lose control of her emotions.

Michelle walked over to Kelly and put her finger in Kelly's face.

"Listen, Kelly, don't talk to me like that! I'm not gonna have you accuse me of doing something I damn well know I didn't do. I did not get on the Internet last night. I did not kill Susan Knox and I did not set fire to her apartment. Do I make myself clear?"

Kelly was surprised by the sudden outburst from her sister. She had obviously hit a nerve. Somehow, she was not convinced yet that Michelle wasn't hiding something. Michelle had been known in the past to be able to bend the truth.

"Okay, you didn't do any of this. Let me ask you one more question. Where did you go after you left Susan's apartment?"

"I went straight to Patricia's," Michelle replied without hesitation.

Bingo! Kelly knew Michelle was lying. Kelly decided not to let on that Patricia had come by earlier that afternoon expressing her concern about Michelle and her whereabouts the night before. She would tell her parents about her conversation with Michelle and the lie that she had caught her in. If she had told the truth about her whereabouts up to the point to where she had left Susan Knox' apartment, she had to have gone somewhere else before going to Patricia's. But where?

Michelle interrupted Kelly's mesmerizing.

"Is there anything else you would like to know?"

Kelly looked at her sister. She knew that Michelle was going through some turbulent times. Even if everything she had told her wasn't true, she still needed the love and support she deserved in her time of need. She did not believe that Michelle could go as far as killing someone. Still, with all that had happened to her in the past 24 hours, Michelle might not have been thinking coherently. Kelly reached out to her sister and wrapped her arms around her.

"No more questions, okay? I'm sorry I had to do this, but I want to make sure that you're not in any trouble."

Michelle held on the her sister as tight as she could

"I'm sorry for putting you through this," Michelle started.

"Hush now! Don't say anything else."

When they finished their embrace, Michelle let on that it was time for her to go home. She kissed Kelly good night and walked out the door. Kelly stood in the doorway and watched her sister drive away. Tears were flowing down her cheeks. She suspected the worst, hoped for the impossible.

47.

Hope Olson had mixed emotions about her assignment to the investigate Susan Knox's murder. She felt happy and excited that she had finally managed to get a case assigned to her; on the other hand, she felt sadness that Hinson did not approve of Van Acker. Not that it was any of his business whom she dated; however, she wanted his approval as a friend. She did not think she was going to get it. Hinson had been firm about any involvement from Van Acker into the investigation. She knew it wouldn't be easy to keep him away from the investigation; after all, he had immediate interest into the murder of Susan. She had not yet been able to tell him that he would not be able to stay with her until he was able to move into his house. Van Acker had looked distracted ever since they had left the funeral home. At Hope's he kept pacing the house, walking from the living room to the spare bedroom and back to the living room. Hope, who was in the kitchen fixing dinner, could not figure out what was bothering him. She decided that she would not bother asking him what was wrong, but wait until he felt comfortable enough to tell her on his own accord.

Van Acker had not spoken on the way back from the funeral home. He knew Hope was happy about something, however, on the same token, he could sense that something was bothering her. There was an eerie silence between the two of them that had carried over once they arrived at Hope's house. When asked if he would like to have supper with her, he had said that he would like that. Nothing else had been said between the two of them.

Van Acker, while pacing the house, was trying to figure out a couple of things. First, there was the black piece of fabric he had found hanging on the door lock at the funeral home. Whoever had killed Underwood had brushed up against the lock on the way out and torn their clothing. The piece of fabric would probably not be too helpful. Dimitri made a mental note to send it to his friend Sid in Washington, DC. Sidney Schumaker was a forensic scientist who worked for the FBI. Schumaker enjoyed his work so much that he had made a laboratory and research center in the basement of his house. He could not afford the high tech equipment the FBI used in their labs. However, when his laboratory was assigned new high tech equipment, Schumaker had been first in line to strike a deal with his director and had been able to buy most of the old equipment at extremely discounted prices. Van Acker hoped that Schumaker would be able to find something that might be of help to him. He doubted it.

What bothered Van Acker also was the pencil he had found in the trash can. He could not figure out how a pencil could be used to examine a burn victim. With all the tools Underwood had, why on earth would he use a pencil in conducting the examination? Van Acker could not think of a satisfactory reason. Whatever the pencil was used for, Underwood must have found something on Susan's body. Why else would Underwood have called him? Van Acker felt inside his pocket. The crisp edges of the piece of paper in his pocket touched his fingers. He was tempted to decipher its contents in the presence of Hope. For some reason, he didn't know if he could trust Hope with whatever information the sheet of paper held. She had acted funny when they left the funeral home. He didn't know what had happened. She was not the same Hope that he had frolicked in the grass with a couple of hours earlier. Whatever her boss, Hinson, had told her, must have left an impression on Hope. Van Acker shook his head. He had hoped to find peace and quiet in the small town of Stuttgart, instead, he found murder and complexity building all around him. Was he a bad omen? Was the violence of DC following him? He shrugged it off as coincidence. All this might have happened even if he wasn't around, he thought.

Hope had studied Van Acker's face as he paced through the house. She was amused by the different expressions that filled the man's face. Every time a new thought came to his mind, a different facial expression appeared. She finally couldn't stand it any longer and busted out laughing. Van Acker turned and looked at her with wondering eyes.

"What happened?" he asked.

Hope managed to stop laughing so she could answer him.

"You! You are so funny!"

"Me?" Van Acker asked.

"Yes, you! You walk through this house thinking of God knows what, your face having a different expression every time you walk by. I'm sorry; I just couldn't stand it any longer. What are you thinking about?"

Dimitri thought hard before he answered her question.

"Well, a lot actually. Mainly, I'm trying to figure out how Susan Knox died. You see, for the propane to explode, the apartment must have been filled up with a large amount of the gas. Propane is poisonous and has a strong odor. Most people start coughing when inhaling it. The propane should have woken Susan up. I figure that she was dead before the stove was turned on. Whoever turned the gas on killed Susan and I think Underwood figured out she was killed and called me to tell me of that fact. I just cannot prove it."

"Dimitri, I don't think that Joshua was over there snooping around over Susan's body. He was robbed! All his money was gone!"

Van Acker looked at Hope with piercing eyes.

"You believe there is no connection between Susan's murder and the slaying of Joshua, don't you?"

"Look, it's a little farfetched that whoever did Susan in was watching the funeral home to make sure nobody would go in and examine the body."

Van Acker sat down at the kitchen table. He rubbed his temples as he was thinking.

"Hope, again, how well was Joshua known in Stuttgart?"

"Most everyone knew him. I guess you can say that when one acts a little out of the ordinary, most people take notice."

"Okay, it's safe to say that if Susan's killer is from Stuttgart and saw Joshua's truck at the funeral home, they would know that it was unusual for Joshua to be there on a Sunday afternoon, right?"

Hope just nodded her head.

"Let's assume that you are the killer and you saw Joshua's truck at the funeral home. Knowing what you know about Joshua's habits, what would you do?"

Hope's face lost the smile it had displayed up to this point. She thought about the rhetorical question Van Acker had posed. She could not argue against it. As much as she hated to think that Joshua's death was related to that of Susan's, it became more and more clear that this might be the case. She still wanted to hold on to her original assumption of robbery.

"If I was the killer, I would want to know what the old man

213

was doing there on Sunday. But I would not kill him simply for being there. I'd have to be positive that he was indeed examining Susan's body before I got rid of him. There appeared to be no evidence of Underwood examining Susan's body. I cannot be sure. We shouldn't rule out the possibility of robbery."

Van Acker stuck his hand in his pocket and felt the paper brush up against his hand. He decided not to pull the piece of paper from his pocket but keep it to himself for a little while longer. He wanted to know what was written on that paper before he shared the information with Hope. It might be nothing. Then again, it could be a break into the investigation.

"I hope you're right. I hate to think that Susan's murder has more to it than a crime of passion. If Underwood's death is linked, then we have a dangerous situation on our hands. More people may turn up dead."

Hope didn't say anything. She just looked at Van Acker with worried eyes. She knew that his assumption would prove right. Van Acker noticed the worried look in her eyes. He walked over to her and wrapped his arms around her, holding her tight. She put her head on his chest and closed her eyes. His touch felt good, comforting, and secure. God, did she have to tell him she didn't want him to stay with her?

Hope broke the embrace and went back to cooking supper. She was just about finished. Van Acker asked if he could help out. She told him he could set the table that by the time he finished with that, she would have supper ready. He happily obliged. There was still so much he wanted to talk to her about, yet, he didn't know how to approach her. He felt that there was something she was holding back, something important. He would ask her over supper. He did not want anything to stand in the way of their relationship. Van Acker looked forward to spending the night with her. He hoped Hope felt the same way.

48.

Julie Sutton drove into her driveway. She looked around to see if anyone was out in the street. She did not want anyone to see her the way she looked. Satisfied with her observation, she opened the door of her car and rushed to the side door entrance. She fumbled with her keys. She was nervous and could not find the right key. She dropped her keys. She looked around. Good! Still nobody around! She bent down and picked up her keys. Again, she fumbled with them. She found the right key, turned the lock and pushed the door open. She jumped into the house and slammed the door shut behind her. Quickly she turned the dead bolt latch. She was safe! Her heart was beating at an accelerated pace. She walked through the corridor holding on to the walls and finally stumbled into the living room. She made her way to the couch and flopped down on it. She was exhausted from worry. Most of all, she felt dirty and cheap, like a slut. Never before had she felt this way. What had possessed her?

For a brief moment, she thought back on the encounter with Lester, or whatever his name was. He had appeared to be such a nice man. He had sweet-talked her into following him to what he said was his house. She had accepted the drink. What happened next, she had no recollection of. She knew that he had raped her. She was naked on the bed when she woke up. No doubt he had sex with her. The bastard! And her panties and panty hose, they were gone. She would put money on it that he had kept them as a souvenir. A cold chill ran down her spine. It made her sick to think that some pervert would be sniffing her panties while getting off and reliving the fun he had with her.

Julie got up and walked upstairs. She stepped into the bathroom and took off her clothes. Looking in the mirror she saw her mascara smeared face. She had been crying on the way home and the tears had done a job on her face. She took a long hot shower trying to clean her body from the filth that she knew was covering it. After she finished and dried herself, she walked over to her closet and found a simple white cotton nightgown. She slipped it over her head and let if fall over her naked body. She grabbed a pair of white cotton panties from her nightstand and put them on. She noticed how

215

good they felt against her skin. Julie walked back into the bathroom and removed the rest of the mascara from her face. She picked up her silk blouse, skirt and black lace bra and threw them in the trash can. She put on her robe and walked back downstairs. In the kitchen she poured herself a tall glass of iced tea and sipped on it while walking into the living room and taking a seat in her chair. She felt better now and she closed her eyes.

Julie Sutton's thoughts floated from one subject to the next. First there was Tom. How could he have treated her the way he did? He made a mockery out of their marriage and brought shame to her family. And Susan! Julie knew Susan had problems with her sexual feelings. She still could not understand her sister treating her the way she did. Then, Julie remembered the dark figure sneaking around Susan's apartment. Who could it have been? Was the person responsible for the death of Susan? Her face contorted as she though of Susan lying in her bed, the apartment burning up around her. How horrible it must have been! A cold chill ran down Julie's spine. Who would want her sister dead? So many people had shown up at Susan's apartment that night before the fire. There had been Tom. She had seen him drive by Susan's apartment. Dimitri Van Acker had visited Susan. He had stayed a short while. She doubted seriously that he had anything to do with her murder. After all, he stood to gain business by Susan being alive. Bryan Scarboro had been parked on the opposite side of the street facing Susan's apartment. He had shown up after the fire had started. Could he be the killer? There was a possibility.

Two other people had been around Susan's apartment. Julie did not know their identities, but she suspected that one of them was Susan's killer. The first had sat in a black car about 200 feet from Susan's apartment. No attempt had been made to get out of the car. There had been a lot of body movement inside the car. However, the person never did leave the car and took off after about 20 minutes. The last person was the one Julie suspected to have killed her sister. That person had snuck around the apartment and had more than likely entered the apartment. From her viewpoint Julie could not see Susan's front door. The person had disappeared around the building for about 10 minutes and had left as inconspicuous as the person had come. The black clothing was a definite sign of an attempt to remain as unnoticed as possible. Julie opened her eyes. She got up and walked over to the window. She stared at the ruins of her sister's apartment. The remains of the black charred framing of the walls had an eerie look in the moonlight. Ghostly shadows were cast on the ground around the remains. Julie felt tears well up in her eyes. She said a quiet prayer for Susan.

Julie looked over at the clock on the wall. It was getting late. She turned off the lights downstairs and headed up the stairs. Shortly after, she fell into a troubled, uneasy sleep.

49.

     Tom Sutton looked around the bar. Larry's Lounge was busy for a Sunday evening. Most customers were there to watch the Atlanta Braves play their rival the NY Mets. Braves' hats and shirts were the attire of choice by most of the customers. The bar was noisy and filled with cigarette smoke. Sutton, not used to cigarette smoke, coughed as he was trying to find a familiar face.

     Sutton had met Eddie Jovanovic a couple of months earlier. Andrew Hinson had arrested Jovanovich in a traffic-related incident. Jovanovich, who was from New Jersey, was on his way to Florida when Hinson had pulled him over for speeding. Jovanovich was doing 73 in a 55. Not knowing that in Dawson County going more than 15 miles over the speed limit ends you up in jail, Jovanovich found himself behind bars. Hinson had called Sutton and told him about his catch. A background check revealed that Mr. Jovanovic had a long crime record, ranging from failure to pay child support to aggravated assault and domestic violence. The last five years he had been clean. Sutton and Hinson figured that Jovanovich had just been released from his parole and was on his way to Florida to start anew.

     Sutton had been looking for someone to do some dirty work for him. He figured that Jovanovich would be perfect. He obviously did not care about the law too much and if he could strike a deal with him, he might be able to help keep Jovanovich's records from expanding. Sutton went and talked with Jovanovich. The traffic fine was set at $400.00. Sutton produced a paper indicating the fine. In reality, the fine was only $85.00, but Sutton had told Hinson he had a purpose for this man and needed to keep him around. Sutton told Jovanovich that he would pay the fine and in return Jovanovich would have to do some work for him. At the question of what type work Sutton was referring to, Sutton told Jovanovich that it was private investigation work. He had looked at Sutton with small, questioning eyes. Jovanovich was a seasoned crook and knew he was being taken advantage off. He told Sutton he'd rather spend time in jail and pay the $400.00 off that way than work for a dirty lawyer. Tom Sutton was surprised by the reaction but did not let on that it bothered him. He then made Jovanovich a sweetheart deal he could not resist. He would pay off the fine and pay him $1000.00.

Jovanovich had thought about the offer for a moment. A thousand dollars would come in handy. Jovanovich decided to push his look a little further. He would do it, only if Sutton picked up his motel room expenses while he stayed in the area. Tom Sutton agreed. Jovanovich was released from jail and the plan was set in motion.

Tom Sutton was now at Larry's looking for Eddie Jovanovich. He hoped whatever Jovanovich had with him would prove to be valuable. He didn't like paying a thousand dollars for nonvaluable merchandise. In the back of the bar, Sutton spotted Jovanovich. He was sitting at a table with a bottle of beer in front of him. Jovanovich looked as if he had started celebrating early. He was talking to one of the waitresses in a way that showed he was in a slight state of inebriation. Jovanovich had his arm around the waitress' waist and was holding her hand with his free hand. Both were laughing with whatever Jovanovich was telling her. Sutton moved in closer to Jovanovich's table. He was curious what he was telling the waitress. He moved to within eavesdrop distance and hid himself behind some of the other customers.

"So Sally, you tell me you're not married, eh!"

"That's right, John."

Sutton smiled to himself. Jovanovich wasn't using his real name. He was sure this was a regular thing for Jovanovich. He continued listening.

"Like I said, I'm staying at the Hilton tonight. If you feel like it, you can come over and party with me after you get off."

Sally giggled.

"Oh, you naughty boy," she played the game along. "What would a respectable girl like me do in a hotel room with a complete stranger?"

"I'm sure I can show you when you get there," Jovanovich said, sounding confident.

"Well..., I don't know..., you see, my girlfriend Angie and I made plans to get together tonight. We're gonna watch a movie and such. I don't wanna disappoint her."

Sally looked Jovanovich deeper in the eyes. She gave Jovanovich a pouty look.

Jovanovich who still had his arm around Sally's waist pulled her closer and said, just loud enough for Tom to hear:

219

"Why don't you bring her also? We'll all watch a movie together."

Again, Sally giggled. She worked her way out of Jovanovich's embrace and stood a little straighter.

"Let me call her and see if she likes that idea, okay? I'll be right back!"

Sally tiptoed away from Jovanovich's table. As she passed by Sutton, he noticed that she was not all that beautiful. Her face was caked with make-up trying to hide huge pits left behind from acne or chicken pox. Her nose was crooked and her teeth were yellowing and not taken care off. Her hair was bleached to a white blonde. Dark black roots were sprouting at the scalp. She wore a T-shirt that was probably two sized to small for her frame. The contour of her bra was clearly visible. Obviously her conversation with Jovanovich had excited her and Sutton noticed her erect nipples pushing up the fabric of her bra and shirt. She wore stonewashed blue jeans shorts that hugged her hips and left nothing to the imagination. Your average trailer-trash slut, Sutton thought as she brushed by him. Sutton emerged from behind the customers shielding his presence from Jovanovich and acted as if he just walked in.

"Eddie, hi, there you are!"

Jovanovich took a draft on his cigarette and blew the smoke in Tom Sutton's face. Sutton coughed. Jovanovich smiled and motioned for Sutton to sit down.

"Tom, my friend, how are you? Want a beer?"

Sutton took a seat and motioned to the waitress. He ordered a beer. His eyes lingered on the buttocks of the waitress as she walked back towards the bar.

"Nice piece, ain't she?" Jovanovich cackled. "Gonna get me some of that tonight!"

He smiled, ear to ear.

"Good for you." Sutton said, making Jovanovich feel good about his catch.

Tom Sutton couldn't find a better way to describe the situation. Jovanovich had caught the girl. Not that the waitress wasn't a willing participant. She had 'easy' written all over her. He wondered if Jovanovich would tape their escapades too. He was almost certain he would.

"Where's the tape?" Sutton broke Jovanovich's concentration on the waitress.

"It's in the car, safely tucked away until I see some green come out of your pockets."

Sutton smiled. He looked around the room. Nobody was paying attention to them. Everybody had their eyes on the TV screen as the televised baseball game was coming to an end and the excitement rose. He reached inside his jacket and produced a thick envelope. He handed it to Jovanovich. He opened it up and looked inside. Twenty-dollar bills stared him in the face. He closed the envelope, folded it and put it in his pocket.

"I guess the whole amount is there?"

"Every bit, just as I promised."

"It better be there, if not I go talk to your wife about our little arrangement."

Tom Sutton bit his lower lip as he controlled his anger. He knew he was taking a risk by employing a lowlife to do his dirty work. Calmly he responded.

"I want you out of the State by sundown tomorrow. I can arrange for a personal escort if need be, or you can drive into Florida on your own accord. It's your choice. If I see you again, it better not be in Dawson County. Understood?"

Jovanovich looked at Tom Sutton with small slatted eyes. He was no fool. He didn't trust Sutton one little bit. He had learned a long time ago never to trust a lawyer, especially a crooked one.

"No worry, my friend. After I have my fun with Sally over there, I'll be heading down South and out of your way."

"Good. Now let's go get the tape."

Sutton finished his beer and got up. Jovanovich was right behind him. He motioned to Sally that he was coming right back. No way was he going to miss having fun with her.

Outside Larry's, Eddie Jovanovich walked towards his car. He opened the trunk. Sutton looked inside and could not believe his eyes. Among dirty laundry and various porn magazines, Jovanovich produced an 8-mm tape. He handed it to Sutton.

"Here you go, my friend; a film of your gorgeous wife getting

221

it on with yours truly." Jovanovich smiled.

Tom Sutton put the tape in his pocket.

"Remember; don't ever set foot in Dawson County again!"

Her turned around and walked off towards his car. He did not look back. He got in his car and drove off. Eddie Jovanovich followed Tom Sutton with his eyes as far as he could. He was going to do more business with that man, whether he wanted to or not. He knew exactly how as he closed the trunk to his car. He headed back inside the bar to finish the deal with Sally.

50.

Kelly Murphy had sunk herself into her couch after her sister left. She did not understand what had come over her little sister. Everything Michelle had done in the past couple of days was completely out of character. Sure she had lied her way through a couple of events when she was younger, but what teenager hadn't tried that? Otherwise, everything she stood for, everything she believed in had been violently thrown out of the window. One night of giving in to her feelings rather than to her convictions had caused a whirlwind of trouble and anxiety. Maybe Michelle was responsible for Susan's death. After all, Susan was the one that had been the key source for the AIDS virus. She wondered how long Susan had known. Kelly shook her head as she thought off all the young and not so young men that Susan had lured into her lair. How many married man had visited her through the years? How many of those were infected and had ultimately infected their spouses? A frightening thought. As far as Kelly could imagine, half of Dawson County could possibly be infected by the virus.

A chill ran down her spine as she thought of how risky she had led her teenage years. She had not exactly been the poster child for teenage abstinence. She recalled the first time she had ever been with a man. She was sixteen at the time. Looking much older, she had been able to win the heart of a high school senior. Logan had been his name. Much to her father's dismay, she had dated him for a couple of months. The first time they decided to have sex had also been the last time that they had seen each other. It had been a fumbling experience from the beginning. Kelly remembered the pain she had felt as he entered her. She had not been ready. On the other hand, Logan was more than ready and pounded away at her, not caring how she felt or enjoyed the experience. Luckily it had not lasted long as Logan climaxed rather quickly. He had dismounted her and put his pants back on, asking how it had been. Kelly remembered that she had cried and screamed at him to take her home. That had been the end of their relationship. Since Logan, half a dozen other boyfriends had bedded her, each with varying results. Never once had she reached complete ecstasy by the doings of another. She had not thought of the risks it involved. She could have gotten pregnant or gotten a sexual transmitted disease. She had preached to Michelle that she should not be promiscuous. She had confided in Michelle about her bad experiences and the pain and hurt she'd felt. There was nothing beautiful to lovemaking! She had convinced Michelle of those facts. Yet, Michelle had been lured by the same kind of man Kelly had warned her about. And of course, the predictable result had happened. It could not have gotten any worst for Michelle. One time was all it had taken to destroy forever the beauty of lovemaking. No matter how wonderful a husband she may find, no matter how good a lover he may be, Michelle would never be able to enjoy a truly orgasmic sexual relationship. The experience with Bryan would linger in her mind for a long time. Sure Bryan was to blame, but most of the blame lay with Michelle. She was the one who took it upon herself to drink, to give up her ability to think coherently. As bad as the actions of Bryan had been, Michelle's actions were the source of her lifelong misery. Kelly just hoped the HIV virus had not found its way into Michelle's body.

The memory of her sexual experiences brought one image to mind that she had never been able to get rid off. Dimitri! She had been fourteen when Dimitri Van Acker started living with them. She had felt it from the first time they met that she was attracted to him. That he was almost seven years older had not bothered her. She had been scared to let him know how she felt. Many times when she had been alone with him, she had wanted to tell him that she loved him. She wanted so much to kiss him and feel his body pressing up against hers. She had never been able to do so. Mostly she had been scared of his rejection. He had basically been a grown man when they met. She saw him go out with different women. Susan Knox had been one of them. She recalled that he had dated her for a long time. Then, without warning, their relationship had ended. He would never talk about it. And then, there was Hope Olson. She had been the flame that lit his eyes. Unfortunately, her life in the Navy had pushed sticks in the wheels of their relationship. Van Acker gave up on having a relationship with her and moved to DC. Doing that, he had broken more than one heart. Hope had been heartbroken when she came back after being discharged from the Navy. She had hoped that he would have waited for her. Her hopes came crashing down when she found out he had left Stuttgart.

The other heart that had been broken was Kelly's. She had hoped that as she grew older and more mature, Van Acker would start noticing her. The only way he looked at her though, was as a little sister. That's not how she wanted to be looked at by him. She wanted him to see her as an attractive woman who might interest him as spouse potential. Kelly knew that Van Acker had his sights once again set on Hope. She also knew that the feeling was mutual. Kelly let out a long breath. Could there be a way to win Dimitri's heart? Maybe she should not be passive any more and take control. Total control! Show him how she feels! She smiled at the thought, a crazy idea for sure. Van Acker was too strong-minded to give in to anybody coming on to him, except Hope of course. But what did she stand to loose? Nothing! She did not have Dimitri now. If he dismissed her, she would not have him then either. If she tried it, the only thing that could happen was that he might not feel about her the same way as he did now. Would he still want her to work for him? She had to take that chance. As she sat and pondered on what she might do to win his heart, she imagined his body against hers, his strong muscular arms around her, holding her tenderly, protecting her, making her the safest and most loved woman in the world. She closed her eyes and smiled. If only it could come true.

51.

Hope Olson and Dimitri Van Acker had been quiet at the dinner table. Van Acker enjoyed Hope's cooking and showed so by taking seconds. Hope looked at him with glistening eyes. She was glad that he loved being in her company. She rather enjoyed being with him too. She hoped he realized that, especially when she was going to tell him that she could not let him stay with her during her investigation. She had quietly hoped that he would come back to Stuttgart some day, at least for a visit. She had never imagined that he would come back to stay. She had been feeling like a high school teenager these past couple of days. Her hopes had come true. Van Acker had come back and he had paid her the attention she had wanted him to show her. They picked up where they had left off so many years ago. He had changed, though. He was in better physical shape than she remembered him. What impressed her most was his knowledge of the law and law enforcement. She could tell that he had spent a lot of time with the DC law enforcement, even though he had been defending criminals. He would be a great addition to the small town of Stuttgart. He would be a good antidote to the clique attitude of the establishment, the clique that had ruled Dawson County for generations. She could see him enter the local political scene. With his outlook on life and his European background and believes, she knew that he would be able to make a difference.

Eyes full of admiration, Hope looked at Van Acker. An uneasy feeling in her stomach kept creeping up as she tired to get her nerves together and tell him what was on her mind. She looked away from him for an instant. She picked up her fork and moved it around in circles on her empty plate. She was thinking of how she would start.

Van Acker picked up on her uneasiness. As a lawyer he had learned to sense what a person's emotions were. In Hope, he knew she was nervous or uneasy about something.

"Care to tell me about it?" he said in a soft voice.

Hope's head shot up and she fixed her eyes on his. She tilted her head and took a deep breath.

"Oh honey, I don't know where to start."

"Does it have to do with me? I know I have changed and

maybe you don't like the new me. Let me know now. I don't want to waste your time."

Hope sat upright, reached across the table and grasped Van Acker's hands in hers.

"No, no! That's not it at all. I like the way you are. You've changed, but you're still the same person to me. I think I like you better now than I did before."

Hope turned a shade redder as she told Dimitri her feelings. Dimitri was showing signs of scarlet himself.

"Does your conversation with your boss have something to do with it?" he probed.

Hope looked down at the table and tried hard to get her sentences in order. At least he knew how she felt about him; maybe that might lessen the pain a little.

"Please believe me that I wish this could be different." She raised her head and looked at Van Acker.

"Andy doesn't like you for some reason. I think he sees you as a threat to the ways things are run around here. I don't know for sure. Him being good friends with Tom Sutton may have something to do with it, I don't know. But whatever the reason, he warned me that if you as much as come near the investigation, he'd pull my butt from it and will put me on probation. As much as I would like to tell him to go to hell, I cannot do that. I have been waiting for an assignment like this since I joined the department. He has a lot of respect for me. He treats me like one of the guys, which is not what you can say about most Sheriff or police departments around here. But when he tells me he's going to pull me, believe me, he's telling the truth. I don't want you to feel like you're second choice over the investigation. If you feel that way, I can understand, but I wish you wouldn't."

Van Acker looked at Hope with curious eyes. He was wondering what Hinson had on Hope. With Hope's abilities, education and intelligence, she would be able to find a job; a better paying job at that. He had always imagined her joining the FBI or some similar agency after she got out of the Navy. The local Sheriff's department had not exactly been what she was most capable off. He knew what was about to follow wasn't something he necessarily wanted to hear.

"Dimitri, I love you! I have always loved you and having you here with me, in my house, has made me feel so great and complete. I knew I asked you if you wanted to stay here with me until you could close the deal on your house, until your furniture arrives. Now, I'm faced with the fact that if Andy finds out you're staying with me, he'll know that you will be open to any information I have on the investigation. It will complicate things for me at work, but it may also complicate things for you. You have to think about Susan's rights. Even though she is no longer with us, there is still a lot that needs to be done about the legal aspects of her death. There's the court order for the autopsy. I know you will need to talk to the family about that. It will seem strange that you as an outside lawyer will be handling the legal dealing of Susan while Sutton is right there in the family. You see, I don't want us to complicate things by living under the same roof, even if it is only for a short while."

Van Acker took in all the information Hope had hurled at him. He could see that she was sincere about her feelings for him. Hope had been close to tears when she told him what was on her mind. Her eyes had become watery. He could see that she did not want him to leave. He knew it was best for both of them that they did not live together. He had never thought about staying with her until the deal with his house was finalized. Of course she was right. After their romantic interlude during their picnic that afternoon, and her request for him to stay with her, he knew that it was only a matter of time before they would be sharing the same roof. The unfortunate events that had taken place and the stress on them both because of it might make things work out for the better. It would be better for their relationship if he didn't stay with her. The distance between them would make them appreciate each other more. The longing for each other's company would make their bond stronger as they got to know each other better.

"Hope, I'm not upset. You're right. Not only do I think it would be better for me not to stay here because of our respective professions, but also, and most importantly, I don't think I need to stay here because of our love for each other. Our relationship, during this courting period, will benefit far more from us being apart from each other than if we were under each other's feet at all times."

"Do you mean that?" Hope asked, not sure what to expect

from his response.

Van Acker stood up and walked around the table. He placed his hands on Hope's shoulders and gently massaged them. Hope felt the tension leave her body as his strong hands did miracles to her. Hope closed her eyes as Van Acker's hands kneaded away the tension in her body. Her breathing became more controlled and she felt as if she could go to sleep. Van Acker bent over and kissed her neck.

"I love you, Hope Olson," he whispered in her ear.

Hope reached behind her and grabbed his hands. She gently squeezed them.

"I love you too, Dimitri."

Van Acker helped Hope clean up the dining room table and helped with the dishes. He knew he had to leave soon. He was sure that Hinson would check up on Hope. He knew this investigation was important to Hope and he did not want to complicate things for her. So he was going to do the one thing he hated doing the most. Leave! He had not let on his concern about Hope handling the investigation. If Susan Knox' killer was able to eliminate Joshua Underwood, then surely Hope could be taken out too. He would try to keep a close eye on her even when he wasn't around. He needed to get going. There was a lot of work he needed to do on his end of the investigation; work that Hope did not need to know about now. They kissed and held each other for what seemed like a lifetime before she watched him pull away from her house.

52.

Michelle Murphy dreaded going home. Her conversation with her sister had become a little heated. She knew that things around her were starting to fall apart. It had been crazy to get on the Internet and call up a website such as PERFECTCRIMES.COM. She had been in a hurry, not knowing whether she would find what she was looking for or not. She had found a perfect and barely traceable way for killing a person. She had printed out the information and put it inside her pocketbook. As Van Acker had come back inside, she had been forced to exit the website rather quickly and had not been able to erase any traces of her search and where she'd been. Now, she had been discovered. There was no way that she would confess to looking up the website. Her parents would no doubt question her again about it. That was if Kelly hadn't already called them and told them of their conversation. She shook her head as she drove into the driveway. The last two days had been a roller coaster ride. Two days ago, her life had been normal, almost to the point of boredom. Now, she was caught up in a whirlwind of events that she had no control over. At least that was her take on the situation. Everything she had done had been the direct cause of actions taken by others. Of that she was convinced.

Walking up the steps of the front porch, she took a deep breath and then entered the house. Allen and Helen Murphy sat at the kitchen table, looking gloomy and holding hands. They were in the middle of a silent prayer. Every time they had difficult times or tragedy struck their lives, they would turn to intensive prayer, asking their beloved God to help them through the difficult times ahead. It was something they had done since they had been married. Up to this point, both of them strongly believed that they were able to get where they were through the help of divine intervention. Their actions, they felt, had been guided by the wisdom and knowledge of God. Now, with their youngest daughter possibly having been exposed to the HIV virus and maybe having committed the gravest of sins, they were once again asking for some divine intervention.

Michelle walked passed them as quietly as she could. She did not want to disturb this sacred tradition of the Murphy household. As Michelle made it past her parents and was trying to head to her room, Allen Murphy stopped her in her tracks.

"Wait just one minute, young lady! You're not going anywhere until we talk to you."

Michelle felt her stomach drop.

"Yes, sir," she replied.

"Sit down, Michelle," Helen told her daughter.

Michelle took a chair and sat down.

"Michelle," Murphy started, hesitantly. He had been both furious and worried about the whereabouts of his daughter. Now, he had a hard time not losing his temper with her.

"I'm going to ask you to be straight with us. I know that I have not been able to talk to you yet about what happened with Bryan Scarboro. I understand the two of you made love and that somehow he then called you to let you know that he might be infected with the HIV virus. Am I on track so far?"

Michelle stared at her father and managed to nod her head. Yes, that was indeed what had happened.

"Now, what happened between the time when you told Kelly about Bryan's news and when Dimitri came inside to talk to you? Did you access any Internet sites within that time frame?"

Michelle was tempted to sink her head down on the table, start crying and tell her parents everything. An unknown strength from deep within her gave her support and made her hold her head up straight. She looked at her father, and then drifted her eyes to her mother.

"I don't know what you're talking about. Kelly had some crazy thought like that too. I didn't get on the computer after talking to Kelly last night. Besides, there was not enough time between Kelly walking outside and Dimitri coming in the house to do anything on the computer. What is it I'm supposed to have looked up?"

Murphy looked at his wife. They both knew that Michelle was smart. If she had committed the crime and if she thought that someone might be on to her, she was smart enough to play the game along. They would have to choose their words wisely.

"Michelle," Helen started, "the Internet site that you accessed was called up around the same time you talked with Kelly and Dimitri. I double-checked the computer clock with my wristwatch.

They are within thirty seconds from one another. So telling me the computer clock is off won't work. Do you want to keep going on with 'I didn't have enough time to access any sites' or will you come up with a different lie?"

Michelle's eyes shot fire at her mother. They were better prepared that she had thought. She didn't know if she could go on. The web she had woven was slowly being torn apart. She decided to give in on the Internet story.

"Okay, I'm sorry! I did get on the computer. The fact is that I was on the computer before Kelly and Dimitri arrived. The system was still online when I got off the pone with Bryan. For the first time in my life, I understood what it felt like to feel hatred. Kelly came in and tried to help me get back up and get a grip on the situation. Then when she went outside to fetch Dimitri, I decided to look up something on the web. For some reason, the screen I called up transferred me to PERFECTCRIMES.COM. I had little time, so I quickly moved through the links and found a nice way to kill someone. I printed out the result and then cut off the computer. Dimitri walked in just as I sat back down on the couch."

"Why would you want to find out a 'nice' way to kill someone?" Murphy asked.

Michelle took a deep breath.

"Daddy, you must believe me when I tell you that I did not kill anyone. Maybe I thought about it, but I did not kill Susan Knox!"

Murphy shook his head in disbelieve.

"Michelle, I have a hard time believing anything you're telling us right now. I looked up the website. The description of the crime matches closely with what happened to Susan. There are a few noticeable differences. However, if the law looked at the website, they would be tempted to think that whoever looked up the site would also be the killer."

Michelle cut her father off.

"Look, I don't know anything about killing someone or covering up a crime. If I would have done it, don't you think I would follow the exact instructions of the website?"

"Maybe, maybe not! It depends on so many variables once you committed the crime. A lot of things can happen that the website doesn't touch on or that it cannot predict. The slightest thing can make it where the crime would be committed in a completely different way."

"Dad, like I told you, I didn't do it!" I don't know how Susan died. I don't know how she got killed. I didn't even know she was killed. I thought it was an accident. In Christ's name, believe me!"

"Michelle," Helen shouted, "watch your mouth!"

Michelle slumped in her chair. She had told them the truth about the website. She felt better. Still, she knew that it would not be the end. She looked at her father who was staring at her with hurt, disappointment and sad eyes.

"Okay, Michelle, I believe you. I just hope that when everything is said and done, your story holds. Because if it doesn't, not only will you spend time in jail, but you'll never set another foot in this house! Understood?"

Michelle swallowed hard. The mentioning of the word 'jail' made her uneasy. The threat that she would never be allowed to set another foot in her parents house, made her scared. The one place that she had thought she would always be able to come back to, no matter what happened, would be off-limits. She shuddered at the thought.

"I understand, Daddy."

Helen looked at her husband with hurt eyes herself. She did not like the threat of having her daughter kept from her home, no matter what she had done or didn't do. She would not stand for it.

"Michelle, did you go by Susan's place?"

Michelle looked at her mother with calm, icy eyes.

"Yes. I was parked outside her apartment and thought long and hard about going up there and confronting her. Maybe I even had thoughts about killing her. The fact is that I did not have the guts. I was too chicken. I'm not a murderer, Mom."

Helen stood up and walked over to Michelle. She knelt down and took Michelle's hands in hers. Tears flowed freely down her cheeks. Michelle didn't know what to do. With great difficulty, Helen muttered her feelings.

"Michelle, I love you. You're dad loves you too. We will always love you. I never thought that we would have to be in a position to where we have doubts about what you're telling us. I want to believe you; however, right now, all fingers point in your direction. Even if you didn't do it and the investigation turns in your direction, there is enough circumstantial evidence to have you arrested. Don't forget that."

Michelle nodded her head, indicating that she understood.

Helen stood up. She was exhausted. She kissed Michelle on the forehead and announced that she was turning in for the night. Michelle and her father were left sitting at the table together. With anxious eyes, Michelle eyed her father. He was staring at her with great intensity, as if he was trying to read her mind, her brain.

"What's wrong?" she asked.

"I need to ask you a question and I want to make sure that I ask it the right way. If the answer is right, I'll feel a lot better. If I'm wrong however, I'll pick up the phone and call Andrew Hinson."

Michelle's eyes started to get bigger.

"Okay, ask away," she said uneasy.

"Assume for a minute that you would commit the murder, exactly the way it was described on the website. After you killed the person, how would you continue?"

Michelle looked down at the table, rubbing her fingers over the small crack made by the divider piece in the table. She had studied the printout closely while she was parked outside Susan's apartment. She also knew that her father had carefully read the items on the website. What she didn't know was what her father had found inside the apartment when he performed his inspection of the apartment.

"Well, I would turn the stove on, making sure the gas escaped; then I would take a timing device and find a place near the stove. Then I would leave."

She thought for a moment, making sure that she did not leave anything out. She had her tracks covered.

"That's it," she said nonchalantly.

Allen's eyes narrowed. The description she had given him was too close to reality for comfort. He needed to have more details. He needed her to be more specific about the placement of the timer. He wanted to know if she would turn on one eye on the stove or if she thought it was necessary to turn on all four.

"Okay," he started, "a couple of things I want to ask you.

Would you place the timer as close as possible to the gas stove? Say, there's an outlet in the kitchen, would you put the timer in that outlet?"

Michelle scratched her nose as she thought about the question. Her eyes lit up.

"Yeah, I'd put it as close to the stove as possible. That's were the largest amount of gas would be, and that would create an explosion."

Allen breathed a little easier. Then again, she could be playing him. She was a smart young woman and could outwit him if needed. He prepared himself for a second question.

"Would you turn on one of the eyes on the stove or all of them?"

Again, Michelle scratched her nose. This time it took her a little longer to think about her answer.

"It wouldn't be necessary to turn all the eyes on. If you tried to make it look like an accident, which would be the result you want in a case like this, it's better to turn on only one; part of the way. It's easy for someone to forget to turn the knob off all the way, especially of one is distracted. I've caught myself doing it a time or two. If I didn't want to create immediate suspicion, I would only turn one knob part of the way on. Give it about a good hour maybe an hour and a half and there will be enough gas in the house to create the required effect."

Allen looked at his girl with admiring eyes. If she had committed the crime, she would have done a better job than whoever had committed it. He knew she was innocent. Dimitri and he had found the source of the gas leak too easily. Whoever was responsible for Susan's dead was not as smart as it appeared at first. Allen had found a flaw in the crime.

"Honey, I'm glad I had a chance to talk to you about this. I know now that you didn't kill Susan. Still, I'm disappointed that the thought even crossed your mind in the first place. If this situation with Bryan got you so upset that you had thoughts of killing another human being because of it, you should have talked to your mother or me before taking any action. I hope that you learned your lesson."

Michelle nodded her head affirmatively. She was glad she had convinced her father that she had not committed the murder. At least for now, she was in the clear.

"I'm glad you finally believe me, Daddy. I think I will turn in now. Goodnight."

She got up and walked around to her dad. She gently kissed him on the cheek and gave him a hug.

"I love you, Daddy."

"I love you too, sweetheart. Goodnight."

53.

The light of the sun filtering through the window blinds woke Dimitri Van Acker. He opened his eyes and looked around, a bit disoriented. Then he realized where he was. He was at Kelly's. However, he could barely remember arriving at Kelly's. It had been late. After leaving Hope's he had driven around for a while; gone back to Susan's apartment. He had looked for possible clues on the ground. Maybe the killer may have left some footprints in the mud around the apartment. That had been idle hope. The heavy thunderstorms that had battered Stuttgart the night of the explosion had destroyed any possible remnants of footprints. He wondered if someone had seen movement around the apartment. The Knox' probably would have been in bed at the time the killer moved about their daughter's apartment.

Across the street was the Sutton home. From what he understood, through the rumors Hope and he had picked up in town, Julie had kicked Sutton out. Would Sutton have been able to commit murder? He doubted it. Tom Sutton was one of those who had a big mouth, but when it came to performing, Van Acker seriously doubted he would be capable of doing the act. Van Acker thought about Julie Sutton. Susan had slept with her husband since she had known Sutton. No doubt there had to be much resentment; years of deceit and lies. Maybe Julie was the killer. Would she be knowledgeable enough to set up this kind of explosive situation? Van Acker had smiled at his thoughts. Explosive situation! It had sure turned out to be just like that. Finally he had returned to Kelly's. Kelly had already been in bed, and Van Acker had quietly snuck inside and collapsed in his bed.

Dimitri Van Acker got up and walked into the living area. Looking at the clock on the wall, he noticed that it was just a little after seven. He tried to be as quiet as he could, as he looked for coffee and coffee filters. Finding the required items, he started a pot of coffee. Despite his attempts not to make too much noise; he managed to wake up Kelly. Sleepy eyed, she walked into the living room. "Hi stranger," she said rubbing sleep out of her eyes.

Kelly dropped herself down on the couch. She eyed Dimitri Van Acker as he starting making breakfast. Her eyes were full of admiration.

It wasn't long before the two of them sat at the kitchen table helping themselves to eggs, grits, bacon, toast and coffee. Kelly enjoyed the breakfast and told Van Acker so. It was also the first day that she did not have to go to work at Sutton's. It felt weird. Actually she was already at work. She laughed out load, to the surprise of Van Acker.

"What was all that about?" he asked.

"You know, I just thought about the fact that I don't have to go to work at Sutton's today. I'm already at work, sitting right here at my kitchen table with my pajama's still on. Isn't that a hoot?"

Van Acker smiled at the observation. He had not thought about that fact either.

"You know, I guess I'm at work too then. Let me tell you something, though; don't expect me to keep cooking you breakfast every day. Once I'm in my office, you'd better have breakfast before you come to work."

"I know," she answered, "but until then, I will sure enjoy this."

They continued the small talk a little longer until Van Acker got a serious look on his face. His thoughts had traveled back to the events that had happened the day before. Kelly noticed the serious look on his face.

"What's wrong?" she asked.

Van Acker looked at Kelly. He had to trust her. She was the only one that he could share this information with. After all, she would have to help him with the evidence that he had found.

"Joshua Underwood was killed yesterday."

He looked Kelly dead in the face. The reaction he got was one of total surprise. Kelly's face turned pale and she grabbed her stomach as if she was going to get sick.

"Are you sure?"

"Oh yeah, Hope and I are the one's who found him."

Van Acker told her the story about Underwood leaving a message on his phone, and then not responding to his returning phone call. He explained to her about going out there and finding Underwood drenched in his own blood and the inside of his head

238

being splattered on the wall.

Kelly shook her head in disbelieve.

"What was Joshua doing at the mortuary on a Sunday? As far as I can remember, he hasn't worked on Sunday since his wife died. Something must have triggered him to go to the mortuary."

"I'm the one that triggered it. I told him about the possibility that Susan might have been killed and to hold up with embalming the body until I could produce the necessary paperwork from the judge."

"Well, you're not to blame for his death, Dimitri."

"I know, I just wish that I wouldn't have told him about the possibility of murder."

Van Acker shot up from his chair and headed towards the door.

"Wait just a minute," he told Kelly. "I have something I need to show you."

He headed out the door and within a few minutes came back in, holding a plastic canister and an envelope in his hands. He put them on the kitchen table.

"What are those?" Kelly questioned.

"Those are items I got from the mortuary."

He pointed at the piece of paper.

"In a couple of minutes, I will be able to tell what was written on here. Remember the old high school trick of sending blank pieces of paper through the room? It was one way to send notes around without anyone picking up on what was written on it?"

Kelly nodded her head in agreement. She had done that once or twice while in high school.

"Underwood had written something on the piece of paper that was directly above this one. I'm going to find out what that was."

Kelly looked worried all of a sudden. Something was wrong about this.

"Dimitri? I think that maybe you need to turn this over to the Sheriff's department. That's evidence."

Van Acker's face turned cold suddenly. He looked Kelly in the eye. She felt a shiver run down her spine. Never before had she seen that look in his face.

"The Sheriff's department is going to look at Joshua Underwood's death as a robbery gone bad. Whoever wanted

239

Underwood dead made it look like that. I believe Underwood found something on Susan's body and he wanted to let me know. That's why he called me.

"How can they be so sure it was a robbery?"

"Joshua's empty wallet was found."

Kelly shook her head. She now understood where Van Acker was coming from.

"Kelly, I have a hunch about this. Susan's death and Underwood's death are connected."

Kelly looked at the film canister.

"Did you take some pictures of the crime scene?"

Van Acker smiled.

"No, I've got some more evidence in there. Whoever killed Underwood is missing a good chunk of fabric from a shirt or pants. I found it hanging on the lock of the door at the mortuary. Again, I took the liberty to collect the evidence as I presumed it would either not have been found or simply ignored."

"What are you going to do with it?"

"A friend of mine in DC is a forensic scientist for the FBI. He has his own lab at home. If there's a fly dropping on this piece of fabric, he'll find it."

Kelly laughed at the expression.

"He's that good, huh?"

"Oh yeah, he's brilliant!"

A silence felt between them. Both of them had their own thoughts on the matter. Van Acker knew that he could never use the results of his findings as evidence in a trial. It was obtained illegally. He planned on turning it over to Hope as soon as he had the results back. Kelly didn't know what to think about Van Acker's actions. He was obstructing justice by removing evidence from a crime scene. What if it was a setup?

Van Acker broke the silence.

"Do you have a pencil?"

Kelly shook her head and found him a pencil.

He gently rubbed the pencil over the piece of paper he had recovered from Joshua's office. The carbon of the pencil rubbed over the paper, filled the indentions of the writings and revealed the hidden message. Kelly looked in awe as the words Joshua

240

Underwood had written down slowly appeared. She looked at Van Acker to see his reaction. His eyes were almost shut; however, he was looking at the words. She knew he was in deep thought. She had seen him like this before when he was studying. He had been right that Joshua Underwood figured out Susan had been killed. The message revealed that all too well.

Van Acker looked over at Kelly. There was a cold, icy look in his eyes. The blue of his eyes seemed to have changed from the warm sky-blue that they usually were to a cold steel blue. She shuddered as she saw that look.

Dimitri read the message out loud:

"Susan was killed! Bullet hole under left breast!"

He leaned back in his chair and rubbed his hands through his hair. He took a deep breath and let the air slowly leak out of his lungs.

"You know, Kelly, when I looked around the embalming room, I found a brand-new pencil in the trashcan. I could not figure out for the life of me what it could have been used for. I must say, old Joshua was smart."

"You mean he used a pencil to detect the bullet hole?"

Van Acker nodded his head. Kelly continued:

"Underwood's death was not a coincidence, was it? The robbery theory doesn't hold ground. Whoever killed him saw the note and took it. A robber would have had no use for that information or for that matter, wouldn't have cared if the authorities discovered the note. Whoever killed Joshua also killed Susan, right?"

Van Acker had the same mind-set. He had had that mind-set ever since Hope and he discovered Joshua's body. He had been right. God, he hated to be right about this.

"Will you tell Hope?"

Van Acker looked down at his feet.

"I need to."

"Yes, you do."

He sighted. It was a tough decision to make.

"I will tell her when I get the information back on the piece of fabric that I found. Hopefully it will reveal some information about the killer."

"Don't wait too long. I hate to see you get in trouble over this. You know, you could be disbarred because of this, maybe even go to jail. Obstruction of justice is serious."

Van Acker looked at Kelly with a sense of pride. She had done well for herself. From the little girl who hated to go to school and being disinterested in anything but shopping and staying on the phone with her friends to a well educated young woman. If given half a chance, she would be able to make something of herself besides remaining on the sideline. She had potential and could easily make it to the top if she tried. He hoped that one day she would reach her potential. He stood up and walked around to Kelly's seat. He let his hands rest on her shoulders.

"I know I can get in trouble for this. But don't you worry, okay? I know how to push the limits. And believe me I'll push the limits on this one!"

Kelly turned her head towards his. She felt an attraction to this man she had never felt before. Was it the suspense of the events of the last couple of days? She didn't know.

"Please be careful. I don't want anything to happen to you. I wouldn't know what to do without you!"

She was surprised at her own words. She looked Van Acker in the eyes and found him smiling at her; a warm, reassuring smile.

"Don't worry you won't get rid of me that easy!"

Van Acker announced he was going to take a shower and prepare for his visit with James and Phyllis Knox. He was also going to talk with Julie Sutton about her sister and about the pending lawsuit. He had a full day ahead of him.

After showering and jotting down some notes, he gave Kelly an address in Washington, DC and instructed her to mail the piece of fabric to the address. He quickly wrote a short note and asked her to put in the package. As he grabbed his keys and headed out the door, he gave Kelly a quick kiss on the forehead. Kelly blushed. A warm feeling flowed through her body. She had a chance, she thought. Slim as it may be, she had a chance.

54.

Judge Julia Snelgrove arrived at the courthouse at her normal time, ten minutes till nine. She had her routine and did not stray from it. She was punctual and expected the same from her employees. She walked into her office. The morning paper was already lying on her desk. Janice Wallace, her personal secretary had already placed it on her desk. Julia made herself a cup of coffee and sat down behind her desk, looking at the headlines of the newspaper. She dropped her cup of coffee when she saw the main headline: *"Daughter of prominent farmer James Knox dies in raging fire"*. Janice who heard the crash of the coffee cup against the hardwood floor came rushing in.

"Miss Julia, are you alright?"

Julia sat down in her chair, ignoring the mess on the floor. She looked up at Janice.

"Yes, I'm all right. Did you see the headlines?"

Janice looked at the chair sitting in front of Julia's desk and sat down in it.

"I've seen the headlines. I'm surprised that you hadn't heard already. It happened Saturday night. The whole town's been buzzing about it."

"John and I were out of town this weekend. We got back late last night. I have no idea what happened here this weekend."

"Well, from what I understand, there was a gas leak. Anyways, Susan ended up dead. Then to top it off, and the newspapers haven't picked up on this yet, Joshua Underwood was killed yesterday."

"What?" Julia exclaimed.

"Yeah…, for some reason he was at the funeral home yesterday and apparently he was robbed. They shot him twice in cold blood."

Julia clasped her hands together. She looked at Janice. Her eyes told the story of a woman who was disturbed by the news she'd just received.

"You know, Janice. I've been Judge in Dawson County for fifteen years now. As far as I can remember, I've never had to deal with a murder. I am glad for that. I was glad that I finally found a place where murder is not the number one reason people come into my courtroom. And now, we have one, Joshua of all people. Are we at the point where it will be impossible to look at our small community as being immune to the dangers of the big city? I sure hope this was an isolated case. I hope I don't have to deal with another murder case soon."

Janice nodded her head agreeing. She got up and straightened her skirt. It was time to get back to business. But first she needed to clean up the spilled coffee and broken cup. As she walked out the door, she turned around.

"Miss Julia? Some guy named Dimitri Van Acker called and asked if he could see you first thing this morning said it was important he talked to you. I hope you don't mind, but I pushed him between the Walker divorce and the Jones-Davis land dispute at 9:30."

Julia was surprised by the name.

"Dimitri? He's back in town? Yeah, 9:30 will be fine."

Julia Snelgrove sat up straight in her chair. She pushed the paper aside and grabbed the Walker divorce file. She opened it up and looked at her notes. Somehow, she could not concentrate on its contents. She had received one chock after another since she had walked into her chambers. Susan Knox was dead. Joshua Underwood had been killed. Dimitri Van Acker had returned to Stuttgart. Dimitri Van Acker. How long had it been? It must have been at least six or seven years since she had seen him. She wondered what had become of him. The last she heard he had moved to Washington, DC to become a defense attorney. Did he fail in that? Somehow she doubted that. He had always been interested in the law. She could not recall the countless hours he had followed her, asked her questions, and basically pestered her while he attended law school. She somehow had not minded. It was nice to see a young man like Dimitri to be as interested in his profession as he was. He would make a good lawyer and if he wanted might just make it all the way to the top and become a judge. She could hardly wait to see him.

Nine o'clock came around and it was time for Judge Julia Snelgrove to do her job. She had to make a judgment in a nasty divorce case. Janette and Charles Walker. It was a clear case of a

244

wife who could not get enough satisfaction from her husband and who entertained various lovers while her husband was at work. A simple case from that point of view; however, there was a little boy involved and both of them were fighting for custody. It was a difficult decision to make on Julia's part. She had two children of her own and she would have hated if one or both were taken from her. She was going to rule in the father's favor on this one. The child would have a much better chance of receiving a good upbringing under his father's supervision than with the sluttish lifestyle her mother was leading. It wasn't an easy decision, but one that she had to make in the best interest of the child.

Julia returned to her chambers after the divorce settlement. Janette had hurled all kinds of obscenities at her. She had threatened her and promised that nobody takes away her child from her without paying for it. Judge Julia had ruled and that was that. Janette had one more outburst, which had landed her in jail for an indefinite amount of time. Judge Julia, as everyone in the county knew, did not put up with having her courtroom disturbed, much less being threatened. Now, Julia was sitting behind her desk. Her next case was at ten. Dimitri would see her at 9:30, which left her with a little time to review her next case. She grabbed the file on her next case and started reviewing it.

The knock on her door made her look up from her notes. Julia Snelgrove looked at her watch. It was almost 9:30. That would be Dimitri. Unconsciously, Julia brushed her hair in place and straightened her clothes.

"Come in," she said, sounding as professional as possible.

The door opened. The man in the doorway was not whom she expected to see. Instead of Dimitri Van Acker, Andrew Hinson stood in the doorway. The smile on Julia's face was replaced by a frown.

"Good morning, Judge. What? Not happy to see me? I bet you were expecting someone else, right?"

Julia bit her tongue. She had never cared for Hinson's rudeness. She had hoped that he would not have been reelected after his first term in office. However, the good folks of Dawson County thought otherwise and he had easily won reelection; much to the dislike of Judge Snelgrove. She did all she could not to snare at him.

245

"Andrew, what a surprise! What do I owe the pleasure of you coming to see me this morning? And please, make it rather quick. I have a busy schedule ahead of me."

"Oh, Judge, always so busy!"

"Get to the point, Andrew!"

"All right. I just wanted to tell you that we had an interesting weekend. It seems that all the fun starts when you're not around."

"If you're referring to Susan Knox' and Joshua Underwood's deaths, I am already aware of it. I just hope that you are in the middle of an investigation into the fire as well as into the robbery. I hate to see our taxpayer's money going to waste."

Hinson was taken back that Julia was already aware of the events of the past weekend. He figured she had seen the headlines in the newspaper about the Susan Knox event. He could not figure out who might have told her about Joshua Underwood. Unless... No, he didn't think that foreigner had told her yet. From glancing at her appointment book, he knew Van Acker was supposed to meet with her in a little while. Who then told her? With questioning eyes he looked at her.

"I see you are well informed. It's amazing how fast news travels in these small towns. Anyways, to answer your question; yes we are busy with both investigations. I am personally handling the Joshua Underwood case."

"And who's running the Susan Knox investigation?"

"I have Hope Olson working that investigation. Olson's been with us a long time and I think that she's ready to take on the responsibility. However, I'm keeping a close eye on her. Just making sure she doesn't screw anything up."

"Good. I would like to be kept abreast in the progress of both investigations. I want whoever killed Joshua behind bars. Understood?"

Andrew Hinson shook his head.

"Yes, Judge. Anything else?"

"Actually there is. I have a lot to do, so if you don't mind, please leave."

Hinson was surprised at the tone of Judge Snelgrove's voice. It was no secret that she didn't like him, but she had never been short with him or snared at him before. He left her office and headed down the stairs.

Halfway down, he ran into Dimitri Van Acker.

"Van Acker, we meet again!"

Van Acker looked at Hinson. He extended his hand. Hinson did not return the gesture.

"Boy, I don't know what you're doing here, but I suggest you keep out of whatever it is you're getting involved in. You don't think you'll be able to establish yourself here, do you?"

Van Acker looked up at Hinson, who was standing a couple of steps up.

"I hate to be rude Sheriff, but I've got an appointment. Maybe we can talk some other time. Maybe we can meet at "Langston's". From what I've been told, they serve good food there. What do you say?"

Dimitri Van Acker pushed past Hinson and hurried up the steps, not waiting for an answer. Hinson balled his fists. Who the hell does this kid think he is? What gave him the right to waltz in here like that and try to take over? He had no right! His face red and blood pressure up, Sheriff Hinson headed out of the courthouse.

Dimitri Van Acker knocked on Judge Snelgrove's door after he exchanged greetings with Janice. Inside, before telling Van Acker to come in, she went through the same hair and clothes straightening routine as before.

"Come in."

Van Acker entered the Judge's chambers.

"Dimitri! How good to see you! Come over here and give me a hug."

Van Acker met Julia halfway into her chambers and gave her a hug.

"Hi, Judge Snelgrove, how are you?"

Julia gave him a stern look and said:

"Listen, Dimitri, from now on, you can call me Julia, unless of course you see me in my courtroom.

"Okay…, Julia."

"I'm fine. How about you? How are you doing?"

"Well, I left the bright future of a crooked defense attorney behind to practice law in this little backwards town. I have decided to leave all the violence behind. And guess what? It seems like the

247

violence followed me."

"What do you mean?"

"Well, the first day that I'm in town, Susan Knox' apartment becomes an inferno with Susan in it. And to top it off, the next day, the town's undertaker Joshua Underwood gets the life shot out of him. I tell ya, I could have stayed in DC and found that same violence."

Julia was not sure where Van Acker was headed.

"How about being a bit clearer, Dimitri?"

Van Acker explained to Julia about his suspicions about Susan Knox being killed before the apartment catching fire. He withheld the information he found on Joshua's note. He did not want to set himself up. He told her that he doubted a proper autopsy would be performed. As Susan Knox' attorney he wanted Julia to make sure that Susan's body would not be embalmed before an autopsy was conducted. Julia told him that she would make sure that she ordered the autopsy and that no one was to see the body unless they had a court order. Dimitri also told Julia that Hope and he were the one's who found Underwood's body. He understood that everyone thought that Underwood was killed during a robbery. However, he did not and thought that somehow Underwood's death was related to Susan's death. Julia sat back in her chair and mesmerized about what Van Acker had told him. She was wondering if she should let Van Acker in on the fact that Hinson was handling the Joshua Underwood case. She decided not to. She needed, after all, be unbiased to any investigation.

A half hour later Dimitri Van Acker walked down the steps of the courthouse, court papers in hand to keep everyone away from Susan's body except her parents, Julia Sutton, the medical examiner, Hope Olson, Andrew Hinson and himself. He was going to be present at the autopsy. No one would stop him. He knew Andrew Hinson would try to stop him. However, with the court papers, even Andrew Hinson could not stop him from being there. Whatever would be found would come to his knowledge first. No room for distorted stories or facts, or even worse, distorted records. Van Acker smiled. Next, he had to go talk to Susan's parents. Feeling as if things were coming together, he got in his car and drove off.

Across the street, Andrew Hinson watched Van Acker leave.

He wondered what he had been so excited about. He had to watch him closely. He was not stupid. Hinson thought he was a whole lot more intelligent that his counterpart Tom Sutton. He liked Sutton though. He could make the crooked lawyer eat out of the palm of his hand. Hinson had too much dirt on Sutton; more than Sutton ever imagined.

55.

Julie Sutton was ready to head for the funeral home around nine o'clock. She had put on a black skirt and white blouse with a black blazer over it. She had her hair put up. Looking in the mirror she noticed that she looked older. A couple of sleepless nights had left black circles around her eyes. Nightmares of Lester coming down on her had kept her awake and bathing in sweat. Finally, around five o'clock, she had gotten up and taken a shower. Feeling refreshed, she had made herself some breakfast and read the morning paper. The fire at Susan's apartment had made the headlines. She had quickly scanned the story. No mention of murder. It was ruled an accident according to the paper. Maybe that was for the best. She was ready to put the pain and suffering her sister had caused behind her; the best way, she thought, was to put her sister to rest as quick as possible. She would be there when Joshua Underwood arrived at the funeral home.

The trip to the funeral home didn't take long. Julie Sutton drove a little faster than usual. She knew Joshua Underwood arrived at the funeral home exactly at nine o'clock every morning. As Julie drove into the parking lot, she noticed the yellow crime scene ribbon across the front door. She stopped the car in the middle of the parking lot. What was this all about? Why would there be crime scene ribbon strung across the entrance? Had something happened at the funeral home? A break-in? Julie parked her car in a spot closest to the entrance. As she got out of her car, a deputy standing guard at the funeral home approached her. Julie did not recognize the young man. He must have been a recent addition to the Sheriff's department. She thought she knew everybody on the force.

"Excuse me ma'am? May I ask what your business is here?"

Julie looked at him in disbelieve.

"My business? You want to know my business? I'll tell you what my business is! My sister is in there. She died Saturday night and I want to make sure that proper arrangements are being made for her funeral!"

The young deputy looked flustered.

"Eh, I'm sorry, ma'am, I didn't know. You must be Julie Sutton? I'm sorry about your sister dying in the fire like that. Must be horrible!"

"Well, I guess I shouldn't have gotten bend out of shape like I did. I apologize. Now, can you tell me what's going on here?"

The deputy followed Julie's gaze to the yellow ribbon across the front entrance.

"I guess you haven't heard yet, huh? Mr. Underwood was killed yesterday."

Julie's jaw dropped. The color in her face drained to an icy white. She clamped her fingers around the steering wheel.

"Killed, you said?"

The deputy shook his head.

"Yes, ma'am. For some reason Mr. Underwood was here yesterday afternoon. Someone came in and robbed him, killing him in the process."

"A robbery? Are you sure?"

"Oh yes, ma'am. We found Mr. Underwood's empty wallet on the floor. There was no money in it."

Julie looked straight ahead, her mind wandering. What was Underwood doing at the funeral home on Sunday? She had never known him to work on Sunday. What had possessed him to come in yesterday? Did it have something to do with Susan's death? She looked back at the deputy.

"When will David get here?"

"We called his house earlier but we couldn't get an answer. We suspect he's already on the way over here."

Julie didn't answer. She stared out the window not focusing on anything in particular.

     ***

David Johnson had not made it back to his house after his Saturday night out. As usual, he had gotten extremely drunk and had spent the night at his girlfriend's house. On Sunday, he had once again had too much the drink and had spent the night again. It was almost a ritual for him and his girlfriend, that on weekends, he would get drunk to the point of passing out. Underwood did not approve of his behavior but as long as Johnson showed up on Monday morning to do his job, he looked the other way. At 29, Johnson was short and overweight by at least 100 pounds. He had a head full of long curly red hair, a puffy face covered with freckles and piercing green eyes. He had learned everything he knew from watching Underwood. Johnson had come by the funeral home at the young age of 15 and had wanted to know everything there was to know about the profession of mortician, as he so eloquently called it. After graduating high school, he held various jobs; none capable of supporting his drinking habit. The people he called his friends took advantage of him and made fun of him behind his back. Many a night, Johnson had found himself stranded on the side of the road, his car in the hands of some self-proclaimed friend in need. His goodness and gullible nature were his downfall. At 21, he had approached Underwood and was offered a job as Underwood's assistant. Joshua Underwood had made it possible for David to attend Gupton-Jones College of Funeral Service. Johnson had at first struggled with attending college, but Underwood was patient and pushed him till he received his degree. Johnson kept working under Joshua Underwood's tutelage and after a few years was able to pass the State Board Exam for funeral director and embalmer. Over the past 8 years, he had become a skilled mortician and was mostly performing the work by himself now. Underwood stilled helped with the paperwork, however, when it came down to it, Johnson would be able to run the funeral home by himself.

David Johnson looked surprised as he drove up into the funeral parking lot. He started feeling uneasy about the Sheriff's car being in the parking lot. Yellow crime scene ribbon was pulled across the doorways. He started sweating. Nervously, he wiped sweat from his brow. He parked his car in its usual spot and walked towards the back entrance of the funeral home. The young deputy, who had been talking to Julie, approached him.

"David Johnson?"

David felt the sweat pushing through his pores. His scalp started to itch.

"Yes."

"Mr. Johnson, I'm sorry but you will not be able to enter the building."

"What happened? Did someone break in? I've warned Joshua about this. The chemicals in there can give someone a high."

He looked around the parking lot. He had been so nervous about the Sheriff's deputy being around that he had not even noticed that Underwood's truck was not in the parking lot.

"Mr. Johnson, I'm sorry to tell you this, but there was a break in yesterday. Apparently Mr. Underwood showed up to do some work, and was shot during an apparent robbery."

Johnson's face turned a shade whiter than his already fair complexion. He felt his knees go weak. He leaned up again the building.

"Is Joshua alright?

The deputy lowered his head and slowly started shaking now.

"I'm afraid that Mr. Underwood did not survive the shooting."

Tears started to well up in Johnson's eyes. This was unbelievable. Joshua was shot during a robbery?

"Shot..." Johnson said more to himself than to the deputy in front of him. "….who would shoot the old geezer? He never had any money on him. A few bucks maybe, but not worth killing for."

He looked towards the back entrance.

"I really cannot go in there?"

"No sir. It'll be at least tomorrow before you can go in there. We're investigating the crime scene and no one is allowed in.

"Tomorrow, huh?"

The deputy shook his head affirmatively.

David Johnson turned his attention towards Julie Sutton's car. He knew the woman inside from sight, but could not place her name.

"Who's the woman in the car over there?" he asked the deputy, pointing at Julie's car.

"That's Julie Sutton. Her sister was killed in a fire Saturday night and her body is in the funeral home. She came by to find out when the funeral could be held. It'll be a couple of days I suspect."

"As soon as you guys get out of here, I'll be able to perform the work. The funeral could be held day after tomorrow."

"Maybe you need to go talk to her and tell her that, okay? It might make it a little bit better for her."

Johnson looked at the deputy, and then focused his attention on the woman in the car again.

"Sure."

With as much grace as he could muster, David Johnson walked over the Julie Sutton's car. As he approached, he adjusted his pants, making sure his shirt was tucked in. Sweat was starting to bead up on his forehead again. Heavy droplets flowed down to his eyebrows and stung his eyes. Nervously he wiped his eyes. Reaching the car he tapped his fingers on the window of the driver's side door.

"Miss Sutton?"

Julie snapped out of her daydreaming. She rolled down the window.

"Hi, David, how are you?"

Johnson nervously played with a button on his shirt. He shuffled his feet.

"I… I'm sorry about your sister, ma'am. I… I guess we'll be able to arrange for the funeral tomorrow. They won't let any one in today… something to do with the investigation into Joshua's murder."

"Okay, I guess that'll be fine. Let's say that you would be able to start preparing tomorrow, when could we have the funeral?"

"Oh, I would say by Thursday for sure. I don't foresee any problems at all."

"Thanks, David. I'll check with you in the morning and see how things are going."

"That'll be fine, Miss Sutton. If anything should come up, I believe I have your number in the office.

"Thanks."

Julie Sutton rolled up her window, starter her car and drove off. Johnson followed the car with his eyes. His face turned a bit scarlet as not so pure thoughts entered his mind. He cursed himself. He could not be thinking that way now. He had to think about the funeral home. With Underwood gone, it was up to him to keep the funeral home running. Thank God Joshua Underwood had always looked into the future and had made him a partner in the business. With the death of his wife and children, he had made sure he was prepared for the unexpected. Johnson was thankful for that now. He would have to change his way of life. No more drinking till he dropped. No more not caring where you slept or fell down from

254

drinking too much. He had to stop. He had to get his life in order. He had more important issues to worry about now. He would have to pay the bills, keep the funeral home running. Most of all, he would have to change his appearance. He needed a haircut. Most of all, he needed to lose weight. As he watched Julie Sutton's car turn the corner of the parking lot, he made up his mind that he would continue in Joshua's fashion and make sure that everyone in town respected him. He would no longer be the laughingstock of his generation. He would show them all that he could do better than he had been doing. They would look up to him.

56.

Bryan Scarboro arrived at his father's office around eight o'clock. He knew his father wouldn't be there yet. Weather permitting; his father had a standing weekly meeting with a group of jogging partners on Monday morning. Scarboro had plenty of time to take care of business before his father's return. Dr. Earl Scarboro had given his son the keys to his office and told him to go through the appointment schedule and see what the morning would look like. He also told him to go ahead and start searching for a new secretary. Usually, Scarboro would not have been excited to be up this early to start work, but this morning was different. He was more than happy to oblige to his father's wishes, something that had not gone unnoticed to the elder Scarboro. Dr. Scarboro wondered what his son was up to.

Taking position in Susan Knox' chair, he started examining the computer. Thankfully, Susan had been a great organizer and neat freak. It didn't take long; with a few strokes on the keyboard and a few shuffles of the mouse, Scarboro had the appointment schedule. Only three appointments. That wasn't too bad. He wondered how many walk-ins there would be. This time of year most of the patients were young mothers with crying babies or older children who had gotten into trouble and cut themselves or stepped on something sharp. He hoped that it would not be a busy day. He looked at his watch: just a few minutes past eight. He had plenty of time to do what he needed to do and decided to start with calling the newspaper to place an advertisement for a new secretary.

***

Outside Dr. Scarboro's office, Michelle Murphy had taken up position across the street. She was closely following Bryan's movements. She had had a restless night and had been up at the crack of dawn. She had thought back to her conversation with her parents. I had been an uncomfortable confrontation.

Michelle got out of her car and walked towards Dr. Scarboro's building. She peered through the window and saw Bryan Scarboro disappear down a hallway towards the examination rooms.

She tried the doorknob. It turned and the door swung open. Quietly she entered the waiting room. She looked around, her head moving from side to side. A smiled appeared on her face. On her tiptoes she crossed the waiting room. She stopped by the receptionist desk, scanning it. Next to the computer screen she noticed two vials. She looked at the labels. She noticed the symbol, skull and crossbones. She knew that these should not be sitting out in plain sight for anyone to be able to grab. She wondered if Scarboro had put them there. And if so, why? Michelle again scanned the waiting room and looked through the windows. Nobody was in sight. She grabbed the two vials. She peered down the hallway. Clear. Quickly and as quietly as he could, she moved past the examination rooms and turned the corner at the end of the hallway. She pressed her back against the wall and listened for any tell tail signs that Scarboro was coming towards her. All remained silent. She poked her head briefly around the corner checking the direction she had come from. Everything was still clear, the hallway empty. Michelle moved down the hallway and stopped in front of a door that read: "Dr. Earl Scarboro". She tried the doorknob. It turned. She opened the door and slipped inside the office, silently closing the door behind her.

     ***

Bryan Scarboro hated the morning tasks. It was something the nurse was supposed to do, but she was on vacation this week and his father had requested that he'd take over the job for the week. With Susan gone, he would have to do more than just play nurse; he'd also have to attend to the front desk. He hoped a replacement for Susan would be found quickly. He prepared both examination rooms: cleaning out trash cans, and depositing hazardous waste bags in the proper containers. He made sure there were plenty of cotton swabs, tongue depressors, and in general making sure that everything his dad needed to perform a basic examination was were it was supposed to be. It didn't take him long to finish and by 8:30 he was finished. Plenty of time to do what needed to be done. He walked back to the front desk. The color drained from his face. The vials were gone. He scratched his head. He knew he put them on the counter when he had first sat down. He eyes were bulging and he

257

started to sweat. His head moved from side to side, looking. Maybe he had accidentally knocked them down when he was getting up. He hurried around the desk and dropped to his knees. Nothing! Scarboro started to panic. Beads of sweats started forming on his forehead. His hands were starting to feel clammy. What happened to the vials? He scratched his scalp. His eyes lit up and he rushed into the first examination room. He scanned the room. Nothing! The second examination room got the same treatment. Again, nothing! A queasy feeling invaded his stomach. He rushed outside to his car. Again, no vials to be found!

***

Michelle sat behind Dr. Scarboro's desk looking through files. All the patient files were in the front by the receptionist desk; all except for some confidential files that Dr. Scarboro found necessary to keep in his office. She had gotten that information from Scarboro during one of their dates. She had asked why. The reason given was that Dr. Scarboro wanted to keep those files in his office because of the sensitive information contained in them. Michelle had found the right filing cabinet and was scanning through the files. Most of the files were old and of patients who were no longer alive. She scanned through the names. Her sight and fingers froze as she crossed the name Murphy. She looked at the first name. Kelly! Why did Kelly have a file back here? Michelle pulled the file from the drawer. She laid it on the desk and opened it. Quickly she scanned the contents. She sighted with frustration. How can anyone understand these terms? She tried to find a date on the papers. One of the forms, one with her mother's handwriting on it, showed a date. Michelle quickly calculated how old Kelly must have been. Five. This was an old file. She had been a baby herself. Michelle wondered what had been wrong with her sister.

Michelle returned the file to its proper position and scanned the rest of the files. Reaching the letter K, she slowed down. Knox, Susan! There it was. Quickly she pulled the file. She opened it and rustled through the papers. She looked through them carefully. One paper caught her eyes. It had names of what look like different diseases on it.

"Coeurnechol".

She took one the vials and read the inscription. It was the same medicine. Michelle scanned the paper for information on the medicine. She noticed a section highlighted in yellow marker with a big red exclamation mark next to it. Michelle read the passage half-loud.

"Susan suffering from congestive heart failure due to HIV. Possibly 6 months before fatal. Careful administration of Coeurnechol must be followed. Overdose is fatal. Administer maximum 1 ml per day by injection only".

Michelle looked at the contents of the vial. It was a 10-ml vial. She shook her head. Bryan Scarboro had put two vials on the desk. If he was Susan's killer, and he administered 20 ml of the drug, Susan would have died quickly. But were these two vials the only one's he had taken? And where did he get the vials from? She scanned the room and noticed a cabinet in the corner opposite the door. She got up from behind the desk and walked over to the cabinet. She tried to open it, but it was locked. She looked at a folder hanging on the side of the cabinet. Susan's name was written on the inventory form inside the folder. Next to her name was the number 1, the name of a drug: Coeurnechol; and the date the drug was removed from the cabinet. Susan was getting the medicine from Dr. Scarboro. The last time she had received the medicine had been the day before her death. That meant that with a 10-ml vial she was good for at least 10 days. Why would Scarboro take two or more vials with him only to return at least two of them? She wondered why he had taken the drugs from his father's office. He obviously had not known about the AIDS before Susan had told him about her condition. Did he know about her heart condition? Suddenly it hit Michelle. Scarboro had done the same thing she had just done. He had reviewed the file and knew what drug Susan was taking and what its potential deadly effects could be. The information in the file about her having AIDS was inconsequential at the time he took the medicine. He was already aware of it. So Scarboro had also thought about killing Susan, only he wanted to kill her using her own drugs, making it look like an overdose. Michelle looked at her watch and noticed the time. 8:43. Dr. Scarboro would be coming in soon. She needed to get out.

***

Bryan Scarboro sat down behind the computer. What could he do? The two vials would eventually come up missing. His father would know. He would know that he had lied about the keys. There had to be something he could do! He stared at the computer screen. Maybe, just maybe, he might get away with it. Scarboro typed something on the screen. An inventory page appeared. He studied it closely. Sure enough, five vials of Coeurnechol showed up as being in inventory. He moved the mouse to the Coeurnechol line. He clicked once on the number five. It became highlighted. He then pushed the number three button on the keyboard. The number was accepted. However, when he tried to get out of the screen a message appeared. It asked for a patient's account number. Scarboro turned pale. He looked at his watch, almost time for his father to show up. He got up and hurried down the hall to his father's office. Susan's account number would be on her file. He turned the knob and opened the door. He hurried behind the desk and opened the file drawer. The account number was printed on the tab. He tore a piece of paper from a notebook on his dad's desk and grabbed a pen. He scribbled the number down on the paper. Quickly he replaced the file in the file cabinet and hurried back to the front desk. He punched in the account number praying that it would work. The computer screen returned to its original position. Scarboro breathed a sigh of relieve.

***

Michelle had opened the door to Dr. Scarboro's office slightly and peeked out to see if the coast was clear. As she was about the head into the hallway, she heard Scarboro heading towards his father's office. From the sound of it, he was in hurry. She quickly closed the door and looked around the room. She only had a few second. She noticed a door at the far corner of the room. She hurried across the room and opened the door. To her surprise, she found herself on a small porch at the back of the building. She locked the doorknob and as quietly as possible closed the door behind her. She froze for a moment as he heard Scarboro storming in and moving around inside the office. She leaned up against the wall and took a deep breath. That had been close! She looked at her watch. Almost 9 o'clock. She needed to get away. She took the stairs to the back porch two at a time and found herself in the alley besides the office building. She walked towards the front of the building. She took a peek around the corner. All was clear. She jogged across the street and got into her car. She put the two vials of medication on the passenger seat. She started the car and took off.

57.

After his meeting with Eddie Jovanovic, Tom Sutton had returned to his office. Even though he had his clothes at the hotel in Pinegrove, he did not feel like driving back out there. He had been exhausted and crashed on the couch in his office. It was still dark when he woke up. He hadn't slept well. The couch was no substitute for a bed and his bones were aching. He'd returned to Pinegrove, took a shower and changed his clothes. After eating breakfast at one of the local restaurants, he returned to Stuttgart. He had a busy day ahead of him. With Helen Murphy more than likely not coming back to work, he would have to handle everything himself.

Tom Sutton sat down behind his desk. He had a stack of files in front of him. He had a court appearance that afternoon. He needed to make sure that he was properly prepared. His opponent in the case was Elisabeth Stanton, a tough, take no prisoners lawyer from Macon. To top it off, Judge Snelgrove would be presiding. She had a dislike for him, despising his arrogant behavior in her courtroom. He knew she was looking for a change to hold him in contempt of court so she could throw him in jail for a little while. He wanted to make sure that he had all angles of the case covered, hoping no unforeseen surprises reared their ugly head. He carefully read through the pages, looking up and staring in front of him on occasion, imagining himself in the courtroom. For some reason, he did not seem to be able to concentrate on the task at hand. His mind kept wandering. He looked towards his safe. The tape of Eddie Jovanovich and his wife was safely stored inside it. Would she ever be surprised when she filed divorce papers against him for infidelity? He was going to turn the tables on her. She had no evidence of his fooling around. All she had was hearsay. On top of that, her key witness in her possible defense was dead. Susan was the only one who could testify against him if Julie took him to court. Now with Susan out of the way, he was in the clear. She would not be able to find out whom else he'd slept with over the years. He refocused his attention to his upcoming case. He laid out his defense. Carefully he jotted down some notes on his legal pad. It wasn't the easiest of cases, but he was sure he could create enough reasonable doubt to sway the jury his way. That's all he wanted. An acquittal would be wonderful, but he would be more than happy with a hung jury. He jotted down some more notes. He stared at the safe again. A wicked smiled formed on his face.

Tom Sutton pushed the case file to the side and got up. He retrieved the incriminating tape from the safe and pushed it in the VCR. After a little static, the picture became focused on the TV screen. He could see Julie, lying on the bed, naked. God, she did have a beautiful body. Too bad she didn't know how she was supposed to use it. A wicked grin appeared on his face. According to the tape he was watching, it appeared that his wife did indeed know how to use her body. A naked Jovanovic appeared in the picture, obviously very aroused as he slowly approached the bed. He leaned over Julie, massaging her breasts and running his hands over her naked body. Sutton sat down on the couch and relaxed. He watched as Jovanovic mounted his wife and started to go down on her like a wild man. Jovanovic turned out to be quite the lover and it took him a long time before he was done violating Julie's body. Watching his wife together with Jovanovic somehow turned him on. He had never thought himself a voyeur, and he was surprised of his own body's reaction to watching the scene on the TV. He felt uncomfortable with it; however, there wasn't a whole lot he could do about it. When the screen went blank after Jovanovic finished his business and was seen walking towards the camera to cut it of, he pushed the rewind button, and replaced the tape in the safe. The tape would do miracles and he could not afford to loose it. As he closed the safe and turned back towards his desk, he jumped.

"Good morning, Tom!"

"Andy, what the hell are you doing here? You scared the hell out of me!"

"Just thought I'd drop by and give you a little update on our buddy Van Acker."

"What about Van Acker? I don't have time right now."

Andrew Hinson smiled.

"Seems to me that you have all the time in the world," he said, pointing at the TV. "I didn't know you and Julie were into the swinging scene."

Sutton turned pale.

263

"On top of that, wasn't that the guy who I arrested for speeding? What's his name...? Eddie, isn't it?"

"Look, this is none of your business, Andy."

"Well, I don't know, Tom. I've always liked Julie. She reminds me of my wife when she was younger and still alive. I would hate to see her getting hurt, no matter how or by whom. You know what I mean?"

Sutton sat down behind his desk. His original fright ebbed away and now he was ready to jump to the offense.

"You see, Andy. I wanted Eddie to hang around a while to do some work around the house. I come home one afternoon and find him in the kitchen chatting away with Julie."

Sutton looked Hinson straight in the eyes. Hinson did not reveal any emotion. Sutton continued.

"I became suspicious. You know, Julie's not the type to be talking away like that with strangers. So, I put up a camera in the bedroom closet. It's one of those that activate when there's movement in the room. Paid a lot of damn money for it too! Anyways, last week, I finally got prove."

"Prove of what? That's she's fooling around?"

"Yeah, man. I couldn't believe it either. But the tape shows it clear as day."

Andrew Hinson rubbed his chin. He knew Sutton wasn't being truthful with him. He knew as well as Sutton did that Julie had been set up.

"Let me ask you something, Tom."

"Okay."

"If Julie is having an affair, and she so obviously loves having sex with this man, then why in hell is she laying there like she's dead?"

The pale color returned to Sutton's face.

"My dear man, if I were the one making love to her, she'd be jumping up and down with excitement. There's no way in hell that she'd be laying their like that. What's going on, Tom?"

Sutton leaned back in his chair and propped his chin in his hands. He looked past Hinson out the window. He found himself in an awkward situation. Hinson obviously had not bought his explanation. He contemplated telling the truth. He chose not too.

"Well," Tom Sutton started, taking a deep breath, "you see, Andy…"

"Yes?"

"Julie and I have a strange relationship. You may say that we're not your average straight couple."

Sutton stopped and swallowed, looking at Hinson, trying to find the smallest hint of facial expression. He could not see the slightest hint of either believe or disbelieve.

"You see," he continued, "we've been getting involved with other couples."

"You mean like swinging or swapping?" Hinson asked.

Sutton swallowed hard before continuing.

"Yeah, kind of like that. I tell you though, I don't think that it's any of your business what my wife and I do in the privacy of our own home."

Hinson leaned back in his chair. He had obviously hit a nerve with Sutton. Never before had Sutton raised his voice at him. Now, he was getting more and more agitated as the conversation focused on his personal life."

"Tom, correct me if I'm wrong, but didn't Julie kick you out of the house?"

Sutton sat straight up in his chair.

"Yes, she did. And again, I'm telling you Andy, it's not of your Goddamn business!"

"Okay. I won't press the issue; just as long as Julie doesn't get hurt."

"You've got my word."

There was a long silence between the two men. Hinson had his eyes focused on a picture of Julie hanging on the wall. Sutton was staring out the window. He broke the silence first.

"So, Andy, what was it you came to bug me about before you got into my personal business. I hate to be rude, but I've got a case this afternoon. I want to prepare a bit more before I go into the dungeon."

"Well, talking about the dungeon. Guess who went to see the executioner this morning?"

Sutton scratched his head. He couldn't think of anyone.

"No idea. Humor me."

"Our mutual friend Dimitri Van Acker."

"What was he doing there?"

"I don't know. All I know is that he was there at 9:30. He left about a half an hour later. The only thing that I did notice is that he was not carrying anything going in, however, when he left, he was carrying a stack of papers."

Tom Sutton rubbed his hands together as he thought about what Hinson had told him about Van Acker. He had no idea that he knew Judge Snelgrove. He shook his head in disbelieve.

"You know, Andy, I've got all the forces working against me on this one. I want to get rid of Van Acker as bad as you do. I don't like him a bit. I don't like Snelgrove. You don't either from what I've heard. Both of them together could be trouble around here."

Hinson turned his eyes to slits. He looked at Sutton for what seemed the longest time.

"Tom, I've told you before, and I will tell you again. You don't worry about Van Acker. I'll take care of him. Snelgrove, I'm afraid, is out of my reach. But I'm sure that you can do some work in that department. Let me worry about Van Acker and I'll let you worry about Snelgrove."

Hinson stood up and walked towards the door. As he opened it he turned around and faced Sutton.

"Tom..."

"Yeah."

"I'm serious about Julie, you know! Anything happens to her and you'll be the first I'll come see!"

"Are you threatening me?"

"No, not threatening, just warning."

Hinson walked out the door into the reception area. He looked at the empty desk. He turned around and stepped back into Sutton's office.

"Say, where's Helen?"

"She quit on me Friday."

"Is that so? What about Kelly?"

"She quit too."

"Now isn't that interesting. What'ya do, Tom, try to convince both of them to go swinging with you and Julie?"

Before Tom Sutton could answer, Hinson was out of the

building, laughing. Sutton was furious. Why did he put up with Hinson's mouth and attitude? He should just face him one good time and put him in his place. He slumped down into his chair and looked up at the ceiling. God, what was he going to do? He didn't want anyone to know about the tape and now, the worst possible person in the world knew about it. He'd have to take care of Hinson in a different way. He could not let any loose ends float around. When the time was right, he would use the tape. No one, absolutely no one could throw a wrench in his plans. Andrew Hinson had to be dealt with. Sutton straightened himself up and focused his attention back to his upcoming case. He only had a few more hours left before having to go to court. Today, for the first time in his career, he was not looking forward to going into court.

58.

Hope Olson wasn't due at the Sheriff's Department till late in the afternoon. At 10 o'clock, she was sitting behind her desk going through her notes on the Susan Knox case. She had called Allen Murphy and received his written report on the findings of his investigation of the fire at Susan's apartment. She was excited to be handling the case. She didn't know whether she would get overtime pay for the extra time spent investigating the case, but she was so full of energy and determination that she didn't care. She was sure Sheriff Hinson would be able to cover some of her time as overtime.

As Hope looked over Murphy's report, she jotted down some notes on a notepad. The one fact that most intrigued her was that Susan had not known about the gas being released inside the building. Had she been dead before the fire started? Hope wrote down something on her notepad: "Gas-phase electrochemical test". She paused as she underlined the words. She knew of the test from when she was still in the Navy. A friend of hers had died in a fire and foul play had been suspected. The test results showed hat her friend had died before the fire had started. As far as she could remember, the test, also know as GPE test, measured the levels of carbon monoxide in the victims tissues, therefore indicating whether the victim inhaled carbon monoxide or not. If the carbon monoxide levels in the tissue were much higher that what is considered normal, then the victim must have been alive when the fire started. And if the carbon monoxide levels were within the normal range, then that would indicate that the victim had died prior to the fire. If no physical markings were found on Susan's body, then the GPE test would be the only method of finding out whether or not she had been dead prior to the fire. She would wait until the autopsy was completed. If nothing out of the ordinary was found, she would take further steps to get the test done.

Hope rubbed her temples as she tried to put the pieces of the puzzle together. If Susan had been killed; and it seemed likely, who could have done it? There were several possibilities. She and Van Acker had run down the list the night before. One possible suspect stood out: Bryan Scarboro. She reached inside her breast pocket of her uniform and pulled out the bracelet she had found in the alley.

She wondered if Scarboro was missing it yet. She decided that she would go talk to Scarboro and gauge his reaction. Other names popped into her mind. How about Tom Sutton? He had had an affair with Susan. He had every reason in the world to get rid of her. His name would be ruined forever if the news came out that he might be infected with the HIV virus. From what she had heard, the word was already out on the street. She could see dim times roll in for Sutton. He was sure to lose a lot of business. Well, that would be good for Van Acker.

Dimitri Van Acker. Hope's mind wandered off. She felt a warm feeling flow through her body as she thought about him. She was glad that she had waited to get involved with anybody. As if by destiny, she had not pursued any relationships. Van Acker coming back was a dream come true for her. She had never stopped loving him. Never before had she felt so happy about having someone in her life. Hope's daydreaming came to an abrupt end when the phone on her desk started the ring. Bewildered, she answered it.

"Hello?"

"Hi beautiful, how are you?"

A smile appeared on her face.

"Hi to you, too! I'm doing fine. Actually, I was just thinking about you."

"Really? Listen, are you gonna be busy around lunch time?"

"No, I don't think so. Why?"

"How about meeting up with me at Langston's?"

"Okay, that sounds good."

"Great, see you there."

"Dimitri, I love you."

"Love you too."

Softly, Hope put the receiver back down. She felt a little warmer than before. A smile ran across her face. She definitely felt happy.

The phone rang again. She looked at it in disbelief. Who knew she was already at work? She picked up the receiver.

"Hello?"

"Hope, Andy here."

"Yes, sir?"

"Listen, I've gotta run to Pinegrove this afternoon in

269

reference to last weeks chase across county lines. I was wondering if you could go with me."

"I don't see why not. What time?"

"I'm leaving here around twelve. I'd like to get something to eat in Pinegrove before the meeting. Don't worry; I'll pay for your meal too."

Hope felt silent. As fast as her happiness had built up to a euphoric state, her disappointment came even faster. She had committed herself without knowing any specifics. She had let her guard down. She definitely could not let Hinson know that she had made plans with Van Acker. That could mean her dismissal from the Knox case. That was something that she did not want to have happen. She would have to cancel with Van Acker.

"Hope? You still there?"

"Hmm, yeah. Hmm, I'm sorry. That sounds good. I'll wait for you here at the station."

"Great. I'll pick you up at twelve."

Hope returned the receiver. She held her hand on it, disappointed about her lack of concentration. She was mad at herself. As a former Navy Intelligence Officer, she could not accept that failure without shame. She could have told Hinson that she couldn't go with him. Instead, she had felt the need to suck up to him. She wanted so bad to be on his good side that she had been willing to jeopardize her beginning relationship with Van Acker. She hoped that Van Acker would understand. Then again, if he didn't, she couldn't blame him. She felt low. She needed to let him know that there would be a change in plans. She picked up the receiver and dialed his cell number.

59.

Michelle Murphy was sitting in her car at the edge of the road, a few miles outside Stuttgart. She didn't know what to do. She knew that Susan Knox had been killed. How? That she didn't know. She had planned to kill Susan, but someone had beaten her to it. After leaving Susan's apartment, not having the guts to go in and confront her, and possibly kill her, she had returned to the apartment. She had parked her car a short distance from Susan's apartment and as she walked towards the apartment, she had seen a dark figure walk up to Susan's apartment. She had seen the light of a flashlight moving through the apartment. Then the figure had come out and walked away from the apartment. Michelle knew that nothing good had happened inside the apartment. She had waited hidden behind a tree thinking if she should go and check things out. If Susan had indeed been murdered, she would be able to sneak back out and feel a sense of satisfaction. If she hadn't been murdered, she would take care of it herself. She knew exactly what to do. However, as she carefully approached the apartment, looking around, making sure that no one was around to see her, she had nearly been killed herself. When the gas in the apartment ignited, she had been a mere 30 feet from the building. A piece of timber had nearly hit her in the head as the force of the explosion pushed her down. The timber had landed just a foot away from her. With difficulty she had managed to scramble to her feet and make her get-away. She did by no means want to be discovered. She had never looked back as she drove away from the scene. She needed to get rid of the items she had brought with her to do what someone else had beaten her to. She drove towards the river and down to the boat ramp, crushing everything with the tires of her car before throwing everything in the river. Finally, tired and sore from being thrown to the ground by the force of the explosion, she had returned to Stuttgart and found refuge at Patricia's.

Now, sitting in her car, thinking back to the events that had taken place that Saturday night, she felt a cold shiver run down her spine. It seemed that all fingers pointed in her directions. She wondered if her father would tell anyone about what he had found on the Internet. She had been so careful not to leave any tracks. Still,

271

she had forgotten that the last 20 website addresses were displayed in the website history file. She wondered who would have thought about the same thing she had. Making the apartment explode was a brilliant way to get rid of Susan. Still, the plan had been flawed from the start. Her father was brilliant when it came to investigating the source of a fire. By now, she knew that he had figured out how the explosion came about and where the fire started. The only question Michelle still had was something her father had said. She didn't think much of it at first. He had not been interested in whether or not she might have killed Susan before preparing for the explosion. He had been interested in the way the explosion had been set up. He kept coming back to it as if he wanted to make sure about the way she would have done it. Maybe that's where the other person made the mistake. Whoever killed Susan must not have followed the procedure that she had described to her father. Maybe, just maybe that might be enough to get her out of trouble. The only question still out there was whether Susan had been killed first. She would need to find out. She looked at the two vials lying in the seat next to her. She would have to be careful not to be discovered with them. She needed to hide them. She opened the glove compartment and put the two vials inside. She sat back straight.

She felt her stomach contract as she looked out the window of her car. Parked in front of her was Dimitri Van Acker's car. She could not see Van Acker in it and when she turned her face to the side, she came face to face with him. He motioned for her to roll down the window.

"Hi sweetie, are you okay?" he asked.

Michelle who was caught of guard did not know what to say at first. She felt her face starting to turn red.

"I'm doing fine. I just pulled over for a couple of minutes to think about something."

"Anything I can help you with?"

"I don't know. So much has happened since you came back. It's hard to believe that all this is just a coincidence. I mean, you coming back, Susan getting killed, me finding out that I may have HIV. God, it's almost too much to handle!"

Van Acker looked at her with questioning eyes. She had mentioned Susan getting killed. How would she know that Susan had been killed?

"Did you say: Susan getting killed?"

Michelle realized her blunder as soon as she said it. She had hoped Van Acker wouldn't have caught it, but what did she expect. He was after all a lawyer, trained to pick up the slightest slip of the lip. She did some quick thinking.

"Yeah, I talked with Daddy last night. He thinks that Susan didn't die because of the fire, but that she was killed before the explosion went off."

"Why did your father talk to you about the explosion and Susan possibly having been killed?"

Michelle sensed that Van Acker did not know about the Internet situation. She was glad that Kelly had not told him. That would leave her in the clear, at least for now, from being questioned by Van Acker about it. On the other hand, she did want him on her side. It would be helpful to have a lawyer knowing her side of the story. He did not have to know about her being at the scene when the explosion happened.

"I'd rather not talk here. How about we go to Langston's and talk over there?"

Van Acker looked at her with great curiosity. What did she know? In his mind, Michelle was a suspect in Susan's murder. He agreed to go to Langston's with her. Since Hope had canceled their lunch-on, he was looking forward to some company.

"How about I call Kelly and have her join us? She is working for me now and I want her to be as informed as possible about this case. I know that she is emotionally involved since it is you, but she will have to learn to put emotions aside when it comes to the law. Besides, I want to buy both your lunches."

Michelle nodded her head agreeing with Van Acker. She liked that she would not have to talk to Van Acker by herself. She never had formed the same bond with him that her sister had. She didn't feel comfortable around him. Maybe it was the age difference.

"I'll call Kelly and tell her to meet us at Langston's. I'll see you there."

Van Acker walked back to his car and drove off, Michelle close behind.

273

60.

Julie Sutton had returned home after her visit to the funeral home. The depression she had fallen into after her meeting with Lester started getting worse. She didn't understand why all these things were happening to her. On top of losing her sister and being raped, she had lost a good friend. Joshua Underwood had been a friend of hers. She had visited him on many occasions. She loved talking with him. He was intelligent and witty. Now, that too was lost. Julie buried herself in the couch and silently cried. The crying did not relieve the pain she felt. She looked at the clock; nearly noon. Her normal routine of doing household chores and making sure that she watched her religious shows on TV had been broken. Here chores were falling behind and she felt the same way. She could not get her body in gear to take on the day.

A little energy flowed her way when her eyes fell on the letter that Susan had written her. She felt cold thinking about Susan and what the letter was about. She needed to make a decision on the matter. Would she continue her sister's crusade against the wrong-doings of their father? Would it make a difference now? It had been a long time ago. So much had happened since then. So much had happened because of the sexual abuse. Never did she think about the effects that her father's actions might have had in their lives. But after all, they had enormous effects. It was as if you were running blindfolded through the woods. After much stumbling and getting back up, eventually you'll run into a tree or worse, reach a cliff at the edge of the woods. Susan had reached her edge of that cliff. Along the way she had managed to drag several people with her. She had managed to take of their blindfolds while keeping hers on. Only the others had not helped her take her blindfold off; instead, one of them had pushed her over the edge of the cliff. Julie could think of no better way to describe the events of the last 20 years. She was glad in a way that her blindfold had been lifted. Now she could see the light. She knew where to step to avoid falling or run into the trees. Now, she knew when to stop and not take that final step over the edge of the cliff. She made up her mind that she would not be ignorant of this. Something needed to be done about what had happened. She needed to go through with what her sister had started.

If not for her own sake, then those thousands of little girls and boys who were in the same danger as she and Susan had been 20 years ago. It needed to be made public. Her coming forward and bringing out the accusations against her father could save someone else's life. If she saved only one, then her efforts would have been worth it.

Julie, feeling her strength come back after her deliberation, went upstairs and changed her outfit. She put on something a little cooler. Ten minutes later, she returned downstairs in a pair of shorts and a t-shirt. She grabbed Susan's letter and walked out the door. She had no idea how to get in touch with Dimitri Van Acker. As she got in her car, she tried to remember who he would be staying with. She had been a good many years older than him when he lived here before and didn't pay that much attention to him. The only thing she could remember was that he hung around Allen Murphy a lot. She decided to take her chances at the Murphy farm. Maybe he could point her in the right direction.

After a short ride, Julie arrived at the Murphy farm. She parked near the farmhouse. She walked up the porch and knocked on the front door. There was no answer. She looked around to see if anyone was moving about the farm. She could not see anything. She walked back to her car, disappointed that her little trip had not paid off. As she was about to get in her car, she saw a truck pull up into the yard. It pulled up next to her. Allen Murphy rolled down the window.

"Hi Mrs. Sutton, anything I can help you with?"

Julie was a little nervous and rubbed her hands back and forth over her hips, trying to get rid of the moist feeling on her hands.

"Hi Allen, I'm looking for Dimitri. Do you know where I can find him?"

Murphy scratched his head and thought for a moment.

"Well, I haven't seen him this morning. I suspect that he's up and about trying to get settled in around here. He's staying with my oldest daughter Kelly. You might be able to find him over there. If not, I think since it's about lunchtime, he might be over at Langston's. If I were you, I'd check there first."

"Okay, I'll try that. Thank you."

"Sure thing"

Julie turned around and opened the door to her car. Murphy

looked Julie over as she turned around to get in her car. He wondered if the rumors were true. Why would Tom Sutton fool around if he had a beautiful wife like that?

"Miss Sutton, uh, I'm sorry about what happened to your sister. If there's anything I can do the help, in any way, please don't hesitate to get in touch with me or my wife for that matter. I know that Helen just quit working for your husband, but I'm sure that she can look past her personal problems with him to help you out, should you need the help."

"Thank you, Allen, and please, call me Julie," she said, giving him a warm smile.

"Okay, I'll do that."

Julie got in her car and drove off.

61.

Sarah Jackson was busy in her kitchen cleaning up from lunch. Sarah was a stay-at-home mother whose husband worked two jobs to support his family and to be able to let Sarah take care of their three children. At 33, she had kept her youthful appearance that had attracted her husband to her. Her reddish blond hair hung in waves down to her shoulders. She had soft green eyes that seemed to be sparkling all the time. A pair of naturally bright pink lips that lined her pouty mouth accentuated her fair skin. Even though she had given birth to three children, she had retained her slender figure. Sarah enjoyed staying at home, especially now that it was summer vacation for the children. She enjoyed hearing their laughter in the house and outside in the yard. Her youngest child was only 10 months old and could not yet frolic with the others. Her son Robbie was 10 and her daughter Katie had just turned 6.

With her husband Gary, they had bought a little farmhouse after Katie was born. It needed a lot of work. For three years, Gary had worked every day to make it into the dream home that they wanted. The walls and ceilings received new sheetrock while the floors had been done in hardwood. A new modern kitchen with a view of the backyard had been installed. The three bedrooms had not been enough when Sarah got pregnant with their third child. But with a little convincing, they had managed to get Robbie and Katie to bunk together till the new baby would be old enough to share a room with one of them. Katie had hoped for a sister, while Robbie wished hard for a brother. Katie had won. Caroline was the apple of her eyes. Even though Katie admired her brother and thought that he could do anything, she lost some of her admiration for him when Caroline was born. Now, she spent more time with Caroline than she did with Robbie. Robbie at first had felt a certain loss, but he had turned his attention to the new video game system he had gotten from Santa Claus. It was for both him and Katie, but Robbie got the most pleasure from it. Katie really was too young to enjoy the games.

That afternoon, however, Robbie and Katie had decided to go venture out in the backyard together. Gary and Sarah had explained to them that they could go no further than the edge of the pasture. The backyard was a pasture occupied by two goats. The goats kept the grass short and it made and excellent play area for the kids. Robbie had convinced Katie to go with him beyond the boundary of the pasture; and they had walked to the edge of the woods. Chicken wire with barbed wire on the top edge of it nailed to trees marked the boundary of their playground. Robby, however, had found a tree that was easily climbable. In no time, he was over the wire fence. He helped Katie scale the fence and the two of them headed into the woods. Robbie made sure that he marked the way they had come. He pulled out his hunting knife and carved markings in the trees. Katie stuck close to Robbie, as she was not too sure about their adventure. A couple of times, she had insisted that they return to the boundaries of the pasture. Robbie had told her that if she wanted to be as brave as he was that she needed to stick with him. So she did.

Robbie felt like an explorer venturing out into the unknown. He was having a good time leaving his markings on the trees and looking at different insects. Katie, who had been following close, finally felt a little bit more comfortable and looked around herself. She looked at the trees and plants, found a butterfly and tried to catch it. Unfortunately for Katie, it flew off. Katie chased after it. It landed on a flower a few feet away. Quietly, Katie sneaked closer to the butterfly. She was within a foot from it. She sat down on one knee, extended her arm and tried to catch the butterfly. Again, it took off. Katie's face turned into disappointment. She got up and chased after the butterfly. Once again, it landed on a flower. Katie made another attempt at her prey. Again, she was unsuccessful. She had forgotten that she needed to stay with Robbie. As her pursuit for the butterfly continued, she came upon a clearing in the woods. As she reached the clearing, she realized that Robbie was no longer with her. She turned around to see if she could see her brother. There was no sign of him. Frightened, she looked around the clearing. The grass was tall and she could not see above it. She called out to her brother.

"Robbie? Robbie? Where are you? Help me, Robbie!"

Robbie had wandered off in the opposite direction of his sister. He had seen a deer move in the distance and ventured out after it. He forgot to leave markings as he was too intense on following the deer. The deer had positioned itself on a little hill and was searching its surroundings for anything threatening. Robbie sat

278

behind a tree and spied on the deer, amazed by its size and beauty. He placed an imaginary riffle to his shoulder and took aim. Just as he was about the squeeze the trigger, he heard the cries of his sister. The deer heard it too and took off. Robbie tried to listen where the cries were coming from. He wasn't certain. He closed his eyes and listened. Again, he heard his name called out. This time he could clearly distinguish the location of the screams. He started running. Over his heavy breathing, he could hear Katie's cries; they became louder. Even though tears of fear were running down his cheeks, he felt a joyous feeling. He would find his sister. Again, a cry reached his ears. Louder still! He was on the right path. He would find her soon. In the distance, he could see the light shining brighter. He was reaching the edge of the woods! He stopped, confused. Where was Katie? He knew for sure the cries had come from this direction. Hadn't they grown louder and louder as he ran towards them? Robbie felt his tears welling up in he yes. He needed to be strong, but could not find the strength to do so. Katie was not here. She was nowhere in sight. What had he done? He had taken her into the woods and forgotten to look after her. Now, she was missing! Robbie's face lit up as he heard Katie's cry. He was on the right track! The sound came from where had seen the light shine brighter. She must be out of the woods!

Katie didn't know what to think. She had been calling out Robbie's name for some time now. He had not responded. Was he lost too? She sat down on a tree stump and started sobbing. She was lost! No one would find her! She would be left here alone! What would mommy do? She would be so sad.

"I'm sorry, mommy. I didn't mean to get lost. I'm sorry. I love you, mommy."

Katie looked around, wiping tears from her eyes. Maybe she could find a way out and ask for help. If only she could make it to the highway. She knew the main highway was a good ways away from their home. They had to run onto a dirt road to get to their home. Maybe if she reached the highway, a trucker or maybe a policeman would stop and take her home. She got up. Maybe she should try to call out for her brother one last time. Maybe this time he would hear. If not, she would start walking in the direction that she thought would lead her to the highway.

"Robbie? Where are you? Robbie?"

She listened. Nothing! Tears started rolling down her cheeks. Her shoulders low and her chin on her chest, Katie started walking in the direction of where she had seen a patch cleared out. She was only 10 feet along when she heard it.

Robbie came running out of the woods into the clearing. He was taller than the grass and could barely see his sister in the tall grass.

"Katie! Katie! Over here!"

Katie turned around as soon as she hard her name called out. She could barely see where she was going, but she was running as hard as she could in the direction she had come from.

"Robbie, over here!" she yelled as loud as she could.

Robbie shouted her name some more and guided her towards his voice. The two of them collided when they finally reached each other. They gave each other a long hug and Robbie planted a kiss on his sister's forehead.

"We need to get back home," Robbie said.

Katie took hold of his hand and shook her head.

Robbie looked around. As he could look above the tall grass, he wanted to see where this clearing lead to. At the far corner away from them, he could see a path. What was more surprising to him was that he thought he could see the top of a car. To Katie's surprise, Robbie changed directions and headed in the direction she had been walking in before he found her.

"Robbie, where are we going?"

"I thought I saw a car over there where that path is. I wonder why nobody was trying to come to you when you were calling my name."

Katie felt a little frightened knowing that she might not have been the only one out there. She squeezed Robbie's hand a little tighter.

It wasn't long before brother and sister where at the place where the car was parked. It was a black Oldsmobile Toronado. Robbie let go of his sister's hand. Slowly he approached the car. He motioned for Katie to stay where she was. Katie did not have to be told twice. She was scared to death. Robbie reached the driver's side door. He looked in the window. Robbie's face instantly lost all color. He fell backwards and scrambled to get away from the car.

"Katie, run! We gotta run! Hurry!"

As lost as he thought they were, Robbie had no trouble finding the way home. His markings were meaningless. He could not have kept up with them. Robbie was running as hard as he could, Katie crying and screaming for him to slow down. She was a good 20 yards behind him. Robbie reached the fence of the pasture. He didn't want to climb over it. He ran alongside the fence. He knew that eventually he would be able to run the corner and head home. When he finally reached the corner, Sarah Jackson heard her children's screams. She headed out the backdoor, the baby in her arms.

Robbie reached his mother first, out of breath. Katie dragged herself towards them, exhausted, her face dirty from falling down and crying.

"Robbie, what's wrong? Where were you?"

Robbie looked his mother in the eyes. He knew what he had done had been wrong. He knew he would never leave the yard again. He hated to tell his mother. But first, he needed to tell her about the car and what he'd seen.

"Mommy,... black car,... horrible,... blood everywhere... dead man."

Sarah didn't wait for the rest of the story. She ran into the house and called the Sheriff's Department.

62.

Hope Olson was not in a good mood when Andrew Hinson came by to pick her up. She had her hopes set on enjoying lunch with an Acker. She was angry with herself for giving in to her feelings for him. Was it that she was afraid? She didn't want to be caught in the middle between her investigation into the Knox fire and Van Acker. Yet, the warning Sheriff Hinson had given her back at the funeral home put her in that middle position. If she was seen around town lunching with Van Acker, she was sure that word would reach Hinson faster than anyone could imagine.

So now, she was on her way to Pinegrove. She felt a bit uncomfortable riding with Hinson. She had never felt this way before, but off late, it seemed he was paying her more attention than usual. Was it because of the investigation, or was it because she paying Van Acker all the attention? She didn't know. She sat straight in her seat, looking out the side window. She watched the grass and trees go by, her mind far away from work and a murder investigation.

Hinson noticed that Hope had her mind somewhere else besides being with him in the car. He had an idea what Hope was thinking about. His warning had been stern. He meant what he had said to both her and Van Acker. He didn't trust that fellow. What was he up to? Why would anyone who was remotely successful as a lawyer in Washington, DC come to live in a godforsaken place like Stuttgart? No! There had to be something else there. He needed to find out. Suddenly a smile appeared on his face. What was he? A dummy? He could kick himself in the butt. Of course! He had been mad that Van Acker had been part of the discovery of Joshua Underwood's murder. He did not like him snooping around. It was *his* county. *He* was in control. Nobody came just waltzing in here to take over. He needed to find out information on Van Acker. What better way to do so than to pry information out of Hope? Why keep her away from him? The closer she got to him the more information she might be willing to share with her co-workers. It was a brilliant idea. He just needed to find a way to reverse his decision and present it to Hope to where she would not become suspicious of his intentions.

Hinson glanced over towards Hope. She looked somber, staring out of the window. He coughed to draw her attention. She did not respond. Again, he coughed. Nothing! Not even a wink of the eyes. He called out her name.

"Hope?"

Wearily she turned her head in his direction.

"Sir?"

"Hope, I can't help but notice that you seem to be upset about something. It's not like you to sit there and stare out the window like that. I asked you to come along because you usually keep me entertained and amused. What's wrong?"

Hope looked at Hinson with questioning eyes. Was he sincere or was he playing with her emotions?

"Nothing much, just some personal problems."

"It wouldn't have anything to do with Mr. Van Acker, would it?"

Hope's eyes fixed on Hinson. Sparks shot up from deep inside and flashed at him. She didn't say anything. She just shook her head in disbelieve. The nerve this man had.

Hinson knew that he had hit a nerve. He needed to approach this topic carefully.

"Look, it's not that I don't like him. I just don't want any of my deputies getting mixed up in something that could hurt the department directly or indirectly. I don't know Van Acker. I'd never met him until yesterday. Naturally I have my reservations about him. You cannot blame me for that. I have the welfare of my deputies and the citizens of the county to worry about. I'm obviously going to worry when one of my deputies starts dating, if I may call it that, a stranger who has potential skeletons in his closet."

Hope closed her eyes and took a deep breath.

"Andy, I respect you a lot. I look up to you and I've learned a lot from you. One thing I want to make clear: don't mess with my personal life. I've been committed to the department for a long time. Never, not even once, have I jeopardized the department or the people I work with. I don't intend to start now. If there's one thing that I've learned in the Navy, it is that the crew comes first and nobody gets left behind. I may not have been on the front line like some of my friends, but I was there when they were brought back.

My personal life stays at home; I don't bring it to work. I have never brought it to work and I don't intend to start. I care for Dimitri. I've known him a long time. He is loyal, trusting and on our side of the law. He is not a criminal. As to your doubts about why he has returned to Stuttgart after all these years, as to why a successful lawyer from Washington, DC wants to settle in small-town USA; it's because he is honest and just. He could no longer accept his role in the big world of crime and injustice, where the big crooks get off and the little innocent people get punished. Anyone with a conscience would not fill those shoes for long. He is moving back down here to get some peace of mind, to be able to serve the citizens that you are so worried about protecting. He wants to protect them too. He wants to protect them from the people that can get away with crime. We're not the only one's that can protect them. People like Sutton and Dimitri can protect them too, although, I believe that Dimitri can do a far better job than Sutton."

Hope stopped her monologue to catch her breath. She had gotten worked up and her face had turned a light color of scarlet. Hinson admired her passion for this man. He had hoped that she would come to his defense. It had been more than he had expected. She felt passionate about this guy. He had her right where he wanted her.

"You know, Hope, I think I might have overreacted a bit. I want to apologize. If I offended you in any way, I hope you can forgive me. It seems that I might have misjudged Dimitri. It's just that my first encounter with him was at a crime scene. I cannot help being suspicious when a lawyer is present on a fresh crime scene. I will trust your judgment on him. I know I cannot tell you not to socialize with him. However, I don't want you to share information with him on the Knox case. From what I've heard through the grapevine, Van Acker is the power of attorney for Julie's estate. I want him to stay clear of our investigation. I know that he will be conducting his own. Let him do his own dirty work. When the time is ripe, we can work with him. Right now, I don't want him to get any information."

Hope looked at Hinson.

"Like I said before, sir, I will not compromise my department or my crew in any way. I do appreciate you realizing that you cannot stop me from seeing Dimitri. As far as the case is concerned, I do not plan on sharing information with him, no matter what state of mind I'm in."

"Good," Hinson said, looking over at her smiling, "I'm glad we got the tension out of the way."

Hope looked over at Hinson and just smiled. She had a feeling that he wasn't as sincere as he wanted her to believe he was. Still, she could not understand where the feeling had come from. She should trust her superiors. She hoped that time would tell.

Both Hinson and Hope were torn out of their individual thoughts about Van Acker when the Emergency Alert Signal on the onboard radio activated. Someone at the Sheriff's station had activated it. Hinson grabbed the speaker and responded to the signal. Both heard the message. Another dead person had been discovered. Hinson looked behind him in the rearview mirror, saw nothing was behind him and turned his patrol car 180 degrees from the direction they were going. The meeting in Pinegrove would have to wait. He turned his warning lights on and sped up the car in the direction he had been given by the dispatcher.

63.

Michelle Murphy felt uneasy sitting across the table from Dimitri Van Acker. She wasn't sure anymore whether to confide in him or not. Having her sister, Kelly, present did not ease that feeling. She needed to convince the both of them that though she had been at Susan's apartment at the time of the explosion, she had nothing to do with it. With the evidence that could be connected to her, all fingers would be pointing in her direction. Did she have a choice? Could she take the chance and hope the investigation would not take a turn in her direction? Even if she told Van Acker, she knew that he could not prevent the authorities from arresting her. The only thing he could do then was to represent her and hope he could convince the jury to get her off; create reasonable doubt. She hoped it wouldn't have to come to that. She looked down at her plate. The food smelled delicious and Van Acker and Kelly were almost finished. She had only taken a few bites. She was not hungry. She had too much on her mind to be thinking about her stomach.

Dimitri Van Acker noticed the absent look on Michelle's face. He knew that she was debating if she would confide in Kelly and him. Was it about what had happened to Susan Knox? He hated to think that Michelle had anything to do with Susan's murder but his instincts told him that she had either done it or knew who had done it. Even though her personality was that of someone who was drawn to herself, she seemed a little too much drawn in. Something was eating on her. The stress lines on her forehead didn't lie either. Whatever was bothering Michelle, was serious. He hoped that he would be able to help her open up and confide in him. He looked over at Kelly. She was finishing her lunch. She had a worried look on her face also. Unlike her sister, she would result to eating in times of stress. He was dealing with a potentially explosive situation. Even though he had hired Kelly to work for him and she promised him to be professional, he couldn't overlook the fact she was Michelle's sister. She would be emotionally affected by whatever Michelle confessed or confided in them about. He would have preferred to talk to Michelle one-on-one, but he feared that he would not accomplish anything taking that route. So, he had to take the risk of having his only employee emotionally involved in what he feared was going to be his first defense case.

If Michelle was guilty of Susan's murder, he felt that it was his duty to see to it that she would get the least possible sentence. Surely, she could not have premeditated the murder. There just hadn't been enough time between her receiving the phone call from Bryan Scarboro and the explosion at Knox' apartment. She was bright though. She was smart, excelled in math and physics. It would not have been too difficult for someone with her smarts to have figured out a close to undetectable murder and how to cover it up. The one thing he wondered was whoever had committed the murder was not smart enough to open only one burner on the gas furnace. All four had been turned to the open position, a careless action of a desperate person who wanted to make sure the apartment would blow up. He took a deep breath. Michelle could be the killer! There was one event that gave him doubt though: the murder of Joshua Underwood. It was his believe that Susan's and Underwood's murderer where one and the same person. He did not buy the burglary story the Sheriff's department was using as an explanation. Underwood was smart too and Van Acker knew he had found something on Susan Knox' body that would prove she'd been murdered prior to the explosion. Why else would he have tried to get in touch with him? Where had Michelle been when Underwood was murdered? She had been at Kelly's and at home. He needed to find out the time when she was at Kelly's and when she had been at home. He needed to ask Helen. Still, he could not believe that Michelle would commit two murders in two days. If she had, the first one was surely not meditated. The second one could not have been either. An emotional reaction to seeing Underwood's truck in the parking lot of the funeral home? No! Not Michelle!

If she was not guilty of Susan's murder, then there was nothing to worry about. But she would have to be able to present a good alibi about her whereabouts at the time before the explosion. Thus far, no such alibi had been presented. Impossible to put up a good defense starting with the information he had. He needed to get all the information out of her that he could get. It might mean the difference between life or death for Michelle. She surely would get the death penalty in this county. Majority conservative and the victim the daughter of a well-known, respected citizen. No he needed to have all the facts. But, he was getting ahead of himself. He needed to talk to Michelle first and see what her story was; then and only then could he start worrying about what the future for her would bring.

He looked over at Michelle. She was still playing with her food, taking little bites, but mainly just swirling her fork through her food. Her eyes where fixated on her plate. Van Acker broke the silence.

"So, Michelle, what's on your mind?"

Michelle looked up at him, then turned her head towards Kelly and then looked back down at her plate.

"I don't know."

She looked back up at Van Acker, looking him straight in the eyes.

"I just don't know."

Michelle looked around the restaurant. They were the only one's left from the lunch crowd. Pam Langston glanced in their direction every so often. It was curiosity more than anything since Van Acker had told her that they might be a while and that they needed some privacy. She had an idea of what was going on, especially after talking to Patricia about Michelle's mysterious appearance the night of the explosion. But, she kept to herself and stayed busy in the kitchen, preparing for the evening crowd.

"Look, Michelle, if you're afraid that you cannot trust me, please think again. Your family has helped me a lot over the past decade. Without them, I would not be what I am today. No matter what you tell me will be confidential. If you need a lawyer, then please, let me represent you. If not, then let me just be a listening ear. Trust me!"

Michelle looked at him, tears welling up in her eyes. She fought them back. She took a drink from her iced-tea.

"Okay, I guess you're right. Let me just make it clear that I did not do anything illegal."

"All right, so you did not kill Susan Knox. Why the worry then?"

Michelle felt her stomach contract as she began to tell the story. Sweat starting popping up on her forehead and her back and chest started to itch as her sweat glands produced anxiety sweat.

"I was going to kill her."

A look from Van Acker in Kelly's direction told him that this did not come as a surprise to her. She just turned her eyes down to the table as if praying to God that someone had beaten Michelle to it.

"But you didn't," he spurred Michelle on.

"No! Someone beat me to it. I was sitting in my car outside Susan's apartment trying to build up courage to go in and take care of the bitch. But I was too chicken. I could not bring up the courage to go inside her apartment and kill her."

Michelle started to cry as she recalled the events of that night.

"I left. I drove off and parked my car in a dark spot a little ways up the road from the apartment. I did some more thinking and the more I thought the clearer it became that I could do it and that I had to do it to prevent her from spreading anymore of her disease. I had to be able to justify doing it. Keeping her from spreading any more AIDS seemed a good justification in my mind. So, I headed back towards the apartment. When I got close, I saw someone moving around in the apartment with a flashlight. I hid behind a tree and watched. Then the person left. I was scared and stayed hidden behind the tree. I knew that whoever was in the apartment did what I was planning on doing. I just knew. I don't know how long I stayed there hidden; making sure that no one would see me around the apartment. After a while I decided that I needed to make sure that what I thought that person had done really happened. So I started to sneak my way towards the apartment. I was about 30 feet from the apartment when the explosion happened. I was almost killed myself. A large piece of timber just barely missed hitting me in the head. So I scrambled up and ran as fast as I could to my car. I was barely in my car before people everywhere came out of their homes to look at the disaster. I just drove and drove, as far away from Stuttgart as I could. I was almost in Pinegrove when I realized that I needed to get rid of whatever it was I had brought to make her apartment explode. So, I drove to the river, crushed everything that could incriminate me and threw it in the river. Then I returned and went to Patricia's to spend the night. You have to believe that is what happened! I did not kill Susan Knox."

Van Acker rubbed his chin as he listened to her story. She

289

sure seemed sincere. Either she was a good actress or she was telling the truth.

"Let me ask you something," he said softly, looking her in the eyes and putting his hands on hers.

"How were you planning on killing her?"

Michelle took a deep breath and pulled her hands from underneath Van Acker's.

"You don't believe me, do you?" she said, offensively.

"No, I believe you. But I've got to have more details. The authorities will not believe you. It sounds too perfect to blame someone else when you're right there at the scene with the tools to commit the crime. Could you describe the person that you saw?"

"It was dark. All I saw what a person dressed in black. There was some sort of pouch hanging from his belly. I guess like on of those carryalls where you can put your billfold or camera in."

"Did you say *his* belly?"

"I guess I did."

"So you think it was a man that you saw?"

Michelle thought for a moment.

"I couldn't tell for sure."

"Think hard Michelle. It's important that you try to distinguish between a man and a woman. Even though you are still going to be a suspect in the murder, you are my only witness. You are the only one that could place another person at the scene of the crime. If you try to remember what the posture of the person was, then we can try to find a match. Otherwise, you will be laughed right out of court."

Michelle breathed hard. She had watched the person long of time. She should be able to tell more about him, or her. She thought hard for a second.

"Well, I remember that the person was not tall. I can't tell for sure, but there is a tree close to the apartment that has a low limb on it. The person was, from where I was standing, about a foot shorter than the limb."

Dimitri nodded his head and urged her to continue.

"Let see. The person was athletic."

"Athletic, in what sense?"

"Well, when he left, or she left, the movement was very

290

smooth. Like someone who is used to running."

Van Acker smiled. He knew that when pressed, most witnesses could remember more about what they saw then they thought they did. It was just a matter of making the brain bring out the details.

"Well, that helps some, Michelle. We're looking for an average height, athletic person. I believe that rules out some of the suspects I had in mind. Now, back to my original question; how did you intend on killing Susan?"

"I had planned on suffocating her with a pillow. I know that I'm stronger than she is. I could have easily held her down until all the oxygen was gone from her body. It wouldn't have been too hard. Then I would have turned one of the gas furnace knobs to the "on" position. I had a cheap timer with me that would create enough spark to ignite the gas. The fire spreading through the apartment would destroy any evidence of the strangulation. No sign of fibers from the pillow around the face to be detected. In other words, the perfect crime."

Dimitri shuddered at the description Michelle had given them. It was exactly as he had imagined what had happened that night. Except, all knobs had been turned on, not just one. He needed to believe that Michelle was telling the truth, as hard as it was. Her descriptions were too on the money to be coincidental. As smart as she was, she could have changed her story about the knobs to throw him off.

Kelly who had been silent during the entire conversation decided to add a little drama to the event.

"Why don't you tell him about the web site," she said nonchalantly.

"What web site?" Van Acker asked, looking from one sister to the other.

Michelle looked at Kelly with hurt eyes. She had not wanted to go into that. Now, she had no other choice.

"I accessed a web site name "PERFECTCRIMES.COM". On it, I found the way I planned on killing Susan Knox."

"My God!" was all Van Acker could say.

All that he had hoped for to save Michelle had been blown clear out of the water. Not only was she at the site of the crime, she had also left behind evidence that she researched the crime. His crime of passion defense had just taken an abrupt turn towards premeditation.

Michelle looked at Van Acker's expression. She knew that it didn't look good for her. An experienced criminal defense lawyer as Van Acker was, showing the expression he had just given, meant that not much could be done to convince the jury of reasonable doubt. She swallowed hard as she though of the possibility of receiving the dead penalty. She realized that she needed to find out who had killed Susan to keep herself from being killed. Could she find out on her own? She didn't know. She was sure that Van Acker would start an investigation himself. She did not want to rely solely on him. She needed to investigate on her own.

64.

Julie Sutton arrived at Langston's a few minutes after Dimitri Van Acker and the Murphy sisters had received their lunch. She had seated herself as far away from the threesome as possible. She did not want to give the impression that she was eavesdropping. They seemed to be involved in a serious conversation. She could tell from looking at them that the mood at the table was tense. She wondered what the conversation was about. With Van Acker having just returned from Washington, DC, she would have thought the reunion would have been a happy one, not a tense one. Unless of course Van Acker's return wasn't as happy as one might have thought. Who knew what had happened between him and one of the sisters. Julie cursed herself for judging. She said a quick prayer, asking for forgiveness for her judgmental mind. So much had happened the last couple of days that she had allowed herself to slip away from her Christian habits and believes. The trip to Larry's Lounge had proven to be a disaster. She still could not figure out why on earth she would have gone out to a place like that. What was she trying to prove? All it got her was a horrible experience that no doubt would haunt her for the rest of her life. Would she ever be able to trust another man? She thought about that question. Since she had been a little girl, men had manipulated her life. Her father had molested her, her husband had cheated on her, and the one man she though would be a listening ear for her problems had raped her. She quietly shook her head. How could so much unhappiness and disaster happen to a God-fearing Christian woman? What was it she needed to do to find happiness? Was God just testing her, as he had tested Job? Would she like Job, be strong enough to withstand the tests and not lose her faith? Those were all questions that she could not answer. The last few days she had felt like deserting God, abandon all her Christian believes and see if there was something else out there that would provide a little happiness in her life. Each times those thoughts had entered her mind; she had told herself the Devil would be all too happy to have her on his side. He had tried for 30 something years now to bring her down, to make her stray from the righteous path. He had succeeded with Susan. Susan had had all the fun. She had tried all the vices life held: drugs, alcohol and sex. They had all led to her destruction as well as destroying several other people in Dawson County. There was no telling how many people had contracted the HIV virus because of her actions. The Devil must have smiled and chuckled when he trapped Susan in his miserable web. And now, he had reached his final goal: Susan's death. Julie wondered if God was a just God would Susan be in Heaven or in Hell. She felt that Susan needed to be in Heaven. Sure she had committed sins against God and against many people; but was she the one to blame for what had happened. Not in her mind Susan wasn't. Her father ought to be the one who went to Hell and burn in it for eternity. Maybe, if God was just, her father would one day burn in Hell.

With her inner conflict brewing, she had not noticed that Pam Langston had approached her. When she saw a shadow come over the table, Julie's head shut up and she looked bewildered at Pam.

"Hi, Mrs. Sutton, are you alright?"

Julie straightened herself in her chair and nodded her head.

"Yes, thanks, I was just thinking about something. I'm sorry."

"Oh, please, don't apologize. You've been through a lot the last couple of days. I believe that you have a right to be distracted and upset."

"Thanks."

"Can I get you anything? I can fix you a nice plate."

"No thanks, Pam, all I want is a glass of tea."

"Are you sure?"

"Yeah, thanks."

Pam turned on her heels and disappeared behind the counter.

Julie looked at her in admiration. She knew Pam had struggled a great deal when her and her husband had first started their business. But now, she looked energetic and happy. Life was good for the Langston's, she could see that. Julie wished the same for her. She had never had to struggle to get anywhere. Everything she had, had always been there. Her college had been paid for; she had stayed out of the workforce after she married Tom, never having to work a day in her life. She wished it had been different. She wished she had been poor and had to work for what she had. Maybe then, everything might have turned out differently. She could only wonder. She would never find out.

Pam returned with Julie's tea. She sat down opposite of Julie. She crossed her hands in her lap and looked at the weary face in front of her.

"Mrs. Sutton, if you ever want to talk, woman to woman, please know that I love to listen. You can even call me at home. Okay?"

Julie felt her emotions bubbling up. Tears fought their way into her eyes. She could not remember anyone reaching out to her, offering her help, even if it was only to listen. She was touched by the gesture.

"Thank you, Pam; I will keep that in mind. And please, call me Julie."

"Okay, I will."

"Pam? How long do you think Mr. Van Acker is going to be tied down with the Murphy girls?"

"I don't know, Julie. He asked me that they not be disturbed. They seem to be talking some serious business. Legal stuff, you know." Pam winked at Julie.

"Gee, seems like he chose the right county to come to. I didn't know there were so many legal problems in Dawson County. I thought Tom had everything in check."

Pam looked at Julie with questioning eyes. Most everybody in the county knew by know that Julie had kicked Sutton out. She wondered if she was being sarcastic or not. She decided to try her luck.

"You know, Julie, a lot of people don't like your husband that much. I don't want to talk bad about anybody, but his reputation is not the best."

Julie's eyes looked as cold as ice. She ran her tongue over her lips, moistening them. Her nostrils flared a little as she prepared to respond to Pam's observation.

"You're right, Pam. If you had told me that a week ago, I would have been offended and furious with you. Now, I know the truth. As hard as it is to accept, and to admit, he's been cheating on me for a long time."

Julie leaned in a little closer to Pam. Pam in turn did the same. She knew something juicy was about to be revealed. She

295

enjoyed a little dirt now and then, especially when it came from the horse's mouth itself.

"Keep this to yourself, okay?"

Pam nodded affirmatively.

"He was cheating on me with my sister!"

"No!" Pam said, trying to look surprised.

She had known that fact for a long time now. One evening, late after coming back from a convention, she had returned to Stuttgart with a little too much to drink. She had taken it slow, making sure that she did not attract too much attention to herself. She had to pass by Susan's apartment to make it home. As she drove by, she looked over at the apartment. The lights were on and there had been a crack in the curtains. She had slowed down even more. She had always been the curious and nosy type and being a Peeping Tom excited her. She had seen Tom Sutton and Susan, both naked, in an embrace. So Julie telling her that Sutton was finding his kicks at Susan's didn't come as a surprise. Still, she acted as if it was.

Julie had gotten tears in her eyes telling Pam her horrible secret. She wanted to tell her more. Tell her about the AIDS and the possibility that she might also have it because of her husband and her sister. But that would have to wait for another day. She was here for a different reason. She needed to talk to Van Acker. Julie looked over towards his table. Everybody looked somber. They must have been discussing some serious problem for everyone to look so distressed. She turned her attention back to Pam.

"When he comes to pay for his meal, can you please ask him to come see me before he leaves? I need to discuss some legal problems with him myself. I just don't trust my husband with my legal problems."

Pam wasn't too chocked. She had a good idea why Julie needed legal help. She was sure that Julie was going to divorce Sutton. Good for her! She deserved better.

"I will," was all Pam said as she left the table and moved back behind the counter as Van Acker, Kelly and Michelle were getting ready to leave.

Kelly and Michelle went outside while Dimitri Van Acker settled the bill with Pam. Pam turned her eyes towards Julie, telling for him to take a look. He turned around, pretending to be looking at

296

the Murphy sisters. He saw the woman sitting at the table in the far corner of the restaurant. He turned his attention back to Pam.

"She wants to talk to you. Legal stuff!"

"Now?"

"I guess so. She asked me if I'd send you her way before you left."

Van Acker shook his head. Things were getting more and more interesting.

"Well, at least business seems to be picking up," Pam commented, giving him a little wicked smile.

"Yeah, faster than expected!"

Van Acker pocketed his change and walked over towards Julie Sutton's table.

"Mrs. Sutton?"

"Yes, Mr. Van Acker, please sit down."

"In just a minute ma'am, I need to let my two lady friends outside know that I will not be joining them right away. If you'll excuse me?"

"Sure, I'll be waiting right here."

Van Acker walked outside and explained the situation to Kelly and Michelle. Kelly told him that she needed to go to he Post Office and that she had some paperwork at home to complete. Van Acker knew exactly what she was talking about. Michelle gave him a long and tight hug. He was surprised by the sudden affection Michelle was showing him. She'd always been distant when it came to him. Well, maybe stressful situation made people realize who looked out for them and who didn't. Van Acker return inside the restaurant and walked over to Julie Sutton's table.

"Okay, Mrs. Sutton, how can I be of service to you?"

65.

When Hope Olson and Andrew Hinson arrived at the clearing in the woods where little Robbie Jackson had discovered the car and the body, other deputies had already made work of the area. Yellow caution tape was stretched between trees and fenceposts, marking the horrible scene. As they drove up and saw the car, Hinson immediately recognized the car. He felt his stomach contract and felt like he would need to throw up. As strong as he was, he could not handle the fact the body he was about to look at, probably distorted and carrying a sickening odor, was that of his good friend Gerald Radcliff. How was this possible? How could something like this happen? Was it murder; or suicide? Those questions raced through his mind as he opened the door of his patrol car.

Hope recognized the car as well. She was shocked but not surprised. She knew from her conversation with Van Acker that Radcliff had been a lover of Susan's. No doubt, she had told him about the AIDS virus. Another thought occurred to her: could Radcliff be Susan's killer? A murder-suicide was a likely possibility, especially with a person of his position. A cover up would not be too hard. It would never have to be revealed that he had killed Susan. She played for a second with the idea to tell Hinson about Radcliff's involvement with Susan Knox. Then again, she started to get some reservations about being able to trust Hinson. Sure he had told her he had overreacted as far as Van Acker was concerned; however, Hope instinctively felt there was another reason for the sudden change in attitude. She would keep her knowledge of Radcliff's involvement with Susan Knox to herself and make it a part of her investigation into Susan's murder. Besides, she did not want to jump to conclusions. It seemed too easy. Would Radcliff even be able to commit murder? She would definitely consider him as a suspect; yet, she would pursue other possibilities as well. She felt the contour of her breast pocket making sure the bracelet she had found was still there.

As she made her way to the black Toronado she noticed Hinson's face turn white as snow as he recognized the disfigured face of his friend. Tears started coming to his eyes as he leaned up against the car. Hope held her distance, not knowing what to do to

298

console her boss. She had never seen him this way. He had always seemed strong and unemotional to her. Yet, here he was, fighting back tears and trying to look professional. He was clearly in no state of mind to take control of the situation. The other officers on the scene stood around wondering what to do next. They had never been on a crime scene like this one before. They had no idea where to start. They looked at Hinson for guidance, but found none. Hinson was in shock and not able to give out orders or tell his officers how to continue. Hope decided to take control of the situation. She walked back to Hinson's patrol car and grabbed the evidence bag from the trunk. She spread it out on the hood of the car and sorted through the contents. She had a box of rubber gloves, sample bags, carbon dust, sticky tape, a couple brushes and a digital camera.

"Baker and Gonzales come over here," she ordered.

The two deputies walked over towards Hope looking at the articles on the hood of the car.

"Okay, Gonzales, you dust for fingerprints on both doors and as best as you can on the inside. Baker, we need to put the gun in an evidence bag, but please be careful not to smudge any fingerprints. Use a pencil or pen to pick it up with.

Both Baker and Gonzales looked at Olson with contempt in their eyes, but still, they put on rubber gloves, took the tools and went to work. They didn't like being bossed around by a female deputy of the same rank as they were, but still, they realized that she knew what she was doing.

Hope took the digital camera, two memory cards and walked over to Radcliff's car.

After taken pictures of the crime scene, both outside and as best she could inside the car, she removed the memory card from the camera, inserted a new card and repeated the process. One card was going the crime lab, with the gun and any possible fingerprints that were found. The second card was going to go home with her for her own use on her laptop computer. She decided to hold on to the gun for now, just in case Susan's autopsy revealed that she was shot before her apartment becoming an inferno. She was reasonably sure that Susan did not die of smoke inhalation and that she perished by other means.

As she collected all the evidence found in and around

Radcliff's car, she walked back to Hinson's patrol car slipping the second memory card in her shirt pocket. She hoped that Van Acker would be able to help her. Even though she knew what Hinson had told her about Van Acker's involvement in any of the department's continuing investigations, she wanted him to help.

David Johnson and the county coroner, Jason Crew had been contacted about the dead body. The dispatcher at the Sheriff's office had failed to tell them that it was a suicide. Jason Crew was the first on the seen. He'd seen plenty of dead bodies during his tenure as coroner, but he had to admit that this was one of the most nauseating scenes he'd been to. It was obvious that Gerald Radcliff was dead. He made a note on the paperwork he had brought with him. The victim was identified as Gerald Radcliff; cause of dead appeared to be suicide pending further investigation. Time of dead was impossible for him to tell, all he knew was the body had been exposed for at least a couple of days; his best guess being 2 days. Other than that, there wasn't much he could do to contribute. He walked over to Sheriff Hinson, shook his hand, told him his condolences, got in his truck and left.

David Johnson felt like the world when he arrived at the scene. He was in charge of the funeral home; actually, the funeral home was his. He was going to make the big money now. No more being underpaid for doing the dirty work. He hated to embalm bodies. Flushing a body was a clean procedure, but the smell and the risk involved were getting to him. He wouldn't have to put up with that much longer. He would hire someone, train them, and put them through funeral school, just as Joshua Underwood had done for him. Then he could sit back in the office and handle the public relations of the funeral home, just like Underwood had done. He would finally be able to afford those expensive suites, drive a better car and live in a nicer home. A smile covered his face as he drove up at the scene. He saw the somber faces of the deputies, even the Sheriff. That was a new one for Johnson. He had never seen the Sheriff somber about anybody's death; except for the death of his wife. Who was this fellow who had died? Johnson pulled up as close to the cars as he could. Deputies Baker and Gonzales guided him in backing up the hearse. Johnson got out and adjusted his pants. He could feel the heat of the afternoon coming down on his back and instantly sweat droplets were starting to form on his forehead. Sweat rings seemed to almost instantly appear on his clothing. His body just wasn't made for these hot Georgia summer days. He walked over to the black coupe, full of confidence; sure that this would be an easy pick up. Probably someone who had gotten off the road, feeling chest pains and died of a heart attack. As Johnson approached the car he sensed a foul odor coming from the car. With questioning eyes he looked at the deputies. As he came close enough to the car to witness the body behind the steering wheel, David Johnson felt his midriff contract and pulled to the side, leaning against the car, emptying his stomach. As hot as it was, suddenly his body had chill bumps running over it and he felt weak. The color had drained from his face and he looked pale. He finally composed himself as best he could and took another look at the body in the car. The back of the man's head was gone, dried blood, bone and brain matter covered the headrest, the rear passenger side window and part of the rear window. Where once the back of his head had been, there was only a big gaping black hole. Because of the heat, the body had swollen and the belly of the guy was pushed into the steering wheel. He looked over at the deputies.

"What the hell happened here? You expect me to take that with me?" he said, pointing at Radcliff.

"Well, let see," Baker started. He had never liked David Johnson. He looked at Johnson as a looser by nature who would never amount to anything.

He continued: "We got our dear mayor in here who decided to put an extra hole in his head; and yes, I expect you to take care of it!"

Johnson looked at Baker with hateful eyes. He knew the deputy didn't like him. Since they had been in school together, there had been friction between the two. Johnson didn't understand where it came from. He never knew how to react to the verbal and sometimes physical abuse that he'd received from Baker. Still to this day, he didn't know how to deal with it. He stood sheepishly, leaning against the car trying to find words to fire back at Baker, finding none.

"Well Johnson, what's it gonna be? You gonna get a move on or not?"

Johnson turned his look away and found the eyes of Hope Olson who was observing the situation. She felt he was trying to find support in his struggle against his foe. She didn't understand the history between the two; however, she felt that she needed to intervene. Not only was Baker acting unprofessionally and no becoming a deputy; there was a job to be done here. This was not the place or time to work out some age old feud.

"Gonzales, why don't you help David with the corps? Baker and I will go and talk with the Jackson's, okay?"

Gonzales didn't like the order, but he realized that it was the best for the situation. He didn't care for Baker either. He was always cracking Hispanic jokes at him even though his family had been in the States for over three generations now, legally. He nodded his head at Hope and got to work.

Hope and Baker got in Baker's patrol car and drove off towards the Jackson home. The air in the car was tense and nothing was said during the short ride over. Hope decided she'd have a word with Hinson after this ordeal was over. Baker was a bad apple and the bad spot either needed cutting out or the apple needed to be tosses altogether.

66.

Bryan Scarboro had worked at his father's practice before, however, with Susan Knox gone, he had to fill her position rather than work with his father in the examination rooms. He hated it. He did not like to sit still, greet people and do paperwork. Maybe it was better that he was tied down to the front end of the business as his mind was not focused on helping in medical examinations. He was bothered by the fact the 2 vials of Coeurnechol had vanished. He knew for sure he had put them on the desk when he walked in. He had searched high and low to find the medication, to no use. He was glad that he had been able to alter the information in the computer. Still he did not feel he had covered all his tracks. His father was a strange creature and possibly had other ways of keeping track of this information. The morning crowd had been slack. Now, early afternoon, the waiting room was empty. Two patients were listed on the appointment book. They were scheduled for 2:00 and 2:30. He had already finished all the paperwork that needed to be done for the day. It hadn't been easy, but with the help from other files, he was able to follow Susan's procedure and finish the paperwork as required. Susan had been so efficient at what she did; he was sure his dad would have a hard time replacing her.

As he sat waiting for the 2:00 patient to arrive, he wondered if anyone would be able to trace him back to Susan. Sure he had told Michelle; but would she tell on him? He didn't know. Could he take the chance? No! Michelle had to be dealt with. She knew too much. She could drop his name to the authorities. He wondered if they already knew how Susan had died. He hoped that they would never investigate any further than the fire. If they did, they could find evidence of his being at Susan's. That would make him a suspect. He hoped Susan hadn't kept a diary. If she did, then he knew his name would be in it. Would they investigate him if his name were discovered at Susan's or by other means? He hoped the fire had destroyed any paper evidence that was present in the apartment. He was not too worried about his name being discovered that way. Michelle was the one that could blow it for him. He needed to make sure that she didn't talk. He needed to scare her. He needed to scare her so bad that she wouldn't talk. A smile ran across his face as he thought about how he could scare her. Unconsciously, his mind flashed back to the encounter he'd had with her in the hotel room. She was so innocent, so ignorant in the matters of making love. It was hard to believe that at 19, she had still been a virgin. Scarboro felt his body react to his thoughts. He closed his eyes and enjoyed the pictures flashing through his head. She had been his first virgin, at least as far as he could remember. It had been wonderful…

Dr. Earl Scarboro, upon arrival in his office, had noticed that something wasn't right. The items on his desk were not in the same place that he had left them in on Friday night. He hated disorder. He hated even more that someone had been in his office. What would he do with his son? He was unorganized, and did not conform to the required discipline a doctor must follow. He had concerns. He planned to ask him if he had been in his office. His mind flashed to his keys. They had been in disarray yesterday morning. Could it be possible that his son had taken them anyways and had come to the office? He hated to think that his son had lied to him.

Dr. Scarboro had some time between his patients and was sitting at his deck in meditation. He thought about Susan. She had been such a lovely woman. She was sweet, attentive, smart… Why on earth had she gotten her life in such a mess? Her being the carrier of the HIV virus had been a chock to him. He had tried to help her, given her an experimental drug. It hadn't worked. Then she started having heart problems. The Coeurnechol had helped; still, Susan's days were numbered. Now, she was gone. Dr. Scarboro dropped his head in his hands and slowly swayed his head from side to side. She had been in need of a job so bad when she came back to Stuttgart. She did everything and anything in her power to make sure that she had a job and could support herself. He looked up and muttered the word out loud:

"Anything."

He looked at the dark spot growing on his arm. He had thought it to be skin cancer when it first appeared. He had not been too concerned about it. Then, it started spreading. At that point, he had it examined. The unfortunate news had been given to him on his anniversary. Somehow, he had been infected with the HIV virus. On his 24th anniversary, the news had been disturbing. How was he going to tell his wife? He knew the cause of the infection. He swore he would never reveal his condition to anyone, not even the person whom he contracted it from. How could he have been so stupid? One moment of losing his self-control had led to this.

Dr. Scarboro remembered the event as if it had happened only yesterday. It happened seven years earlier. Susan had come to him to get a job. The job interview had gone well; still he had his doubts about hiring her. He knew how she had been as a teenager. Always the rebel, not sticking to the laws and rules presented to her. He had told her that he would review his notes on her interview and get back in touch with her. Susan had looked disappointed. He guessed she thought she would be hired on the spot. He felt sorry for her. Young and inexperienced, she was not what he was looking for. And then it happened. When she crossed her legs, she parted them just a little too much for just a little too long. He couldn't help himself. His eyes followed her moving legs and what he saw made his body react. Susan had played him like a well tuned piano. Her not wearing panties had stirred his sexual desire. At the risk of being slapped with a sexual harassment suit, he proposed Susan. She had greedily accepted. There had been no emotion involved in their actions. They had gone into one of the examination rooms; she had lifted her dress and bent over the bed. He had dropped his pants and underwear and taken her. Susan had agreed to it to get the job; Dr. Scarboro had acted out of pure animal instinct. Less than 10 minutes later, Susan had walked out of his office, only to return the next day, dressed professionally, ready for the job. The ten minutes of lust, of primal need had caused him to catch one of the world's most fatal diseases. How stupid had he been!

He'd known about his situation for a little over 3 months now. He had not told anyone, yet. He needed to tell his wife about it. But how much did he tell. As a doctor, he could have contracted the disease through the blood of one of his patients. All it would take was a prick of an infected needle, bodily fluids coming in contact with a scrape or cut on his hands. Even though he did now, he had not always been in the habit of wearing surgical gloves when examining his patients. Should he tell her the whole story? Intimate relations were out of the question no matter what the story. Should he confess to his infidelity and make her even more devastated that she would already be? No! He would not tell her about his one time with Susan. He shook his head again. One time! That's all it took for the virus to take hold of his body.

He had not told Susan either. He had wanted to tell her. But he hadn't. She had come to him with her condition right before he had found out about his own misfortune. Susan had been in a more advanced state of the disease than he was. Susan had ignored her physical problems for a long time, hoping that she might get better. Finally, she had given in and asked for advice. Her heart condition was the major disease she had suffered because of the virus. The medicine he had prescribed had helped. She was able to control her heart rate with it. It was a dangerous medicine. Too much could easily make your heart slow down to barely anything and that would cause the major organs to start shutting down. An overdose would cause heart failure within 10 minutes, without the taker knowing that anything was happening. The reduced heart rate would send the patient into a coma and would cause the body to shut down within 5 minutes. That's why he kept the medicine in his secure cabinet and kept a tight inventory control on it. He felt sorry for Susan. As nice as she was, she needed not suffer like she had. At least now, she was no longer in pain. She had gone on to a better place. Not a place he would see, with the sins of the past and present hanging over him.

He was jolted from his mesmerizing when a knock on the door announced that it was time to go back to work.

67.

"So tell me Mrs. Sutton, how can I help you?"

Dimitri Van Acker looked at Julie Sutton. He saw a young woman who was carrying the burden of the world on her shoulders. Being in her early thirty's, she looked a whole lot older right now. She looked as if she had lost her youthfulness a long time ago. He wondered what the reason was; her husband? He could only guess at this point.

"Mr. Van Acker,"

"Please, call me Dimitri."

"All right, as long as you call me Julie."

"Sure."

"Dimitri, I have a letter here that my sister wrote probably a couple of days or even the day before she died. She mailed it to me registered mail."

Julie handed the letter over to Van Acker. He read over the letter and looked at Julie with questioning eyes. Julie's eyes were focused on a coffee stain on the table. She avoided looking him in the eyes.

"Do you mind clarifying this a little further, Julie?"

"Which part?"

"The part about your father doing the both of you great injustice."

Julie looked up at Van Acker now. Tears were starting to form in the corners of her eyes.

"God, where do I start?"

She swallowed hard and took a sip from her iced-tea that Pam had brought them.

"I guess when I was about 12 years old and Susan 10, it all started. Daddy would come in our room, make us strip down naked and lay on the bed. He would then take off his clothes and force us to have sex with him. Most times, he would visit both of us, one after the other. At first, it was only oral. But when Susan was about 12, he would force himself on us and have sex with us, both vaginal and anal."

Julie paused as tears started flowing down her cheeks. Her face was blushed as she told this total stranger about her nightmare.

307

Van Acker grabbed Julie's hands and held them in his.

"Take your time, Julie. I understand that this is difficult for you."

Julie nodded her head.

"It continued with me till I went to college. I was at the point where I did not care anymore. He always threatened us; said he would hurt us if we ever told. So, we kept quiet. From what Susan told me, she was able to get a camcorder and set it up in her and mine closet and filmed Daddy and herself and me, time after time. Apparently there is 4 hours of footage."

Again, Julie took a break. Van Acker acted as if he heard the story for the first time. His face was that of total disbelieve. He was glad that Julie Sutton was backing Susan's story about her father. He knew what was coming. With Susan's death, he had figured that nothing would happen against their father. Now, with Julie picking up the pieces, the lawsuit was on again.

Julie continued:

"I guess you know that Susan was going to sue Daddy for whatever she could sue him for. I have thought long and hard about it. I think that I'm ready to go through with it. Not only is he responsible for my sister's death, but he has also ruined my life."

Van Acker wanted to make sure that he heard right.

"Did you say he's responsible for your sister's death?"

Julie turned her head away and looked out the window, looking at nothing in particular.

"Yes, I did."

"Can you explain how you come to that conclusion?"

"I don't know what you know. What I'm going to tell you may be old news to you or it may shock you. Susan's death was not an accident."

"Well, I've figured that much. I believe the explosion was staged. Besides that, I believe, and I may be wrong, that she was killed before the explosion took place."

"I don't know about her being killed before the explosion. I do know, however, that someone entered the apartment while she was asleep."

"Did you witness anything?"

Julie looked at the floor. She should have come forward with this when it first happened. Would she be viewed as an accessory for not trying to stop a crime in progress? She needed to take that chance.

"I saw someone entering the apartment. I don't know for sure who it was. The person was dressed in black and in the dark it's hard to recognize anyone from my window all the way across the street."

"What can you tell me about the person you saw?"

Julie thought for a moment.

"Well, there were two people. First there was on sitting in front of the apartment for a long time. That person drove off. Then there was the person who entered the apartment. While the second person was in the apartment, the first one came back towards the apartment. When the intruder left Susan's, the other person approached the apartment. The explosion happened before he made it to the apartment."

"Did you say 'he'?"

"I don't know. It could have been a woman too. I just don't know."

"What can you tell me about the person who entered the apartment?"

"Not much, except that he, or she, was dressed in black. He or she was athletic, not too tall."

Van Acker thought for a moment. Julie's story coincided with Michelle's description of the events; that made him feel better.

"Is there anything else you can tell me about the person who entered the apartment?"

Julie thought hard.

"Yes, whoever it was drove a black sports car. Actually, the other person was driving a black sports car too."

"Do you have any idea what kind of car it was?"

"No. When it comes to cars I don't know how to tell one from the other. If I cannot see the name on the car, I don't what it is."

"Don't worry, that's not that important right now.

A silence fell between them as both thought about the explosion. Both were thinking different thoughts.

Dimitri looked at his watch and decided that it was time to leave. He had some phone calls to make.

"Julie, I hate to have to leave, but I have got some work I've got to finish today. If it is okay with you, I'd like to come over tomorrow so we can discuss this matter some more. Would that be okay?"

"That's fine, but I have more."

"I'm listening."

"Dimitri, I want to hire you for something also."

Van Acker looked at Julie full of anticipation.

"I have decided to leave Tom. I want to divorce him. I hope that you'll be able to represent me."

Van Acker folded his hands.

"I'll be glad to represent you. You must know that when it comes to divorce law, I'm not familiar with the process, but I guess if I'm going to be practicing law in Dawson County, I'd better learn, right?"

"I guess so. So, are you going to represent me?"

"Yes, I'll represent you."

"Thanks."

"Sure."

Van Acker produced a big smile and shook his head.

"What's so funny?"

"Well, I knew that I would have to content with your husband. I knew that it wouldn't be easy or pretty at times. I had never thought that my first major project would be to represent his own wife in a divorce suit against him. It's ironic if you asked me."

"Well, I'm sure that you'll do just fine. I've heard a lot of good things about you."

Julie stood up, realizing that she had taken up enough of Van Acker's time. She extended her arm and shook his hand.

"I'm looking forward to working with you, Dimitri."

"Likewise."

Julie waked out the door; Van Acker staring after her. Damn, what a shame! A beautiful lady like herself being so messed up. She deserved better; a whole lot better! He looked towards Pam. She smiled at him and gave him the thumbs up. He returned the smile and shrugged his shoulders. Who knew what was going to happen? Waving at Pam, he headed out the door. He had a lot of work to do.

68.

It was late afternoon when Hope Olson made it back to her desk. She was tired and weary. Instead of working on Susan Knox' case, she had been pulled in every direction possible. She was an hour into her shift and felt as if she had already worked two. Hinson had told her that she could stay in the office for a while, making sure she rested up before she went out on patrol. She was glad for that. 12 a.m. felt a long way off. She could use some rest. The warm sun had played its part in making her tired. Glad to be making the overtime, she wondered if it was worth it. It had been today!

Hope leaned back in her chair and stared at the papers lying in front of her. She was bothered by something. Would Radcliff have murdered Susan Knox prior to committing suicide? She doubted it. It just didn't fit the character. Even if he had gotten mad after receiving the bad news, would he just go out and murder her? She didn't know for sure, but something told her that Radcliff was not responsible for Susan Knox's death. She picked up the handgun and studied it through the plastic bag, a .44 magnum. She pushed the release button for the clip. It fell into the bag. Careful, making sure that she did not tear the bag, she unloaded the clip. It was a 6 bullet clip. She dropped the bullets one by one to the bottom of the bag. She counted 5. One missing, unless Radcliff loaded one in the chamber and then added another bullet to the clip, which she doubted was the case. She still could not rule him out as a suspect in Susan's death. It was still possible that he went in the apartment, turned the gas stove on and planted the timer. But what was the possibility that Susan had been murdered before the explosion? She would have to wait. Not until the autopsy would she be able to draw her final conclusion.

Hope leaned back in her chair. She closed her eyes and thought about Dimitri Van Acker. How much she had to tell him! So many developments that could affect the result of her investigation had popped up. But how much was she willing to share? She surprised herself by asking the question. What caused her to pose that question? Was it the pressure she felt from Hinson? She wasn't sure how to approach Van Acker at this point. One moment she's being threatened with losing her job if she so much as associates with him, the other, she's being told that it wouldn't hurt if she did spend time with him. And what about Van Acker, how would he feel about the new position Hinson was taking on their relationship? He would be suspicious; there was no doubt about that. Would he think that she was trying to set him up? She couldn't take that chance. God, why was everything so damn complicated? She decided to wait for Van Acker to make the first move. If he was willing to share information about what he had found then and only then would she share some of her information with him. She took a deep breath. She opened her eyes. She saw the message light on her phone was illuminated. She had missed that when she first arrived at the station. She pressed her security code and listened to the message.

"Hope, this is Dimitri. Give me a call when you have a chance. Better yet, if you're patrolling tonight, come by Kelly's and see me. I need to talk to you about something. It's important. See you then. I love you, bye!"

Hope produced a smile when she heard the message. She felt better. Some of her doubts had vanished. Obviously, Van Acker had found something and wanted to share it with her. She could hardly wait to go on patrol. She wasn't going to call him. She wanted to see him, feel his body pressed against hers, and feel his lips touching hers; a warm feeling flowed through her body. Some of the tension that had built up started ebbing away. She was relaxed, at ease. She felt ready to take on the evening. She would complete her paperwork before she'd go on patrol. Hopefully by then, Van Acker would be waiting for her to come by, full of anticipation. Hope's face was gleaming as she picked up her hat and put on her jacket. She couldn't wait to get her patrol going.

69.

Andrew Hinson had gone home after he dropped Hope off at the station. He felt miserable. He had lost a good friend. He could not understand why a successful man such as Gerald Radcliff would want to commit suicide. Something must have happened for him to reach for his gun and finish his life. But what?

Taking a shower and eating supper put him in a better mood. He sat down in his lazy chair and stared out in front of him. His mind wandered off to earlier that morning. The conversation he'd had with Hope about Van Acker had been difficult for him. As much as he detested Van Acker's presence in Stuttgart, he knew that he needed to get on his good side. He would have to warn Sutton about his plans. He hoped that Sutton would understand his position. He needed to understand that what he was trying to do was for the both of them. Both Sutton and he would be better-off with Van Acker gone. To reach that objective, Tom Sutton needed to understand that what he was doing was necessary to reach that goal. He managed to produce a smile. Poor Sutton! How was it possible that he had gotten himself in such a mess with Julie? His reputation had taken a terrible blow the last couple of days. He had heard the people in the street talking. It seemed the entire town knew about Julie kicking him out of the house. A few had picked up the words AIDS. It hadn't taken long for the speculation train to start moving through town. Sutton was in more trouble than he probably realized.

Hinson tried to put thoughts of a more pleasant nature in his mind; however, there were none. For a long time now, pleasant thoughts had been a thing of the past. He had received bad news and experienced misfortune far too much these last couple of years. It was time that changed. He wished he knew how. Thoughts of Gerald Radcliff filled his mind once more. He had had some wonderful times with Gerald. The many times that they went fishing and hunting together, the times that they had watched the ball games and races on TV and had gotten too drunk to drive anywhere. Those had been fun times. Now, they were gone; for what? He wished he could figure that out. He needed to find answers.

Hinson got up and walked out the door. He would go by Radcliff's house and see if there was anything in his house that would suggest why he had taken the drastic steps that he had. Gerald lived only a few miles away.

Hinson felt eerie entering his dead friend's house. The door had not been locked. The A/C was still blowing full power and it felt cold in the house. The light in the living room was on. Hinson looked around the room. He noticed the broken ceramic lamp on the floor. The television was still on, the volume rather high. He turned the TV off. He scanned the room. Nothing struck him as being out of place. He walked over to the bedroom area. Hinson raised his eyebrows as he noticed the broken window. He examined the window more closely and saw the empty whiskey bottle lying in the grass. He suspected that Ratcliff had slammed it through the window. He looked for a scrap of paper, a suicide note, anything that would suggest why Radcliff had taken his own life. Hinson looked through the entire house. No notes, nothing that suggested distress. He looked at the phone. What if Radcliff had gotten a telephone call that had set him off? He picked up the phone and punched *69. The phone produced a ringing sound. Then there was an answering machine. Hinson put the receiver down. Disconnected; that figured. He picked the phone back up and looked at the caller ID. Somehow, Radcliff had not subscribed to get caller ID on his phone. He would have to call the telephone company in the morning and see if they could tell him who had called Radcliff in the last 72 hours. He wasn't sure if it would be that easy, but he had to try something

Disappointed, Hinson drove back to his house. Instead of turning onto his street, he continued. He had someone to visit.

70.

Tom Sutton felt exhausted when he returned to his office late that afternoon. Judge Snelgrove had given him total hell. His opponent, Elisabeth Stanton had done a good job herself in making him look bad in front of the jury. He thought he had a good case built against the evidence, but unfortunately, Stanton had done better and researched deeper than he had. He allowed himself some latitude on the case. He had not spent as much time on it as he needed too. Now, with probably half a day remaining in the case, he did not know if he could convince the jury in his favor. He was sure that Stanton would be ready for him. For sure, after today, she smelled blood in the water and she had a reputation for digging the knife in all the way to the handle when the time was right. He knew the time would be right when she gave her final arguments in front of the jury. He had much work to do.

Sitting with his head between his hands and his eyes closed, Tom Sutton's mind drifted off. He saw himself at Susan's apartment. Susan was sitting on the couch, naked. God, she was beautiful. He was there too. He was naked also. Susan got up from the couch, her slender body gliding towards his. She embraced him. He felt the pressure from her curves; her naked breasts, with hard nipples, pushing against his chest. It excited him. He could feel her lips touching his. They were moist and warm. Her tongue slid inside his mouth. He savored the feeling. He wrapped his arms around her back and grabbed her ass, lifting her up. She wrapped her legs around his waist. He could feel his hard on, touching her skin. Slowly, he walked into the bedroom, still kissing her, trying not to stumble along the way. He reached the bedroom and put Susan on the bed. Then it happened! She was stuck to him. He tried to break away from her body, but couldn't. Their bodies were stuck. He pulled away from her, but nothing happened. Their flesh did not let go. Panic started setting in. He pulled harder. Finally, with one final pull, he could feel his body separating from hers. He felt relieved, until he looked at Susan. Fright overcame his face. He looked down to his midriff, hoping that he was dreaming. His eyes shot back to Susan's body. But she wasn't there. Something was there, but it wasn't Susan. It was some sort of monster. Sutton could

315

see his midriff still attached to the monster's belly. He screamed. The monster laughed. Susan's body, now in the form of a monster, started another metamorphoses. Slowly, the ugly skin turned to soft pink, a fluid pink, nothing you could touch. Then it turned to a crimson red; the red of blood. Again, Tom Sutton screamed. He wanted to run, but couldn't. His legs were not attached to his body any longer. His private parts were gone, melted into the monster. He just floated there, staring at the creature in front of him, changing into what? Julie! Sutton saw the head of Julie on top of the crimson red liquid. She was laughing out loud. She was whispering something to him. He couldn't hear. Slowly she started speaking louder and louder, until she was screaming.

"You will pay for this! You will burn in Hell! Go! Go down to Hell and burn!"

Tom Sutton shot up from his chair. He looked around his office, bewildered. Cold sweat was flowing from his face, dripping onto the floor. His breathing was hard and irregular. He leaned up against the table. He was not sure whether he would collapse on the floor or not. All his strength had left his body. He hadn't realized that he had dozed off. What was happening to him? He had never felt any guilt for cheating on Julie. Why suddenly would he have nightmares about her; both her and Susan? He managed to sit back down. He looked at Julie's picture he had still sitting on his desk. He turned it face down. He was ready to put this chapter of his life behind him. It was time to get out. A smile appeared on his face. After he divorced her, he would move away from Stuttgart. It was time to move on. He had spent enough time here; it was time to find bigger and better things.

Sutton got up. He would give his work a rest. Who knew, maybe tomorrow, he might not be practicing in Stuttgart any longer; maybe he would have found something bigger. A smile covered his face. What if he never came back? That would solve his problems. It would solve his problems with Julie, with Susan's death. Everything would be better. He made up his mind that tonight would be his final night in Stuttgart. He would put closure to his life in this godforsaken place. He would wave goodbye to Stuttgart and Dawson County. He grabbed his paperwork from his desk and deposited it in his filing cabinet. Another smile crossed his face.

Dimitri Van Acker. Well he'd have a lot of new clients. In a way he felt bad about leaving and proving himself wrong. He had hoped to see Van Acker return to Washington, DC with his head on his chest, a failure in small town law. Instead, he was going to give him a golden opportunity. He wished him all the best. He walked towards his safe and removed the contents: the tape of Julie and Jovanovich, files with personal information on some of the town's people, and some stock certificates. He put everything in his suitcase.

Walking out his office, he turned around and looked over his office one more time. He would miss coming here, odd as it was. But he needed to get out, get as far away from here as possible. He locked the door to the building and got in his car. Without looking back, he drove off, away from his troubles. He had one more stop to make, one more piece of unfinished business to take care off. Then he'd be on his way.

71.

After leaving Langston's, Dimitri Van Acker had gone to the Murphy farm and gotten permission from Allen Murphy to use his office. He needed to make some calls. He checked with Albert Jones on the status of the contract on the purchase of his house. Jones told him that everything was in the works and that Van Acker would be able to take possession of the house in a couple of days. Another call was to a friend who worked for the police force in Washington, DC. When he posed the question about the use of a pencil in the investigation of the body, he got a lot of laughter as a response. He finally called his buddy at the FBI. He had wanted to wait to call him till he knew for sure that he had received the package Kelly was supposed to have sent; however, he needed an answer to that question. Sidney "Sid" Schumaker was surprised to hear the voice of his best friend. When posed the question about the pencil, he answered by posing Van Acker a question. Is the body suspect to having been shot? Van Acker knew the answer to that from Underwood's note. Of course, the pencil had been used to find the bullet hole, an ingenious idea by Underwood. Van Acker told Schumaker of the package that was coming his way and urged him to take a look at it as fast as he could. Schumaker promised that he would examine the materials the same night they arrived.

After making the phone calls, Van Acker wrote down information and details about his conversation with Julie Sutton. He also made a note on Julie's recollections of what she had seen the night her sister had died. He'd been glad that her story coincided with Michelle's. Still, he could not rule out Michelle. She could after all have been the person inside Susan's apartment while someone else was trying to enter the apartment. For now, he would try not to think along those lines and believe Michelle. He was tired but felt exhilarated by the events of the day. It was time to go home, or at least the place that he temporarily called home.

When he arrived at Kelly Murphy's house, he was surprised by the smell of good country cooking. Walking through the front door, he saw the dining room table was set for two. Candles were lit and a bottle of white wine was cooling. He looked around the living room to see if Kelly was around. He figured he should have called

318

Kelly first. He had no idea that she had company coming over tonight. Looking over his shoulder like a child trying to put his hand in the cookie jar, he lifted the lids of the pots to see what was cooking. He found fresh squash, carrots and snow peas steaming in one pot, chicken roasting in the oven with home made biscuits and a pot of mashed potatoes. Dimitri licked his lips. This looked to be a delicious meal. He envied the young man who would be filling his belly with the food. He took a deep breath and tried to figure out where he would be eating tonight. There was nothing open in town besides Langston's and he did not feel like eating there again, good as the food was. He would have to go to Macon to fill his stomach. That wouldn't be too bad. He could look around and see if he could find some furniture for his new house. He decided to change his clothes before heading to Macon. He disappeared into his room.

Kelly walked out of her bedroom just as Van Acker closed his door. She felt euphoric. He was home! Great! She knew that he must have seen the table set and smelled her food cooking. She hoped that he would like it. After leaving Langston's, she had gone grocery shopping and had spent the rest of the afternoon trying to put a meal together that she though he would like. This would be her chance to make her move. Her attraction to him was growing by the minute. It was almost like a drug and she was in need of it badly. She could feel her body react to her thoughts. God she hoped this would work. She needed relief from the ache her body was feeling. She walked back in her room and took another look in the mirror. She had fixed her hair, put on make-up, but most of all, she had chosen the most revealing outfit she had in her closet. She was wearing a light flowery cotton dress. It was tied in the neck with a strap that held the front part of the dress in place. Over half her back was exposed. A semi-tight elastic in the back kept it from gaping open. The dress stopped halfway down her thighs. It wasn't too short, but a little bit longer would have made her more comfortable. Still, she had a mission to complete and wearing the dress was all part of the plan. She had not been able to wear a bra. The bare back kept her from doing that. She hoped that she would be able to control her excitement. She had looked through her lingerie drawer and found a pair of lacy thongs that she thought he would find sexy. She hoped that she would be able to get that far with him.

Her self-admiration was interrupted when Van Acker walked out of his room. He was dressed in a pair of shorts and a silk shirt. He saw Kelly standing in front of the mirror. His eyes moved over her body in admiration. She sure had grown into a beautiful woman. He had never though of her this way before, but he couldn't help for a few seconds admiring her. Kelly noticed him staring at her.

"Hi, Dimitri," she started, "I'm glad that your home."

Van Acker felt a bit confused. He would have thought that she would be trying to push him out of the door.

"Really? I thought that you had made plans with someone. I think I'll be on my way. I don't think it would be a good idea for me to be around when your date arrives."

Kelly's look on her face changed.

"What? You think that I have some guy coming over to have supper with?"

"Well yes. I figured that you had made plans before I came back and just forgot to tell me about it. Which, if that's what happened, don't worry about it, I'll just go out and eat."

Kelly walked over to Van Acker and hugged him.

"Dimitri, I did all this for you. There's nobody else coming over. It's just you and me."

Van Acker looked at her with curious eyes. She had caught him off guard. He wasn't sure what to make of this.

"I don't understand, Kelly. What's the occasion? My birthday is not for a couple of months."

A smile appeared on Kelly's face, as she kept mysteriously quiet. Without answering his question, she lit the candles on the table, walked over to the CD player and started a CD with romantic favorites. She then turned off the lights and walked towards him. She wrapped her arms around him and gave him a big hug. Letting go, still not having said a word, she took a bottle of champagne from the fridge, pouring two glasses, offering one to Van Acker.

"So," she whispered mysteriously as she gave him his glass of champagne, "what do you think? Could you get used to coming home to something like this every night?"

Van Acker found a chair, as he needed to sit down. What was going on? Why was Kelly acting this way? He felt uncomfortable.

"Well, let's see, I don't think I could handle champagne every night if that's what you're asking."

"I know the champagne would be a little much every night, but how about the rest? Would coming home to a home-cooked meal sound good to you?"

Van Acker had to admit that it had been a long time since he had come home to a home-cooked meal after working all day. He admitted to that fact.

"Now, for the tough questions: would you be able to come home to *me* every night?" Kelly asked seductively.

"Well, for now, I think I can handle coming home to you every night," Van Acker answered with a smile.

"For now?" Kelly asked acting hurt.

"Well, at least until I have a chance to move into my new house. This will be at least another week."

Kelly felt disappointment hit. She should have taken this a bit slower. Pushing herself on him like this had made him confused and had put him in a defensive mode. She needed to slow things down. She needed to work him a little better.

"Oh, well that makes me feel a little better."

Van Acker felt that he had disappointed Kelly with his response.

"Kelly, I love coming home to you. And I love you cooking for me like this. I do appreciate it."

She felt a little better.

After drinking their champagne, dinner started. Both were quiet during dinner. They casually talked about Susan's murder and about how Michelle had gotten involved. Van Acker assured Kelly that Michelle would be fine. He would make sure that nothing happened to her. After dinner, Van Acker helped with the dishes and that finished they both sat down on the couch. Kelly needed to make a move soon before the chance would slip through her fingers. She figured if she did not act soon, Dimitri Van Acker would be lost from her forever. She knew that if Hope happened to come by, her chances of further seducing him would fall through. She didn't know if she could handle that. For so long, she had wanted him. She had felt an attraction for him ever since they first met all these years ago. Silently she had admired him, tried to become part of his world, be as close to him as possible. He had never, not even once, made a move towards her. What was wrong with her? Was she not attractive? She knew that she wasn't necessarily the prettiest, but she wasn't ugly either, and she took great care of her body. Still, in secret, not letting anyone know, she had quietly loved Van Acker. He had always acted as if she was his little sister. He had always protected her, watched out for her in her personal life as well as in her school life. And she had not minded at all that he paid her attention. In fact she loved it. It meant that she got to spend time with him, giving her feelings for him a chance to grow. But the fact remained; she wasn't his sister anymore than he was her brother. To even think that was crazy. They were in no form related to each other. And that made her feelings for him even stronger. She was attracted to him and that feeling was growing more and more intense with the minute, especially having him sit on her couch. She looked at him as he was writing down some notes in his notebook. It was now or never! She got up and scanned her CD collection. She found one with nothing but love songs on it. She put it on and looked over at him to see his reaction.

Van Acker lifted his head as he heard the familiar tunes of a love song from times gone by. It reminded him of a girl from his past, a girl he wished he could have gotten to know better but who had found love in someone else's arms. It brought back memories of regret for missed opportunities that would never be offered him again. Memories of young love flowed through his mind. And here stood Kelly in front of him, her hand extended, asking him for a dance. Why not? One innocent dance with someone he cared deeply about wouldn't hurt. He got up and wrapped his arms around Kelly, holding his hands just above her hips. Kelly in turn had her arms wrapped around his neck and had her head resting on his chest. A feeling of total delight overpowered her body. She could barely stand on her legs. At this moment, she felt as secure and happy as she had ever felt. Slowly, they danced like that throughout the duration of the song. As the song ended, Van Acker released his hands and moved towards sitting back down on the couch. Kelly on the other hand held on to his neck and forced him to have another dance with her. He felt funny about it; still, he gave in to her wishes. The next song again brought back memories of a lost teenage love.

He didn't know why, but it felt good holding Kelly close to him. For the second time tonight, he noticed her in a different light. He felt the contour of her body as it pressed against his while they were dancing. Never before had he paid any attention to the physical pressure of her body when they hugged. Now, he felt her body. He felt her soft breasts pressed against his midriff, the curve of her hips underneath his fingers. Unconsciously, he moved his hand more towards the middle of her back, right above her buttocks. He could feel Kelly's body react to his touch. She pressed her abdomen a little more into his. She was obviously feeling his touches too. He held her a little closer and tighter as their chemistry began to mix. His mind was not functioning in its full capacity; passion was starting to set in. Thus far their relationship had been one of friendship and trust. He had always felt a bond with Kelly, but never knew how to explain it other than friendship. That friendship and trust had brought them to this moment. There had been a passion in their relationship that had never surfaced until now. How could he have missed it all those years? Van Acker looked down at Kelly. She raised her chin so their eyes could meet. He felt his body react to the tenderness and love that was expressed in those big brown eyes. Their faces moved closer together and their lips touched. Kelly felt her heart beat hard and fast. She was scared that Van Acker would notice. She felt her face grow hot and knew it must be as red as a tomato. But as their lips locked and formed into a passionate kiss, she regained control of her emotions. She stood on her tiptoes so she could reach his lips better. Van Acker had moved one hand up towards the middle of Kelly's back while his other hand had moved lower, lifting her buttocks; both hands supporting her in their kissing.

Whether it was the alcohol or the music, or both, Van Acker didn't know. He had lost all sense of time and logical thought. Without much effort he untied the strap from around her neck and her dress slipped to the ground. He took in the sight of her naked breasts, nipples as hard as they would get protruding from them. Kelly in turn unbuttoned Van Acker's shirt and dropped it to the floor. She then pressed her half-naked body into his. Dimitri picked her up and carried her into her bedroom. Soon, sounds of passionate love making reached the outside of the double wide.

Hope Olson, who had been eager to see Van Acker, walked

up to the front door. She was ready to knock on the door when she decided to look through the window instead. Why she had the urge to do just that, she would never know. She wished she hadn't looked. What she saw shocked her. She saw Kelly and Van Acker in an embrace, their lips locked together in a passionate kiss. She then witnessed rest of their seduction up to the point where Van Acker carried Kelly into the bedroom. Hope leaned up against the side of the double wide, sliding down until she was sitting, tears flowing down her face. All of her energy had disappeared into thin air. She couldn't get up. After a hard day at work, the only thing that had given her any energy was the prospect of seeing Van Acker and spending a few romantic moments with him. Now, she had nothing left. The romantic moment she had craved would not come; at least not for her. Slowly she managed to get back to her feet and make it to her patrol car. Sobbing louder now that she was in her own private space, she dove off into the night, not knowing where she was going or what she was going to do.

72.

Andrew Hinson drove up into the driveway. He sat quietly and looked at the house in front of him. What was he doing here? The question had bothered him on the drive over. The facts that he knew were too much for him to keep quiet. But telling the truth might cause more hurt for a family that was already hurting a lot. Was it right to add more fuel to the fire? He was sure that what he was going to do would create more hurt; however, he needed to share the information. He took a deep breath as he stepped out of his car and made his way to the front door.

Julie Sutton was surprised to hear her doorbell ring. She had been in the kitchen fixing some supper. She had taken it easy after coming home from her meeting with Dimitri Van Acker. She actually felt better now that she had taken her life back into her own hands and felt that she was finally heading in the right direction. She straightened her hair as she opened the door.

"Andy? Hi, what a surprise. Come on in."

Andrew Hinson walked in and stood in the foyer, feeling sheepish. He didn't know how or where to start. He felt more like a shy little schoolboy than the Sheriff of Dawson County.

"Have a seat, Andy." Julie spurred him in the direction of the sitting room.

Both sat down, opposite one another. Still Hinson didn't know why he had come. There was so much he needed to tell Julie; so many secrets. He didn't know where to start or whether he should tell her everything. Telling her everything would be too much for Julie to handle right now. He needed to tell her a little at a time. He looked at her and admired her beauty. She had not changed much in the past couple of years. She still had that same youthful appearance when she smiled. God, he loved her smile. Why was he here? Was it to be in Julie's presence or was it to talk about what he had found out? He knew that her marriage with Tom Sutton was as good as over. It was no secret that she had thrown him out. He wondered about the tape Sutton had been watching in his office. Had Julie been a willing participant in the actions that had taken place or had it been a setup to get back at her? He was sure that Sutton had paid to have the tape made. Jovanovich sure didn't seem to mind doing the dirty deed. He wondered how many other women Jovanovich had treated the same way. He made up his mind to tell Julie only part of the information.

"Julie, hmm, God, where do I begin?"

"What's wrong, Andy? What are you trying to tell me?"

"Well, it's not easy and it's probably not my place to tell you. However, I consider you a good friend and I do care for you a lot. You know that Tom and I are good friends too, but I'm afraid that our friendship is coming to a close. I cannot accept what he's been doing to you."

"Like what?" Julie asked, feeling uneasy about where the conversation was headed. She started to rub her hands back and forth over her thighs.

"Well, I know that by now, you know about his long-standing affair with Susan."

"Yes, Susan told me. Tom still has not admitted to it, but I have to believe Susan."

"Susan was telling the truth. I've known about the affair for as long as I've known Tom. He used to brag about his adventures with your sister."

Hinson looked down at the floor, ashamed, knowing that he was admitting to helping Sutton keep his dirty secret. He did not feel good about having kept it from Julie all these years.

"Look, Andy, I understand why you never told me. I know that you tried to keep the peace and probably thought that what I didn't know wouldn't hurt me."

She paused for a second, moistening her lips before she continued.

"In the long run, it probably was better that this came full circled as it did. I think that I was able to handle it better coming from my sister than if it would have come from you. So don't feel bad."

"Thanks. But there is more. I talked with Tom this morning. I believe that he's going to file for divorce."

"Well, I think that I'm ahead of the game then. I have started divorce procedures against Tom this afternoon. I have hired a lawyer to represent me in the divorce. I can guarantee you that it won't be pretty."

326

Hinson had a good idea who it was she had hired. He hated to think that Van Acker was starting to get business. He hated that his own friends were seeking council with Van Acker; not that Julie had a lot of choice, but she could have found a good divorce lawyer in Macon. He knew he had to turn the heat up on Van Acker if he wanted to prevent him from settling in Dawson County.

"Julie, you need to be careful when going after Tom. He's a good lawyer and he's sly. Watch out for him! Watch out what you do and where you go. He may try to trap you into doing something that would look like infidelity."

Julie burst out laughing. She thought the mention of infidelity was funny, especially when it was directed at her.

"How can he get anything on me for infidelity? Everybody in town knows that I am not that type of person. If you were talking about Susan, I could understand. How did you come to that conclusion?"

Hinson didn't know if he had told her too much at this point not to tell her about the videotape. He was sure that it would embarrass Julie if he mentioned that he had viewed a tape with her on it, naked on a bed, making love to a total stranger. At least, that's what the tape would produce as evidence, whether Julie was a willing participant in the action or not. He was almost positive that Julie had been drugged to make the video footage of her lovemaking to Jovanovich. How would she handle the revelation?

"Andy, tell me, how did you come to that conclusion?" Julie pushed.

"Did Tom tell you that he'd be trying to catch me with another man?"

She didn't think it was funny anymore. She grew more and more concerned with the way Hinson was acting. He obviously knew something and had a hard time sharing it with her. She tried to think of when she would ever have been in a public situation that could be construed as cheating on Sutton.

Julie turned white and started rubbing her hands nervously over her thighs again. She had figured it out. That son of a bitch! Lester! The bastard! It had been too easy. She had been the perfect target. He must have been one of Tom's clients from whom he needed a favor. But what had happened after she passed out? No! It couldn't be! Would Tom be able to stoop so low? She had no problem answering her own question. She turned her eyes to Hinson. Tears started to appear in them.

"Andy? Is there a tape of me?"

Hinson looked down, avoiding her eyes. He had to tell her. He needed to prepare her for what was coming.

"Julie, I'm sorry. I saw the tape. Tom was watching it when I walked into his office this morning."

Julie's head dropped to her chest and she started to cry. Tears were flowing down her cheeks and her chest heaved as she tried to breathe. Hinson got up and sat next to Julie, wrapping his arm around her, trying to give her comfort.

"Julie, tell me, did you have an affair with that man?"

Julie looked up at Hinson in disbelieve. How could he ask such a question?

"Of course not!" she said, almost screaming.

Hinson wasn't satisfied with her answer.

"Julie, where did you meet that man and how did you end up naked in bed with him?"

As hurt as she was, at this point she felt more anger than pain. She got up and faced Hinson. She pointed her finger at him.

"Don't you sit there and judge me! I have done nothing wrong! I was raped! I was drugged! I had nothing to do with that man, nothing!"

She turned her back towards Hinson as she felt a new flood of tears finding their way into her eyes. God! When would all this end? She'd received nothing but bad news the past few days; Tom cheating on her, Susan's death, being raped, and now there's a tape of her with the rapist. She didn't think she could handle it any longer. She turned back to Hinson.

"Andy, I'm sorry, but I'm going to have to ask you to leave. I want to be alone."

"Listen, I can stay if you need someone to talk to."

"No! I want you out! The more I think about it, the more I'm blaming you for not telling me about all of this. If you're the friend that you say you are, you should've told me a long time ago. None of this would have happened then. None! I want you out, and I don't want to see you around here again. Do I make myself clear?"

328

Hinson realized that coming to her with the information had been wrong. Slowly, he got up and walked towards her. He tried to give her a hug. Instead she turned away from him. Julie held her arms tight to her chest and pulled away from his touch. He quietly walked to the front door, opened it, walked outside and quietly closed the door behind him.

Tom Sutton had watched Andrew Hinson's meeting with his wife, wishing he knew what the two had talked about. Obviously, whatever it had been had upset Julie. He had an idea what the conversation had been about. Damn you, Andy! Why did you have to tell her? Well, it just made it all the more certain that he needed to get the Hell out of Stuttgart. It was time to start over. But first, he needed to wrap up some unfinished business.

73.

James Knox was standing in the dark in front of his bedroom window. He looked over at the destroyed remains of his daughter's apartment. He could think of only one thing: where were the tapes? He thought Susan would have hidden them in her apartment, but his search had revealed nothing. Was he sad that Susan was gone? He couldn't say what emotions he had to the passing of his youngest daughter. He felt sadness and a great sense of loss; however, his mind was not reacting the same way his body was. In his mind, he could not help but think of what was going to happing in the next couple of months. From overhearing the conversation between Julie and his wife, Phyllis, it appeared that Julie was going to continue what her sister had started. It would no doubt bring shame to the entire family. His business would most definitely suffer, if not be destroyed because of this. He thought back to the tapes. Those tapes were the only evidence that existed of his pedophilic activities with his daughters. Without them, it would be Julie's word against his. If he could find those damned tapes, he might be able to come out of a trial without too much damage. He needed a good lawyer. Tom Sutton was out the question. He was family and that would not work. What about that new lawyer in town? What was his name again, Dimitri Van Acker? No! He was out of the question too. From what he knew, Susan had hired Van Acker to start a lawsuit against him. He was already involved on the wrong end of the case. Damn, why did Susan decide to this after all this time? He needed a good lawyer. He would have to consult some of his friends in Macon. Maybe there he could find a lawyer who was willing to defend him. Money, of course, was of no concern. He would pay whatever it took to have his name cleared. But first, he needed to get a hold of those tapes. Knox leaned up against the wall, arms spread out on either side of the window. He looked across the street to Julie's house. Slowly, he shook his head. God, what had he done? He had tried to resist his urges. Why he felt the way he did, he had no idea. He had first become attracted to his daughters when they were still little. He had felt attracted to a lot of little girls, but his daughters were the only one's who were available to him. He had been able to hold off acting on his urges and needs until their bodies had started to develop. It was at that point that he couldn't hold back any longer. As much as he tried not to, he could not resist to his needs. Why was it that he wasn't able to resist his daughters in such a way? Was it because as a teenager, he had never been close to any of his female contemporaries? Was it because he was more powerful than they were and knew that he had total control over them? He had a lot of questions, but no readily available answers. He had gotten satisfaction from his actions. It had felt good and he had never once thought about what he was doing to his daughters. He had never even considered how they felt about what he was doing to them. Never once did he ask himself the question if he was hurting them in one way or another. Never once had he considered what he was doing to their young bodies and minds. He had no concern with that at the time. The only thing that mattered was his pleasure and his satisfaction. He only thought about how good it had felt as he zipped up his pants, leaving them in their room, crying, ashamed, depressed and wondering why they deserved to be treated that way. Now, it looked as if he was finally going to have to pay for his pleasures, his satisfaction, and his sins. He shook his head and bowed his head. Nothing came for free.

With his mind working overtime and his attention drawn to the burned-out apartment of his daughter, James Knox had not seen his wife Phyllis walk in. She stood quietly by the door, watching her husband; the man she had loved and married, the man who had given her two beautiful daughters. She had never imagined for one moment that the man she so loved and adored was the source of her daughter's problems. She had often wondered where she had gone wrong with her two girls. Both had a normal childhood, but they had changed rapidly in their late preteen years. They had become distant, withdrawn, rebellious and not as she had foreseen them to become as young women. As far as Julie was concerned, she could not have hoped for a better behaved child. Even though sometimes withdrawn and quiet, she had always been the one who was reading from her bible and excelling at everything she did. She guessed that had been her way of dealing with the stress, the hurt and the confusion of being sexually abused and raped by her own father. Susan's path on the other hand had been one she had never been able to figure out; that is, until now. Susan had brought shame and hurt to her family.

331

Susan had been an embarrassment to her family. It had started in middle school and carried on into high school where she had quickly developed a reputation for being the school slut. Phyllis had hoped that Susan joining the Army would straighten her out. Those hopes had not come true. Her husband was the only one who knew what exactly had happened while she had been enlisted. All these years, he had kept the secret; such a horrible secret indeed. Her baby girl had become a whore. James had never told her what he had found in New York. If she'd known, she didn't think that she would have agreed to let Susan stay in the apartment. Now she understood why her husband had been willing to put up with her lifestyle. It had been guilt, but mostly, it had been a way to keep Susan quiet; to keep Susan from revealing to the world the dirty Knox family secrets. She would tell her story if he didn't take care of her. And what a story it was! Not even in her wildest dreams could Phyllis ever have imagined that her family had been so dysfunctional. Her whole family had fooled her for so many years. Her whole family had fooled the entire county, except of course for all those involved. How many were affected because of what had happened in the Knox house? Counting everybody who had slept with Susan at some point during her adult life, it wouldn't surprise her if many families would be affected by her daughter's actions, by her husband's actions. From what she'd heard, several married men had visited Susan to take advantage of her services. A tear came to her eyes as she thought of what had become of her daughter. Was it true that all Susan had been her entire life was a toy for men to use and abuse? Had Susan been nothing more than a willing sex toy for men to enjoy before heading back home to their families? All of them had wanted the fun, but none had wanted the commitment. What a distasteful world she lived in! And the source of much that distastefulness had originated with the man standing by the window, her husband of 35 years. He was the one guilty of what had happened to both Julie and Susan. What about herself, was she guilty as well? It was a hard question to pose. It would take much soul searching to answer that question. On the surface she did not have any guilt in what happened. Anger is what she felt on the surface, but what lay beneath the surface? Only time would tell, she guessed. She had not yet confronted her husband about the accusations that were hovering over them. She needed answers, truthful answers.

"Jim?"

James Knox turned around to find his wife standing only a few feet away from him.

"Yes, honey?"

"Jim, is all of it true?"

James Knox looked away from his wife. He couldn't look her into her eyes. He loved Phyllis very much and to think that he might lose her because of all of this was hurting him.

"Jim, I need to know the truth!"

"The truth," he said, barely audible, "You know the truth is a funny thing. There are so many truths out there. Which one will you believe? Susan's truth? Julie's truth? My truth?"

"Don't play mind games with me, Jim! I want to truth that God knows. That's the only one I'm interested in."

Knox turned his back to his wife. He closed his eyes and felt his stomach contract. What was the sense in it? The truth would come out sooner or later; no matter whose truth it was. It all came down to the same thing, really. He could not hide that he had molested his own daughters. He could not hide that he'd had sex with them, that he had raped them. He turned back around and looked Phyllis straight in the eyes.

"What's true is that I love you. I've loved you since I first lay eyes on you and I will continue to love you more and more every day. But I'm afraid that my love for you will not be enough for you to keep on loving me.

"I have done wrong. I don't know what exactly it is you have heard or what it is you've been told."

He paused and walked over to the bed. He needed to sit down. He pointed next to him and motioned Phyllis to sit down next to him. He took her hands in his.

"Honey, for some reason beyond my control, I've done with my girls what only I should have done with you."

Phyllis tried to pull her hands away from his grip, but he was too strong.

"No! Please tell me it's not true!" she pleaded with him.

"Telling you it never happened would be a lie. Far too long have we been living a lie. It's time to come clean. I hate it has to be

333

under these circumstances. I wish I could have done this a long time ago when at least we could have given the children some professional help. It's too late for that now. I believe that Susan's death was because of what I did to her so many years ago.

"The life that she lived was the not the life that I intended for her to have. Still, I pushed her into what she was, into what she became, into how she lived her life. There's nothing I can do to change that now."

James Knox broke down and started to cry uncontrollably. Phyllis had been crying during his confession. She had hoped, in the back of her mind, that it was all a lie, instead, she found out that she was the one who'd been living a lie. Ironically enough, the truth had been the lie. Never again would their lives be the same, would their lives be normal. She would never be able to go to church again without being judged. No matter what the Bible said about judgment and forgiveness, she knew that in real life, the teachings of the Bible were not followed to the letter and she would be judged by her peers. She would be an outcast in her own community. People would ask her how it was possible for her not to have known about what was going on in her own house. They would have their mind made up that she must have been part of this horrible secret that had been played out behind closed door inside the Knox home.

"Why?" she managed to ask her husband.

He shrugged his shoulders, wishing that he had an answer to that questions, a question he'd asked himself so many times, for so many years.

"I honestly don't know."

"What are *we* going to do?"

Phyllis was surprised by her own question. She knew that twenty years, even only ten years ago she would not have posed that question. She would have known what to do. She would have left her husband and made sure that he was locked up for the rest of his life so he could not hurt any more little girls. A thought just hit her. Where there others? Did he molest other children? Oh God please let that not be the case! She had to know. Would he be honest with her? She needed to ask.

"Jim, were there others?"

"What do you mean?"

334

"Did you molest other children? Did you do things with more than just our daughters?"

James Knox quietly shook his head. God knew he had thought about it, but he had never had the courage or the guts to approach another child.

"No, I haven't. I've thought about it, fantasized about it, but no, I've never touched another child."

Phyllis breathed a sigh of relief. That would be all she needed. God, how could she not know her own husband? Thirty-five years of marriage and she had no idea what went on in her husbands head; she had no idea what this man who she shared everything with was capable of doing. What was she going to do? It was hard to believe that it had been thirty five years that they'd been together. She had stood by James through some hard times and she had enjoyed the good times. It had taken a lot of work and sacrifice to get where they were now. Was it worth it to lose all of this and start over? She was not 30 or even 40 anymore. Even though she was in good physical health, the aches and pains she felt after each workout told her the story. She was getting older. If she left him, would she get anything? And even then, would it be enough to see her through? It was a hard decision that she needed to make; a decision she needed to make before it was too late. She had loved James unconditionally; she had trusted his decisions even though she had not always agreed with them. She had been the picture-perfect wife for him; and how he had repaid her for that was the question she needed to ask herself. Sure, he had given her all she wanted. They were well off, had a booming business, a nice house and nice cars; but was all that enough to stay with him after all he'd done to their daughters, her babies? She could find a job, she supposed if she needed to, or if it came down to it, she could learn to run the business. It wouldn't be the first time that a woman took over a business from her husband for whatever reason. If she stood up and cast her own judgment on James, then maybe she could save the wrath of the community.

Phyllis did not wait for Knox to answer that question for her. She got up from the bed and walked to the door. She looked back at the man that had given her everything, but who had on the same token, made a fool out of her. It was a tough decision to make. It would not be easy, still, it had to be done. She walked out of James' bedroom and silently closed the door behind her. Tears were flowing down her cheeks as she made her way to her own bedroom and collapsed on the bed.

James Knox knew what was going to happen. He could not blame Phyllis for feeling that way. Would he be able to save her name, her reputation? Not too many choices remained available for him to be able to do that. Coming forward and turning himself in would show her that he was sorry for what he had done. No! He would not give up this easily. He could live his life without Phyllis. He could move and start over. But first, they had to fight him! And by God, he would fight back! He balled his fists as the thoughts of an embarrassing trial crossed his mind. He would put up a fight! But first, he needed to track down those damned tapes Susan had made of his sinful actions.

74.

Hope Olson was not paying attention to her patrol route. Her mind kept flashing back to images of Van Acker and Murphy, their naked bodies pressed together. How could he do this to her? Damn him! For once in her life she had thought that she had found a man she could trust, a man she could rely on. Once again, she had hoped for the impossible. What had happened to the Van Acker who had told her that he loved her? Were his words just idle talk designed to make her feel good and get her into bed? Maybe Hinson had been right about him; maybe he was trouble. What was he trying to prove? She could not understand what would have turned him on to Kelly Murphy. Was it his initiative to make love to her? Maybe Murphy was behind it, had seduced him and lured him into her bedroom? She would be capable at seducing him. She was always looking at him with those big admiring eyes. Still, if he could not resist Murphy's advances after letting on he cared for and loved her, what would he do once they were involved in a deeper relationship? Hope shook her head. No! If he loved her then he should be able to resist the advances of any woman, no matter what she tried. Tears were flowing down her cheeks again. She had to pull over on the side of the road. She found a driveway that led into a pasture. She pulled into the driveway and was able to turn the car around so it was facing the road. What was she going to do? She needed to go on with her life. She just would have to forget about Dimitri Van Acker. Three days of happiness had just vanished in thin air right in front of her eyes. No, she could not let herself get hurt; not by Van Acker or any other man for that matter. She was a strong enough woman to be able to take care of herself. She did not need anyone to mess up her life. She was set in her ways and she was happy. She managed to produce a smile at the fact that indeed, her life was not as bad as it seemed. She had a good job, she came and went as she pleased, and she did not have to worry about making sure that she took care of the household needs on a daily basis. If she didn't feel like cleaning her house, that was just fine, she didn't do it. With a man living in the house, more than likely she would not be able to get away with that. Yes! She was better off without him. She opened the cruiser's window and let the musk evening air enter her car. The smell of fresh cut hay reached her nostrils. She took a deep breath and inhaled the country air. It helped to clear her head.

She put her cruiser in drive and drove off. She had a job to do. She needed to make sure the businesses were secure and she needed to work some more on her investigation into Susan's death. She realized that it would be impossible to perform her investigation and not be confronted with Van Acker. She would handle that when the time presented itself. She reached for her breast pocket and felt the bracelet. She needed to go talk to Bryan Scarboro. He was a suspect. What was he doing at his father's office that late at night, trying to make sure that nobody saw him? It was suspicious behavior. She decided to talk to him first before she patrolled the businesses. Coming into town, she turned towards the Scarboro home. As she did, a black coupe, one that she didn't recognize, came from the direction of the Scarboro home. She looked in her rearview mirror. She wondered who it was. The windows had been tinted and she had not been able to take a look at the driver. She hated those tinted windows. Even though there was a law about how much they could be tinted, it was still too much in her opinion.

Arriving at the Scarboro home, she parked her cruiser and walked up to the font door. Ringing the bell, she looked inside through the sidelight. The home was neatly furnished, she noted. Mrs. Scarboro must take great pride in her home. The door opened.

"Yes?"

"Good evening, Mrs. Scarboro, my name is Hope Olson, I'm a deputy Sheriff. I was wondering if Bryan was available."

Mrs. Scarboro looked Hope up and down with small suspicious eyes.

"He in trouble?" she snapped at Hope.

"Well, I don't think so. I believe that I found something that belongs to him and I would like to return it."

"Well, you can give it to me. I'll make sure he gets it."

Hope had a hard time not smiling at Mrs. Scarboro's rudeness.

"Actually, I think that I want to give it to him myself. I have a couple of questions for him…"

Mrs. Scarboro looked at Hope as if she were crazy.

"…it's about where I found the particular item."

"Oh. I see. Well, let me see if he's in."

Mrs. Scarboro shut the door in Hope's face. Hope looked at the door in disbelieve. She could not figure out why she was being treated this way. Something must be going on here. She didn't know what, but something wasn't right. She decided not to worry about it. It was probably just a family problem.

A few minutes passed and the door opened. Bryan Scarboro was standing in the doorway, his mother close behind him. Scarboro looked nervous. Hope could feel the cool air from the air-conditioner flow over her face; still Scarboro's forehead was covered with sweat drops. She didn't like the way Mrs. Scarboro was hovering over him. She needed to talk to him alone. This might not lead anywhere; still she did not want to get Scarboro in trouble over nothing.

"Bryan, why don't we take a little walk," Hope said, motioning towards the driveway.

Scarboro looked at his mother, the look on his face that of someone guilty of something.

"Okay," he said.

Both walked off the porch and towards the driveway. Hope made sure that they were out of eavesdropping distance before she took the bracelet out of her pocket and showed it to Scarboro. She noticed that he turned a shade paler when he saw the bracelet.

"I found this a couple of nights ago behind your father's practice. I thought that it belonged to you."

"Thank you. I've been looking for this. I must have left it when I left my father's office.'

"Can I ask you what you were doing at his office that late in the evening?"

Scarboro didn't want to admit that he had been at the office that faithful night. But how much did Olson know? He hated Olson had been the one who found his bracelet. He knew that she didn't like him much. He was buddies with most of the other deputies, but he'd never been able to butter his way up to her.

"What do you mean late in the evening? I left from there in the afternoon as usual."

He was looking for a reaction from Olson. He didn't get the reaction he'd been expecting.

"Bryan, I'm investigating Susan Knox' death and right now,

we believe that she was killed before her apartment exploded. You are one of the suspects in her killing. I also know the bracelet was dropped in the alley sometimes after 10 o'clock that night. It wasn't there on my first patrol. I found it during my second patrol just before midnight. So if you lost it, it had to have been after 10 o'clock. Besides, I believe that you were in the alley when I was doing my patrol. I can't prove it was you, but someone was in the alley."

"Are you accusing me of murder?"

"No. I'm telling you that you're lying about when you lost the bracelet and that you're a suspect in Susan's murder."

"No I'm not. I'm not lying and I had nothing to do with Susan. No matter what, you can't prove it!"

"You're right, I can't. But I'll be keeping an eye on you."

Hope threw the bracelet up in the air and turn around. Scarboro caught the piece of jewelry. He watched as Hope Olson got into her cruiser and drove off. Exactly how much did she know? He had to be careful with her. She could be trouble. If she dug deeper, she might find something and he could not afford that. Right now, he needed to go back inside and face his mother. Why in God's name had Michelle called her and told her about the HIV?

Hope Olson drove off, looking at Scarboro in her rear-view window. She knew she had something here; Bryan Scarboro had just become her first suspect in Susan Knox' murder. There was motive. Scarboro, being the son of a doctor and a medical student himself, had access to drugs and knew how to use them. He could have drugged Susan before setting the timer, which might explain why Susan never noticed the gas filling up her apartment. She had more questions she wanted to ask; however, they would have to wait for now.

75.

Sitting across the street from his house, Tom Sutton was carefully planning his next move. He could not let anything go wrong. It was essential that he did everything right. He could hardly wait. He was ready to leave Stuttgart behind and there was only one thing he had left to take care. He cranked his car and drove across the street and into his driveway. The lights in the sitting room were on and he could see Julie's silhouette through the curtains. Carefully, without making too much noise, he closed the car door behind him. He walked up the steps to the front door. Hesitation swept over him. He slowly backed away from the door and moved to the right, peeping inside the sitting room. He could see Julie sitting in her favorite chair. She was looking down at something but he couldn't make out what it was. Walking down the porch stairs, he moved towards the side door. He needed total surprise; failure was not an option, not when so much was at stake. No, with his decision to leave town, he could not afford to blow this one. He slipped his key into the lock and turned the doorknob. A faint sound came from the lock as the cylinder turned. Sutton pushed the door open a bit. He knew that when it was humid, the door squeaked at times. He took it slow, making sure that hardly any sound came from his direction. Once inside, he left the door standing open. The hallway in which he stood was dark except for the light coming from the sitting room. The rest of the house was engulfed in an eerie darkness.

Stealthily he moved towards the sitting room. Could he make it up the stairs without being seen? He thought he could. Careful not to stumble into anything, he pressed against the wall and made it to the bottom of the stairs. From around the corner, he could see Julie sitting in her chair, still looking down at whatever it was she had in her hands. He turned the corner and started up the stairs. He reached the top without any problems, having skipped the fifth and eight risers, knowing that they creaked. From the landing he looked down. Nothing! Good, he had made it this far. Quickly he entered his and Julie's bedroom. A smile appeared on his face. It wasn't his room any longer. Strange, he thought, that after all these years, he had no regrets for what he had done. It was all Julie's fault, having been so turned off from anything sexual. Well, he wouldn't need to worry about her turning him down any longer.

He slid the top of Julie's nightstand open and revealed a secret hidden compartment. He reached into his pocket. The dim light from the night-light illuminated the steel blue metal of Julie's .380 handgun. Sutton took a handkerchief from his pocket and rubbed the metal clean. He did not want his fingerprints found on the gun. He placed the gun in the hidden compartment and slid the top back in place. He headed for the door when he heard the sound of footsteps coming up the stairs, a distinctive squeak as the fifth and eight risers were being stepped on.

***

After Hinson had left, Julie Sutton felt as if all the problems of the world rested on her shoulders. The news that her husband had set her up with Lester had come as a shock. However, looking back at the situation, she was not surprised. After cheating on her for all these years, she believed that he was capable of anything. Mentioning the videotape and knowing Hinson had seen the tape made her feel dirty. She had a hard time looking Hinson in the eyes, knowing that he had seen her naked and being taken by Lester. Would he see her as she was, or would he look at her as if he knew what she looked like naked? No matter what, she would not be able to look him in the eyes ever again. Tom Sutton had stooped low this time. If she could get her hands on him, she would teach him a lesson. The events of the past days had made her stronger. She did not feel like the weakling she had been before everything had come tumbling down around her. She felt a surge of adrenaline building inside her body. She needed an outlet before she would do damage to herself or to her home. Her rage was building fast. She had taken the letter Susan had written her and had read it over and over for what seemed like a million times. Susan somehow knew what was going to happen. More than likely, she knew her killer too. Did she look him in the eyes before she was killed? Was she killed at all by the explosion? So many questions, so few answers. She felt tired. She needed to lie down. She had a busy day coming up and she wanted to be rested. She got up and turned the light in the sitting room off. Walking to the stairs, she did not see the side door standing open. Reaching the top of the stairs, she turned in the direction of her bedroom. She hesitated. Something wasn't right; she could feel it. Her stomach contracted at the thought that someone had snuck into her home. She turned towards the stairs and looked down. If anyone was downstairs, she needed to stay upstairs. Tom's study! She walked to the other side of the stairs, looking down from the landing, making sure that nobody was coming up the stairs. She opened Tom's study. She turned the reading light on the desk on. Where was it? She opened drawers and grabbed through them. He had a gun here somewhere! The bottom drawer was locked. She felt her heart beat faster at the thought that she wouldn't be able to get to the gun to defend herself. She was devastated, scared and angry. Again, an uneasy feeling overwhelmed her as she sensed that she was no longer alone in the house. She hunched down behind the desk. As she did, she bumped into the bottom drawer and the lock was released. She heard it click. She opened the drawer and found a small .22 handgun. She grabbed it and cocked the hammer. She was so frightened that she forgot to check to see if there were bullets in the gun. She held her breath and listened. She could hear it now; footsteps. She crawled on her knees to the edge of the desk. She glanced around the corner out the door and unto the landing. She couldn't see anything. She realized that she was a perfect target with the reading light on. She sat up and reached for the desk light when she saw the figure standing in the doorway. She was blinded by the light and couldn't see who it was. All she saw was a dark figure moving in on her. Without thinking, she held the gun in front of her and pulled the trigger. One, cock; two, cock; three, cock; four, cock; five, cock; six cock; nothing, cock; nothing, cock. She fired all bullets into the person in front of her, repeatedly pulling the trigger and cocking the handgun even after all bullets had been fired. The sound of the gunpowder exploding impaired her from hearing the person yell out for her to stop. She was frozen, sitting on her knees, one hand on top of the desk, the other hand hanging on to the gun. She finally started regaining her hearing. She heard load moans coming from the person on the floor. Fear overtook her again. Damn it! She hadn't killed him! She got up off her knees and carefully reached for the phone. She dialed the emergency number

343

and told the dispatcher what had happened. Slowly, she put the phone down, finally laying the gun down on the desk and sitting down in the chair.

***

Tom Sutton who had been curious why Julie had turned away from her bedroom and gone into his study, left the bedroom and snuck up to the study's door. He watched Julie rumble through the drawers. What on earth was she looking for? He decided that maybe it would be better to announce his presence, knowing he kept a .22 handgun in his bottom drawer. He also knew the drawer didn't lock properly and the slightest bump would cause the lock to disengage. As he moved into the doorframe, he could see Julie sitting on her knees behind the desk, trying to turn of the reading light. As she saw him, before he could say anything, she raised the gun and pulled the trigger. Sutton fell to the floor. He was in horrible pain. His shoulder was burning and he could feel the warmth of his blood flowing against his skin. One bullet had hit him in the shoulder, while another had hit his right thigh, just above the knee. Another bullet had struck home as he went down and he could feel blood flowing from his right buttock. Luckily, the other three bullets had not found their target. Still, he was in a lot of pain. He could not feel his right leg and blood was flowing freely from the wound in his thigh. She must have hit an artery. He was scared to call for help, worrying that Julie might reload the weapon and fire another salvo at him. He was still in the dark. He was glad when he saw Julie pick up the phone and call for help. When he saw her sitting down, he tried to call out her name. He had gotten weak from the rapid blood loss and was slowly falling into a coma. His eyelids were starting the feel heavy and the last thing he saw was Julie putting the gun down on his desk.

76.

Dimitri Van Acker opened his eyes. He looked around and sat straight up. Where was he? What had happened? Sunlight was flowing in through the slits in the blinds. He saw clothes scattered around the room. Some where his, others were a woman's. He looked at the other side of the bed. There was nobody but himself in the bed, but someone had obviously been sleeping next to him. He was naked. Suddenly he felt an uneasy feeling flow through his body. Who had he slept with? Rubbing his eyes he looked around the room again to see if he could find anything familiar. Besides his own clothes, he recognized an outfit lying on the floor; a flowery dress that tied in the neck. Kelly! Van Acker shot up out of the bed and ran out of the room, forgetting in his anger that he was not dressed.

Kelly Murphy had gotten up early. She was in a good mood. She had enjoyed the night with Van Acker. He'd been a great lover, even if he had been drugged and probably didn't remember much. She realized that she had to be careful. More than likely, he would be upset when he discovered what had happened. The trick would be to make it look is if it had been his idea, not hers. She needed to convince him that he had been the instigator and that she resisted, thinking it would not be fair to Hope, but finally giving in as her emotions took over. If he ever discovered that she had set him up by drugging his drink, she would lose him forever. She had fixed a light breakfast, set the table and put the newspaper next to the plate where Van Acker would sit. She was ready to pour some coffee when the door to her bedroom flew open.

"What the hell is going on here?" Van Acker shouted, looking Kelly straight in the eyes.

Kelly saw that he was naked and started blushing, barely being able to control a giggle.

"What are you talking about?" she asked innocently.

"Wha... wha... what am I talking about?" Van Acker stuttered. He could feel his anger building and he was close to losing control and his ability to speak English. His native language somehow took over when he was angry and he could feel one of those episodes coming up.

345

"You don't have to scream at me and act like I did something horrible here. If anyone should scream it should be me," Kelly responded assertively.

The tone in Kelly's voice stunned Van Acker and he was short of words. He still did not realize that he was naked. He walked over to the sofa and sat down. Only then did he realize that he was not wearing any clothes. His face grew a dark crimson and he stumbled and fumbled trying to make it to Kelly's room so he could put his clothes on. Kelly busted out laughing and followed him into the bedroom.

"Get out!" What do you think you're doing? I don't want you in here!" he shouted.

"Would you calm down? You're gonna blow a blood vessel, if not my eardrums! Besides, you are in *my* bedroom."

Van Acker looked around. He continued to put his clothes on while Kelly stood in the doorway and watched him.

"You know, you could give me some privacy. This is embarrassing."

"What's so embarrassing? You didn't mind taking off your clothes in front of me last night!"

"I did what?"

"You don't remember? After dinner last night, we danced a little and then you started kissing me. Then you started to undress me! You're lucky that I feel attracted to you too, because I could get you arrested for attempted rape!"

"Wacht eens.. I mean, wait a minute. I did what again? Kiss you? Undress you? Rape you?"

"Well, you didn't rape me. I was a willing participant after I recovered from the initial shock."

"Don't you think that I would know if I had done those things? You know, I remember having dinner with you and I think I remember dancing with you, but after that, I don't remember anything at all until I woke up a little while ago."

"Well, you did have a lot to drink. You drank just about a whole bottle of wine."

"I've drunk whole bottles of wine before, Kelly, and they have never left me in a state of mind where I don't know what I'm doing, much less where I don't remember what I've done. I don't

346

know what you're up to, but I don't like it!"

"What do you mean: what you're up to? I should be asking you that question. I'm not the one who started this. You made the first move. You're the one who undressed me and made love to me."

Van Acker turned white at the words "made love to me". He found the edge of the bed and sat down. He looked at Kelly, his mouth slightly open, wondering what all had happened.

"Kelly, you've got to believe me that I don't remember anything. For all I know, you could be putting me on. You said that we made love. Did we use protection?"

"I made sure that we did, Dimitri. I don't want to get pregnant!"

Van Acker breathed a sigh of relieve. He was slowly regaining control of his emotions and his mind was racing trying to find answers for his strange behavior. Or was it his behavior? He could not help but wonder if Kelly had not tried to get him in her bed. He could never have thought that she would be that infatuated with him. He knew that she had a crush on him when he was in college and lived with her family, but she had never tried to get him in her bed. The most she had done back then was flirt with him. Could she have become so obsessed with him that she could possibly have drugged him? That's what he felt like. He felt as if he'd been drugged. His head was hurting and his mouth was dry. He would have to see if the glass he had used was still dirty. He hoped that it was. Then again, if Kelly had drugged him, why would she leave evidence lying around? No, he was caught in a dangerous web. And what about Hope? She was supposed to have come by. Oh God, what if she had seen him and Kelly? She would be devastated. He hoped and prayed that she did not have a chance to come by and witness the horrible actions that had taken place. He shook his head. Well, he couldn't say that the actions had been horrible. He didn't remember. From the way Kelly looked and felt, he gathered that she had enjoyed last night. All the more reason he was suspicious about the events and how they had taken place.

"Kelly, what did you think when I started to undress you?"

Kelly was surprised by the question. She had let her guard down a bit, feeling that she had convinced Van Acker that he had been the instigating party.

347

"Eh, I don't know. I guess I was flattered. I felt attracted to you last night. I... I really didn't mind."

"What happened last night; is it something that you wanted to happen?"

"I... I can't say that I've never fantasized about it. I just never thought my fantasy would ever come true."

Van Acker managed to smile at her.

"Well, it looks like it came true, didn't it?"

"Yeah, who would have thought?"

"Was it everything you had ever dreamed it would be?"

Kelly produced a smile that seemed to reach from ear to ear.

"It was great! The best lovemaking I've ever had."

"Really? You talk about lovemaking. Don't you mean the best sex you've ever had?"

"What do you mean?"

"Well, for it to be lovemaking, I think that you should love the person that you're doing it with. Are you trying to tell me that you're in love with me?"

Kelly Murphy blushed as she felt that her charade was falling apart. She had been trapped. She should have known better than to think that she had a chance to trick Van Acker. He was after all a lawyer; and a brilliant one at that, from what she understood.

"Why did you do it, Kelly?"

"Do what?" she said defensively.

"Why did you drug me?"

"I didn't drug you! You came on to me. I thought that you loved me, thought that you cared for me."

Kelly started to cry. Tears were flowing down her cheeks and her voice was getting weak.

"Kelly, I do love you, and I do care for you. But I don't see you as my lover. I see you more as a soul mate, someone whom I can turn to in times of need. I see you as someone I can come to when I need a shoulder to cry on, and someone who is there when I need someone to talk to. Look, I didn't know you felt this strongly about me. If I had, I wouldn't have stayed with you. I would have stayed in a motel. It's hard for me to look at you now and not feel embarrassed. Besides, you put me in a hard spot, especially with you working for me.

"You've broken the trust we had. That to me is more sacred than anything else in this world. To know that I can trust you no matter what, means the world to me. Now, I don't know if I can ever trust you again. It will take some time before I can look you in the eyes and tell you a secret, tell you something confidential. I don't know right now if I can trust you working for me. You need to think hard about what you did. Not only that, but what if Hope had come by and saw or heard what we did? I can easily have lost everything that was ever dear to me, just because you wanted to convince me that you loved me and that you were right for me.

"Kelly, I know that you love me; and I want you to know that I love you too. But the love that we share is not the kind of love that makes two people jump in the bed and have wild passionate sex. Our love is the kind that is built on friendship, on mutual understanding and respect for one another. I know that it is hard to see the difference between the love that we share and the love that I share with Hope. My love for Hope right now is built on nothing more than feelings. I still have to build the friendship, the mutual understanding and the respect. I already have that with you. But the one thing that I'm not looking for in you is the sexual attraction. I can feel a whole lot closer to you without being sexually involved with you than I could if we would be involved."

Van Acker took a deep breath. Kelly was sitting next to him on the bed, sobbing, her eyes red and tears running down her cheeks and nose. She was looking down at her feet, feeling like an idiot. She should have known that Van Acker was way out of her reach. She should have known that she didn't stand a chance. At least she had tried. Even though she had failed miserably at her attempt, she had at least enjoyed the closeness she had longed for. She looked Van Acker in the eyes and managed a smile.

"You know what?"

"What?"

"You are the most understanding man God has ever put on this planet."

"Why is that?"

"You should be furious with me, wanting to slap me around and try to hurt me and mess up my life. Instead, here you sit next to me and explain why we can never be lovers. You amaze me, Dimitri

349

Van Acker."

"Well, don't count on me not being furious with you. I'm hot about this whole situation, but I also realize that *slapping you around* is not going to do either of us any good. I'll have to think hard about keeping you on as my secretary. Also, I'll move out today and will get in touch with you when I'm moving into my new house. That should be within the next couple of days. Until then, I want you to think real hard about what happened. I'll keep you on my payroll until I make a decision."

Van Acker took Kelly's chin between his fingers and pulled her head up till their eyes met.

"Now, promise me something."

"Okay."

"Promise me that you'll never pull another stunt like this again."

"I'll promise."

"And one more thing."

"Yes?"

"If for some reason Hope knows about what we did last night, I want you to go to her and apologize for your behavior and confess to the whole thing. I'll be the bad one in her eyes unless she's told differently by the guilty party. Deal?"

Kelly worked her chin loose from between Dimitri's fingers and looked down at her lap. She took a deep breath and focused her eyes back on Dimitri's.

"Okay, if needed, I'll confess to her."

"Thank you. Now, I do believe that I have to go take care of some things."

Van Acker freshened up and changed clothes. Kelly left the house without saying a word. Van Acker sat down at the kitchen table and looked at his notes. He was to go with Julie to the bank today. He wondered what he would find. He also made a note to call Schumaker in DC to find out if his package had arrived and if he had found anything yet. He had a feeling that Susan's murder might have set off a chain reaction in town that was going to be hard to stop unless someone came up with some answers soon. He hoped that he would find those answers. He looked at the clock. It was nearly 10 o'clock. He reached for his phone and dialed the number. He hoped

350

it wasn't too early. He shook his head at that thought. No, he hoped it wouldn't be too late!"

77.

Andrew Hinson was sitting with his head resting in hands in an uncomfortable seat in the waiting room of The Medical Center. It had been a restless night and he had not gotten any sleep. The call had come just after he had gone to bed. The dispatcher on duty had told him that Julie Sutton had just shot her husband. Without much regard for his personal appearance he had hurried out of the house and left for the Sutton home.

Julie Sutton had been in shock. She was rambling and nothing she said made any sense. Hinson tried to make her call her lawyer; however, she said that it was self-defense and that she did not want to speak to anyone. She had collapsed on the way down the stairs. Tom Sutton as well as Julie Sutton had been committed to The Medical Center. Tom Sutton was in life-threatening condition and Julie Sutton had been kept overnight for observation. Hinson had made the decision to post a guard by Julie's room. He hated to think that she had shot Sutton in cold blood. He did not want to take any chance on her slipping out of the hospital and disappearing forever. He could not let that happen. He shook his head thinking about the situation. Not a half hour before the call had come, he had visited with Julie. Did she call Sutton to come over? Maybe he was at fault here. He had told her about the tape. Was that a mistake? He couldn't say; either way, his best friend was fighting for his life.

He looked at his watch. It was 6 am. He'd been up for a little over 24 hours now. A few catnaps in the waiting room had done nothing to bring some relief to the tension he felt in his body. He needed some coffee.

***

Julie Sutton woke up and looked around the room she was in. A hospital room! She closed her eyes and tried to remember how she had gotten here. The last thing she remembered was talking to Hinson about what had happened. Then there was nothing. She had shot Tom! Oh God, forgive me! She felt fear overtaking her body. Would she go to jail? What if no one believed her that it was self-defense? Was it self-defense? Her husband had not carried a weapon. He had just come into the room, his office. Why had he not announced that he was coming over? He could have called out her name! But no, he had snuck into the house for God knows what reason. She didn't understand it. Tears were rolling down her cheeks at the thought she would be going to jail. She had heard terrible stories about women's prisons. Could all of them be true? No, she could not allow herself to get weak and collapse. She needed to be strong. She needed a good lawyer. Dimitri Van Acker! A slight smile appeared on her face as she though of him. Who could ever have imagined that she would need the use of a lawyer in so many ways in such a short period? And to be married to a lawyer on top of that! It all seemed hilariously funny to her. But it wasn't funny at all. She had shot her husband. If he died, she would be charged with murder. No matter what degree of murder she would be convicted off, she would be send to prison. That thought did not appeal to her.

Julie's head jerked to the side when the door opened. It startled her. She expected a nurse or a doctor to come through the door, instead she watched as Andrew Hinson entered the room.

"Good morning, Julie."

"Good morning."

She looked at him with suspicious eyes. He was supposed to be her friend. Would he treat her as a friend or as a criminal? She could only wait and see.

"How you're feeling this morning?"

"I feel all right, I guess."

"Have you thought about what happened last night?"

"Yes, I have."

"Speaking as a friend, I suggest that you call a good defense lawyer. If Tom lives, I can guarantee you that you will need someone good."

"I understand that. I have someone in mind. Don't worry about that. By the way, how is Tom?"

"I haven't heard anything yet. He was in surgery for most of the night. They told me he was in critical condition. He lost a lot of blood. You hit a main artery in his leg. He's lucky you called for help when you did. Otherwise he more than likely would have bled to death."

353

"Lucky for him and lucky for me."

Hinson looked at her and knew what she meant. If Sutton stayed alive, she would be charged with aggravated assault with a deadly weapon, a felony. However, it was better than murder.

"When can I leave?" Julie asked.

"I'm not your doctor, Julie. Speaking as the Sheriff of Dawson County, I will not arrest you. However, if Tom dies, or if he presses charges against you, then I will have to come and arrest you. You do realize that, right?"

Julie nodded her head. She all too well understood what could happen.

"Thank you, Andy."

"Don't thank me yet. I still don't know what happened last night. All I know is that you emptied a revolver at your husband. Why or what the circumstances were, I don't know till you tell me. Still, I don't want you to talk to me without consulting your lawyer first."

"I can tell you that I didn't know it was Tom till after I shot him."

"Stop, Julie. I don't want to know any more. Whatever you say to me, can be used against you. If I think that it is relevant to the case, friend or not, I've got to make a note of it. My notes will be used in a trial, if there is one."

"But I didn't kn…"

Julie was interrupted as a nurse came in. She looked at Julie than at Hinson.

"Mr. Hinson?"

"Yes."

"The doctor asked me to come tell you that your friend Mr. Sutton is being upgraded to stable. His injuries are no longer life threatening."

"Thank you, nurse."

Hinson looked in the direction of Julie and smiled at her.

"Well, it looks like you will not be classified as a murderer after all. The most that you can be charged with now is aggravated assault."

"It doesn't make me feel any better."

Hinson didn't respond. What else was there to say? He

354

could only imagine how terrible she must feel. Shooting her husband and not knowing if he would file charges. He needed to talk to Sutton as soon as he could, get his side of the story. He needed to talk Sutton out of trying to sue Julie. It just wasn't worth it.

Hinson announced that he would go check on Tom. He kissed Julie on the forehead and left the room. Julie's eyes followed him out of the room. She felt funny. Hinson had never expressed his concern or his care for her as he had done just then. She shook her head. Men! She would never understand them. Or was it that she refused to understand them because she was afraid of what they were capable off? She laid back and rested her head in her pillow. She needed to get out of the hospital as soon as possible. She rang the bell. She needed an answer soon. She had a lot to take care off.

78.

Hope Olson looked at the phone. It had been ringing for about a minute now. She couldn't decide if she should answer it. From the number on the caller ID she knew who was calling. She had promised herself that she would have nothing else to do with him. After what he had pulled the night before, she could not make herself face him. How could he! Invite her over and then treat her like that? Having that slutty Murphy woman all over him, kissing on her, having her naked body against his? What did he think she was? Stupid? No! She would not put up with it. She had her life and she didn't want him to be part of it. Or did she? God, the feelings she had for this man. They were stronger than she could have imagined. The phone kept on ringing. Hope grabbed the portable receiver and answered the call.

"Hello?"

"Hope, it's Dimitri."

"What do you want?" Hope responded short.

The tone of her voice must have startled Van Acker. There was a notable silence on the other end.

"I was wondering why you didn't come over last night."

Hope's grip on the phone tightened. That slime! God, he was trying to play her.

"Well, the fact is, I did!"

Again, there was silence. Hope almost smiled at the reaction. She thought it was humorous to be able to play the game from her end. She'd make him squirm.

"You did?"

"Yes. But you were too busy to realize that I was there."

This time the silence annoyed her. He was obviously looking for an excuse of why he had made love to Kelly.

"Listen, if you don't want to have this conversation, just hang up the phone and leave me alone, you son of a bitch!"

"Hope, no! I do want to have this conversation. What exactly did you see?"

"Isn't it bad enough that you had the pleasure of fucking that bitch, you want me to tell you about it too? What is going on? Are you over there jerking off, enjoying making me feel miserable?"

This time she expected Van Acker to be silent. She got her way. She was sure that he would be surprised by her outburst and by her language. She didn't like using bad language but her father had told her once that there was a time for everything. And the time to use bad language was definitely now.

"Hope, I cannot explain this over the phone. Please let me come by and tell you what happened. Even though I know that you will not believe me, I need to tell you this in person. I will see about bringing Kelly with me so she can explain her side of the story. I want you to know that I didn't have any control over what happened."

"That's a good one, asshole. What, you two are plotting something against me? No way in hell am I going to have you and her over. I have a hard enough time deciding whether to let just you come over. If she's anywhere near my house, I'll arrest her for trespassing. You can come over and when I think that you have shown me reasonable doubt about the fact that you had no control over what happened, then I'll consider talking to her."

"That sounds fair, Hope. When can I come over?"

"How does right now sound? Unless you're too busy?"

"I'll be there in 10 minutes."

The phone went dead.

Hope sat down on her couch. She slumped back and looked at the ceiling. She didn't know if meeting Van Acker was a good idea or not. Something inside her told her to hold on, not to let go. She wondered what story he would tell her about what had happened and why he was not responsible for the actions he took. The thing that kept bothering her was that Kelly would back his story up. If she was in love with Van Acker, it seemed that she would do everything in her power to keep him away from her. Hope shook her head. It didn't make sense.

Hope got up and made herself another cup of coffee. There were other matters to consider in this too, she thought, as she poured the hot liquid in her cup. He was involved in the investigation into Susan's death. He knew a lot and without his help, it might take a lot longer to figure out the mystery surrounding Susan's death. She would have to wait and see. Thinking about Susan's death, Hope made a mental note to call the medical examiner, an autopsy needed

357

to be performed. By now, the funeral home should be cleaned up from Underwood's murder. The embalming room should be ready. She could hardly wait to see what they would find.

79.

Just like the day before, Michelle Murphy was sitting across the street from Dr. Scarboro's office. She had been there for a little over half an hour, the engine cranked and the A/C pumping cold air. She could not decide whether to confront Bryan Scarboro with the two vials of medication. She had looked up the name on a medical Internet site, but had not been able to find out anything else beyond what she had read in Susan's file. She wondered if Scarboro had somehow been able to inject Susan with a deadly dose of the medication. She needed to get her name cleared. There was enough circumstantial evidence to put her away. There was motive and evidence. Who could the other person have been?

She sunk down in her seat as Bryan Scarboro left the building and headed for his red BMW. Michelle put her car in gear and followed Scarboro as he drove off. She made sure that she stayed a good distance behind his car. She didn't want him to know she was following him. Not yet! She wondered where he was headed; it was too early for lunch. It had seemed a bit slow and she was sure that between the nurse and Dr. Scarboro, they would be able to handle the patients.

***

Bryan Scarboro had told his father that he couldn't concentrate on his work and needed to get out for a little bit. Earl Scarboro had agreed. He understood the strain his son must be in right now. He hoped that he had not contracted the disease. It was bad enough that he had contracted it from Susan. It would not look good if both father and son had contracted the same disease from the same woman.

Bryan Scarboro had taken blood and it was ready to be sent off to the lab. I would take a couple of days before he would get an answer as to whether of or not he had the disease. He hoped that nothing would show up. Of course, he would need to be checked every six months for the next two years. He still couldn't believe Michelle had called his mother and told her about the chance of him having contracted the virus. She had also told his mother whom he could have contracted it from. He would deal with Michelle Murphy. When he got through with her, she would think twice before she talked to anyone else about his affairs again.

Bryan Scarboro figured that Murphy was working and headed towards Langston's. Michelle Murphy, who was keeping a safe distance from Scarboro, realized where he was headed when he took the last turn. Unconsciously, she slowed down a bit and increased the distance between them. She had a good idea what or who he was looking for. Her! Calling his mother had been hard to do. After things had settled at home, she had gone on the computer and research the subject of HIV and AIDS. If she had contracted the disease, she read, she had at worst 10 years to live. She was too young to die! Even ten years from now she would still be too young. No, the consequences of her sleeping with Scarboro and having sex with him, even if it was with protection, could be devastating to her, and his family as well. She had met his mother a couple of times and she liked Mrs. Scarboro. She felt that she needed to do the right thing and tell her about the possibilities because she felt Scarboro would not be truthful. Had she crossed her boundaries? She hated to think that someone would have called her mother with that kind of news, but realized at the same time that it would be for the better if the immediate family was involved. A family was always stronger than just one person. Even though she hated Bryan Scarboro for what he did, she wanted him not to have to suffer by himself but felt that he would need the support of his family. Little did she know that telling the secret had brought on the wrong reaction, on both sides of the field. She realized, following Scarboro to Langston's that he had not appreciated her telling his mother. What she didn't know or realized was that Scarboro's mother had not appreciated it either, but for different reasons.

Bryan Scarboro pulled up into the parking lot and looked around. He could not find Michelle's car. He banged the steering wheel. Where was she? Scarboro parked his car and walked into the store. Michelle positioned herself behind some bushes across the road and watched.

Scarboro walked up to Phil Langston and asked if Michelle Murphy was working. Langston told him that she was scheduled to work that afternoon. Michelle could vaguely see Langston pushing his finger in Scarboro's chest. She had a good idea what he was telling him.

The finger poking him in the chest surprised Scarboro.

"Listen here, punk, I can't keep you from coming in here and spending your money. But if I so much as see you come in here and try to give Michelle any trouble, I promise you, you'll have something coming your way."

"Sir," Scarboro said, trying to act innocently, "I don't know what you're talking about. You can't prevent me from seeing Michelle or talking to her."

"That's what you think. I own this place and I can ban you from coming in here. This is private property. If I don't want to see your mug in here, then by George, I'll make sure that it doesn't come in here. Now get the hell out of here!"

Scarboro started to say something, but the look in Langston's face told him it would be wise not to do so and to get out as told.

***

Michelle Murphy produced a smiled as she guessed at what had been said inside the store. She figured that Patricia Langston had told her parents about what had happened to her. She hoped that she wouldn't have said too much. She watched Scarboro get back in his car and drive off, tires spinning and leaving black rubber marks on the concrete parking lot. Inside, she noticed Phil Langston shouting something. She knew that he was furious now. If there was something he despised more than anything it was someone laying rubber in his parking lot. Michelle again followed Scarboro. She knew where he was headed. She hoped that he was actually not crazy enough to try to go to her house. She looked at the clock. Her father would be at the farm, however, with her mother no longer working...

She pushed the gas pedal down and accelerated until she was right behind Scarboro's car. She waited for the curve in the road. Just past the curve was a small stretch of straight away road. She pushed the accelerator down and passed Scarboro, honking her horn while she did so. When the cars were side by side, she looked over at Scarboro and shot him a bird. She then finished passing him and sped up even more, reaching close to 80 mph. Michelle hoped and prayed that no deer would decide to cross the road and she also hoped that no Sheriff's cruisers would be out on this side of the county.

The honking of the horn surprised Scarboro. Looking in his rearview mirror, he saw the car starting to pass him. What an idiot! When the car was next to him, he decided that he would take a quick look to see if he knew this idiot. Surprised to see Michelle Murphy, he slowed down a bit and his face turned crimson when he saw her throw up her middle finger at him. He had her now! As soon as Michelle had passed him, he punched down the accelerator. His BMW had a little bit more get up and go than Michelle's older sedan. It didn't take long for Scarboro to catch up with her and he was riding her bumper. His rage was growing. He was going to hurt her. He checked his mirrors. Nothing was coming. He pushed down the accelerator some more and started a passing maneuver. Michelle Murphy's car was going at least 85 mph and Bryan was slowly pulling up besides her. He was sweating profusely by now, both excited and mad. His excitement came from the high speed and the danger involved in what he was doing. The madness came from knowing that Michelle Murphy had destroyed his life. He didn't want anyone to know that he might be infected with the HIV virus; least of all his mother! God, she was impossible as it was. Now with Michelle's revelation, it had become even worse. He was determined he was going to take care of Michelle. He looked over at her car next to his. He could see her, holding the steering wheel as best she could to keep from losing control of her car. She looked over at him for a brief moment. He could see the fear in her eyes. Seeing her like that excited him even more. He turned his attention back to the road in front of him. His face turned white. In front of him, not 400 feet away, a log truck was headed in his direction. Black smoke emerged from the back of the truck. He looked down at his speedometer for a brief moment. He was doing right at 95 mph.

***

The driver of the log truck had seen the red BMW just a moment too late to be able to pull to the side of the road. An empty feeling in his stomach was all he could feel as he pushed the brake pedal of his truck down as hard as he could. The rear tires of the truck locked up and produced black smoke. The same happened with the tires on his trailer. All eight tires on the trailer locked at the same time and produced more black smoke as the rubber was melted away from the tires. The weight of the logs on his trailer made it difficult to calculate how much room he was going to need to come to a stop. He looked at the red BMW coming closer. Maybe, if he could come to as near a stop as possible, the impact would not be as bad. The driver noticed the sedan that was now side by side with the red BMW. Oh God, this doesn't look good!

***

Bryan Scarboro scanned the side of the road for a clearing where he could possibly drive off the road. He didn't have much time to consider what to do. The gap between him and the log truck was closing fast. There was a ditch to his left, a pasture with no ditch in front of it to his right. Without thinking about the consequences, Scarboro hit the brakes of his car as hard he could and threw his steering wheel to the right.

***

Michelle Murphy had seen the log truck as soon as it came around the curve a good 600 feet away. She hoped that Scarboro would realize that it was coming. With the high speed of both cars it was hard to tell what would happen. Michelle's face turned white when she saw the truck lock up his tires. She had seen too many movies where the trailer would go sideways when the tires locked. She didn't want the truck to land on top of her. She looked for a place to run off the road and hopefully, be safe. She couldn't see anything in sight.

***

The truck driver saw the maneuver Scarboro did and breathed a sigh of relieve. He eased up on the brakes a bit. He knew the

363

driver would more than likely get hurt going through the pasture. He would have to go see and help him. Then the sedan caught his eyes again.

***

Michelle Murphy had never been in a situation like this before; nowhere to go and the possibility of a log truck trailer headed her way, she pushed the accelerator down. Her car vibrated and objected to the abuse it was receiving. It soon reached its maximum speed. The engine was overheating and the oil was deteriorating at a fast rate. The pistons where pushing in and out and faster and faster with less and less lubrication protection from the oil. The four-cylinder car was pushed to its limits. Michelle could feel that something wasn't right with her car. She knew that she had pushed it to the limit. Smoke was starting to come from underneath the hood. Metal to metal sounds were audible. She looked at the log truck. She was about 70 feet away from it. Almost!

"Come on, car, we're almost there! Please make it past the truck!" she shouted.

***

Bryan Scarboro felt his car leave the paved road and enter the grass area. A fraction of a second later he heard the barbed wire fence make contact with his car. With both rear wheels locked, the wetness of the grass made his car start to spin. He panicked. Never before had he been in a car that was sliding and spinning. He turned the steering wheel. Unfortunately for Scarboro he turned it in the wrong direction. This made his car spin even faster. He could feel his stomach contract as his car lifted off the grass and started flipping.

***

Michelle Murphy's car didn't make it past the log truck before her engine locked up. The friction and consequent heat caused between the metal parts of the engine and lack of lubrication from the deteriorated oil locked all moving parts within the engine. A brief second after the tires locked, they came loose with a snap as they detached from the transfer case. The tires locking up followed shortly by being turned loose again made Michelle lose control of her car for just a second. She could see the rear of the log trailer heading her way. The longest logs were sticking out behind the trailer a good 4 to 6 feet. She could see the end of one coming closer to her windshield. As by miracle, the trailer made a sudden move away from her car. Michelle pushed down the brakes and stopped on the left hand side of the road, facing the wrong direction. She lowered her head to her steering wheel and started crying.

***

Bryan Scarboro's red BMD finally stopped after flipping through the air for what had seemed forever. The car landed on its tires. Scarboro was conscious. He could feel a sharp pain in his chest. He looked down and found himself trapped in his seat with the steering wheel pushed tight against his chest. Breathing was getting harder to do. He suspected that several of his ribs must have punctured his lungs. He was crushed over the steering wheel and could feel to top of the car pushing down on his head and neck. He couldn't move. Blood was flowing freely from his nose. He tried to move his fingers but couldn't. Somehow, the pressure from the top of the car on his neck was pinching a nerve somewhere, making it impossible for him to move any of his body parts. He was taking short breaths trying to keep air in his lungs. He needed help soon.

***

The log truck driver had seen the sedan leave the lane it was in. Applying the brakes had caused his trailer to slide to the left. He let go of the brakes and with the renewed speed, the trailer straightened itself out, just enough for the sedan to miss the logs. He applied the brakes again and stopped 200 feet away from where the red BMW had left the road. The truck driver got out and looked towards the sedan. The driver looked to be all right. He then looked towards the red BMW. He would be surprised if anyone in that car would still be alive. He reached into the cab of the truck and grabbed his cell phone. He dialed 911 and gave them the location of the wreck and what had happened. He switched off the phone and started to run towards the red BMW, hoping that it would not be too late.

***

Michelle Murphy lifted her head from her steering wheel and looked in the rearview mirror, witnessing the truck driver heading into the pasture towards Bryan's car.

"I hope you're dead," she muttered quietly to herself.

She then grabbed her cell phone and called home. She explained to her mother what had happened. Yes, she was all right. Her car was wrecked, but she was all right. The line went dead. She laid the phone next to her and reclined her seat. She would sit and wait.

80.

Dimitri Van Acker rushed over to Hope Olson's house as fast as he could. He knew that it would be hard to convince her that he was mentally unaware of what happened between Kelly and him. He hoped it was not too late.

It was just 10 o'clock when Dimitri Van Acker drove into Hope Olson's driveway. He hurriedly got out and made his way to the door. Before he could knock, the door opened and hope stood in front of him. She had on her uniform and looked upset.

"Can I come in?"

Hope looked at Van Acker with penetrating eyes and finally moved to the side and motioned him to come in.

"Thank you."

Van Acker felt out of place, not knowing whether to sit down or to stand up. He played with a button on his shirt and looked at the ground.

"Why don't you sit down?" Hope asked.

"Thanks."

Hope sat opposite of Van Acker and stared at him. Van Acker could barely raise his head to meet her eyes. He could feel her eyes burning holes in the top of his head. What was she thinking? Would she ever be able to trust him again? Slowly he raised his head and met her stare. He looked at her. She was sitting there, in her uniform with her hair still loose. She was absolutely gorgeous. He would be a fool to go to someone else and let her slip through his fingers. He had been a fool; or had he? He doubted himself now about his feelings for Kelly. Was she just like a sister to him or had it been unavoidable that they would get hooked up as lovers? No! He was not attracted to Kelly sexually. He was attracted to her mentally, as a friend and as a sister he'd never had. He made that clear to her this morning. Would Hope understand? Would she believe that he had no feelings for Kelly Murphy and that what she had witnessed was nothing more than a set up by Kelly to try to win his heart? Tears popped into Van Acker's eyes at the thought of losing Hope and being left with nothing.

Hope was studying Van Acker's face. He looked like a beaten puppy. He was obviously too ashamed to look her in the eyes. She tried to think of how she would feel if she had been in his situation. She didn't know Van Acker well enough yet to figure out exactly how he reacted to situations like these. Obviously he was disturbed by it. When she saw him lifting his head and noticed the tears running down his face, she knew that whatever had happened between Kelly and him had not made him happy. She knew that he was sincere about his feelings for her.

"Dimitri?"

Van Acker swallowed before he replied.

"Yes, Hope."

"I need to know for sure if you have any feelings for Kelly Murphy. I can see that you are upset about this whole situation but I need proof."

Van Acker lowered his head slowly then looked back up at Hope.

"What do you want me to do or say? What can I do to make you see that I am not in love with Kelly and that I don't have any sexual attraction for her?"

Hope shook her head.

"You know, Dimitri, it's hard for me not to suspect that something is going on between you and Kelly. You used to live with her family. I've seen the looks that Kelly used to give you when you lived with them, and now that you've come back, she's still giving you those looks."

"You're right. But have you also noticed that those looks were and are one directional? I cannot remember once giving her a look that would make her believe that I was interested in her beyond the relationship that we have."

"Except for last night!"

"Hope, please understand. I was unaware of what was going on. Kelly used a drug on me, you have to believe that!"

"Dimitri, as much as I want to believe that, the fact remains that I saw you kissing her, that I saw you caressing her naked body. From everything that I witnessed, I can only assume that you were aware of what was going on. I did not see you laying on the couch, passed out, being left to her every whim and want."

Van Acker lowered his head again.

"Hope, I know I did not do anything last night that I wanted to do. I have never dreamed of having sex with Kelly Murphy. When I woke up in her bed this morning I was as surprised as I could be. I did not remember how I got there or what had happened. I questioned Kelly and she finally confessed to me that she had drugged me and that she was in love with me."

Hope got up off the couch when she heard about Van Acker waking up in Kelly's bed. She had a hard time coping with these revelations, especially since she felt so strongly attracted to him.

"Hope, I told Kelly I was moving out today. I don't want to stay with her any longer. The only relationship I will have with her is that of an employer and employee. I also told her that if she tried something like that again I would fire her instantly and never have anything to do with her, ever again. Is that enough for you to realize that I am not looking to have a relationship with her?"

"How can I know for sure that you're not making all this up as you go along? How can I be sure that you will not secretly see her? You're telling me that you will not even interact with her as a friend? I cannot believe that. You are too close to her family not to interact with her!"

Van Acker thought for a minute, he needed to choose his words carefully. Hope was bright and picked up on every little detail. He felt as if he were in a courtroom trying to get some murderer from going to jail. The thing was, the murderer in this case was innocent but the accuser had evidence that the murderer did it. The prove was there. He was guilty of having sex with Kelly, but did a person commit a crime if someone else held their hand on the gun and pulled their finger back on the trigger? Even if there was a witness who saw the gun in the person's hand, it doesn't mean he consciously pulled the trigger. This was exactly what he was faced with in this situation. He needed to get the responsible party to admit to their crime. Even then, it would be hard to convince Hope that he had not felt an attraction towards Kelly that night. He needed to get in touch with Kelly and have her confess to Hope what she had done.

"Hope, I guess it doesn't matter whether I tell you the truth or not. You will not believe me until you have evidence that I was indeed drugged and had no conscious participation in the actions you witnessed. Therefore, I will leave here with a heavy heart, knowing that I might lose you forever. I am asking you to please contact

Kelly Murphy and get her side of the story. She has told me she'd tell you the truth. I believe that she realizes now that I can never be part of her life the way she would like me to be. She'd be a fool to try to hold on to something she can never have. She may be wicked and sly but she's not stupid. So for your sake and mine, get with her and let her put your mind at ease."

Van Acker got up and walked to the door. He turned around and watched as Hope sat back down and held her head in her hands. Tears were flowing down her cheeks. She turned her head towards Van Acker as he opened the door.

"Dimitri, I want to believe you so bad. I just don't want to get hurt again. You've left me once, don't leave me again!"

"I am not going to leave you, Hope. But until you can come to grips with what happened last night and realize that I had no control in what happened, I don't think we need to see each other. I hope and pray that you'll talk to Kelly today because I don't want to be away from you for long. Hope, I love you more than I've ever loved anyone. I have always had you on my mind. I always hoped that one day, I could come back and you'd still be here. Now I'm back and you're still here. You're still here, waiting for me. I'll be waiting for you till the day comes that you can realize that you're the only one for me. Goodbye, Hope!"

Van Acker opened the door and walked out. Hope sat on the couch, tears flowing freely down her cheeks. She wanted to get up and run after Van Acker and tell him that she loved him too and that she didn't want him to leave but somehow, she couldn't. Somehow, in the back of her mind, a little voice was telling her to be careful, to be careful of a skilled lawyer who could talk his way around anything. Was Van Acker really like that? He had shown his emotions too. He had sat there in front of her and cried. She could not remember ever having seen a grown man cry. He had been the first. She needed more time, more prove. She could not let her heart be played with. She looked out the window as Van Acker dove off towards town. Ever so softly she whispered:

"I love you, too, Dimitri. I love you more than you'll ever know."

370

81.

The log truck driver made it to the BMW after tripping over grass mounts and stepping into cow manure. He looked inside the car. The driver was bleeding severely from the nose. The roof of the car was crushed and the driver was pressed against the steering wheel.

"Can you feel anything?" he asked Bryan Scarboro.

"No!" Scarboro responded with great difficulty. Breathing had become a hard task to do. It was almost impossible for him to bring air into his lungs.

"Don't move! Help is on the way! I'll go check on the woman in the other car and see if she's okay."

The truck driver ran back towards the road.

***

Bryan Scarboro closed his eyes. It had been stupid of him to try to outrun Michelle and then force her off the road. Sure his car was faster than hers, but he had underestimated the power her old car could produce. He had no idea if she had wrecked or if she had been able to reach the side of the road in one piece. He hoped for the former. It had been his plan to make her wreck and hopefully kill her. He had never really cared for her. She had been easy pray for his sexual wants. Everything had worked out. But then Susan Knox had revealed her horrible secret to him. He felt obligated to Michelle Murphy to tell her the truth. He had not foreseen her turning into a monster of gigantic proportions that he did not know how to tame except by killing it. Now, he was almost dead himself and he was sure the monster was okay. How ironic!

***

Michelle Murphy jumped when she heard the knock on her window. She looked over and saw a man standing next to her car. She didn't know who it was, but she was sure that it had been someone who had witnessed the wreck. She moved her seat back to the upright position and opened her door.

371

"Miss, are you alright?" the tuck driver asked.

Michelle looked around to see if anyone else had stopped or maybe seen the accident. No one else was present and the only other vehicle around was the truck. This must be the truck driver.

"Yes, I'm fine. I didn't think I was going to make it. I came close to hitting your truck."

"Yes, I know. It was all I could do to keep it from jackknifing. You're a very lucky young lady."

"Thanks."

Michelle Murphy looked over towards the pasture. She pointed in that direction.

"And that car?"

"Pretty bad situation; the man is crushed inside the car. He's alive, but if help doesn't arrive soon, I'm afraid we'll lose him."

"I see."

Michelle Murphy got out of the car and started walking towards the pasture. She could feel the stare of the truck driver in her back. She knew it wasn't a concerned stare. He was admiring her body. She couldn't believe that even in this bad situation, he would be no better than if they'd met in a bar.

"Ma'am, I wouldn't do that if I were you."

Michelle didn't respond. She kept on walking. She walked over the loose barbed wire and struggled towards Bryan Scarboro's car. She was careful not to step in any cow manure. Just before she reached the car, she turned around and checked to see where the truck driver was. He was walking back towards his truck. She waited till he climbed into the cabin and then continued towards Bryan Scarboro.

***

Bryan Scarboro had managed to keep his breathing to a minimum. He had opened his eyes when he heard the grass rustle nearby. Maybe it was the truck driver again. Maybe he would have some tools with him to help him out of this situation. He took a breath. His face turned white as the pain he felt in his chest was worst than it had been. He could feel the sharp pain in his lungs with every breath. His ribs pushing deeper and deeper, letting more and more blood flow inside his lungs. He moved his eyes up as far as he could. He wanted to move but couldn't. It wasn't the truck driver; it was Michelle Murphy. He could not believe what he saw; not a hair was out of place. It was as if nothing had happened. Next to the whitish look on her face, you would not be able to tell anything was wrong.

"What the hell were you trying to do?" Michelle asked Scarboro. "Were you trying to kill me?"

Bryan Scarboro tried to wet his dry lips. With difficulty he managed to rub his tongue over his lips, but his tongue was also dry. His mouth felt as if it were leather.

"You know, I don't care what happens to you. For all I care, you can die right here. It's your own fault you're in this situation. I don't know what your plans were with me, but I know that it was something I wasn't going to enjoy."

Michelle moved a little closer towards Scarboro and bent down so she was face to face with him.

"To think that I once believed that you were the right one for me; God, I should have listened to everybody else. I should have never gone on my feelings. All these years I've been able to control my emotions, but with you I figured that it would be all right to let go. I figured that you would be true to me. Boy, I was so wrong. You were the worst one of them all. And you know, because of you, I may never know true love; instead, I may be dying a slow agonizing death; just like you are right now."

Michelle cocked her head to one side and looked at Scarboro with spite in her eyes.

"I want to know one thing from you, Bryan. You see, everybody around me thinks that I killed Susan and that I started the fire in her apartment. But I know I didn't do it. I was planning on it, but someone got there before I did. Tell me, Bryan, did you kill Susan? Did you go over there that night and kill her?"

Michelle reached inside her pocket and produced the vials of Coeurnechol. She showed them to Scarboro and she could see the fear in his eyes.

"Look familiar?" she asked as she threw the two vials inside Scarboro's wrecked car.

Scarboro was trying hard to collect enough air in his lungs to give Michelle a response. He was barely able to breathe now; what little air he was able to take into his lungs earlier, seemed to be an impossible task now. The blood was filling his lungs up quickly and the air volume in them decreased rapidly. He could feel his head getting light as lack of oxygen was making its presence known. He looked at Michelle with bulging eyes. All he could do in a form of a response was to move his eyes from side to side. He wasn't able to produce any more sounds. Scarboro knew the end was near when things started to get dark. He was losing his ability to see. His brain was close to being without oxygen. If help didn't arrive soon, he would be dead within minutes. He closed his eyes. He was frightened. He had never been what one would call a believer in God or Jesus. The unknown scared him. Was there such a thing as Heaven and Hell? If so, where would he end up? The thought that came to mind was frightening him. He hadn't lived his live the way he should have. He had been careless and always taking the lives and feelings of others for granted. If God indeed existed, then for sure, he knew he would not make it to Heaven. It became harder to think. He was unable to take any more air into his lungs. He knew the end was near. God forgive me, please be kind and...

Michelle looked at Scarboro. His skin had turned a color she had never before seen on a person. She knew that it wasn't good. She looked towards the road. She heard sirens in the background. They were too late. She knew Scarboro was dead. She stood up and took a deep breath. She started walking back towards the road. She looked up into the sky.

"God have mercy on his soul," she whispered.

***

Allen Murphy had received the phone call from Helen and dropped everything. He had raced to the site of the accident as fast as he could. When coming to the accident scene, he saw his daughter's car sitting on the side of the road. Unharmed, yet smoking from the engine. Than God she was alive! He looked over towards the pasture and saw Michelle walking towards the road. He pulled up beside her and rolled his window down.

"Are you okay, sweetheart?"

Michelle looked at him and smiled.

"Yes, I'm okay, Daddy."

"Bryan?"

Michelle nodded her head.

"Nope, he's dead," she said coldly and looked at the car over her shoulder.

"Are you sure?"

Michelle nodded her head.

"Yes! And he didn't kill Susan as I suspected he had," she added.

The response threw Murphy, but he also realized the pain Scarboro had put her through. He didn't feel bad for Bryan Scarboro. He felt bad for Mr. and Mrs. Scarboro. They were without a son.

"Is Mom coming?" Michelle asked.

"Yeah, she's on her way."

"I'll go home with her then."

Murphy nodded his head. He knew Michelle was under a lot of stress. He watched her walk backs towards the road as two State Troopers and a Sheriff's cruiser pulled up into the pasture. He hoped that Michelle was indeed innocent of Susan's murder and he hoped to God that she had not planned this as well. Someone was eventually going to put one and two together. He was afraid that Dimitri Van Acker was already adding things up.

82.

Kelly Murphy had not felt the best after her conversation with Dimitri Van Acker about the events of the previous night. She felt like a fool for making herself believe that she had so much as a shred of hope to ever win his heart. She knew now that Van Acker was not interested in her the way that she wanted him to be. He would always remain there as a big brother to her. At least, she had been able to love him and care for him the way she wanted to, even if it had only been for one night. She smiled at the thought of their lovemaking. It had been passionate, yet he had been gentle and considerate to her feelings. Too bad he won't remember how wonderful it had been. The drug that she'd gotten from her friend had worked miracles. He had performed to her liking, but for what? It had been a one-night stand, and a one-night stand was all it would ever be. She wanted happiness for herself, but she also wanted happiness for him. She loved him too much to want to hurt him. He was in love with Hope Olson and he was happiest when he was with her. So, she would let him go, just so he could be happy.

Kelly looked at her watch. It was almost lunchtime. She hadn't realized that she had been driving aimlessly around town, her mind far away from what was happening around her. There was something that she needed to do. She needed to make things right with Van Acker. She did not like the distrust that he had for her. Most of all, she did not want to loose her job because of what she had done. The first step in winning back his trust would be to go over to Hope's and confess everything to her. Kelly turned towards Hope's house.

The drive to Hope's house was a short one. Kelly drove into the driveway. She swallowed hard as she pulled herself together. She had no idea what was going to happen. She didn't know how Hope would react to her confession. She rang the doorbell.

Hope Olson opened the door and looked surprised to see Kelly Murphy at her front door. Her eyes were still red from crying.

"Hi Hope. Can I please come in?"

Hope didn't say anything and motioned for Kelly to come in. Kelly stood in the middle of the living room, playing with the hem of her shorts. She was nervous and didn't know where to start.

"You know, it's funny that you came over because I was just about to try to call you to meet with you," Hope started the conversation.

"Really? What about?"

"Dimitri."

Kelly looked down at the floor.

"So you know?"

"Yes I do! I was there last night. I saw you two through the window."

"What did Dimitri say happened?"

"He told me that you drugged him; that he has no recollection of what happened. Is that true?"

Kelly took a deep breath.

"It's true Hope, I set it all up. Dimitri is not involved with me. He's in love with you. He has no eyes for anyone else. What I did was wrong, I know that now. But I'm in love with him and I cannot change my feelings. But I want you to know that I will not pursue him. I'd be a fool. Why chase after something that's not attainable? I will only hurt myself more than I am hurt now. I wouldn't blame you if you never wanted to talk to me again; but I'd like for us to be friends. Dimitri will always be a part of my life and I'll always be a part of his. If you and he become a permanent item, then somewhere down the line, our paths will cross. I'd rather us be friendly when our paths cross than be enemies. It will make things a whole lot easier for all of us."

Hope had sat down and listened to Kelly. As much sense as she made, it was still hard to believe that one could do all of these things without the other person having any recollection of the events. She had read up on date rape crimes where the woman was drugged and then sexually abused. Usually, the victim had no recollection of what had happened. She knew the drugs to accomplish such a state-of-mind were out there. It was scary to think that those were floating around Stuttgart. She had to make a tough decision. She needed to believe Kelly's side of the story. She needed to believe her confession to her. It must have been hard for Kelly to come over and tell her side of the story. From the conversation, she realized that Van Acker had not told her that she knew about what had happened. She had to believe her. For her own sake and for her love for Van

377

Acker, she had to believe Kelly.

"Kelly, I don't know if we can ever be good friends; especially after what you pulled. I do believe that you're telling the truth. I want to thank you for that. If you knew how much Dimitri means to me, you would have never pulled that stunt. I'm sure that if you continue to work for Dimitri, our paths will cross. I'll be friendly towards you but remember, I'll always distrust you when it comes to him. I don't like the thought of you working for him, but that's his decision. If you can show me that you will keep your relationship with him professional, then and only then will I be able to start trusting you."

"Thank you, that's all I ask of you. Now, go get Dimitri and make up with him! That will make you feel better."

Hope produced a smile as Kelly got up and walked towards the door.

"I'll do that. I'll call him right now."

"Good. I'm glad you understand as well as you do."

Hope smirked and pointed her finger at Kelly.

"Don't push your luck. You're not out that door yet!"

"Okay, point taken. See ya!"

Kelly drove off, feeling a whole lot better than before her conversation with Hope. Even though she felt better, tears were flowing down her cheeks, as she knew that Van Acker was forever out of her reach. She shook her head. Hope had said, "if only you knew how much I loved Dimitri!" If only Hope knew how much she loved Dimitri Van Acker herself! Love was so unfair.

Hope sat down after Kelly left. She felt better about the situation. She was glad that she had talked with Kelly. Still, if she and Dimitri Van Acker were going to have a relationship, there were going to be ground rules. She was not going to get hurt. She reached for her phone and called his cell number.

83.

The phone on the nightstand was ringing relentlessly. Andrew Hinson woke up slowly as the annoying ring from the phone reached his ears. He hoped the ringing would go away, however, whoever was calling him knew he was home and needed to reach him. Mad at being woken up after only a few hours of sleep, Hinson reached for the phone.

"Hello?"

"Mr. Hinson, this is Debra. I didn't know whether to disturb you with this or not, but I think it's important that you know."

"Okay, Debra, what is it?"

"Bryan Scarboro, the doctor's son was killed in a car wreck just a little bit ago. It seems that he was in a race with Michelle Murphy. He lost control of his car and rolled it in a pasture."

Hinson listened and he felt his stomach tighten. He was good friends with Dr. Scarboro and he knew that he would take this hard. Even though Bryan Scarboro was a troublemaker and up to no good, Dr. Scarboro loved his son and hoped that one day he would come to his senses and take life seriously. Now, it seems that his worries had come to an end; unfortunately not the type ending anyone would have hoped for.

"Thanks Debra. I'll go visit Dr. Scarboro later this afternoon. I'm still trying to recover from the Sutton ordeal from last night. If anything else comes up, please get in touch with Hope and let her handle it."

"Yes, sir. Will do!"

Hinson put the handle back on the receiver. He dropped his head back into his pillow. The events of the recent days were getting to him. Too many people had lost their lives. The biggest loss to Hinson was losing his best friend, Gerald Radcliff. He could not understand why Radcliff had taken his own life. Had he been involved with Susan Knox and somehow contracted the AIDS virus? If Radcliff had contracted the AIDS virus from Susan Knox, then he understood why he had taken his own life. Radcliff had a lot to lose if the news spread that he had contracted the virus. His career would be finished. The mindset that Radcliff lived by was that it was better to take your own life than to live with the shame and embarrassment of everyone knowing you have AIDS because you screwed around with the town whore.

Hinson took a deep breath. The news of Bryan's early dead had shaken him to the point where he could not go back to sleep. At one time, the loss of a friend's life had not bothered him. He had been in Vietnam and had seen many of his friends die. He had learned to deal with it. Being a pilot in the Air Force, he had seen planes being hit by SAM's and AAA's. He had been lucky never to have gotten hit. He had learned to live with the knowledge that once you took off, you or your friends might not make it back. He had also learned to live with the losses, the loss of friends, and the loss of confidence in the system. He had learned not to question why they were not allowed to fly across a certain line drawn on a certain map. He had learned to follow orders no matter what they were. The key was to fly the missions and try to survive so you could do it all again the following day.

Now, it was not as easy to deal with the loss of a friend's life. He had grown softer through the years. He had lost his hard edge that had made him a survivor during the war. He was thankful for that hard edge, as he would not have been able to survive the hatred he had felt towards him after returning from Vietnam. He had been able to ignore the criticism and the hate he had felt for years after returning from the war. As he had hoped, the hatred had passed and the respect for him and for what he had done, returned. Sure, there were still a few of the hard-line hippies who thought he was a baby killer. Luckily, those were far and few between. The younger generations had lived through the Reagan Presidency and had enjoyed the military built-up against the Soviet Union, against Communism. That younger generation had gained a renewed respect for their military.

Hinson sighted. Too bad that with the coming down of the Berlin Wall, the need for a large military force had also come down. He was glad to be a civilian. He didn't think that he could survive in today's military. The military was spread too thin. Not only that, but it seemed that every other month, forces were being dispersed all over the world to play international police leaving the mainland US unprotected. He hated to think there would be an attack of any magnitude on the US mainland. There was no way the armed forces in place could protect the country now.

Hinson shook his head and looked at the clock. Close to lunchtime. He needed to get started. There were a couple of things that he wanted to check on before someone else did. Hope Olson was tied up with the Susan Knox case. By his own choosing, he was in charge of the Joshua Underwood murder. He needed to close the case. The funeral home needed to be re-opened. Susan Knox' body had to be put to rest as soon as possible. He would have to check with Olson and see where the investigation into the explosion was headed. He hoped an autopsy would not be required but if so, it could take another week or two before the body would be put to rest. That wouldn't be good. As far as the murder of Joshua Underwood was concerned, it was simple. He would write it up as a robbery. Underwood's wallet had been found empty. The burglar had used a .44 caliber handgun to blow Underwood into the hereafter. Case closed. His funeral could be held before Susan's.

As he got dressed, Hinson looked at the cut on his arm. He could not for the life of him remember where he had gotten it. He knew that it hadn't hurt when he cut himself. To his surprise, he had seen the bloodstain on his shirt. Even though it hadn't hurt when it happened, it had become slightly infected. The cut had been deeper than he first thought and dirt had gotten into the wound. He would need to bandage the wound. He wished he could remember what had happened.

After a quick lunch, Andrew Hinson was on his way to the Sheriff's office. He hoped that Olson would come in early and work on Susan Knox's case. He wanted to check her notes and see if there was anything he could help her with. Most of all, he wanted to make sure that Dimitri Van Acker was not too closely involved with the investigation. He didn't like the lawyer. He needed to watch him closely. The last thing he needed was a lawyer getting involved with his department's investigations. No, that just wasn't good business. The less information lawyers had the better. He assumed that Van Acker was conducting his own investigation on the Susan Knox explosion. After all, he was her lawyer and he was sure that Phyllis Knox had retained him for his services. What frightened him the most was that he believed that Julie Sutton was also talking to Van Acker. Was she going to divorce Sutton? He suspected as much, especially with the rumors floating around town that he and Susan Knox had been having an illicit affair for so long. He couldn't blame her. He believed that he would do the same. Still, he didn't like Julie mixing with Van Acker. He was trouble. He was well on his way to upset the order of things in Dawson County. Things were going too well. Hinson smiled. He was in control of the county. Everything was going according to his plan. With help from Sutton, he had been able to shape the county to his liking. Van Acker coming in would more than likely change all that. Van Acker wasn't from around here and he didn't understand that you didn't mess with the order of things in small rural towns. Too much progress wasn't good. First it was big town lawyers coming in; next it would be big town business. It just wasn't good for the citizens. Well... it sure wasn't good for him. He was well on his way to being elected a third time to the Sheriff's position. He wasn't about to have Van Acker destroy that possibility. No! Van Acker had to be taken care off; and as he promised Tom Sutton, that's exactly what he was going to do.

A wry smile appeared on the Sheriff's face. He had a brilliant idea. For sure it would work. His plan to destroy Dimitri Van Acker had already been set in motion. He just needed the right place and the right time. He was sure that he would not have to wait long before the opportunity would arise. Another smile appeared on his face. They had taught him well in the Air Force. Always look for your opponent's weakness. In a one-on-one air battle, no matter how good your enemy is, there is a weakness. It was only a matter of time before that weakness would present itself. Yes! He knew what Dimitri's weakness was. At least he suspected.

Andrew Hinson smiled one last time before he left his house. The one thing they had also taught him in the Air Force and what he had so dearly forgotten, was that you yourself, just as your enemy, also have a weakness. If you didn't find your enemy's weakness fast, surely your enemy will find yours first.

84.

Dimitri Van Acker answered his phone on the first ring. He prayed it would be Hope. However, somewhat to his disappointment, it wasn't Hope.

"Mr. Van Acker?"

"Yes."

"Mr. Van Acker, we need to meet."

"Who's this?"

"That doesn't matter now. What matters is that we need to meet."

"Where and when?"

"Meet me at the back of the old cotton storage hangar about 2 miles south of town. You know where it is?"

Van Acker knew where it was. It was a deserted place that was frequented by teenagers and young lovers on the weekend. It was an excellent place to make out; hidden from the road and dark at night. He had been there a few times himself when he was going out with Hope. He had good memories of that place.

"Yeah, I know where it is. What time?"

"Be there in an hour. It's important that you show up. Things can turn ugly if you don't. Oh, and no cops, if you know what I mean.

"Who is this?"

"I told you that it's not important right now. Just show up and things will become clear."

Instinctively, Van Acker felt under his car seat to make sure that his gun was there. His stomach contracted at the thought of a setup.

"I'll be there."

The line went dead. Van Acker looked at his phone in disbelieve. What was all this about? And who was this person? Was it someone who knew something about what had gone down at Susan's apartment? Or was it the killer? The thought of it possibly being the killer sent a cold chill down Van Acker's back.

The phone rang again. The ringing scared him and he dropped the phone. He reached down and found it. Hesitantly he answered the phone.

"Hello?"

"Dimitri, it's Hope."

He breathed a sigh of relieve.

"Are you alright?" she asked, hearing him take a deep breath.

"Yes, I just had a strange phone call right before you called."

"Listen, we need to talk."

"I agree."

"When?"

"How fast can you get to Langton's"

"Five minutes."

"I'll see you there."

Van Acker hung up the phone and headed towards Langston's. When he arrived at the restaurant, he saw that Hope had beaten him there. She was talking to Pam Langston and exchanging giggles when they looked in his direction. A good sign! He wondered if Hope had talked to Kelly. From the way things looked, she had. He was glad that Kelly had realized that they did not have a future together and that if she wanted to make him happy, she needed to let him pursue Hope. Van Acker smiled as he entered the restaurant.

"Hi gals."

Both women smiled and returned the greeting.

"Any one of you two gorgeous ladies want to join me for a quick lunch?"

"I think I'll let Hope have the honors. Thanks for the invite though."

Van Acker got the reaction he wanted. He wouldn't have minded Pam joining them, but he needed to talk to Hope alone. Not just about their relationship, but also about the Susan Knox case and the mysterious phone call he had received.

"So, you did tell me the truth," Hope started as they sat down.

"I'm glad you realize that now. Did you talk to Kelly?"

"I did. She came by out of the blue. I was going to wait to call her, but she showed up on my doorstep. She told me what had happened and that she only wants you to be happy. She realizes that you are not interested in her and that you only have eyes for me."

"I'm glad she realizes that. Besides, it's true, you know?"

"I know. But, Dimitri, we need to set some ground rules if

384

we're going to make this work."

"I'm listening."

Pam brought both of them the special of the day. Van Acker did not object to Pam deciding for them. He trusted her cooking and was sure that he would enjoy the lunch. When leaving the table, Pam winked in his direction. He had a good idea what it was her and Hope had talked about before he made the scene.

"Dimitri, you can no longer stay in the same house with her. It's obvious that she has the hots for you; and who knows, she may try again. If you want, you can stay with me till your house closes."

"Hope, hold it. I thought we talked about his. I'm not going to stay with you."

Van Acker looked around.

"Too much gossip going around this town already as it is. I'm going to talk to Allen and see if I can use Kelly's old room until I can move into my own place."

"I understand. No problem, but if you change your mind, you are welcome to stay with me. Another thing and I told Kelly this too, I don't like her working for you. I told her that I would be social with her when I come by to visit you at your office. I also told her that I will always view her as a threat to our relationship."

"What did she say to that?"

"She said she understood and that I didn't have anything to worry about."

"Well, I hope you two keep your promises. If it ever would come to a fight between you two, you can count me out on getting in between. I petty Kelly though. I'm sure that you as a former Navy gal can put a whooping on her scrawny little butt."

Both smiled as the tension somehow left the table.

"Hope, I don't have any problems with what you want. You don't have to worry about me doing anything with Kelly. She'll have to drug me again or knock me out before she'll get her hands on me again."

"Good. Just don't have any drinks with her!"

Both laughed.

They ate some of the food in silence. Hope could sense that something was on Van Acker's mind. He had a worried look on his face.

"What's wrong?" she asked.

"Huh, oh nothing."

"Come on, you can't hide it. It's written all over your face. Something is bothering you."

Van Acker put his fork down and crossed his hands, as he looked Hope straight in the face.

"I got a phone call right before you called me. It was a man. He wouldn't give me his name. He said that he needed to talk to me right away. That it was important. He said that if I didn't show, things could get ugly. I'm meeting him in about a half an hour."

Hope looked at Van Acker with concerned eyes.

"I wouldn't take this too lightly if I were you. I'll go with you."

"No! You can't! He specifically stated there were to be no cops. Otherwise, things would go bad."

"Dimitri, I don't think you need to go."

"What choice do I have, Hope? If I don't go, and this guy is a psycho, then who knows what will happen. If I go, then at least I can defend myself with my gun if I have to."

"Let me go along and stay in the background. Where are you meeting him?"

"Behind the old cotton hangar."

Hope was silent for a moment and thought about the cotton hangar. She was familiar with the place in more than one sense. Of course she remembered the times she spent there with Van Acker, but she also remembered being on a stakeout one night to catch a drug deal in the making. She had been hiding opposite the hangar in the shrubbery. The place was perfect for an ambush. It was crowded with shrubbery that hadn't been cut down for years. This time of the year, the brush was thick and barely penetrable. She knew a couple of places where one could hide, day or night, and never be seen. It was not a good place to meet someone.

"I'm going."

Van Acker looked at her in disbelief.

"You must not have heard me! I told you the guy said no cops!"

"Dimitri, the only thing you know about that place is from us making out behind the hangar a couple of times. I know the place for

386

something else too. I was part of a drug bust that happened about two years ago. The deal took place behind the hangar. Perfect place for a drug deal, hidden from the road, especially at night with it being dark. Even car lights can't be seen from the road. It's the perfect place for an ambush! You may be ready with your gun for a man you'll be able to see, but what about the one's you don't see? I don't trust this. That he doesn't want cops around means that he's probably not a law-abiding citizen. If so, I'm sure that he doesn't work alone, and if he does work alone, you'll show up and you'll never see him. The only thing that you will know is the bullet hitting your body, or maybe a baseball bat to the back of the head. I'm not letting you go alone. I'm going or you're not."

Van Acker was surprised by the outburst displayed by Hope. She had gotten loud and some of the other customers were turning their head in their direction. He didn't want everyone to know what they were talking about. There was too much gossip going around already. He motioned for Hope to be quiet.

"Will you calm down some? Don't be some damn loud! You want the whole town to know by tonight that I was meeting some obscure person behind the cotton hangar? You wanna come with me? Fine! Just don't show up where you can be seen. Oh, and I suggest that if you go, you better not take your patrol car. That might be a bit too obvious."

Hope threw him a frowned look. She did not enjoy the sarcasm that had come with his reply. All she wanted to do was make sure that nothing happened to the fool. He might be good at dealing with big city crooks; he sure as hell didn't know how dangerous a country crook could be. It was a whole different ball game out here in the sticks. A lot more places to hide behind. Even during the daytime, it was a lot easier to hide somewhere than it would be in the city.

"Okay. I'll go home and get my personal car. Go ahead and go out there, but wait by the road till you see me pull of the road. There is a driveway about 100 yards before you get to the drive way to the hangar. I'll park in there. I'll walk through the field and behind the cover of the shrubbery to the hangar. Give me about 5 minutes. Then drive in and proceed. Dimitri, make sure your gun is cocked and loaded before you drive in there. This situation has a bad smell to it. I hope I'm wrong, but I don't think this is a friendly call."

"Well, at least we agree on that much," Van Acker snickered.

He looked at his watch. He had about 20 minutes before the meeting. He motioned to Hope that it was time to go. Hope left while Van Acker paid Pam.

"Dimitri, I couldn't help but overhear some of your conversation. Be careful!"

"Don't worry, darling, you're not gonna lose one of your best customers.

He padded her on the hand as he left.

Across the road from Langston's a man sitting in an old dusted down black Chevrolet watched Van Acker waving Olson goodbye taking off towards the cotton hangar. He cranked the car and followed Olson. He had to make sure the deputy Van Acker had lunch with would not show up. He had to be careful. He didn't know how much the deputy knew. Either way, it would be dangerous for him is she knew he was meeting with Van Acker. Anonymity was the most important part of the meeting. He knew too much. He hoped Van Acker would honor his request not to use his name or ask him to appear as a witness in the trial. Coming to the intersection where the deputy turned to go to her house, the man followed. He was allowed to be late for the meeting, but first, he needed to make sure all his bases were covered.

85.

Dr. Earl Scarboro had been notified of the car wreck that his son was involved in. They had not told him that Scarboro had died in the crash. Arriving at the scene, he noticed Michelle Murphy's car sitting on the side of the road. He looked around. She was nowhere to be seen. He wondered if she had been involved in the crash of his son's car. Dr. Scarboro walked the distance from the road to his son's wrecked BMW aided by a deputy Sheriff. He knew that it did not look good. The fact the ambulance was not heading into the pasture was not a good sign.

When he came to the BMW, he saw the fire department was cutting the top of the car with a cutting torch. A fire blanked had been placed over Scarboro's body so that sparks and pieces of hot metal would not touch his body. The last metal burned through and the top was lifted by four volunteers. Earl Scarboro saw the body of his son, as the blanket was removed, pressed down against the steering wheel. It would have been a miracle if he would have survived the impact. He wondered if his son had suffered at all, or if the crash had killed him instantly. Tears welled up into his eyes. His only son, his only child, lay before him, dead. He had tried so hard to talk sense into the young man's head. Had he not warned him just a few days ago that he was headed for disaster if he didn't pay more attention to the way he was driving? Now, it was too late. All the preaching and begging in the world wouldn't help now. Scarboro turned away from the wreck and headed back towards the road. There was nothing he could do now. He hoped that his son was in a better place.

There were two questions that kept coming back to him. What was Michelle Murphy's car doing on the side of the road, and where was she? He knew that his son had been upset with her. For that matter, she had been upset herself. He guessed with good reason. He had taken advantage of her youthful innocence. He had taken away her pride in her body. She had every reason to be upset with him. He wondered how many women his son had slept with while away at college. He hoped that he wore protection while engaging in sexual intercourse. If not, the results could be disastrous.

Earl Scarboro was jerked from his daydreaming when he felt

a hand on his shoulder. He looked around and stared in the eyes of Allen Murphy. Murphy had been a good friend for a long time. They had been going hunting for as long as he could remember. It had been nice to see their kids hook up together. At least it had been for Earl Scarboro. Michelle Murphy was a good-hearted churchgoing woman who could bring stability in his son's life. Maybe she was too good for him. He would not have treated her right. That he knew. He wondered how Murphy felt about the situation.

"Earl."

"Hi, Allen."

"I'm so sorry about Bryan."

"Thanks."

"If there's anything that Helen or I can do, please let us know."

"I will."

Scarboro looked at the ground. He didn't know how to ask if Murphy knew what Michelle's car was doing here, as well as where she was. He held their friendship dear and he hated to think that asking the wrong questions might risk that. Still, he had to know.

"Allen? There's one thing that bothers me. I hope you don't mind me asking."

"What is it, Earl?"

"Well, I see Michelle's car parked over there on the side of the road, but I don't see Michelle."

Scarboro didn't have a change to finish his full question before Murphy cut him off.

"She was involved in this, Earl. She gave a full statement to the deputy about 10 minutes ago. Helen came to get her."

"What happened here, Allen?"

Murphy took a deep breath. He knew it would look as if he were defending his daughter. It was hard not to defend one's child. There was no one else to blame but Bryan Scarboro for the accident. While they walked back to the road, Murphy explained what had happened to Scarboro. A grim look formed on Scarboro's face as Murphy finished telling the events.

"Do you think that maybe Michelle provoked the race?"

"I can't tell. She said that she didn't want Bryan to go

looking for her at home. She knew that Helen was home and that more than likely things might have gotten ugly. Helen's been upset about the whole HIV thing. It looks to me like Bryan was trying to run Michelle of the road and got caught by the log truck. I don't see any other explanation."

Scarboro looked Murphy straight in the eyes. Again tears were forming in the doctor's eyes. Knowing the temper of his son and the situation that he had gotten himself into, it made sense. He would be able to come to terms with it, at some point. He was worried about his wife. She might not understand. She didn't understand about the HIV thing either. His son had caught the devil the night before about that. It wasn't hard to see that Bryan was going to take revenge on Michelle for telling his mother about the HIV and sleeping around with Susan. God, if only she knew! He'd kept it a secret for so long now. Sexual relations between the two of them had seized long ago. She had lost all interest. For that he was glad. Too bad he had tried to find satisfaction elsewhere. God's punishment was harsh. He never would have thought that breaking one of the commandments would put such a curse on him.

He looked away from Murphy as thoughts kept scrambling around in his head. Scarboro extended his hand to Murphy.

"Thanks. I'll give you a call sometime soon. We need to talk, friend to friend."

"Anytime, Earl."

Murphy's eyes followed the doctor leaving the pasture and heading back to his car. A broken man, no doubt. It could have been him walking back to his own truck, having lost Michelle. But no, luckily she had been spared any harm. He was glad for that. He hated to think the way he did, but somehow, Bryan Scarboro had it coming. He had pushed the envelope of luck too far. Eventually, it had to catch up with you. For Bryan Scarboro it had. He was going to be there for Earl Scarboro. He would not desert a friend. Murphy knew that he would never be able to speak his mind about Bryan Scarboro. He was sure Earl Scarboro knew. Still, it wasn't something you did.

Murphy walked towards his truck as the black Cadillac pulled into the pasture and ventured towards the wrecked BMW where the medical personnel had been able to remove Scarboro's remains from the car. Murphy shook his head. Four people dead in four days, what was happening to Stuttgart? Why did all this happen at one time? Where all the deaths somehow related? He was wondering and questioning.

86.

Hope Olson checked her watch as she ran into her house. She didn't have much time to spare. She wanted to make sure that she was in time to assist Van Acker in case he needed help. She did not feel safe with the situation. If the meeting place had been in a more public place, she would have felt better. She didn't know whether it was her combat training, but something inside her told her the meeting was not going to end without violence.

Hope grabbed her extra handgun, a Glock 9mm. She checked the clip. Full! She had an extra clip in her gun cabinet. She grabbed that one too and checked for bullets. She felt a little better with the extra firepower. She looked in her closet and found a pair of loose fitting khaki pants. She wanted to have as much freedom of movement as the situation would allow. She also found an old camouflage T-shirt. She changed into them as fast as she could. She grabbed her service pistol and slit it in her holster. Her Glock, she pushed in the holster under her arm. She slipped the extra clip to her Glock inside her pocket. She was ready. Adrenaline was rushing through her body as she thought about what might happen. She hoped she would not have to use her guns.

***

The black dusty Chevrolet stopped about 20 yards from Hope Olson's driveway. A black man in his midforties got out and walked towards Hope's front door. In her hurry to get ready to give Van Acker support, she had neglected to close the door behind her. Stealthily, the man entered the house. He pulled a gun from behind his back. He looked around the kitchen and the living room. He noticed how everything was neat and well placed. Then he made his way into the hallway. He reached the first room to the left and opened the door. Spare room the man thought. The door to the next room was a bit further up to the right and was open. He suspected that to be Hope's room. With his back to the wall, he sidestepped his way to the door. He could hear movement on the other side of the wall. Carefully, he checked his gun. It was ready. Without making a sound, the man moved to the other side of the hall and walked into the doorway. Hope had her back towards him and was holstering her weapons.

Hope had no idea there was an intruder in her house. With her back to the door, she looked in the mirror and moved a couple of locks of hair in place. She needed to get a haircut soon, she thought. Her bangs were getting too long. The mirror was placed to where she couldn't see the doorway when she stood in front of it. That was a mistake. As quietly as the man had entered Hope's house, he entered her bedroom and stood in the doorway. He lifted his arm and aimed the gun in the middle of Hope's back. His right eye flickered as unexpected nerves entered his body. He had never shot anyone in the back. It just wasn't right. The person you shot should be aware what was going to happen to them. He needed her to turn around. Her gun was holstered. No danger of getting shot himself and there was no time for her to pull her gun fast enough.

Hope felt the look the man was giving her. A cold shiver ran down her spine as she realized that she was not alone in her room. She flexed her fingers. She started to feel her Glock pushing in her side. She had never experienced this feeling until now, but the mental realization that she was in immediate danger made here nerve endings react more sensitive to her surroundings. Calmly, she lifted her right hand and brought it to her chest.

"Slowly, very slowly," she told herself, as she slid her hand towards her gun. Almost had it!

The man noticed the change in Hope's behavior. He knew that she knew he was present in the room. How one could feel the presence of another person in the same space without the knowledge of the other person being there was beyond the man's understanding. He had had that feeling and at times it had saved his life. He watched as Hope raised her right arm and ever so slightly her left arm lifted just enough to grab the gun.

"Stop right there with the hand!"

The blood drained from Hope's face. Her stomach tightened and she could feel her legs starting to tremble. She needed to control her emotions. Shut out everything else except the fact that there was an intruder in her house.

"Turn around slowly."

Hope didn't recognize the voice. From his speech pattern,

she knew the man was black. She closed her eyes and turned around. She made up her mind that she wasn't going out without a fight. When she opened her eyes, she was face-to-face with the end of a gun barrel.

"Now, I want you to know, I don't like doing this. But I have to protect my anonymity. I'm not here to hurt you."

"Then why do you sneak into my house and have the open end of a gun pointed in my face?" Hope shot back.

"You can either cooperate with me or you can give me trouble. I'd rather you cooperate. Either way, I will get my wish."

"What is this about?"

Hope was confused. The man was talking about getting his wish either way, but was not intend on harming her. She could not put those two together. Her first thought was rape, but that involved harming her, with or without her cooperation.

The black man continued:

"I'm the man who Van Acker is meeting with. I have information that he's looking for. I'll only talk to him. Don't show up at the hangar!"

"How do I know that you're telling the truth? Maybe you're the one behind all of this. Who's to say you're not going out there to kill him, like you killed all the rest?"

A smile appeared on the man's face and for the first time, Hope didn't feel as threatened anymore.

"Dear Miss Olson, if I wanted Mr. Van Acker dead, I would have done it the first chance I got. And there have been plenty. I cannot reveal to you why I have to stay anonymous, but you have to believe that I intend no harm to either you or Mr. Van Acker."

"I'm sorry, Mr. Whoever The Fuck you are, but I don't believe you don't intend harm when you're pointing a gun at me. Besides, I promised Dimitri that I'd meet him and that I'd cover his back, so, unless you stop me, I'll be there."

The black man shook his head.

"Don't be foolish, miss. I will shoot and you're not quick enough to stop me. Don't forget who's pointing the gun."

Hope had never felt this desperate before in her life. She was faced with the most difficult decision she had ever encountered. Could she trust this man? Her instinct told her not to. The man was right; nobody in her position could be quick enough to take the gunman out. On movies and TV series, maybe, but not in real life. She was faced with an impossible situation. She had to do something. Pulling her gun was out of the question. She wondered how close he would let her get to him if she walked towards him. If she could get close enough to do a leg swipe, maybe then… She moved towards her intruder.

"Don't, Miss! I'm warning you, don't!"
Hope wasn't listening.
The gun went off with a thundering sound. The small size of Hope's bedroom made the explosion of the shot sound a lot louder than if it would have been outside. It temporarily deafened the man. Hope grabbed her chest. It wasn't anything like she had expected it to feel. All she felt was a little sting right above her left breast. Why was she still alive? Why was she still breathing, seeing? She watched as the gunman left the room. Wait a minute… She looked down at her chest. No blood! Her shirt was clean all except for the little blue dart that was sticking from her chest. Then she realized the man had spoken the truth. Either way, she wasn't going. None of it made any sense to her. She felt her knees go weak and she fell to the ground. She tried to get back up but couldn't. The tranquilizing dart was taking effect and she felt her head become light-headed. All the strength had left her legs and her arms. Hope fell forwards. The dart became unlodged as her chest hit the floor. Her head lay sideways, her eyes wide open. The room was spinning. Her vision became blurred. She fell into a deep sleep.
The man closed the door behind him as he left Hope's house. He had hated to put her to sleep like that, but he could not take any unnecessary risks. He didn't know how much she knew and how involved she was with the investigation. He admired her determination. Too bad. It would have meant her death if he had used a real bullet instead of a tranquilizing dart. He shook his head as he drove off into the direction of his meeting place with Dimitri Van Acker. Looking at his watch, he noticed that he would be five minutes late. He was not concerned about being late; the important thing was that he would be there. Feeling relieved that Hope Olson was not going to be at the meeting place; he had let his guard down

and failed to see an old tan Jeep Cherokee following him at a safe distance. The situation was not as controlled as he had imagined.

***

The meeting place was a short ride from Hope's place. The man saw Dimitri Van Acker's car sitting on the side of the road waiting, no doubt, for Hope to arrive. The man turned into the drive and followed it till he came to a clearing in which stood the old metal cotton hangar. It looked more like an airplane hangar than it did a cotton storage hangar. Slowly, the man drove to the back of the building. The shrubbery and grass around the place stood high. There was no visible line of sight from the road to where he intended to park his car. He turned the car around and had it facing towards the road. You never knew. He grabbed his cell phone and dialed Van Acker's number.

Dimitri Van Acker had been waiting impatiently for Hope to arrive. The person in the black Chevrolet was no doubt the one he was supposed to meet with. He wondered who the man was and what he knew. Why all the secrecy? Did this man have something to hide? He would find out soon, he hoped. He checked his mirrors again. Hope still hadn't made it. He was starting to get worried about her. He picked up his phone and was ready to give her a call when the phone rang. It made him jump. That was twice this afternoon that had happened. He answered it.

"Mr. Van Acker, I don't have all day. If you want the information, please come meet me right now. Do not wait any longer. You are attracting too much attention to yourself sitting on the side of the road like that."

"Give me a minute."

"No, Mr. Van Acker. Now! I don't have much time."

The phone went dead.

Van Acker looked in his mirrors again. Still nothing! The only traffic he had seen was the black Chevrolet and a tan Jeep Cherokee. The person driving the Jeep Cherokee had looked familiar, but he had not been able to place the face. Probably someone he had seen around town. With one last look in his mirror, he started his car and drove into the driveway, disgusted with Hope.

397

Where was she?

Van Acker took it slow going down the drive to the hangar. He had his reasons. For one, it would buy him a little extra time and give Hope a change to get there and get into position. Secondly, the drive was littered with potholes and he did not want his car damaged. As he came around the last patch of shrubbery, he saw the black Chevrolet parked next to the building facing him. The place had not changed all that much since Hope and he had met here years ago. The hangar itself was a danger to be around. The old wooden posts were slowly rotting away year after year. The roof had started to collapse in several places as roof trusses rotted away. It wouldn't be long before there was nothing but a pile of rubble left. Also, the shrubbery had grown extensively and there was not much room left to turn around without running in the shrubs. Van Acker carefully turned around in the clearing and parked at the front end of the hangar, making sure he faced the road. He reached for his gun and pushed it inside his pants behind his back. He hoped and prayed that he would not have to use it.

As Van Acker walked towards the hanger, the man stepped out of his car. Van Acker took in his every feature. The man was tall, he guessed 6'-6", with light dark skin, and close cut graying hair with signs of a growing mustache. He was muscular and looked like someone who worked out regularly. The white of his eyes looked yellowed. He was wearing blue jeans and a dark blue T-shirt with NAVY in large golden letters written on the front of it. The sight of the man caused a cold shiver run down Van Acker's back. This man was not one to be messed with. Without saying a word, the man motioned for Van Acker to follow him behind the building. Van Acker noticed the gun tucked in the man's pants. Somehow, he was not surprised.

"So what is it you wanted to tell me?" Van Acker said with a stern voice, trying to hide his fear. It was all he could do to keep his voice from trembling.

"First of all, you don't know me, you never met me. Right?"

"Whatever you say, man."

The tall black man looked around as if looking to see if anyone was hiding in the shrubbery. Seeming to be satisfied, he leaned up against one of the hangar posts.

"Mr. Van Acker, I know that you are looking into what caused the explosion at Susan Knox' and if she was killed prior to the explosion. I have information in regards to the explosion that might be useful to you."

"How do you know my name?"

A smile appeared on the man's face.

"Mr. Van Acker, this is a small town. People talk, all you have to do is listen. People talk over lunch, they talk at the gas station, they talk in the grocery store, and they talk everywhere. You just have to listen and you can learn a lot. That's what I do. I listen. I was trained to listen in my previous profession. But in this case, I also saw. I believe what I saw will solve your mystery."

"What mystery is that?"

"You have to promise me that you will not reveal your source. I'm in a position that I cannot be identified. I have too much to lose. If it wasn't for that, I might have been able to stop the explosion. I couldn't have stopped the murder of Susan Knox though."

"What do you know and how do you know it?"

"I know that Knox was shot. The person who shot her was careful not to make much noise while pulling the trigger. It may seem rudimentary, but without a silencer, a pillow, or towel wrapped around the gun reduces the amount of noise that is made when the trigger is pulled. It still makes noise, but not as loud and sounds more like a "pop" rather than a "bang". But, let me start with the how I know."

He walked back over to his car and leaned up against the hood.

Van Acker kept his distance, watching every move the man was making. He could feel the hairs on his neck stand up. This was not a good situation. He hoped that Hope had been able to make it and that she was in a position where she could come to his rescue if need be.

The man continued:

"You see, I'm driving down from Tennessee to go spend some time with a friend in Miami. I'm not in a hurry. I hate driving down the Interstate, so I planned this nice trip from where I stay near Knoxville all the way down to Miami using the old roads. The way people used to go to Florida on vacation. You know what I mean?"

Van Acker just nodded his head.

"Okay, so the other night I drive through this here Godforsaken place and I'm almost out of gas. The gas station is closed and I'm tired and I need to get some sleep. Not much, just a couple of hours so I can get back on the road. But guess what? This place ain't got no motel! I decided to park in the church parking lot, get some sleep, gas up in the morning and be on my way. Sleeping in the car is never comfortable. I woke up early and decided to get out and stretch my old bones a little before I crawled back in the car. That's when I saw it happening. I had a clear view of Knox' place from where I was standing. I saw someone enter the place. I could see the light of a flashlight dancing around in the dark in there. Then I heard the gunshot. Real muffled, like it was suppressed by something. It sounded real familiar to me. No doubt about it, it was a gunshot. Then the lights danced around the place some more and then the person left. Next thing I know, a car pulled out from between the buildings where the person disappeared. I cranked up my car and followed the car. It was a black sporty thing. Couldn't read the tag number 'cause the tag lights weren't working..."

Van Acker interrupted. For someone who was in a hurry, this guy sure knew how to tell a story.

"You're telling me you saw everything, followed the person home and you're not willing to testify?"

"That's right. I saw the whole damned thing. And you're right, I ain't willing to testify. I'm sorry Mr. Van Acker but it's gotta be this way."

Van Acker rubbed his chin. Was this man telling the truth? Who was to say he wasn't the one who killed Susan and was now trying to put the blame on someone else, while he fled the State? Van Acker had looked at the license plate of the man's car. He had indeed Tennessee tags. The passing through story could be true. But why stay around for this long? He needed to ask.

"Why did you wait this long to approach me with this? Why stay around if it's not necessary?"

"I wanted to make sure that you were the right person to talk to. Small towns have weird ways of dealing with shit like this. They love to cover up something like that. The explosion was supposed to be that cover up.

"Mr. Van Acker, I'm not a criminal. I'm a law-abiding citizen who knows too much. That's why I'm telling you my story. I want justice."

"Then why won't you testify?"

The man dropped his head.

"Mr. Van Acker, I've seen a lot of bad shit in my lifetime. I've paid a heavy price for it too. I've lost my family, I've lost my friends and I've lost a job that I loved very much. It took a long time for me to come to peace with everything that I went through, everything that I've seen, and everything that I've done. I can't testify because if my face shows up in any kind of paper, then my life will be in danger. You ever hear of the witness protection plan?"

Van Acker nodded his head.

"That should tell you enough. I can't tell you much more, just that I can't be recognized. If some of the characters I've helped put away find out that I ain't dead like the papers said I was, then I will surely be dead once they find me."

Van Acker lowered his head and relaxed a bit. This guy was dead serious and deadly afraid of what could happen. He really couldn't blame the guy. If the roles were reversed he would not want his picture and new name out there either. But he still needed the name of the person this man had followed that night.

"So, who was it you were following?"

The black man gave Van Acker a hard look. Giving a name was the hardest part. He knew that Dimitri had seen his tag number. He could still come after him if he wanted. He needed to make sure all of his bases were covered. He could not leave a trail behind.

"I've gotta have your word, man. Don't mention my name or any association with me. I give you a name, you figure out how you gonna put the pieces of the puzzle together. And I need a new car, man. I've got the money for it, just don't wanna be seen buying it.

"I understand, you've got my word." Van Acker cut in, getting impatient.

The man moved towards Van Acker, extending his hand.

"Thanks, man..."

***

From a little over 100 yards away, hidden behind the thick shrubbery, the driver of the tan Jeep Cherokee was just able to hear the conversation. Thank God there was just a slight bit of wind coming from the hangar so the sound of their conversation carried. Damn! There was a witness after all. A rifle was put up against a shoulder. Aim was taken at the chest of the black man. The sight moved over a little to the right and stopped at Van Acker's chest. It was tempting but there was no way that both could be shot. Not enough time to reload. The crosshairs moved from Van Acker's chest to the head of the black man.

***

"One more thing. Keep this information to yourself! Don't go sharing this with your cop lady friend till you got everything ready. I want justice, not a dead lawyer or a dead cop!"

"You've got my word. Now, give me a name."

The bullet hit the man right in the temple and exploded out the back. The black man fell to his knees and then down on his chest. Van Acker dropped to the ground. While going down, he grabbed his gun. He heard rustling in the shrubbery south of where they were positioned. He got up and crouched down to take cover behind the black Chevrolet. Slowly he lifted his head and looked over the car. The rustling in the shrubbery had stopped. A little ways off, Dimitri heard an engine crank. Damn! He ran to his car and got in. As fast as he dared he started towards the road. The potholes in the drive made it a rough drive and he hoped there would be no permanent damage to the undercarriage of his car. Reaching the road, he turned to the right, the direction in which he had heard the engine crank. Carefully he drove along the edge of the road, looking for signs of a car. He found tire marks in the tall grass that let into the woods. Black marks on the road showed evidence of tires spinning. Whoever had shot his witness was gone. Whoever had shot his witness was Susan's killer. It was hitting too close to home. A foot more to the left and it would have been his brains that were covering the side of the hangar. It was time to get serious.

402

***

The tan Jeep Cherokee was moving away from Stuttgart fast. The driver was smiling. A perfect shot. After a short drive, the Cherokee pulled off the road, into a driveway that led a long ways into the woods. There, the driver stopped next to a black coupe, transferred the rifle and got in. A few minutes later, the black coupe was headed towards Stuttgart.

***

Van Acker returned to the hangar and called the Sheriff's department. Next he called Hope.

87.

Mary Scarboro was sitting on the couch when her husband came home. She had received word of her son's accident from the Sheriff's office dispatcher. Even though no one had told her that her son was dead, she knew. Something inside her was missing suddenly. She could not explain it, but she knew when the accident had happened. She had been in the kitchen unloading the dishwasher when a sharp pain went from the bottom of her spine up to her neck. Just as sudden as the pain had come, it had disappeared. She had read about such experiences, however, a disbeliever in the supernatural, she had never believed a word of what she had read. Now, she thought differently about that supernatural feeling that mothers have when something happens to their children. The feeling had frightened her and the remnants of the broken glass that she dropped when she experienced the pain, were still on the kitchen floor. She had found her way to the couch and had sat their, waiting. When the call from the Sheriff's office came, her feelings were confirmed. Something had happened to her son. He was not going to come home again. She had started crying, hard at first, then softly. Why did this have to happen to her? Why her son? Why not someone else's? The thought made her flush, but she could not help the way she felt. Too much injustice had been handed them. Bryan, from what that Murphy girl had told her, could be infected with the AIDS virus. She had suspected her son was sleeping around. What college boy with his good looks wasn't? But that he would be careless enough to sleep with the town whore? No! That went beyond what she could grasp. Maybe she had blame in that. She had never warned him about sex. She had always expected her husband to take of that part of their son's upbringing. She was sure they had their talks, but did they go into depth about the consequences of having unprotected sex. It's one thing to talk about sex and how things work, it's another to be able to send the message that sex and "sex" are not the same. She knew now the serious sex talk never happened. And now, Bryan was dead. If he had been infected with the virus, maybe dying in the car wreck was the best way to go. Quick! Not suffering in a hospital, watching your body decline and disappear before your eyes. Maybe his dead was a blessing to all.

404

She looked up at her husband. She had never seen him this way. It was as if he had been beaten. His shoulders were hanging and his eyes where puffy and watery. All the dreams he had for Bryan had vanished now. Even the news about the possibility of AIDS infection had not touched him this hard. She guessed being a doctor; he had hope that one day soon, the infectious disease researchers would come up with a cure. That was the doctor in him. But the father and husband that she knew, was not taking it that well. Even violent death is something even doctors cannot do anything about. Now, the defeat showed. The loss of his son was finally sinking in.

"Bryan's dead, isn't he?" she asked.

Earl Scarboro looked at his wife. His eyes were tearing up again and he swallowed hard. Tears started to flow down his cheeks. Total disbelieve is what his face portrayed.

"Why? Oh God, Why? Why did you have to take my son?"

Scarboro fell to his knees. He laid his head down in his wife's lap and cried. His body shook hard, as he could no longer be strong. It was too much to bear. Crying helped to relief some of the hurt, but I wasn't the loss of his son that hurt him the most. What hurt him the most was the guilt and the secret that he lived with since that day in his office when Susan Knox and he had sex. Since then, he had felt the hurt. Every time he looked at his wife, who had stood by his side for so long, had seen them through hard times, had never strayed, the hurt got worse. It had become almost unbearable at the revelation that he had contracted the AIDS virus. As a doctor, it would have been possible to contract the disease from a patient, but he knew better. No patient of his had given him the disease. No, his infidelity towards his wife had caused that. A short period of weakness, of fun, of lack of self-control had given him the disease. What a fool he had been! Was it time to come into the open and tell his wife? What reaction would he get? Right now wasn't a good time to tell her, he decided. Better to let her recover from Bryan's death. But when would be a good time? Would the time ever be right for him to confess his sins to her? He had asked his God for forgiveness and hoped that He would be a fair and just God. To ask God for forgiveness had been easy. To ask his wife for forgiveness would not be. No, he wouldn't tell her, couldn't tell her. Not for his sake, but for hers.

These thoughts raced through his mind as he felt the comforting touch of her hands on his head. The soft rubbing of her hands through his hair made him feel better. Crying less hard, he was thankful for her, thankful for her softness, her caring touch. Too bad he would soon have to miss those things about her that he loved so much. It was now of all moments that he remembered his marital vows: "In sickness and in health, for richer for poorer, for better for worst". His marriage to Mary had meant more than the sexual attraction he had felt for her. It had turned into a lifelong project of which now, he finally saw the benefits. He had taken his vows for granted for too long. It was time to rediscover his marriage, to rediscover his bride. He would be honest with her, tell her everything. Tell her when the time was right. Now wasn't the time.

88.

The phone kept on ringing. There was no end to the noise the little plastic unit emitted. Whoever was calling was in desperate need to get in touch with her. Allen Murphy had stopped by to ask her a couple of questions about the Susan Knox case. Finding both her patrol car and her personal car in the yard, he hoped that she'd be home. His knocking on the door had not provided the desired result. Where could she be? Was she with Dimitri Van Acker? That possibility occurred to him. Still he found it odd the phone kept on ringing. That wasn't normal. No one let a phone ring that long without anyone answering it. What was it now, 20 to 30 rings? He tried the door handle. It turned and he heard the lock come loose. That was strange. Would Hope leave her door unlocked while she went out? Maybe in another time and place, but not in today's world, no matter if they lived in a town without relatively little crime. No! Something was wrong. He pushed the door open. With caution he looked inside. There was nothing to be seen in the living room. Slowly he pushed the door open all the way and stepped inside. An awkward feeling crept over him as he looked around. He felt guilty for some reason. He felt as if he were invading on Hope's privacy. But something was wrong, that he was sure off. Annoyed he found the phone. It was still ringing. Should he answer it? He decided to wait it out; see if it might for some obscure reason stop ringing. He looked around and started into the hallway to the bedrooms. He looked into the room to his left. Empty! Careful, trying no to make any noise, he moved on to the next room. He turned the corner and froze.

On the floor in the middle of the room, he saw the body of Hope Olson. She was face down on the carpet. He fell to his knees and felt for a pulse. She was alive; however, her heartbeat was slow. Careful, not to hurt her, he turned her over and checked for any possible wounds. There were none. His eye fell on the blue dart laying a little ways from them. He picked it up and looked at it. It was the same type of dart used to sedate cattle. He looked at Hope then back at the blue dart. He wondered why someone would do this. Why would you want someone to be sedated? He went into the bathroom and grabbed a washcloth that he wet with cold water. He rubbed it over Hope's face.

The coldness of the water made Hope stir. Slowly she was coming out of her sedation. She opened her eyes. The room looked as if it were in a mist. She tried to get up but couldn't even make it to her knees before she collapsed back to the floor. She felt a hand on her arm. Feeling threatened and not seeing clearly, she reached across and twisted the hand that was on her arm and brought the owner of the hand to the floor.

"Don't you touch me!"

Stunned by the sudden attack and the anger in Hope's voice, Murphy decided to make his identity known.

"Hope, don't worry, it's me, Allen."

"Allen? What are you doing here?" she asked, trying to make sense of things.

"I came by to ask you about the Knox investigation and found you on the floor here. What happened?"

Hope shook her head and rubbed her eyes as her sight was slowly returning to normal. With the help from Murphy, she managed to sit down on her bed.

"Dimitri! Oh my God, Dimitri…"

"What? Dimitri did this to you?"

"No, no… Dimitri was meeting this guy who had some information about the explosion at Susan Knox'. He's the one who shot me with the dart." Her face made a grimace and she felt her chest where the dart had hit her. The spot where the dart had broken her skin was stinging.

"He said that he did not want anyone else out there but him and Dimitri, that he could trust no one else."

"Where was Dimitri supposed to meet this guy?"

"At the old cotton hangar."

Murphy pulled Hope up from the bed and wrapped her arm around his neck so he could lead her outside. The drug was losing its effect and soon, he knew, she would be able to walk on her own. He used similar such tranquilizers before when he was helping a friend vaccinate some cattle. He knew the drug was harmless to cattle, but depending on the dosage, he wondered what it would do to humans. As they walked out the door, the phone rang again. Hope started to turn towards the phone. Murphy pulled her out the door.

408

"We have no time for this. We need to make sure that Dimitri is okay."

Murphy managed to put Hope in his pick-up truck and took off towards the cotton hangar.

***

Dimitri Van Acker had given up waiting for Hope to pick up the phone. He had let it ring for over five minutes without anyone picking up the phone. Where could she be? Had anything happened to her? Had the shooter taken care of her first before coming out here? Why was he not shot at? He had too many questions racing through his mind to have answers to any of them. In the distance he heard the sirens of the Sheriff patrol cars. They would drive up any minute. He looked at his hand. He was still holding his gun. He decided to take the clip out, as well as the bullet in the chamber; and turn it over to them. There was no sense in trying to hide his gun; besides, he was not the one who shot the black man. He put the parts to his gun on the hood of his car.

He walked over to where the body of the man was laying. He had not touched anything. He knew the procedure. The shot had come unexpected and had been aimed perfectly. Van Acker looked at the body. The bullet had entered the head of the man in the center of the temple. The exit wound was close to an inch in diameter. From the distance the shot was fired, it had to have been a high powered rifle. More than likely government issue. A military sniper rifle would be able to give this effect from the distance the shot was fired. What about the local law enforcement arsenal? He made a mental note to ask Hope the type of weapons they had available to them. The first patrol car drove into the drive. Hope! He tried the number again. He would hold the phone until the deputies walked up to him. He wasn't hopeful the phone would be answered.

Murphy drove as fast as he could to the old cotton hangar. He heard sirens in the distance and wondered what was going on. As he came closer to the hangar, he saw the patrol car in front of him, sirens blasting and lights flashing. Not to his surprise he saw the car turning into the drive leading to the hangar. He looked over at Hope.

"That doesn't look good."

Hope just shook her head and prayed Van Acker would be all right."

The deputy in the first patrol car got out, gun drawn and pointed at Dimitri Van Acker.

"Put the phone down and put your hands up!"

Van Acker thought it funny. It was almost like a cheap movie line. He could understand the recent developments in the county had the deputies on edge. He obliged to the request. He put the phone down on the hood of his car, next to his gun and raised his arms.

"Now put your hands on top of the car and spread your legs."

Van Acker obliged without any resistance or argument, to the surprise of the deputy.

The second deputy arrived on the scene, followed closely by Murphy and Hope. Hope had regained enough strength to walk on her own. She got out of the truck and ran towards Van Acker. The first deputy hadn't recognized Hope in her civilian clothes and didn't know how to handle the situation.

"Ma'am, get away from the car."

Hope turned around, looked the deputy straight in the eye and scolded him.

"Deputy Roberts, who are you addressing?"

Roberts recognized Hope and turned all shades of red.

"My apologies, ma'am I didn't recognize you without your uniform."

"Apology accepted."

She turned to Van Acker and wrapped her arms around him. He returned the favor then exploded.

"Where the hell were you? I trusted you to be here to back me up. I nearly got my ass shot up!"

Hope understood his anger. She would have reacted the same way. She pointed at the black man on the ground.

"He followed me home and shot me!" she said with a grin on her face.

"Shot you?"

"Yeah, he didn't think it was wise for me to be out here. Said he wanted to talk to you alone that I had no business here. So he shot me with a tranquilizer dart."

Van Acker blushed and realized that he had jumped to conclusions to soon.

"I'm sorry, Hope, I shouldn't have lashed out at you like I did."

"Don't worry about it, Dimitri; I would have done the same thing."

Hope saw that she was the highest ranking deputy on site and took control of the crime scene.

"Dimitri, what exactly happened here?"

Van Acker retold the black man's story, but for his own benefit, withheld some of the relevant information. He wanted to do some investigating on his own before he told Hope the whole story.

Hope ordered deputy Roberts to go search near where Van Acker told her where the shot had come from. The other deputy was told to start collecting evidence from the victim.

"Dimitri, do you know what kind of vehicle the shooter was driving?"

"I'm not sure. The only vehicles that I saw while waiting for you was this guys and an older model tan Jeep Cherokee."

Hope closed her eyes and thought for a moment. She knew who drove an older model tan Cherokee. She opened her eyes as the blood drained from her face. Without saying a word, she grabbed the radio in the patrol car and called the dispatcher.

"Anyone report a stolen tan Jeep Cherokee?"

"No ma'am, not that I'm aware off. I've been here since this morning. Let me check the computer."

Van Acker was curious.

"Who drives a tan Cherokee around here?"

"Patricia Langston."

"Hope?"

Deputy Roberts was waving his arms and shouting her name.

"I need help over here!"

Hope and Van Acker looked at one another and took off towards Roberts.

"Found a casing, ma'am!"

Hope picked up the casing with her pen. She looked at it closely. She shook her head.

"Nothing special about this one! You can buy them at Wal

411

Mart. Plain old 30-06 used to hunt deer with. Anyone can buy these."

"You know, Hope. We need to find the bullet. I don't think that it will match this casing. I've shot with a 30-06 before. From this distance, no way you get that type of clean wound."

"I'll put Roberts on it."

She gave Roberts instructions to look inside the hanger to see if the bullet was somewhere in there. She did not suspect it to have gotten too much further than the inside of the hangar. The velocity could not have been too high after entering and exiting the man's head and then entering the steel siding on the hangar.

"We'll find it, Dimitri."

Van Acker walked over to Allen Murphy. He pulled him away from the crime scene and faced the road to where Hope or her Deputies could not try to read their lips.

"Allen, I need you to do me a favor."

"What's that?"

"Drive south of here, slowly. Look for a place where someone could turn off from the road."

"What is it I'm looking for?

"A tan Jeep Cherokee."

Murphy nodded his head and left.

Hope watched the two of them and wondered what was going on. She approached Van Acker.

"What was all that about?"

"I've got a hunch. I asked him to check it out. I tell you about it if I'm right."

'No secrets?"

'Nope, no secrets!"

89.

Julie Sutton was sitting in her reading room looking out the window at the charred remains of her sister's apartment. She felt as depressed as she'd ever been. The sexual abuse her father had put her through as a teenager was no comparison to what she felt at the moment. Not only had she lost her sister but her marriage was over, she had been raped and she had shot her husband. Deep inside she wished she had killed him, but she was glad, before the eyes of God, that she hadn't. Mistaken identity or not, she did not want any part of killing anyone.

Julie had been released from the hospital and called a friend to take her home. Now in the quiet of her home, her emotions were getting the better of her. Tears started to flow down her cheeks. How was it possible that God put her through such hardship? Wasn't she a good Christian woman, devoted to her God? Had she not spent all of her adult life living in the example of the Bible? Why then was she put to the test like she was? Was it Satan doing these things? Julie couldn't answer those questions any longer. She would have to meet with Dr. Brubaker and see about getting counseling to help deal with what happened to her as well as with her doubts about her religion.

Julie looked down at her table and saw the letter Susan had written her. Tears were flowing faster now. Poor Susan! As much wrong as Susan had done to her she was still her sister and she had loved her no matter what. Even after finding out that her husband had been involved with her for so long, she still loved her. She picked up the letter and read through it again. She checked her watch. It was well into the afternoon. She was supposed to have met with Dimitri Van Acker! She had forgotten! She wondered if he had shown up and had waited for her. How could she have forgotten? It was important that she met with him. She grabbed her phone and dialed the number he had given her.

It was so important that she talked to him in private. Not only was she in need of his services for her divorce against Tom, she also needed him for the content of the safe at the bank. Without him, she or anyone else for that matter could not get it. If Susan had been telling the truth about the videotapes, they would be in the safe. She

413

needed to get her hands on those tapes. She couldn't stand the thought those would be shown inside a courtroom. No! If she appeared anywhere on those tapes, she would destroy them. She hoped she would have a chance to do that.

Aggravated, she put her phone down as she got a message saying that Van Acker could not be reached. She did not want to leave a message. She would have to keep trying. She looked out the window again. Her father was cleaning up some of the debris from the explosion. How she hated that man! He should have been the one that was blown up instead of her sister. He was the cause of all the trouble she was going through. If he had kept his dirty hands off her, then maybe she would be leading a normal life. Maybe! A smile covered her face at the thought of leading a normal life. To have the sounds of little one's running through the house. That would be so perfect. The smile turned to tears. She would never know that joy. Not only was she getting too old, she was also more afraid then ever to commit herself to someone's love. She didn't think that she could ever love again. No doubt, she had loved Tom Sutton. She realized now, that he had never loved her back. He had loved himself. All he had cared about where his needs and kicks. All she had been was a stepping-stone to bigger and larger opportunities. He had used her. For that, she felt like a fool. She would never let that happen again. Ever!

90.

Andrew Hinson arrived at the Sheriff's department late in the afternoon. He looked over at Hope's desk. She wasn't in the office. She must have taken an early patrol this afternoon and planned to do some work on her caseload when things quieted down towards the evening hours. He walked towards the dispatcher and checked the log. Everything that happened around the county was logged and kept up with. Sometimes, those records could be useful in case certain actions taken by the Sheriff's department ended up in the courtroom. He noticed the car wreck in which Bryan Scarboro lost his life. Then he noticed the event that had taken place at the old cotton hangar. He saw the name of the person who had called it in.

"Dimitri Van Acker."

As much as he disliked him, there was something interesting about him. The most interesting part of Van Acker was that he was representing Julie Sutton. He could fully understand why Julie would not go to her husband for legal representation. Sutton was a shrewd lawyer. He also had a twisted personality. It was not normal wanting to be involved with as many women as he was. No, he could not blame Julie for kicking him out. She should have done it a long time ago. Possibly, the revelation of his affair with Susan and that Susan had somehow contracted the AIDS virus had shaken her enough to take that step. But with all the lawyers in Macon, why did she have to choose Dimitri Van Acker, an outsider with no knowledge of small-town affairs. He needed to be stopped before he went too far. However, the time was not right yet. He needed a little more time. Hinson hoped the natural course of affairs would take care of the situation. If not, then he would give nature a helping hand.

Hinson walked over to his desk and grabbed his radio. He was going to check and see where Hope was.

"Charlie 5 this is Charlie 2, come in please.

The line remained silent. He tried it again.

"Charlie 5, this is Charlie 2, come in."

"This is Charlie 5, go ahead Charlie 2.

"What is your 20?"

"I'm at the old cotton hangar, investigating a shooting."

"Yeah, I saw that on the register. What exactly happened out there?"

"Well, Dimitri Van Acker was meeting with a potential witness in the Susan Knox explosion. From what Dimitri told me, the fellow was in the witness protection program. I don't know, I think his past caught up with him."

"You think whoever shot this guy might also be the one who killed Susan Knox?"

"I don't know, boss. Seems to me like whoever shot the poor bastard must have been following him for a while. It must be his past."

"What about Van Acker? Is he doing all right?"

"Yeah, as well as can be expected. He's a little shook up about the whole thing. Six inches to the right and he'd been the one with an extra hole in his head. It's not a pretty scene."

"How are you coming with the Knox investigation, by the way?"

"Doing well, we're doing an autopsy on the body tomorrow."

"Really? You were able to get Atlanta to react that quickly?"

"No. They're behind more than a year with their investigations. I've got a friend out of Augusta coming and performing the autopsy. She's a pathologist at the Augusta School of Medicine. I was stationed with her in Saudi. Super gal. She knows what she's doing."

"What's her name?"

"Shawn Joiner."

"All right, good work. Make sure I have a full report on today's shooting on my desk in the morning."

"Will do, boss."

Andrew Hinson put the radio back on the unit's hook. Just as he thought, Hope Olson was one smart woman. She had the initiative he expected her to have. Pulling in her pathologist friend to do the autopsy was smart.

Reaching for his left arm, he leaned back in his chair. He rubbed over the area where he had somehow managed to cut himself. It bothered him that he had no memory of when it had happened or where it had happened. Rubbing the soreness some more, he smiled. He was in total control and had everyone exactly where he wanted

416

them.

91.

Dimitri Van Acker, although having appeared calm and collected in the moments following the shooting, felt his body shake as the adrenaline rush subsided. He needed a drink. For only the second time in his life, he had felt out of control of a situation.

All through his formative years, he had controlled the outcome of every step he took. Becoming an exchange student had been his decision. With the financial support from his parents, he had succeeded in the endeavor. He believed the year spent away from home at the young age of 17 had been a deciding factor on how he had developed into what he had become. He had endured hardships in the form of language barriers and feeling lost. Even though there had been a nice, warm and welcoming host family there to give him shelter and moral support, he had been alone. The decisions he had made were his. He had learned from his mistakes and cherished the victories. That year he made up his mind that he wanted to continue his quest to live and work in the United States. Accepted at Penn State University, he continued his quest. He majored in Criminal Justice and graduated in the top 10 of his class. Again, he had been backed by the finances of his parents, but again, the decisions that he made were his. He had faltered a couple of times, getting hooked up with the one's who did not see college as the greatest opportunity anyone could have. No. All they wanted to do was party, drink, and get lucky with the girls. The temptations had been out there. A few times he had joined in the drinking bashes. And of course, just as many times he had been drunk to the point he couldn't stand up straight. The turning point had been the time where he had woken up in his dorm room, in his bed, naked, without any recollection of how he'd gotten there or why he was naked. He had lost control of the situation. He later found out that a friend had managed to get him to bed and undressed him after throwing up all over himself. He swore that would never happen again. And it hadn't. Concentrating on his studies, he had managed to get a partial scholarship to Mercer Law, one of the leading Law Schools in the Nation. And now here he was, for the second time in his life he had been faced with a situation he could do nothing about. He knew it would be a while before the image of the man's head exploding only inches away from his own face would fade. He knew that he would have nightmares.

Hope Olson had sensed the tenseness in his voice and body language and ordered him to leave the scene. Van Acker returned to Kelly's house. Looking through the cabinets he found a bottle of cheap whiskey. He poured a glass and sipped on it. The taste was not what he was used to; however, the whiskey produced the needed result. As he sat down, he could feel his body relax. He rubbed his temples and he tried to remember everything the man had told him. Not much really. No name, no description of the person. One thing the man had told him was important. The car had been a black coupe with missing license tag lights. Van Acker gave the man credit for being observant. Not many people would pick up on that detail. Then again, the man was in the witness protection program and was probably used to looking over his shoulders at all times, taking in every little detail around him. It would only be a matter of time before he would be able to pin down who was responsible for Susan Knox' death.

Van Acker leaned back in the chair. He looked over at the clock on the wall and noticed that it was getting late in the afternoon. He realized that he had not considered what he had on his agenda for the day. He got up and walked into his room grabbing his daily planner. As he looked over his notes, he turned white.

"Julie!" he exclaimed.

He grabbed his phoned and dialed her number. It was answered on the first ring.

"Hello?"

"Mrs. Sutton?"

"Yes."

"Hi, this is Dimitri Van Acker. I'm sorry about our meeting this morning. I got sidetracked and completely forgot."

"Don't apologize, Dimitri. I forgot too. I remembered just a little while ago about our meeting."

"Well, that still doesn't make me feel any better. This is no way to start building a business. Do you think we could still make it to the bank in time to get the contents of the safe?"

"Yes, I believe so. Should I just meet you there?"

"Yes. I'll meet you at the bank in say, 15 minutes?"

"Okay, see you then."

Julie Sutton and Dimitri Van Acker arrived at the bank at the same time. They shook hands as they walked towards the entrance. Van Acker had not yet had a chance to open an account in the bank and it was the first time since he got back in town that he visited the bank. The faces behind the counter and the desks did not look familiar. The only person he did recognize was Jackie Stewart. She was the person they needed to see. Jackie saw the two come in, stood up and walked in their direction.

"Julie, how good to see you. I'm so sorry about Susan."

"Thank you, Jackie."

"Dimitri Van Acker, how are you? It's been so long since I last saw you. I understand that you're trying to establish yourself as a lawyer here in Stuttgart."

"I'm doing great, and yes ma'am, I am trying to establish myself here."

"Good for you! I guess you're here to see about the contents of the safety deposit box that Susan had?"

"Yes ma'am, if you'd be so kind as to assist us in opening it."

"Do you have a key to the box?"

Van Acker reached into his pocket for his set of keys. He didn't understand at the time why Susan had sent him a key while he was still living in Washington. Now, he realized that Susan must have had a feeling about the events that would develop in her life. He produced the key.

"Great! Follow me please."

Julie Sutton and Dimitri Van Acker followed Jackie behind the counter and into the vault. They opened the appropriate drawer. Jackie left them in the vault.

Van Acker pulled the drawer open and lifted the lid. Inside were three videotapes and a letter. He handed the letter to Julie while he kept the videotapes. Closing the drawer, they left the vault and thanked Jackie for her help.

Outside, Julie looked at Van Acker for direction. She didn't know how he wanted to handle this. She also needed to tell him about her other legal problems she was facing. She wanted to have him represent her in her divorce from Sutton, but she also knew she needed legal help after she had shot her husband. Van Acker, as if knowing what was going through her head, said:

"Julie, if you don't mind, I would like to go over this material tonight and if possible plan to meet you to discuss the situation in the morning. I know you wanted to talk to me about representing you in your divorce against Tom; I will be able to do that tomorrow also. Is there anything else you would like to talk about or tell me?"

Julie hesitated. She didn't know if she should tell Van Acker now or wait till in the morning to tell him about shooting Tom. She decided that he had enough to worry about without having more work being pushed his way. I could wait till in the morning.

"No, I think if I have anything else it can wait till tomorrow. What time would you like to meet?"

"Let's make it 10. And this time, I won't forget."

They both smiled.

"Okay, Dimitri, I'll see you at 10 tomorrow morning.

Dimitri Van Acker got into his car and watched as Julie drove off. He couldn't help but notice that she looked stressed. Was it the anticipation of waiting to see what the tapes would reveal or was it something else? She knew what to expect from the tapes. He could understand the content would put some pressure on her but he sensed there was something more to Julie than first met the eye. She was not telling him everything. He'd poke at her some more in the morning. He drove away from the bank and headed towards the Murphy farm. He needed to check with Allen Murphy to see if he had found what he was looking for.

92.

"Daddy, I need a way to work."

"What's wrong with the Jeep?"

"I let a friend borrow it and I thought I'd have it back by now. I've gotta leave in 30 minutes."

"Honey, I don't know what to say. I'm tied up at the moment. I don't know when I can break loose. I'm running the counter by myself."

"What about mom?"

"I can ask, but I don't think she'd be able to break loose either. Look at the time. Dinner traffic is fixing to come through."

"Fine! I'll see if I can find someone else to take me."

Patricia Langston slammed the phone down. She was mad. Why on earth had she let someone borrow her only means of transportation? She should have known this would happen. The one person she trusted the most in the county. The one person she thought she could depend on. She would set the situation straight. But for now, who could she call? Michelle? Patricia grabbed the phone and dialed the number.

"Michelle?"

"Hi Patty."

"Hi, listen; can you do me a favor?"

"What's that?"

"Can you take me to work tonight?"

"I don't know. My car blew up this morning."

"What?"

"Yeah, I'm surprised you haven't heard."

Michelle quickly explained what had happened between Bryan Scarboro and her, explaining that Scarboro was dead and that her car needed a new engine.

"Let me see if mom will let me borrow hers."

A few seconds later, Michelle came back on the line.

"Patty, I can take you."

"Great! Thanks a lot, sweetie. I owe you one."

"Don't worry about it. See ya in a few."

Patricia broke the connection. Great, she had a ride. Now she wouldn't have to worry about breaking her perfect attendance record. If she could keep it that way, it would mean getting a significant bonus at the end of the year. She was looking forward to it. The extra money would come in handy.

Patricia retreated to her bathroom to fix her hair and put on some make-up when there was a knock on the door. Her stomach contracted. She hoped it was who she wanted it to be. She rushed to the door and opened it. Disappointment fell over her face as it was not the person she'd expected.

"Hi Patricia. Have you got a couple of minutes?"

"Hi Hope. Come on in. Hope you don't mind talking to me while I get ready for work."

"No, not at all."

"What's going on?"

"Well, I was wondering if you were anywhere near the old cotton hangar earlier today."

Patricia returned a surprised look.

"No, I wasn't. Actually, I don't have my car right now. I let a friend borrow it."

"A friend?"

"Yeah, that's not that strange, is it?

Hope had a feeling that for some reason Patricia was not going to cooperate in giving out the friend's name. She was on the right track.

"Who's your friend?"

Patricia shot Hope a look that didn't show any appreciation for the questions being asked.

"I don't think I need to tell you that. All you need to know is that it is a good friend of mine."

Hope smiled inwardly. She'd been right.

"So, if you don't have your car, how are you going to get to work?"

"My, my, why all the questions? Have I done something to deserve them?"

"I don't know. You tell me. From your reaction, it seems you're hiding something."

Hope paused for a second to let the meaning of those words fall in place. She continued:

"Patricia, I am the lead investigator into what happened at

423

Susan Knox' apartment the other night. Something happened this afternoon that would suggest the same person responsible for what happened at Susan's was responsible for the murder of a potential witness in that investigation."

"And what does that have to do with me. I was right here all day and at the time of the explosion I was right here too. Are you accusing me?"

Hope didn't know why Patricia was being so defensive. She had never known her to be this way. She had always been the nice proper girl who never got into trouble. Why then was she so offended by her questions?

"The reason I tell you this as that this afternoon, a Jeep that matches your Jeep's description was spotted near the place where the murder happened. Now, it might just be coincidence, but it could be that your friend is the one responsible for the events happening around town."

Patricia dropped her brush in the sink, pushing Hope out of the way. She walked to the front door and opened it.

"I want you to leave right now! If you want to ask any more questions, then you will have to arrest me, read me my Miranda rights and make sure that my lawyer is present. Good day!"

Hope exited without saying a word. Something was strange. Something wasn't right. This display of emotion and anger in her voice told her that she knew something or was protecting someone. She would bring it up to Hinson and see how he thought she needed to continue. In her mind, Patricia needed to be brought in for questioning, but he might have a different way of approaching the situation.

Patricia's eyes followed Hope's patrol car as she exited her property. What was going on? She ran to her phone and dialed the number.

"What the hell is going on?"

"Who is this?"

"It's Patty. Tell me what's going on."

"What are you talking about?"

"Where's my car?"

"Your car is safe. I'm sorry I have to inconvenience you like this but I will have it back to you tomorrow."

424

"You know what else?"

"What's that?"

"Hope Olson just stormed in here and asked several questions about why my car was spotted near the site of a murder this afternoon. Is that true?"

"And what if it were true?"

"Where you near the old cotton hangar in my car today?"

"Yeah, I drove by there today, why?"

"Because the murder happened there!"

"Listen, Patty, I've got everything under control."

"Okay, I just don't want that Olson bitch back in my house interrogating me the way she did."

"You won't have to worry about her bothering you any longer. I'll take care of it."

"Will I see you tomorrow?"

"Yes, you'll see me tomorrow."

"Okay, bye and I love you."

"I love you too."

Patricia broke the connection. For some reason she didn't feel comfortable that her friend had everything under control.

Outside a car drove up. Patricia looked out the window. It was Michelle. Patricia grabbed her pocketbook and headed out the door, making sure it was locked. Scared and unsure about what she had learned, she was quiet on the way to the hospital.

93.

After her visit with Patricia Langston, Hope Olson decided to do an early patrol so she could collect her thoughts and think about the evens of the day. Her investigation in Susan's death had gone nowhere to this point. She wondered if Andrew Hinson would be questioning her about that and decide that it was an accident after all and call her off the case. But today, things had started changing. Not only was there a witness to the event, dead as he might be now; there was a link to Patricia Langston. How did Patricia fit into the Susan Knox scenario? That was the one question she kept asking herself as she made her way down the roads of Dawson County. Whoever Patricia's friend was could be the person she was looking for. She wondered if Van Acker would have gotten a good look at the person. Maybe at this point they could find out whether to look for a woman or a man. It made the case harder not knowing the sex of the suspect. With that question out of the way, she felt the investigation would gain new speed and head in the right direction. She needed to check on that with Van Acker.

She wondered how Van Acker was doing. He had looked shaken when he left the cotton hangar. She felt relieved in a sense that it had not been him lying on the ground with a bullet hole to the head. She didn't think she could have taken that. Not after gaining renewed trust in him. She should have known that Kelly Murphy would try to go after him. Poor Van Acker was so blinded by his trust in her that he never saw the "attack" coming. She had to admit that it was a good try on Kelly's part. She smiled at the thought of being cuddled up in his strong arms on a cold wintry night. That would be delightful. Unconsciously Hope turned the AC in the patrol car up to make it just a little bit colder, bringer her daydreaming a little bit closer to reality. She decided that she would ask him to move in with her until he could move into his house. She knew the contract could come back any day, so the stay would be short. Even so, she felt warm inside thinking about the chance to spend all her free time with him. She needed to see if she could get off 2nd shift duty. Now that she had someone special in her life and since she'd always worked 2nd shift since, she felt it was time to start having normal hours. She made a mental note to ask Hinson about that.

Hope reached for her phone and dialed Van Acker's number. It rang twice before the phone was answered.

"Dimitri Van Acker here."

"Hi sweetie, it's me."

"Hi sweetie to you too."

"Listen, I've been thinking."

"Yes?"

"I know you said you didn't want to. But since you're going to move out of Kelly's place and will need a place to stay, why don't you stay with me till you can move into the house?"

There was a short silence at the other end of the phone.

"Are you sure? You're not scared that Hinson will take some action against you? You know, I am working on the Knox investigation myself."

"I don't care what he says. I just know that I want to be close to you."

"Okay, then. If you don't see a problem with it, I'm in. When will you be off?"

"I'll get of at midnight."

"Is there anyway I can get into your house?"

"Can you meet me somewhere so I can give you the key?"

"Sure, I'm at the Murphy home right now and I'll be here for a couple more hours. Just come by here and drop it off. Maybe you can have dinner with us while you're here."

Hope smiled at the word dinner. She wasn't used to hearing that word about the evening meal. It showed that it had been a while since he had lived in the South. She'd have to train him to use the word dinner for lunch and supper for dinner. A bit confusing, but those where the rules if you wanted to be a true Southerner. And she would make sure he followed the rules.

"That sounds good. I'll be on that side of the county in about an hour. I'll see you then."

"Okay, see ya."

"Dimitri?"

"Yes."

"I love you."

She held her breath as she spoke those words. She had

427

promised herself not to say those words unless she felt absolutely sure she was in love with the person. Did she say them too soon? The answer to her question came with Van Acker's reply.

"And I love you more than I've ever loved anyone else."

Hope pushed the end button on her phone. She felt like a little schoolgirl, butterflies in her stomach and a feeling of light-headedness. It was absolutely delightful. But there was another reason she wanted Van Acker around. Not just because she loved him, but because he was indeed working on the investigation. She felt bad about that part of her need to be around him. She justified that by telling herself that she loved him more for what he was then for what he knew. If she could get him to share some information with her then she would have it all. She knew she could never tell Van Acker that her need for his knowledge in the Knox case was part of why she wanted him to stay with her. She knew the dead witness must have been able to tell him something before he got shot. She hoped the information would be useful to her. She needed to start somewhere. Patricia Langston was a start, even though there wasn't much there. She needed to follow up on Patricia's whereabouts and try to figure out who the friend was who drove her Jeep. It would be hard with her working the 2nd shift. She needed to find someone on the force to do some detective work for her, but who? It needed to be someone who was awake when she was sleeping; someone who she could trust. She racked her brain trying to come up with a name but didn't know of anyone. She would tell Van Acker about Patricia's reaction. Maybe he could get her to talk. He was after all good friends with her parents. Maybe she didn't need a detective. Maybe, just maybe, she would be able to use Van Acker for that purpose. Only time would tell. And time was short.

With those thoughts and concerns, she turned on Hwy 346 and headed south to patrol that part of the county. She felt good and set her radar to lock on 70. She would give the speeders a break tonight. Hopefully, Hinson himself wouldn't be out patrolling. He would not appreciate the break the speeders would be getting. Hope stretched her legs and arched her back and nestled herself back in her seat. She grew tired of riding all the time and she had not yet found a comfortable position in her patrol car. She doubted that she ever would. The radar beeped and showed 67. Hope smiled as she passed

428

the car and saw the break lights come on. Her presence on the road was enough to make drivers slow down; especially if they knew the speed limits were strictly enforced.

94.

Andrew Hinson was sitting behind his desk at the Sheriff's office. He was staring in front of him, not paying attention to what was happening around him. Besides the shooting at the old cotton hangar, it had been an uneventful day. Then again, most days in the quiet little town of Stuttgart were uneventful. The stack of paperwork on his desk had been untouched. Even though he had come into the office late, he was ready to go. He felt no need to stay at his desk. The paperwork could wait. There was nothing too important. Some signatures on official documents Julia Snelgrove had sent him. She could wait for them. He didn't like her anyway, and the more headaches he could send her way the better he felt. Sure she was an excellent Judge, and was good for the county, but in his opinion, she was too soft. He hated to think the way he did, but there was nothing he could do about it, she held a job that he thought was not meant for a woman. He felt that as a judge there should be no show of emotion. The judgeship required that one was hard, tough, and uncompromising; and he expected the same from his judge. He would much rather see her replaced than having to put up with her for another couple of years until she decided to retire. He hoped he could hold out till then.

He rubbed his hands together. They felt sweaty. Even with the A/C working overtime, he felt hot. He needed to get out of the office and breathe the hot, sticky air. He got up and walked out without saying a word to anyone. He got in his car and drove off.

The short drive to the old cotton hangar took him less than five minutes. He got out and walked around to the back where the event had happened. Careful not to disturb the surroundings, he examined the wall where the bullet had entered. He found the hole in the middle of a big red stain on the wall. He then walked around to the inside of the hangar. Calculating the approximate location the bullet would have traveled to, he looked over that area. He found a place in the dirt that had been disturbed. Hope had done her job well. She had calculated the same way he had and more than likely she was in possession of the bullet. He admired her abilities. Despite how he felt about women serving in positions predetermined to be held only by men, he felt different about Hope. She was able and she was tough. She was everything he looked for in a deputy. He got back into his car and drove off, away from town. He drove slow, searching both sides of the road. He saw two different sets of tire tracks to his right. Both appeared to be made by large tires, probably full-size pick-up trucks. They disappeared as the marks switched from the grassy shoulder to the pavement. He drove a bit further hoping to see the tracks appear again on the shoulder. Only one set showed up. It led into the woods. Hinson stopped the car. He knew the owner of the property. The man drove a heavy-duty pick-up truck. He turned his car around and headed back into town. Right before he reached the town's limits, he met Hope Olson. He flashed her down. They pulled into the parking lot of a closed down business. Hope pulled up next to Andrew's car.

"Hi Andy."

"Hi. Everything all right?"

"Yeah, nothing unusual to report."

"Great. Tell me about what you found at the old cotton hangar."

Hope grabbed her notepad from her chest pocket and flipped through the pages.

"Okay, let's see. We found a 30-06 shell about 120 yards from the victim. It was near the place where Dimitri said the shot had come from."

"Good. Did you locate the bullet itself?"

Hope felt a blush come over her face.

"No, I'm afraid we didn't find the bullet itself. I tried to calculate about where the bullet would have hit, but we didn't dig anything up. I don't know if it ended up deeper in the ground or not. If it did, it must have been a high-powered rifle. Probably a sniper rifle and then the 30-06 casing was just a decoy."

"Any idea if the shooting is linked to the Knox case?"

"Not real sure about that one. The guy being in the witness protection program and all, I don't know. Could be someone figured out who he was and the past caught up with him. I'll run his name through the FBI database with a flag of diseased and see what happens."

"You believe it was someone from his past? What's your gut feeling about this?"

"Honestly, I don't believe it's his past catching up with him. My gut tells me that whoever shot him is more than likely the same person who killed Susan Knox. As far as I'm concerned the shooting is related."

"You might be right."

"Listen, about this afternoon's shooting, Patricia Langston's Jeep was spotted around the hangar about the time of the shooting. I went and talked to her about it and she got real defensive. She said a friend borrowed her Jeep. She didn't want to say what his or her name was. I think we might have a lead there. She was real agitated and threw me out. You think I need to bring her in for questioning?"

"Patricia Langston? Don't you think you're overreacting a bit? That woman is as straightlaced as she can be."

"It's your call. Personally, I think we need to bring her in; but if you think that I would be a dead-end, I'll let it go."

"I think it's a dead-end Hope. She was upset because she let someone borrow her Jeep and they hadn't brought it back. I'm sure you've felt that way before."

Hope didn't remember ever feeling the way Patricia had acted towards her, especially not over a friend borrowing a car. She couldn't figure out what Hinson was thinking. She had a feeling about Patricia that had been gnawing at her since she left her place. If she couldn't find out information the official way, well, she'd just have to go about it the unofficial way. She knew how. She would surely follow up on it.

"I guess you're right, Andy. Gee, the events of the last couple of days sure got my nerves on end. Guess I'm looking at everybody as a suspect these days."

"There's nothing wrong with that, Hope. You're just being a bit overcautious and overzealous. Try to relax a bit."

"I'll try."

"Listen, why don't you take tomorrow off?"

Hope couldn't believe what she was hearing. Hinson telling one of his deputies to take a day off, especially since it hadn't been on the board for at least two months?"

"As much as I would like that, I do need to be present when Shawn performs the autopsy on Susan Knox. Maybe after that's done, I'll take the rest of the day off."

"You got a deal. Rest up, relax. Go out and have some fun. I'm sure you'd like to spend some time with Van Acker."

"That would be nice. Thanks!"

"Don't mention it.

Hinson rolled up his window and pulled away from Hope waving at her. He looked in his rearview mirror and saw that Hope was shaking her head. He had thrown her off guard with the permission to take the day off. Well, she deserved it. Not that he liked her spending it with Van Acker. Then again, her hanging around Van Acker could help him in his plan to take care of Van Acker once and for all. He smiled as he turned the corner and headed towards Macon. He was going to check on his friend.

95.

Dimitri Van Acker sipped from the glass he had been handed. The smooth taste of Crown Royal Blended Whiskey filled his mouth. It had been prepared exactly the way he liked it. Pure, no ice or water added. He loved the taste and after the second swallow he could feel the effects of the drink set in. His muscles relaxed and he became more at ease. Never before had he felt as scared as when the man's head had exploded right next to his face. He didn't understand how it had been possible to remain calm at the time, pull his gun, hide behind the car and try to find the source of the gunshot. He figured the adrenalin had been rushing at full speed through his veins. Now, sitting down on Murphy's couch, the realization of the event had hit him and he was thankful for the drink.

Helen was in the kitchen preparing one of her famous southern dinners. He looked forward to it. He had to be careful, he reminded himself. Too much of this good southern food would soon show its effects, especially in his gut. He looked over at Murphy who had poured himself a glass too. He however was not as found of the pure taste as Van Acker was and had supplemented his drink with a couple of ice cubes.

"So, did you find anything this afternoon," Van Acker inquired.

Murphy swallowed some of the whiskey before replying.

"Yes I did. I found a set of tire tracks heading into the woods about 4 miles past where the hangar is. I drove in and found an old abandoned barn. No windows, just a big set of double doors as an entrance. The tire tracks lead straight into the barn. There was another set of tracks also. Whoever was responsible for the tracks tried to hide the fact that two cars had been at the site. The second set of tracks lead straight into the first set, trying to match their exact outline. But after the rain we had the other night, that's hard to do."

Van Acker shook his head as if to confirm Murphy's findings. He had figured there had been two cars.

"Did you try to look inside the barn and see if there was a car parked inside?"

"I did but I couldn't see much though. The barn even though old and abandoned is in good shape. There are just a few minor places where cracks have developed. I was able to shine my flash light inside. There was an older model Jeep Cherokee parked inside the barn."

"What color was it?"

"I believe it was a tan one."

Van Acker stroked his chin. How interesting! Hope had told him the only tan Jeep Cherokee she was aware of belonged to Patricia Langston. Was there a connection there? Was Patricia responsible for all that was going on around town? He hoped she wasn't, but deep inside his mind, he could not count out the possibility. Then again, why would she want Susan Knox dead? Did she have a lesbian affair with Susan? If so, could she have the HIV virus? He didn't know if Susan had been into other women, but then again, she wanted sex all the time. Maybe she satisfied her needs with both sexes.

"Allen, do you know of anyone around town that drives that kind of car?"

Murphy thought hard about that question. He knew exactly who drove that kind of car, but just as Van Acker he was troubled by the name associated with it.

"Only one, I'm afraid to say."

Van Acker nodded his head.

"That's all I've got. Patricia Langston?"

"That's right. I should know. She's been over here plenty of times hanging out with Michelle."

"Where is Michelle, by the way?"

"I don't know."

Van Acker looked towards the kitchen. Maybe Helen would know.

"Helen, do you know where Michelle is?"

"Yeah, she took my car to take Patricia to work. Something about someone had borrowed her car and had not brought it back yet."

The two men looked at each other. Both thought they knew what the other was thinking. Both were wrong. Murphy thought the worst and jumped to the conclusion that Michelle was involved with Susan's murder and had now possibly killed someone else. Van Acker's thoughts were far from Michelle. He had already determined that she had nothing to do with the killings. She was at home after all when his witness was blown away. No, whoever Patricia's friend was, was the killer. He had no doubts about that.

"Dimitri, I'm afraid I don't like the way this is going. I was hoping Michelle was not involved in all this, but it seems that she might be after all."

"No, she's not, Allen. I'm not supposed to tell you this, but Michelle was setting everything up to blow Susan away. Only someone got there before she did. She told me that herself and my dead witness collaborated her story be telling me that he saw the killer drive away from Susan's apartment. He made no mention of Michelle, unless she drives a black coupe with missing tag lights? Now, please don't go spreading this around."

"Well, she didn't drive that type of car. Are you sure? And no, I won't go spreading this around."

"Yes, I'm sure she's not involved."

"Good. Thanks for telling me. I was beginning to doubt my daughter's story."

"Allen, can you do me a favor tomorrow?"

"Sure, you name it."

Van Acker leaned closer to Murphy and told him what he wanted him to do.

There was a knock on the door. Helen opened the door. It was Hope. Helen invited her in. The two women exchanged greetings and Helen pointed towards the living room, signaling the location of the person Hope was seeking.

"Hi gents."

"Hi Hope," Murphy responded, eyeing Hope from head to toe. She did look good in that uniform. Van Acker was a lucky guy.

"Hi darling."

"Allen, I hope you don't mind, but I need to steal Dimitri away from you for a couple of minutes."

"No, go right ahead. I'll see if Helen needs any help in the kitchen."

Murphy got up and left the living room. Hope sat down next to Van Acker and tenderly kissed him on the lips.

"Dimitri, I need you to do something for me tomorrow."

Hope explained in short what had happened at Patricia's and

in turn Van Acker revealed to her what Murphy had discovered a short distance from the cotton hangar.

"I'll go talk to her and see if she's willing to reveal the name to me."

"I'll see about putting someone by the barn and try to intercept them. I might have to clear it through Hinson though."

"If you could, I'd rather you not tell him. I've got a funny feeling about that man."

"I don't know why. He's just very protective of his people and of the county."

"Maybe so, but I don't like him. Listen, before I forget, please give me the key so I can get into your house."

Hope grabbed her key ring and managed to get her house key loose from the ring. She looked at her watch and knew she needed to get moving. She wanted to get through with everything she was working on as fast as possible and she had a report to type up before she got off. She kissed Van Acker a goodbye kiss and waved Helen and Murphy bye.

"I'll tell you what, Dimitri; you've got a good woman there. Don't do anything stupid to loose her."

Van Acker smiled. If only she knew that her oldest had tried hard to undo what he had with Hope.

"Thanks, Helen, I won't lose her."

"Well, come on, let's eat."

They all sat down at the table. Murphy said grace and they started their supper. Van Acker felt bad that none of them had thought about inviting Kelly, but then again, he preferred not to be confronted with her right this moment. She had caused enough trouble in his life. It would be nice to be away from her for a little bit. He dug into the delicious meal Helen had prepared and filled his plate to the limit. He needed to go for a jog in the morning. He was putting on too much weight.

96.

Tom Sutton was not pleased with the result of the events of the previous night. His plans to escape Stuttgart had been destroyed. How he had not thought about taking the pistol with him when Julie threw him out of the house was beyond his comprehension. He guessed he should have just knocked on the door and taken care of her in a more direct way. Because of his carelessness, he was now laying in a hospital bed on his belly. The doctor had told him that it would be at least a week before he would be allowed to lie on his back. The bullet had penetrated his thigh muscle and had lodged itself in the pivot point of his hip. It had taken a long and tedious operation to remove the bullet and to stop the bleeding caused by a ruptured artery. He was out of danger and had regained consciousness and felt meaner than ever. He was giving the nurses a run for their money and soon he was known on the floor as the one to avoid. One nurse had caught his interest however. She was a young intern who was being careful not to make any mistakes. She was slender and tall and had a wonderful figure. That had been the first thing he'd seen when she walked in. Her shirt was pressed tight against her body, showing the large size of her breasts. He had felt his body react. He made up his mind that he was going to hook up with her when he got out of the hospital. She was an opportunity too good to pass up. Thoughts of the nurse were disrupted as the door opened.

"What now?" Sutton angrily said not looking at the person entering the room.

"Well, the rumors I've heard about you while walking down the hallway are true. Would you prefer me to leave?"

"Andy! Buddy, no, please stay. I thought it was one of those aggravating nurses again. Sit down!"

Hinson grabbed a chair and placed it next to the bed. He sat down and rested his elbows on his knees, looking Sutton in the eye.

"So how are we feeling?"

Sutton shot Hinson an angry look.

"What the hell do you mean, how am I feeling? I feel like some bitch shot me in the ass, that's how I'm feeling!"

"Enough said. So what are you're plans?"

438

Sutton looked up at Hinson. He knew what he was referring to with "plans". He also knew that he would not like what he wanted to do. For some reason, Hinson as good a friend as he was, always looked after Julie before he looked after him. It bothered Sutton that he came second place to Julie with his best friend.

"I haven't thought about it much, rally," he said, lying.

Hinson closed his eyes and smiled. Poor Sutton, for a lawyer, he sure didn't lie too well.

"Right, and I'm running for the President of the United States."

"Alright! I'm thinking about filing charges against her for attempted murder."

"Tom, I know that is not what happened. I know that you snuck into the house for whatever reason without letting Julie know you were there. She shot in self-defense. I don't believe you stand a chance, especially in Dawson County."

"It's her word against mine, Andy. There were no other witnesses. Everybody in town knows about my affair with Susan by now and gives Julie motive, doesn't it?"

Hinson knew that Sutton was right. The misfortunate event of having his affair with Susan revealed to the entire town was proving favorably for Sutton. It could hurt Julie in more than one way. Not only was her pride severely damaged, she now had shot her husband. Like Sutton said, his infidelity was motive for the shooting.

"Besides, Andy, I've still got the tape of her doing the humpty-dumpty with that other man."

"I thought you told me that was part of your sexual life-style, exchanging partners and such?"

"Yeah, but the jury won't know that! Again, it's her word against mine."

"It is, unless that man in the movie says different!"

"What are you talking about?"

"Just creating a scenario. Julie might be able to get in touch with him and have him testify against you in her favor. He might say that he did it because you paid him to do it. You know, drug her, rape her, have fun with her, give me the tape, here's your money, that sort of testimony, maybe?"

439

Sutton turned red in the face and was glad that he could hide his face in his pillow. Hinson was not stupid. He'd figured out what he'd done. Was he friend enough to keep that a secret? He hoped so.

"Who's going to be her lawyer?" Sutton asked figuring he already knew the answer.

"Who do you think? Van Acker of course! I've seen them together a couple of times now. I'm sure she's also asked him to do the divorce."

"Swell. You know, I wish I knew more about him. Knew what his track record was. You think you can do some research for me?"

"What kind of research?"

"Call the Bar Association in Virginia and see what his credentials are. If there's any dirt on him, I want to know it. I'm going to bury that bastard."

"Not so fast, Tom. Remember what I told you, leave Van Acker to me. I'm taking care of him. Not too much longer and he won't be no trouble to us any longer. So, don't worry about him. You need to rest so you can get out of here."

Sutton nodded his head. Hinson wanted to add to forget about charging Julie with anything but he knew that would be futile. Sutton had made up his mind on the subject. Too bad Van Acker wouldn't be around to defend her. He knew that Sutton was no match for Van Acker. He had seen that just from talking with and following Van Acker around. He was thorough and knew where to look for answers. Too bad he won't see the big shocker coming his way, Hinson thought.

"Well buddy," Hinson said as he stood, "let me go and take care of some stuff. You get plenty of rest and don't be such a pest to the nurses, okay. They're here to make you and your ass feel better."

Sutton didn't respond. He waved Hinson a quick goodbye and dropped his head in the pillow. Damn that made your neck hurt to look at someone when lying on your stomach. He wondered what Hinson was going to do with Dimitri Van Acker. He didn't care. If he could get rid of Van Acker, he might just stay around. He smiled as he closed his eyes and dozed off, dreaming of the young intern nurse. He would have to get with her when he felt better. Most

440

definitely!

97

Eddie Jovanovich was sitting on the side of the road looking at the house. He didn't know what he was doing here. He had enjoyed getting paid for making a tape of himself with this Sutton guy's wife. He sure needed the money. It was enough to get started in Florida. Then why on earth was he sitting here on the side of the road instead of being in Florida? Why was he sitting in front of Julie Sutton's house? Was it that he felt guilty about what he had done with Mrs. Sutton? As much fun as it had been, he could not forget about what had happened and the circumstances under which it had happened. She seemed to be a nice lady, puritan in her beliefs. It had meant drugging her for him to have sex with her. It had not been natural. There was something wrong with the way it had happened. He wouldn't mind if he could do it over with her being conscious and willing. Somehow he knew that was never going to happen. At least he could fantasize about it.

Jovanovich looked over to the passenger seat of his car. He took the video tape and moved it from one hand to the other. Tom Sutton had been an idiot to think that he owned the only tape of the event. No, Eddie Jovanovich might not have been the most honest person in the world and would do anything to get some quick cash, but he wasn't stupid. Something was going on around this town that wasn't right. He had returned to Stuttgart the same night he was told never to come around again. Being careful not to get noticed, he had picked up on several interesting events. An undertaker had been shot to dead, Tom Sutton had been shot in the rear end by his wife, and then this afternoon someone else had gotten shot. Even though he didn't feel safe, knowing the Sheriff might catch up with him at any moment, he felt the need to stay around and maybe profit from what was going on.

He pulled himself together, got out of the car and walked over to the house. He knew she was home. He had seen her move about the house. He rang the door bell. He didn't know how she would react to him standing at her front door. Probably alarmed and frightened. He needed to make sure that she did not attract any attention from her neighbors. He hated to think they would call the law to check out what was going on at the Sutton home. He saw movement through the frosted window of the door and moved back a step. The door opened.

Julie Sutton had been washing some dishes when the door bell rang. She looked at the clock in the kitchen and wondered who would be calling on her at this hour of the evening. Her mother would be getting close to going to bed and she knew her father would not be coming around. Maybe it was Dimitri Van Acker. He probably had watched the videotapes by now and was coming over to discuss it with her. But no, they weren't supposed to meet till tomorrow to discuss the contents. Maybe there was something on the tapes that needed immediate attention. With the mind-set that it was more than likely Van Acker at the door, she opened the door without taking precaution. She turned white as snow as she laid eyes on the person in front of her. She froze and tried to scream but she couldn't. She was too frightened.

Eddie Jovanovich saw the frightened look on Julie's face and made his move. He knew it was only a matter of seconds before she recollected herself and started screaming. Well, he couldn't blame her, especially after what he had done to her. He pushed her inside and slammed the door shut. Julie stood there, motionless, staring up at Jovanovich. Then it happened. Julie managed to catch her breath and a loud scream erupted through the house. Jovanovich dropped the tape to the floor and put a hand over Julie's mouth.

"Would you shut up? I'm not here to harm you!"

Slowly he released the pressure on her mouth to where she could talk.

"Wh.. wh.. what do you want?"

He let go of her and motioned to a chair.

"Please, Mrs. Sutton, sit down."

Julie obeyed, not wanting to go through another rape, or worse.

"We need to have a long talk about your husband. Before I start telling you my story, I need to have your word that I will walk away from Stuttgart without being harassed by the law. I know what I did was a crime, but I'm asking for your word to look past what I've done and to please consider my story."

"What are you talking about?" Julie asked, totally confused.

443

Jovanovich picked up the video tape off the floor and sat down opposite Julie.

"Do I have your word?"

Julie nodded her head, figuring it was the only way to get rid of this man.

Jovanovich put the videotape on the coffee table beside him and told Julie the story about her husband hiring him to do what he did. Julie's eyes grew big at first, not willing to believe that her husband could do something like that. Then, she started crying at the thought that she had been videotaped lying naked on a bed with this filthy man going down on her motionless body. Unconsciously she pulled on her shirt, making sure it was buttoned tightly and covered the outline of her breasts with her arms. Even though she was fully dressed, she felt completely naked sitting in front of this man, the man who had violated her body, who had forced his manhood inside of her, the man who had seen her naked and videotaped her. She shuddered at the thought that he had watched the tape over and over again, pleasuring himself. That thought made her blush. And then it hit her that her husband surely had a copy of the tape. Had he watched it? What had he thought of it? Had someone else seen it? Why was this happening to her? Why was she being tested to the limit? Why was her faith so violently attacked and tested?

Julie licked her lips to moisten them. Her mouth was dry and her throat hurt. She needed some water. But first she needed to get rid of this animal sitting in front of her. She had one question that she needed him before she wanted him to go.

"Do you have any other copies of the tape?"

Jovanovich looked down at the floor as he shook his head.

"No ma'am. Like I told you, it was a great kick at first to get paid to fuck someone else's wife, but I didn't feel right about it. If you had been halfway willing, then that would have been a different story. But I don't like being called a rapist. This tape here is the only copy I have. It's yours now. Do with it what you want. I don't know why your husband wanted to have a tape of the whole thing. I don't think you would have ever found out unless it hit you out of left field. Now you're warned."

Jovanovich stood up, handed Julie the tape, and walked towards the door.

444

"Mrs. Sutton?"

Julie turned around and looked at him.

"Ma'am, I want to apologize if I harmed you in any way. I hope that you can forgive me one day. I'd like to meet you again under different circumstances but I realize that it'll be cold day in hell before that happens; so for now, goodbye and good luck."

Julie sat down staring at the tape in her hands as the car pulled away from the curb opposite her house. She took a deep breath of relieve. What had just happened? Why had it happened? Was it possible for someone with such criminal intent as Lester, or whatever his name might be, to feel guilt about what he had done? She shook her head, not knowing the answers to a lot of questions.

Julie eyed the video cassette in her hands. She felt a gnawing feeling at her stomach. She was tempted to view the contents of the tape, then again, she didn't know whether she could handle it or not. But Tom had a similar tape and he knew what the contents were. That gave him the upper hand. No, she needed to be strong and watch the tape. She needed to be playing in the same court as he was. She told herself that she needed to be one step ahead of him. She stood and put the tape in her VCR. She sat down and watched as the scene in the house she had been in started. She cried hard and loud as she witnessed herself being raped by this awful person. For so long she had blocked out everything that had happened to her. The incest, the problem she had making love to her husband, and now, the rape. It was time she took control of her life. It was time to take the next step, a step she should have taken a long time ago. But first, she needed rest. She needed to make sure that she was ready for battle.

98.

Dimitri Van Acker sat on the couch in Hope's house, looking at the TV screen. The screen showed a deep blue, nothing being shown on the screen. The look on his face was one of total disgust.

After finishing supper with the Murphy's, he had gone over to Kelly's and retrieved his belongings. Kelly had not been home. He was thankful for that. He had hurried in getting everything out of her spare bedroom to make sure he did not have to face her. He was still too upset with her to confront her in a civilized manner. It had not taken him long to put everything in his car and head towards Hope's. There he had unpacked and stocked the spare bedroom with his belongings. That done, he sat down on the couch and watched the tapes Julie and he had removed from the safety deposit box at the bank. He had witnessed a young Susan, he estimated her to be about 12 or 13 years old, having sex with her father. It was obvious from watching the tapes, that Susan had not been a willing participant. She tried to refuse the advances made by her father and it showed a couple of scenes where he violently jerked her around and even beat her. The man was a sick person. He witnessed several tapings where Susan was forced to perform oral and anal sex with her father. The last tape he had viewed was a tape with footage of Julie and her father. The setting was different. Dimitri guessed it was taped in Julie's room. He estimated Julie to be about 14 or 15 years old. Dimitri watched as James Knox entered the room. Julie looked to be doing homework and when Knox entered, she stood up and went over to embrace him. James locked his arms around her back and held her tight. What happened next, made Dimitri jump. Without warning, Knox ripped the shirt of his daughter's body. The look in Julie's eyes was one of total fright. She tried to hide her bra-covered breasts. James did not give her time to do so as he hit her across the face. Julie fell to the floor. She tried to slide backwards, looking to find the bed. Knox started to undo his pants. He dropped them to the floor and stepped out of them. Then he removed his underwear. Julie's eyes grew big at the sight of her naked father in front of her. She tried to scream but he hit her across the face again and she fell down to the floor. Knox stood over his daughter and laughed. He bent down and pulled Julie up by the hair. Scared and trembling, she stood as Knox pushed her bra upwards, exposing her ample breasts. Knox grabbed his daughter's breasts and squeezed them hard. Julie yelped at the pain it caused. Knox then lowered his hand and pulled her skirt and panties down. Julie stood naked in front of her father, staring at him with fear in her eyes. Knox pushed her down on the bed and mounted her. All Van Acker could do was shake his head as he witnessed Knox violently raping his young daughter. The taping ended with Knox getting off Julie, putting his clothes back on and leaving the room. Julie remained lying on the bed, motionless, staring at the ceiling, tears running down her face.

Van Acker had stopped the tape and was now staring at the blue screen of the television. He was too much in chock to turn off the VCR. He had not realized that what Susan had told him before her death was the truth. He had to admit that he had doubted her but now realized the Knox girls had indeed been sexually abused by their father. It was amazing that Knox had gotten away with raping his daughters for so long. And what about Phyllis Knox, where did she fit in all this? She surely had to have known about what had been happening behind the closed doors of her daughter's rooms. He could not see how it would have been possible for her not to have known. Disgusted with the sights he had just witnessed, he got up and walked over to the kitchen to fetch a beer. He shook his head, thinking about what the poor Knox girls had gone through while growing up. No wonder they were so screwed up. Both had dealt with their experiences in their own way. One had gone the path of fast destruction while the other had crawled in a hole and had hidden from the world around her. God, what a sick bastard! He needed to be put away for a long time.

Van Acker returned to the couch and took hold of the last tape he had brought back from the bank. It was clearly marked that it needed to be watched last. He took a long sip from his beer and popped the tape into the VCR. He wondered what this one would reveal. Van Acker sat down as the tape started to play. An older Susan appeared on the screen and he figured the taping had been done recently, judging by the way Susan looked and how he remembered her from their last meeting. Susan started talking:

"Hi Dimitri, at least I hope it is you watching this last and final tape. I know that by now, you must be in chock about what you

have witnessed. Trust me, I have watched the tapes again and again, trying to figure out what I could have done differently while growing up. I have wondered so many times what I could have done different to make this madness stop and go away. Well, as you know, I failed horribly at doing that. Also since you are watching this tape, I am no longer among the living. I knew the day would soon come for me to leave this world. My disease had gotten the better of me and I feel the end coming closer. There is a slight possibility that somehow I died due to other causes than the AIDS virus. Possibly, one of my many lovers may have gotten a hold of me and taken his, and yes, I may as well be honest, or her, revenge. I am ashamed that I have to sit here in front of the camera and tell you this. Trust me; if this would have been a face to face interview, I think I would be even more ashamed.

Dimitri, as soon as I find out when you are coming back to Stuttgart, I will reveal my condition to four people that I had an intimate sexual relationship with. I feel that I do not gain anything by not telling them of my condition. I am glad however, that since I found out about my condition, I have reframed from having unprotected sex. It hurts me right now to think of how many lives I have destroyed because I did not care whether my lovers used protection or not. But like I said, there are only four. However, those four are prominent people in the community or at least are connected to prominent people in the community. Here are their names:

First there is Tom Sutton. Yes, it seems to be unbelievable. Tom was an important part of my life for a long time. I have been involved with him since before he and my sister were married. Do I feel bad about cheating on my sister? Yes I do. It makes me feel even worse to think that she may also have contracted the disease. I will tell her about my affair with Tom. This will happened the day after I tell Tom. I hope that she will be strong enough to take the news. I am prepared to lose her as my sister if it comes to that. However, I hope that we can come to terms. I will need her to help me in my efforts to take our father to court and make him pay for what he has done to us. But let's move on.

The second person that has been involved with me for a long time is Gerald Radcliff. Of all the people I have slept with, he must have been the sweetest of them all. It hurts me to think that I may be the cause of his death. I hope that he will understand that I did not intend for him to contract this horrible disease.

The third person that I have been involved with and did not use any protection with was Bryan Scarboro. God, I love that young hunk of a man. He is so confident, so sure of himself. He is probably the one person that I am most worried about. I know that he's a lady's man and I know that he has his share of lovers while away at college. It is sad that every one of those women can possibly be infected with the AIDS virus. How cruel a world that we live in! Am I therefore a murderer? Or is my father, the one who drove me to be the way I am, the ultimate killer of innocent life? I believe that he is, and that is why I hired you.

Last there is one more person who has been intimate with me and could possibly be infected. That person, who is still dear to me, who showed me that love could be tender, the one who I loved the most, that person is...

The television screen went to static and then to a blue screen. What the hell? Van Acker cursed. He got up and slapped the VCR box on the side, but nothing happened. Apparently the tape had been damaged unbeknownst to Julie. He sat back down and gathered his thoughts. He knew about Tom and about Bryan. He was surprised to hear Gerald Ratcliff's name mentioned. That would explain why Ratcliff committed suicide. Could Ratcliff have murdered Susan and then decide to take his own life? He would have to let Hope know about this last tape. He pressed the rewind button on the remote and found the spot where the tape went to static. He carefully listened but could not make out the name. Damned! So close! He pressed the rewind button again. He reached the spot where the tape went to static. He listened carefully. No, he could not make out what Susan was saying. He balled his fist and hit the couch. Why did this have to happen?

Van Acker's cell phone rang in the next room. He looked at his watch. Who could be calling him on his cell phone this late? He ran to the next room and answered the phone.

"Hello?"

"Dimitri?"

"Yes, Sid is that you?"

449

"Yeah buddy. How's everything going?"

"Not so good, old friend. I've got a murder on my hands and every time I get to the point of finding out who could be the guilty party something happens."

Van Acker went on to explain what hat happened with his client and then that his only eyewitness had gotten shot. He also explained about the tape.

"Too bad I'm not there with my high tech toys, Dimitri. I could lift the static of the tape and find out what is on that part of the tape."

"Damn, you mean they've got a machine that will do that?"

"You bet. Listen, I've got the information you wanted."

"Anything interesting?"

"Well, we've got a piece of cotton, probably from a T-shirt. It had a little blood on it. Suspect in question got A- for blood type. It took me a while to figure that out because there was not much blood and what there was, was dry. That should narrow down your search some since only about 1 in 16 people have A- blood. That is of course, if you can get a hold of everybody's medical records."

"Funny, Sid. Anything more specific?"

"Sure. How about the person who belonged to this piece of fabric has or has had contact with reddish blond hair? How about the person lives or works in an area that has a lot of dust. The dust particles were off the chart! And possibly the subject has or has been near a cat."

"Sid, be serious my friend. There's no possible way you found all that out from that little piece of fabric I sent you."

"Listen, Dimitri, you told me to analyze the fabric and I did. The person whose clothing this came from has a cat because there are cat hair particle on it. The same is true for the dust and the hair."

"Susan," Van Acker whispered to him.

"What's that buddy?"

"I said Susan. Susan Knox is the woman that got killed the other night. She had reddish blond hair. This could mean the person who killed Susan could also be Joshua's killer. I wish I could borrow you for a couple of days and run those forensic tests for me. We'd have our killer in no time!"

"Well, that would be nice but the FBI keeps me busy! That

reminds me; I may come see you soon. I'm taking a week vacation around Labor Day. I might swing down your way."

"Sid thanks for what you did. I owe you one. And I would love for you to come down and visit and meet my lady."

"Wow, you're not wasting any time are you? Well, I've gotta go. Talk to you later."

"Bye Sid."

Van Acker put the phone down. Okay, he had a bit more information to go on. He grabbed a piece of paper and wrote down his notes.

Black coupe
Broken tag lights
Cat owner
Dirt road or near
Blood type A-
Gun owner

Van Acker thought hard for a minute. How much of this information was he willing to share with Hope? He needed to pry and see how much information she had and then decide if he was willing to share some of his. Of course, none of the evidence that he had would hold up in court. But maybe that wouldn't be necessary. He looked at his watch. A few more hours before Hope would come home. He stretched and lay down on the couch. A little nap couldn't hurt. He closed his eyes and fell asleep.

***

Outside a little ways from the house, a black coupe stopped. A person dressed in black got out. The person snuck into Hope's yard and walked over to Van Acker's car. The driver side door was locked. The person walked to the passenger side. The door opened. The person pulled something from its pants. The moonlight reflected from the metal object. It was placed under the passenger side seat. The door was closed carefully and the person returned to the black coupe. The entire process of placing the object in Van Acker's car had taken less than a minute. The driver of the coupe disappeared, heading towards Stuttgart.

***

Two hours later, Hope Olson finally came home. She smiled at the sight of Van Acker lying asleep on the couch. Quietly she went and got a light blanket and covered him. She planted a soft kiss on his lips and rubbed his hair. He did not wake up. She looked over the coffee table and saw his notes. She was tempted to look. He could have information she didn't have that could help her in her case. She decided not to look. She knew that he trusted her not to look. She was not going to betray him. Hope turned off the television and walked to her room, turning off the light in the living room. Ten minutes later, she was asleep also.

99.

It was still dark when Dimitri Van Acker woke up. He looked at his watch. He was surprised to see that it was this early in the morning. He looked around. Hope must have covered him up with the blanket. He yawned and stretched. He got up and went to the bathroom. That done, he took a peek in Hope's bedroom. He smiled at the sight. Hope was stretched out on top of the covers in nothing but her panties. Her hair was in total disarray and it seemed as if she had a smile on her face. He felt the urge to go in and lay down beside her but decided not to. He was determined to take it one step at a time and not to rush into a relationship that was purely physical. He wanted Hope to love him for whom he was, not for how he performed in bed.

He made his way to the kitchen and started making coffee, careful not to create too much noise. Soon the smell of coffee filled the room. He sat down and grabbed his notes and looked over them. He knew the key to solving Susan Knox' murder was written down in his notes. All he needed to do was to put them in the right order and put a face to them. He wondered why Sid had not been able to tell him whether the blood belonged to a man or a woman. If he had been able to figure out the blood type, then surely he could have figured out the sex of the person. He grabbed his phone and dialed Sid's home number. The phone rang. After about 10 rings the phone was answered.

"Hello," said a tired voice on the other end.

"Sid, it's Dimitri."

"Dimitri? What the hell are you doing calling me at this God awful hour?"

"Sid, there is something missing in the information you gave me."

"Oh yeah, what's that?"

"You gave me the blood type of the person, right?"

"Right."

"All right then, if you know the blood type, why can't you figure out the sex of the person?"

"You know, Dimitri, you're too damn smart for your own good. I totally overlooked that fact. Hold on a minute. Let me get to my lab."

Van Acker's palms started sweating as he waited for Sid to make it to the lab and tell him the information he needed.

"Dimitri?"

"Here, go ahead Sid."

"Well, I did run that test, and I don't know why I didn't put it in my notes. Anyways, blood belongs to a male. Other than that I don't have any further information. I can take it to work with me and get Abe to look at it and see if there is any type disease in the blood."

"No, that will be fine, Sid. You've been a great help. Sorry I got you up so soon. I'll make it up to you."

"Sure thing, bud."

The phone went dead. Van Acker smiled. Okay, so he had a male suspect. That made it easier. Who could have committed the two crimes? There were a lot of possibilities on who could have taken Susan out, but that person also took out Joshua and his eyewitness. The choices became smaller. The voice behind him made him jump.

Hope Olson had woken up by a combination of the smell of fresh brewed coffee coming from the kitchen and Van Acker's voice coming from the living room. She had put on a long T-shirt and walked into the living room. She stood at the corner and watched as Van Acker finished his conversation with whoever Sid was.

"I hope you're as much concerned about waking me up as you are about waking Sid up!"

She smiled as she saw Dimitri jump.

"Hope, hi, I... I didn't mean to wake you up."

"I know. The coffee is guilty too."

She smiled and walked over to give him a kiss.

"So, how do you like your coffee?"

Van Acker felt light-headed. He had no idea that it could feel so good to be greeted by a kiss this early in the morning.

"I like it with a little milk."

"Good, that's the way I like it too," she said.

She continued:

"Guess what sweetie?"

"What?"

"Hinson gave me the day off today. Can you believe it?"

He couldn't believe it. What was going on? Did Hinson giving Hope the day off serve him in any way? He doubted it, but still. Wouldn't it be to his advantage if Susan's case came to a close as soon as possible? No, this didn't make any sense.

"That's great, honey. It is hard to believe but at least we get to spend some time together."

"Well, I do have to go over to the funeral home this morning. Susan's autopsy is scheduled for around 10."

Great! He had a meeting with Julie Sutton at the same time. He had hoped to be present during the autopsy. Well, he could call Julie and reschedule. He was sure she would understand the reason; after all, it was her sister's autopsy. She might even want to be present herself even though he seriously doubted it.

"Well, I'm glad you told me. You know I have a court order that allows me to be present during the autopsy. I hope that won't be a problem?"

"No, I don't see why it would be."

"How about Julie?"

"Sutton?"

Van Acker nodded.

"I don't mind if she's present. I don't think that she would enjoy watching someone cut open her sister, but no, I don't mind."

"Good, I'll have to call her then. I had a meeting set up with her about the time of the autopsy. We can meet afterwards. I believe this will work out great."

Van Acker wondered whether he needed to tell Hope about what he had found out about the Susan Knox case. He wanted so much to know what Hope knew. He doubted that she had as much information as he did, but it couldn't hurt. He could always play dumb, pretending he didn't have any leads at all.

"Hope, how are you coming on the Knox case?"

Hope looked at him. She was not supposed to be discussing cases with outsiders. Even though he was Susan's lawyer, she had to be careful with what information she gave out. Not that she had much. The only thing she had going for her was that somehow Patricia Langston was involved.

"Dimitri, to be honest with you, the only thing I've got is what I told you last night. Patricia Langston is my only lead right now. I was hoping the autopsy would be the turning point in my investigation. What about you?"

"I don't have much either. The only thing I have is that I believe the person who was driving Patricia's Jeep was a man. Other than that, I don't have much to go on."

"What about your eyewitness? Was he able to tell you anything before he got shot?"

"Not much. He told me he was parked in the church parking lot, resting for the night, waiting for the gas station to open. He said, he got out to stretch his legs and that's when he witnessed someone going into Susan apartment and coming out a little while later. He said he followed the person but before he could tell me where to person was going or who it was, he got shot."

"So we don't have much."

Hope handed Van Acker a mug of hot coffee. Both sat down on the couch and sipped their coffee, neither willing to go any further into the subject of Susan Knox' murder. Van Acker was the first to stand up. He stretched.

"I'm going to go for a jog this morning; do you want to join me?"

Hope declined the invitation, explaining that she had promised a friend to go work out with her later in the evening.

"Besides, I need to get ready for the autopsy; and I've got laundry to do as well. No, you go on."

"Is the track at the high school still in bad shape?"

"Oh no, they just put a new one in. It's really nice. You should go and try it out."

Van Acker disappeared into the spare room and came out a few minutes later wearing shorts and T-shirt. Heading out the door, he kissed Hope telling her he loved her. Driving off towards the high school, he thought about calling Julie Sutton, but noticing the time, he decided to wait until after his jog. It was still early and he had plenty of time to make the phone call.

100.

Julie Sutton had put on a conservative outfit. She wanted to look professional, so she had chosen a white blouse with a chemise under it and a gray cotton skirt that come down two inches below her knees. She looked in the mirror and seemed satisfied with was she witnessed. The cold shower had rejuvenated her body and she felt good. She checked her watch. It was a little after eight. She had two hours before her meeting with Van Acker. She hoped that everything would go well with the meeting and that Van Acker wouldn't have any surprises. She was worried about the content of the tapes. If truth be known, she whished the tapes wouldn't have anything incriminating on them. Somehow, she doubted it. Knowing Susan, the tapes were filled with revealing footage of both her sister and her. She felt ashamed, knowing that Van Acker had watched the tapes. That he had witnessed her getting raped by her father. That he had seen her body being humiliated by the one person who was supposed to protect her.

She walked downstairs, into the kitchen and made a cup of instant coffee. She grabbed the cup with both hands, as if she were cold, and sat down on the couch. She looked out the window across the street at her parent's house and the burned down remains of her sister's apartment. As she sipped her coffee, she watched her mother pull some weeds from her flower beds. In the back of the house, she spotted her father cutting grass. They looked so perfect together like that. No one driving by, looking at them would ever think what horrible things had gone on inside that house. But she knew better. For far too long, she had kept the secret inside, had kept her silence. Susan's silence had been bought by her father. Her silence had ended with her death. Now, it was time to break the silence. It was time to expose the horrible things that had happened all those years ago. Dimitri Van Acker had the tapes her sister had secretly filmed. On those tapes was evidence of Susan's body being violated by her father and her own body being violated by her father. Those horrible events would be revealed for all to see. But it was a price she was willing to pay. She would finally turn over that horrible page of her past and start on a new chapter in her life. She would start a new chapter without secrets, without the fear of being found out, and mostly without the presence of her husband. She would start anew. She knew it wouldn't be easy but she was willing to put every effort forward to make the best of the rest of her life.

The thought of her husband made her realize that his car was still parked in the driveway. She had never been one to snoop around, but now, she felt the undesirable need to take a look at what was inside his car. Determined in her little adventure, she walked outside. She looked around as if to make sure no one was watching. She smiled. What was she doing? There was no need to look around as if she was trying to sneak into a stranger's car. This was her husband's car! Millions of wives did this every day. Millions of wives looked in their husband's cars. She felt the driver's side door. It opened. Another smile covered her face. This was easy! She sat down in the driver's seat. The car smelled like him. It was a smell she had gotten so used to during their marriage. Now, it made her shiver. It reminded her of the nights were she lay in bed wishing he would reach his climax so she could get up, take a shower and go to sleep. She shook her head. She needed to get rid of these thoughts. It was time to move on.

Julie reached over and opened the glove compartment. She found a set of keys, an owner's manual to the car, an insurance card, and a videotape. She grabbed the tape. It did not have any labels on it. She wondered if that was her husband's copy of her meeting with Lester. There was only one way to find out. She ran back into the house and put the tape in the VCR. Soon the images that were on the tape Lester had given her were filling the television screen. Julie hit the stop button and smiled. Good, now she had both copies. Her husband would not be able to use that against her during the divorce trial. She doubted that he had made a copy. He was too arrogant to think that he would lose or misplace the tape. Julie sat down and took a deep breath as a smile covered her face. Things were starting to look better. She was gaining control over the situation. She was taking over her own life. She was in control of herself for the first time since she met Sutton. She had taken control over life when she first started college. Then she met Sutton and he had taken control over her. Now, it felt good to have control back. It was long overdue, but it was here. She intended to keep it this way. She looked at her watch. It was nearly nine o'clock. In another hour, she would meet with Van Acker. At that point she would take the second step towards total self control. She needed to shed the mental control her father had over her. She leaned back in her chair and closed her eyes. She had not felt this good in a long time.

101.

Dimitri Van Acker drove up into the high school parking lot nearest to the track. The morning air was heavy and anything but cool and he could feel the humidity pressing down on him. He shook his head. Why had he decided to come back to Georgia and endure its harsh summers? He smiled as he could think of at least one reason. He started with some stretching exercises to loosen his muscles. He was in a crunch position when he heard another car drive up. From behind his car, he looked towards the approaching car. It was a black coupe. Dimitri looked closer. He noticed that it was a Mazda RX7, one of the first ones made. Through the dark glass of the windshield, Dimitri could not make out who was behind the wheel. Still in a crunch position, he waited to see who was driving the vintage car.

When Andrew Hinson emerged from the car, Dimitri Van Acker's hard skipped a beat and he almost fell over on the ground. Hinson was the last person he would have guessed meeting this early in the morning. He got up and looked around the parking lot. They were the only two people present. An eerie feeling swept over him. Was this a coincidence or had Hinson followed him out here? Standing frozen, not exactly knowing what to do, he watched as the Sheriff made his way towards him.

Andrew Hinson was as surprised to see Van Acker as Van Acker was to see him. If he would have known Van Acker would be working out too, he would have gone somewhere else to loosen his muscles. The last person he wanted to meet with this morning was Van Acker. Funny how faith can be! Hinson decided to do the right thing and walked over to Van Acker, his arm extended, ready to shake Van Acker's hand.

Van Acker returned the favor and shook Hinson's hand. Van Acker was starting to sweat and he couldn't tell for sure whether his hands were the one's damp with sweat or if Hinson's hand had seemed to be sweating.

"Well, Van Acker, what a surprise to see you out here this early in the morning. You work out a lot?"

Hinson had wanted to tell Van Acker that he had no use for him in Stuttgart, but thought better of it. There was no use stirring things up right now. He had made Tom Sutton a promise to take care of Van Acker. He still intended to do that, but this was not the time or place to do it. His opportunity would come and it would come soon.

"Yes, I do work out a lot. Unfortunately with all the recent events, you know, moving back down here and dealing with my clients being murdered, I haven't had a chance to get at it."

Van Acker kept his eyes locked on Hinson's face. He had chosen his words carefully intentionally mentioning the words "clients" and "murdered". He thought he could see Hinson's face muscles reacting to those words, even though Hinson tried hard not to show any emotion.

"Clients? I thought you had only one client thus far. Besides, nothing has been decided about it being a murder. You might want to be careful using those words. One may start thinking that you know more than you should."

Hinson winked at Van Acker.

"You wouldn't want someone to think that you had anything to do with that."

This time it was Hinson's turn to watch Van Acker's reaction. He'd expected Hinson would come back with a line like that and had mentally prepared himself for it. It didn't throw him; instead, Van Acker produced a look of total surprise on his face.

"Me? You don't believe that I'm behind killing my own client, do you?"

"Well, I'm not at liberty to say, but I'd be careful about what I said if I were you."

Van Acker held a straight face even though he felt like busting out laughing. Hinson was playing the same game he was. Van Acker wondered exactly how much Hinson knew. It depended on how much information Hope had given him and if Hinson knew what Hope knew, then it was little. At least that was what Van Acker had gathered from his conversations with Hope. They were dependent on the autopsy to get a base for their investigation.

Dimitri Van Acker pointed towards the track and asked, "Would you mind if we jogged together?"

Hinson looked at him with a surprised look on his face. Van Acker smiled inwardly and kept track of the score. He was one up on Hinson.

"Don't mind if I do, Van Acker."

They walked towards the track and once on the track, started jogging at a slow leisurely pace. They made it around the track without uttering a word to each other. Halfway through the second lap, Hinson broke the silence.

"Tell me something, Van Acker. Do you think that you will be able to compete with Sutton in this little town?"

Van Acker looked at Hinson and thought carefully about how to answer that question. He didn't want to sound overconfident. He knew Hinson was good friends with Tom Sutton and everything he said would go straight back to him.

"Well, you never know how you will be received when you start competing against the establishment. I know Sutton has made a name for himself here in Dawson County. I guess about the same way I made a name for myself in DC. I had to struggle against the established lawyers there too, but I was persistent and in the end, I was the one that they had to struggle against. I feel that if things are done right, there might be room for the two of us here in Stuttgart and Dawson County."

Hinson looked in wonder at Van Acker as they started their third lap.

"Do you think that Sutton is going to let you take part of the pie after he has had the whole pie for so long? I don't think so. He stands to lose more than just his customers. He's also involved in local politics and if you come in here and started making him look bad, I don't think he'll be too happy."

Van Acker thought about that for a moment. Hinson was right and he knew it. Sutton had as much as told him that he didn't stand a chance, that he was not going to let someone come in and take over. Van Acker decided to approach the subject from a different angle.

"Seems to me that Sutton is doing a good job all by his self to get his name slung through the mud without my help. Everyone knows that Julie kicked him out and why. You think these conservative churchgoing citizens are going to take lightly to him having an affair with his wife's sister? And what about him maybe having contracted the AIDS virus from Susan? If you ask me, I don't think I'll have too much trouble getting myself settled around here."

Van Acker threw a look towards Hinson. Hinson was looking straight ahead, the expression on his face showing what he was trying to hide by not saying anything. Hinson looked mad. The lines around his mouth and eyes could not go unnoticed.

"You know, Van Acker, I'd be real careful spreading accusations around like that. There is no proof that Sutton and Susan had anything going on."

Van Acker couldn't help but laugh out loud.

"Don't tell me you're so gullible to think that his affair with Susan is a figment of Susan's imagination?"

"I'm not saying that. But there is no evidence to point in that direction."

"You're right. There is no evidence to that point. But then again, Susan is dead, most likely killed, and any evidence that Sutton had an affair with her was destroyed in the explosion. Right now, Tom Sutton is high on my list of suspects."

Van Acker watched for a reaction from Hinson and got it.

"Are you accusing Sutton of murdering Susan?"

Van Acker was certain that Sutton had not murdered Susan, but he wanted to see where the accusation would lead.

"Well I must say that he is on my list of people with motive to kill her."

They were starting their eighth lap and Hinson was starting to show signs of exhaustion. He had been pushing to keep up with Van Acker but was slowing down faster and faster. Van Acker had respectfully slowed down too. Now, Hinson stopped and put his hands on his knees, breathing heavy. Van Acker stopped running and walked back towards Hinson. He watched as Hinson was trying to catch his breath. He noticed Hinson grabbing his arm where a wrap covered his skin.

"Tired already?" he mocked.

Van Acker knew he had the upper hand on Hinson when it came to arguing about Sutton's involvement in Susan's murder.

"You seem to have a lot of information into the case, Van Acker. I hope you have been sharing your information with your girlfriend."

Van Acker didn't fall for the mentioning of Hope.

463

"Actually, I have not revealed anything about what I have come up with. Far be it from me to interfere with an official investigation. That would not look too good now, would it? I'll be glad to share any information I have with your office, but only if you can provide me with a court order to do so. Of course you would have to get a court order from Judge Snelgrove and I know how much you two like each other."

Hinson was turning red in the face. He was getting madder and madder. He straightened himself up and looked Van Acker in the face. Pointing a finger at him he said:

"You watch it, Van Acker. I don't know who you think you are, but you're not going to get anywhere with this attitude. I'll make sure of that. If I were you, I'd watch where I went, where I ate and where I slept. Don't underestimate the force in this county. People tend to stick with the insiders, not the arrogant outsiders who seem to think they know everything there is to know about Dawson County. I'm warning you, watch your steps!"

That said, Hinson started towards his car. Van Acker followed him at a safe distance.

"Sheriff, do I have to take this as a threat?"

Without looking back Hinson said:

"You take that anyway you want, Van Acker. I know this county better than you do. You'd better beware!"

Van Acker didn't respond but watched as Hinson got in his car and started to drive off.

Out of habit, Hinson turned his lights on as he drove off. Van Acker's eyes followed the black coupe as it turned the corner and disappeared from the school grounds. What was he missing? He tried to search his mental banks but could not come up with anything. Shaking his head he walked towards his own car, got in, and drove back towards Hope's. He scratched his head as he tried to figure out what he was missing. It had something to do with the car, something that he had noticed about Hinson's car. He pounded the steering wheel in frustration. He knew it would bother him all day, and no matter how hard he tried, he knew he would not be able to let go until he figured it out. He looked at his watch. It was shortly after nine o'clock. It was time to tell Julie Sutton about the autopsy. He grabbed his cell phone and dialed the number as something else he

464

had noticed hit him square between the eyes. The bandage! Hinson's arm had been bandaged! He tried to recall how high on the door into Joshua Underwood's funeral home he had found the piece of fabric. Could it be? He would have to go back to the funeral home and check it out. But first, he needed to shower and he needed to attend Susan's autopsy.

102.

Shawn Joiner was already at the funeral home when Hope Olson arrived. When the two friends saw each other, they fell into a hug. Shaw Joiner was a tall black woman with long straight hair and pretty features. She had served with Hope during the Persian Gulf War, although in different outfits, but in the same town. Hope had been an intelligence officer while Joiner was putting her talents to work in the local hospital camps. She was studying to be a doctor and the Navy had given her an opportunity she couldn't ignore. The two had become close friends and had stayed in touch after returning stateside. When Operation Desert Storm had ended, both women had retired from the Navy to pursue careers in civilian fields. While Hope had chosen law enforcement, Joiner, who had finished medical school through the Navy, had found a position at the Augusta School of Medicine as Chief Pathologist. She was still single and wasn't concerned that she had not found a suitor at the age of 38.

When Hope had called her and asked for help with the autopsy of Susan Knox' body, she had not hesitated to help out her old friend. She did not make a habit of performing autopsies away from the hospital, especially at funeral homes. That was usually a total nightmare. There never was enough room, the supplies available left a lot to be desired and it meant that she had to drag one of her students with her to help her as her diener. She knew that Hope wanted to solve the Knox death as quickly as possible. She also knew that if Knox' body was transported to the crime lab in either Macon or Atlanta, it would take at least several weeks before any pathologist would even take a look at it. So, she decided to make an exception and help her old out. As her diener she had chosen a last year med student. She was bright and Joiner had high hopes for her. She would make a good pathologist, but she had her sights set on child medicine and Joiner could not argue with that.

Alison Hamlin had assisted in many autopsies under Joiner's supervision and she was comfortable with the procedure. She did not mind being a diener even though she did not fit the profile. Diener was German for "servant", and while Hamlin knew what the derivation of the word meant, it didn't bother her as much as it would bother the average diener. Historically, most dieners were African-

American fewer then 10% of which were female. If the autopsy had taken place at the Augusta School of Medicine, Hamlin would have performed the task of prosector, but in this case Joiner was going to perform this task. As Chief Pathologist, she rarely had the opportunity to perform the task of prosector, as she was busy supervising the pathology residents who performed most of the autopsies. So given the task of diener, Hamlin was in the middle of preparing the embalming room. It was her first time helping in an autopsy performed in a funeral home and even though she had only been here a half hour, she already dreaded it. She was used to a well-equipped hospital autopsy suite and the funeral embalming room was anything but equipped. She now realized why Joiner had packed most of the autopsy tools and solutions in the back of her van the night before. Hamlin placed Knox' body on the preparation table and placed the trays holding the scalpels and knives in the required places for easy access.

Around 9:45 Van Acker arrived at the funeral home. He had been able to reach Julie Sutton and while Julie wanted to attend the autopsy, she did not think that she would be able to stand seeing her sister getting cut open and examined. Van Acker, in a way had not objected to her absence. They had rescheduled their meeting for later that afternoon when, he would give her both the news about what was on the tapes Susan had made, as well as the cause of Susan's death. Van Acker entered the funeral home and made his way to the embalming room where he met the three women.

"Good morning, ladies," he announced as he walked into the room.

"Good morning, handsome," Hope responded.

"So, I finally get to meet Mr. Right!" Joiner smiled.

"You must be Shawn?" Van Acker walked over to her and extended his arm to shake her hand.

"Hell, boy, give me a hug. If Hope has a thing for you, you must be alright!"

Joiner grabbed Van Acker by the neck and gave him a hardy hug. Van Acker blushed.

Joiner introduced Alison Hamlin, and Van Acker and her shook hands.

"So, who else is coming to watch the show?" Joiner asked.

"I think this is it. Sheriff Hinson had wanted to be present for the autopsy, but he called me a little while ago saying he had a personal matter to attend to and would not be able to make it."

Van Acker looked at her with a questioning look. Hope returned the look with a shrug of her shoulders as if to say that she had no idea what was going on.

"Are we ready?" Joiner looked towards Hamlin.

"Everything is set."

Joiner moved in front of the table, slipped into surgical gloves and donned a full face shield. Hamlin followed suit. Joiner checked the body block and make sure it was exactly where she wanted it so she could make a nice incision into the trunk of Knox' body. She smiled at Hamlin. As usual, she had done a fine job in positioning the body block. She then checked the toe tag with the name on the chart. She checked a block off on her chart and switched on her voice recorder.

"External examination of the body of Susan Knox, one Caucasian female, 30 years old, 5'2" long, weighing approximately 103 pounds. Apparent cause of death is smoke inhalation with consequent charring of the body due to fire."

Joiner felt the head carefully, letting her fingers run softly over the burned skin, feeling for any abnormalities.

"There are no unusual crevices or knots to be found on the head. The hair, for the most part, has been burned."

She then dropped her hands to Susan's torso. In one hand she held a probe while her other hand slid over Susan's upper chest and down to her breasts. Shawn examined the right breast area with her free hand, and then she repeated the process with the probe, looking for any abnormalities.

"Upper chest area is free from any abnormalities as is the right breast area."

She then proceeded to examine the left breast area. As she reached under Susan's left breast, her hand stopped. The look on her face told the others in the room that she had found something. Joiner grabbed a ruler and pressed the left breast tissue upwards. She measured from the center of the chest to the place where she had felt the abnormality.

468

"Examination of the left breast area reveals a puncture wound of some sort in the fold area of the breast. Puncture wound is approximately 4.2 inches from the center of the chest."

Joiner turned her voice recorder off and ordered Hamlin to write the information down in her notebook. She then continued examining the rest of the body. Finding nothing else out of the ordinary, and recording her findings on her voice recorder, she moved on to the next phase of the examination.

"So what do you think so far, Dimitri," Joiner asked.

"Well, so far so good."

Van Acker now knew what Joshua Underwood had used the pencil for. He had discovered the puncture hole as well, and confirmed his suspicions by poking the hole with a pencil. It was time to fill Hope in on some of the things that he knew in regards to the investigation. He'd wait till after the autopsy was completed.

"Okay, Alison, let's start with the good part now," Joiner said, looking amused at Hope and Van Acker.

"Oh, you mean the part where you start cutting into the body?" Van Acker asked.

"That's right. You think you can handle that?"

"We'll find out soon enough," Hope said, smiling.

"Okay, Alison, give me the scalpel," Joiner instructed.

The scalpel was handed over and Joiner placed it against Susan's body. She placed it at the front of the left shoulder and started making an incision, down underneath the breast to the bottom end of the breastbone. She then copied the procedure on the other side. Where the incisions met between the breasts, she started another incision down to the pubic bone, making a slight deviation around the navel.

Joiner looked at Van Acker. No reaction yet. Hope was still straight-faced as well. She knew it wouldn't last long. The next step was to peel the skin from the breastbone and place it over the face of the corpse. Joiner carefully peeled the skin, muscle and soft tissues off the chest wall and pulled it upward over Susan's face. Opening Susan's chest cavity this way, all present in the room could now smell the gasses escaping from Susan's body. Hope turned up her nose. She couldn't place the smell, but it was not something she would like to get used to.

469

Joiner proceeded with the autopsy and was handed and electric saw. She made a cut up each side of the front of the rib cage so the chest plate and the ribs were no longer attached to the rest of the skeleton. She then pulled back the chest plate with the help of a scalpel. Van Acker could see all sorts of stuff inside the chest cavity but could not distinguish between the different kinds of organs.

Joiner let out a whistle. She turned on her voice recorder.

"It looks like we've got a mess in here. Apparent puncture found underneath the left breast looks to be a bullet wound."

She turned the recorder off.

"Okay, Alison, go ahead with the removal."

Van Acker looked at Hamlin in admiration. He was ready to run for the door and throw up his insides, but she stood by and performed her job without any problems. He looked over towards Hope and noticed that she had turned a few shades whiter herself. She obviously did not enjoy this any more than he did. They both looked at each other and decided it was time for them to leave the room. Hope motioned to Joiner about their intentions and Joiner nodded her understanding. A big smile crossed her face as she admired the both of them for having been able to stay as long as they had.

Outside the embalming room, Hope and Van Acker looked at each other with bewildered eyes.

"How would you like to do that for a living?" Van Acker asked.

"I don't think so. Going to a bad car wreck or to a shooting is enough for me."

"So what do you think?"

"I'd say she was shot," Hope told Van Acker, looking at him intensely.

"I am certain that she was shot."

"How can you be certain?"

"Well, Joshua, I think, was killed because he knew the cause of Susan's death."

"How do you know that?"

Van Acker looked down to the floor as he felt a bit guilty for having held back information from Hope.

"I believe Joshua found the entry hole the day he was killed.

470

I found an unused pencil in the thrash can. Now tell me, why would you throw away an unused pencil? And what would you use it for?"

Hope looked at him with curious eyes.

"You knew this all along?"

"Well, I've had my suspicion. I wasn't 100% sure."

"So what you're saying is that Joshua was killed because he knew how Susan had died?"

"That's my theory anyways. I don't buy the murdered during burglary story."

"I never did either, but we didn't have any proof otherwise. We still don't have proof. All of this can still be purely coincidental. Do you have any idea who might have killed Joshua and Susan?"

"No, not yet I don't. There is something I want to check out before we leave here."

Van Acker walked towards the back door of the funeral home, to where he had found the piece of fabric. He found the place where he had removed the fabric and estimated how high on Hinson's arm the bandage had been. A concerned look covered his face.

Hope Olson saw the chance on his face.

"Dimitri, what is it?"

He looked at her, not knowing how he was going to tell her his findings.

"Hope, do you know if Hinson has a cat?"

"What? What does this have to do with anything?"

"Just answer me, does he or does he not have a cat?"

"He does."

"Does he live on a dirt road?"

Hope looked at Van Acker with questioning eyes but decided to play along. He obviously was onto something and she didn't like it one little bit.

"Not directly on a dirt road. His house is the last house on the paved part of his road, right before it turns into dirt. Why are you asking these weird questions?"

"Hope, the other day when we found Joshua, I found a piece of fabric on this doorjamb here. It wasn't big, but I had it send to a friend of mine who works for the FBI. He's a forensic scientist and he has his own lab set up in his basement. He examined the fabric.

471

He found cat hair on it; he found lots of dust particles on it. He also found reddish blond hair on it. Susan had reddish blond hair! And, he found blood on it. He ran tests on the blood. It belonged to a male with type A- blood."

Hope couldn't believe what she was hearing.

"Dimitri, you know that what you did was evidence tampering. I could get you arrested for that. Besides why did you not tell me about it? What happened with trusting one another?"

"Hope, I'm sorry. But I didn't know how it was going to be handled within the Sheriff's department. I trust you, but I don't trust Hinson. And obviously with good reason! He was here! He was here before we found Joshua because that piece of fabric was on the door jam when we got here?"

"Dimitri, what are you saying? You think Hinson killed Susan and Joshua?"

"I don't know. All I know is that everything points in his direction."

Hope, even though not pleased with Van Acker right this moment, knew that he was right. All of it was still too circumstantial but it was the only lead she had. She didn't feel comfortable thinking that her boss, the Sheriff of Dawson County, could be responsible for everything that had been happening the last few days. She needed to have that piece of fabric. Now that Dimitri had come clean, maybe they could work together on the investigation. She wondered how many more secrets he was hiding from her.

"I've gotta go meet with Julie Sutton and then I'll go by and talk to Patricia Langston. Will you be at home when I get done?" Van Acker asked her, hoping she wasn't too mad at him for keeping her in the dark.

"Yes, I'll be home. I need some time to rest. Be careful."

Van Acker kissed Hope on the lips and left the funeral home.

103.

Patricia Langston heard the door bell ring and hurried to open the door. She kissed the person standing on her front stoop with a long deep tongue kiss. When she finally broke free from the kiss, she looked at the man standing in front of her. He looked amazing to her. She would have never thought that she could have felt an attraction to a man, much less an older man when she was a teenager, especially with her feeling towards other women. Now at 21, she was in a relationship with one. She couldn't explain why she was attracted to this man, she just was. Sure he could be her dad, but what did it matter? As far as she was concerned, there was no age limit when it came to love. He made her feel special and he made her feel safe. He didn't treat her as a child, as most people his age still did; but as an adult, as an equal. She'd been in a relationship with him for a little over eight months now. It had been a wonderful eight months. Not only did he treat her the way she thought a woman should be treated, but he also never pressured her for anything. She remained independent, living in her own place, and living her own life. When they did spend the night together, she would always stay over at his place. He was not comfortable staying over at her place and she could understand where he was coming from. It wasn't as if he wasn't known around town, and his car being seen at her place would raise questions. She was okay with the arrangement. She knew that when he was ready to make their relationship more public, they would probably spend a lot more nights together and be seen in public together more often. Until then, she would enjoy the moments they spend together as best she could. As far as today was concerned, she was glad that she would finally have her Jeep back. It had been inconvenient to be without the Jeep and somehow there had been questions raised about it having been involved in some incident. She wasn't that worried about it, because she knew that her lover had everything under control. As she looked at him walking into her house, she just loved to see him in his uniform.

Andrew Hinson looked at Patricia. God, she was beautiful. He still didn't know how their relationship had started, but he was glad that it had. He never thought that he would find love with another woman after his wife died. He had been in several relationships since his wife had died, but nothing ever panned out. He had known Patricia for a long time, actually ever since she had been a little girl. It had been weird when he fell for her and she in turn fell for him. He was old enough to be her dad, but at this point, he didn't care; he was in love with her. He couldn't even remember how it all had started. He had been at a social at the Medical Center. Patricia had been invited by one of the doctors who had a crush on her. Besides the lovesick doctor, he had been the only one at the party that Patricia had known. She didn't like the advances the doctor was making so she had turned to him for conversation. Surprisingly enough, at her young age, she had been a joy to talk to. They had hit it off right away and he had risked calling on her the following weekend to continue some of their conversations. Over the span of the next couple of months they had been seeing each other more and more. Then one day, she had leaned into to him and kissed him. He'd felt like a little schoolboy who just got his first kiss from the girl he had a crush on. That one kiss had lead to more and now they were in a serious relationship. And now almost a year later, here they were. They had kept their relationship a secret and neither had told any of their closest friends or relatives that they were seeing each other. He liked it that way. But now, suddenly it seemed as if their whole world was falling apart.

Just four days ago, Patricia had received a phone call while visiting him and had busted in tears after she disconnected the call. Through the tears, he finally made out that it had been Susan Knox who had called her and told Patricia there was a possibility that she might have been infected with HIV. As small as the percentages were that sex between two women caused the spread of HIV, it was still a possibility.

Hinson had known that Patricia had lesbian tendencies; she had not hidden it from him, and told him about her sexual preferences when she was a teenager. He had been surprised however that she had been involved with Susan Knox of and on for quit some time. He had asked her how old she was and while turning red, she had told him that she was fifteen the first time she'd had sex with Susan. He had gotten mad. If there was one thing he did not tolerate, it was people forcing their sexual needs on minors.

Patricia had finally convinced him that it had been 100% consensual and that she had been the instigator in the relationship. Patricia told Hinson that she was sorry that she could have given him the HIV virus. She told him she loved him and if she'd known that she would have made him wear protection. Hinson had assured her that she was probably overreacting and that once she calmed down and thought about it, things would be fine. The chances of her having contracted the virus were small.

After Patricia had finally stopped crying, her and Hinson went to bed. It hadn't taken Hinson long to fall asleep; however, Patricia had a harder time finding sleep. She had slipped out of bed once she knew that Hinson was sound asleep. She'd quietly gotten dressed and snuck out of the bedroom. She didn't know what was going on inside her head, but she needed to do something about the pain she felt inside. She felt betrayed by Susan. She had trusted her to show her how love could be tender and special. She had thought that she was special in Susan's eyes. It turned out that she was nothing more than a way to fulfill her sick sexual needs and wants. The more she thought about it, the angrier she became. She sat down at Hinson's computer and searched till she found what she was looking for. Perfect! Quietly she had snuck out of the house, grabbing Hinson's car keys and his .44 Magnum, she knew he kept in a drawer in the kitchen. She had driven to her house, changed in the required clothes and set out on her mission. It had taken all of 30 minutes to complete the mission.

When Patricia had gotten back to Hinson's house, he was awake and dressed.

"What have you done?"

"I did what needed to be done."

"And what is that?"

"Let's just say that Susan Knox won't spread her deadly disease around any longer."

"How is that?"

She had smiled at him while putting his .44 on the kitchen counter.

"You used my gun?"

"I had to. I don't have one of my own. All I have is a shotgun and a rifle. Besides, in about an hour, there will be *fireworks in town."*

"What do you mean?"

"You'll see."

*Hinson had shaken his head and thought about the
predicament he and Patricia were in. If the bullet was found it could
be linked to his gun. But then again, he was the Sheriff and who
would suspect him? He was going to have to play it safe and make
sure that he covered all his bases. What he needed to do was arrest
Patricia for murdering Susan, but he didn't want to do that. He
loved her too much for that and if everything played out right and if
he halfway was right about what she meant with fireworks, they
should be safe.*

*"Patricia, I should arrest you right now. You do realize that,
don't you?"*

*"I do. But you won't. You love me too much to see me put
away for the rest of my life or to see me sit on death row waiting for
the needle. Trust me, we will be okay."*

*Patricia had returned home that night, Hinson not wanting
her to be at his place when the fireworks started.*

Now, four days later, they weren't okay. He should have
done the right thing and arrested her, damned the consequences.
Instead, there were two more people dead because of his actions.
And he was responsible for those deaths. Patricia had nothing to do
with them and he hadn't told her what he had to do to keep their
secret hidden. Unfortunately that damn Yankee lawyer was a lot
smarter than he had given him credit for. Together with the help
from Hope Olson, he was on the right track. It has been pure luck
that he had spotted the black man with the Tennessee license tag
hanging around town. He'd been secretly following him. He in turn
had thrown the man off by borrowing Patricia's Jeep. Again, it had
been pure luck the day he borrowed the Jeep was the day the man
decided to talk to Van Acker. It had been a golden opportunity. He
had loaded up his .50 cal rifle in the back of the Jeep just in case the
opportunity arose. He had also grabbed a spent 30-06 shell to leave
behind as a decoy. It had been tempting to leave the crosshairs of the
rifle on Van Acker's head and take him out instead of the witness,
but he would have his chance soon. If it hadn't been for Van Acker's
quick action with Judge Snelgrove, he might have been able to force

the case closed without an autopsy. But Van Acker had smelled a rat and was one step ahead of him. He knew that by now, they would have found that Susan had been shot. It was time to set the final stage of his plan in action. But first, he needed to get Patricia her Jeep back.

104.

Allen Murphy had agreed to Dimitri Van Acker's plan. Right now, he wasn't so sure that he had made the right decision. Parked, hidden away in some low bushes, he had been staking out Patricia Langston's place for the past two hours. Then a familiar person had shown up. Murphy was surprised to see Sheriff Hinson show up at Patricia's. His first thought was the Sheriff himself was on the same track that Van Acker was on. Then he saw the two of them kiss passionately as Hinson walked inside and all sorts of new and disturbing thoughts started to take over Murphy's mind.

The thought of doing some undercover work had appealed to Murphy. He had gotten up early, nervous and giddy. Would he be able to pull it off? Only time would tell. He had gotten an older truck at his farm, one that he didn't use any longer except for work around the farm when he didn't want his newer truck getting any potential damage. So, if someone spotted him, they would not right away be able to recognize him by his truck. He had driven to Patricia Langston's place and drove by a couple of times trying to find the perfect spot to hide in. He finally found the right spot, easy to back up into and stay hidden behind the low hanging foliage of the bushes. It was also an easy way to get back on the road and follow whoever it was picking up Patricia. He felt a bit like a pervert trying to spy on some innocent girl. But, no, he wasn't; he was here on a mission.

Now, after witnessing Patricia and Hinson kissing he wasn't so sure that his surveillance adventure was such a grand thing. What was going on? Were Patricia and Hinson in a relationship? And if they were, how weird was that? Hinson was old enough to be her father! Murphy shuddered at the thought of any of his daughters being in a relationship with someone who was his age or older. It just didn't seem right. The other thing that was on his mind was that Hinson could have been the one driving Patricia's Jeep. Was he the friend who had borrowed her car? If so, then Hinson could be the one who shot Van Acker's witness.

Murphy's mind wandered some more. Could Andrew Hinson have killed Susan Knox? It was possible, he thought. Hinson would know how to cover up a murder; at least he tried to cover up the murder, if he was Susan's killer. Somehow, the possibility of Hinson being Susan's killer did not fit with what he knew about Hinson. He would not have been so careless as to turn all four burners on the gas stove to high. Then again, in the moment of passion, who knew how one's mind worked? Even the most calculated person made mistakes, especially when they were under stress. And how about Joshua Underwood's murder, was Hinson capable of killing a friend in cold blood to cover up another murder? Murphy just didn't know how the pieces of the puzzle fit with Hinson being the main suspect. It didn't add up. He was obviously making assumptions! No way had the Sheriff of Dawson County anything to do with the murder of at least three people! This had to be a coincidence. It just wasn't possible for the Sheriff, the person who stood behind upholding the law, to be involved in any of this. Hell, he had voted for him in both elections!

Murphy's mind games stopped when he noticed movement at Patricia's front door. Both her and Hinson emerged from the building and headed for Hinson's car. He watched them both get in and drive off. Murphy was ready and had his truck already cranked when they pulled out of Patricia's driveway. He pulled onto the road and stayed back a good distance. He hoped that he would not draw unnecessary attention to himself.

Hinson drove his car at a leisurely pace and it was hard for Murphy to keep his distance. If Hinson was checking to see if he was being followed, it wouldn't take long for him to figure out that Murphy was behind him. It helped that Murphy halfway knew in which direction they were headed. He was almost 100% sure that they were on their way to gather Patricia's Jeep. So Murphy kept his distance. As his gut feeling predicted, they were headed in the direction of the old abandoned barn in the woods. Murphy stayed behind just far enough to where he could make out Hinson's car. As they passed the old cotton hangar, an eerie feeling came over Murphy. It had just been yesterday that an innocent man had lost his life here. He wondered if it came to it, and if Hinson was indeed the killer, would Hinson hesitate to kill him. He told himself that he couldn't think like that and that he needed to concentrate on Hinson's car in front of him. He got he mind back on the task at hand and sure enough, when they got to where the driveway to the abandoned barn was, Hinson turned off.

Allen Murphy looked for a place to pull of the side of the road, park his truck and be able to walk through the woods to the barn. He was curious if there was going to be a conversation between Patricia and Hinson. If there was, Murphy hoped to overhear some it. He found a pasture entrance some 100 yards from the drive Hinson had turned into and parked his truck. He walked to the edge of the woods and started off towards the barn, weaving between trees and low brush, doing his best to stay hidden from sight. As he got to where the barn came into sight, he could see that Hinson and Patricia had just gotten out of the car. Murphy moved as close to the barn as he dared and found a spot behind a large briar patch that would hide him from view.

***

Andrew Hinson opened the doors to the barn as Patricia Langston silently stood by. She didn't understand why Hinson had hidden her car and why they had to be secretive about it. The only thing Hinson had told her was the least she knew, the safer she'd be. Being safe was important to her and if Hinson felt that she was safer not knowing what her Jeep was doing here then she would take his word for it. She was still curious.

"Andy, can you tell me one thing?"

Hinson propped the door he had just opened and looked at Patricia.

"Honey, I told you. The least you know, the better off you'll be."

Somehow that wasn't enough for Patricia.

"I know, but if it involves me, then I want to know. I need to know if you've done anything because of what I did the other night. Tell me you had nothing to do with that man getting shot."

Hinson looked around as if to see if anyone was out there listening. He smiled at the thought. Who would be out here listening? It was just Patricia and him. Still he leaned in close to her and whispered.

"Patty, I've done more than kill that man. I also killed Joshua Underwood. He was smart and had figured out that Susan had been

480

shot. I tried to stop the autopsy and make everyone believe the explosion at Susan's was an accident. But that damned Van Acker wouldn't let go! So I had to make it look like I was interested in getting to the bottom of it. If I could have prevented the autopsy from happening, then we'd be in the clear. Unfortunately, right about now, they are figuring out that Susan was shot."

He looked around again and took a deep breath.

"Damn woman, I wish you would have talked to me first after before loosing your cool and killing Susan. I understand that you were mad, but it would have helped to talk to me first."

Patricia didn't like being talked to by Hinson as if she was a little girl. This was the first time in their relationship that she had felt that she wasn't his equal and that he talked down to her. She didn't like it a bit.

"Don't talk to me like I'm some little girl! I didn't tell you to kill those people. All I wanted you to do is cover up that I shot Susan and that I was at the apartment before the explosion happened. What you did to Underwood and that black man is your fault. So don't blame me for those. If this goes south, then I'll fry for Susan but you'll fry for Underwood and the other guy."

Hinson didn't like the way their conversation was going. Even though they were still talking in whispering voices, Patricia's voice had gotten loud a couple of times and he didn't like it. She'd never raised her voice against him and he wasn't about to let her get away with it. If not for his actions or inactions she would be in jail right now being charged with murdering Susan Knox. No, he wasn't going to let her dictate the outcome of this situation. He was in charge.

"Patty, don't you ever raise you voice at me!"

"I didn't!"

"I think you're getting upset with me over something you shouldn't be upset about! I'm saving your skin here. Don't you get that?"

"Oh, I get it alright. I'm supposed to be all grateful and not question what it is you're doing on my behalf. I'm sorry, but it doesn't work that way. I'm responsible for what happened. I'm the one who lost her cool and decided to kill someone. Yeah, I'm grateful that you tried so hard to cover it up, but I think it's gone too far. I never asked for anyone else to lose their lives."

"You just don't get it, do you? I didn't have to be asked! I did it because it was necessary! "

"Necessary for what? To save poor me? Well, I'll tell you what, Sheriff Hinson, I don't need to be saved!"

Patricia walked into the barn and got in her Jeep. She cranked the car and put it in drive. Hinson stepped in front of the car, keeping her from leaving. Patricia started to cry, feeling the situation was getting out of control.

"Please move! I'm telling you, please move! I need to get out of here. I need to think about this. Please don't make me run over you."

Patricia put the car in drive and started to ease forward. Hinson didn't move. He didn't want her to leave; didn't want her to leave without them talking about their problems. And problems they did have.

"Patty, please, let's talk about this. I don't want you to leave here mad at me. I love you, Patty!"

Patricia started to cry harder. She was in love with Hinson, but she'd never seen him this controlling before and she didn't like it. She just needed to get away from the situation and think about what had happened the last couple of days. Everything that had happened in the past couple of days has started with her killing Susan Knox. She looked at Hinson and shook her head.

"Please don't stop me! Just let me go. We'll talk about this later. Right now I need to go."

She pressed the gas petal and eased the car towards Hinson. He looked at her through the windshield and realized that she was serious and that she needed to get away. He dropped his head and walked out of her path. Tears started flowing down his cheeks as he realized that he might have lost her forever just by trying to protect her. Patricia hit the gas and sped out of the barn, down the dirt driveway and onto the main road, leaving a cloud of dust and gravel in her wake.

***

Allen Murphy, still sitting behind the briar bush, had turned a shade lighter as he picked up on the last part of the conversation. Even if he would have tried to move and make it back to his truck, he couldn't have. He was frozen in place not knowing what to think about what he had just overheard. Patricia had killed Susan Knox. Sheriff Hinson had killed Underwood and the man who had witnessed Patricia sneaking into Susan's apartment. He didn't know how to digest the information. He looked in the direction of the barn and saw Hinson get into his car, back up and drive towards the road. When there was no more noise but the song of birds and chirping of crickets, Murphy decided to get up and ease his way back to his truck. All sorts of scenarios were going through his mind. All he knew was that he needed to get in touch with Dimitri Van Acker and Hope Olson and fill them in on what he had overheard. His phone was in his truck and he needed to get to it as fast as possible. He started to move faster and after much stumbling and a few falls, he finally made it to his truck. He opened the door and looked for his phone. Damn it! He knew he had left it on the seat. Where was it? He needed to calm down. He composed himself, closed his eyes and drew a couple of deep breaths. He looked for the phone again in the seat. Not there! Maybe it had fallen on the floorboard. He bent down and checked the floorboard and underneath the seat. Nothing to be found!

"Looking for something, Murphy?"

Allen Murphy almost jumped out of his skin when he heard the voice behind him. He turned around and was face to face with Andrew Hinson. He knew his face was turning red and he hoped that Hinson would not notice.

"Andy! Man, you scared me. I, eh, seemed to have misplaced my cell phone. I could have sworn that I had brought it with me, but obviously I must have left it at home."

"Is there some kind of emergency? You could use mine."

Confused, Murphy stared at Hinson. Was he on to him or was this just Hinson being the Sheriff checking out a stranded citizen on the side of the road?

"No, there is no emergency. I just hate that I don't know what happened to my phone, expensive as they are to replace them and all. But I do appreciate you stopping and checking on me, though."

483

Murphy managed to produce a smile as he was gauging Hinson to see if he suspected anything. He got his answer when Hinson produced a cell phone from his pocket.

"Would this be the phone you're looking for?"

Murphy turned white at the sight of his phone in Hinson's hand. Hinson started laughing as he reached behind his back and produced a gun.

"Allen, I sure do appreciate your votes in the past two elections, but you've always wanted to stick your nose where it doesn't belong. Why did you follow us today? No, don't answer that! I think I know. Dimitri Van Acker asked you to check on Patty, didn't he? I bet he saw her car drive by the cotton hangar yesterday and he just couldn't leave it alone. First Hope had to stick her nose in it after he told her that he saw Patty's car, and then he had to get you involved."

Murphy was getting more and more scared as he didn't know where Hinson's line of reasoning was headed. So far, he was right on. He clearly knew more than either Van Acker or he thought Hinson knew. He was weighing his options but was not coming up with much in the form of saving his own life. Hinson was out of his reach to try to grab the gun from him; besides, he would never get to him in time. Hinson would surely fire the gun before he could get to him. Then again, he was dead either way. If Hinson was ruthless enough to kill poor Joshua Underwood, then for sure he wouldn't hesitate to kill him. He checked his surroundings to see if there was any way to get away from Hinson without getting shot, but there were no options. If he tried to get into the woods, Hinson would have a clear shot for about a hundred yards. Even if he tried to zigzag his way into the woods, he was at a disadvantage. He could try to get into his truck, crank it and try to get away, but that would take more time than it would take for Hinson to aim the gun and shoot him. The short of it was, he was out of choices. By the look on Hinson's face, he knew it too.

"I'm afraid you don't have many options, Murphy. No matter what you try, you'll fall short of what you'll try to do."

"You're right, Andy, I don't have any options left. I just want to know one thing. Why did you have to kill Joshua?

"To be blunt, Joshua was collateral damage. He was too

smart for his own good.

"You know that's the problem with smart people, they tend to get in the way of themselves. If he would have just stayed home as he always did and not get so damned excited about finding something on Susan's body that would suggest she didn't die because of the fire, he would still be alive. If only."

"You really think you will get away with all of this? Do you think that killing Underwood, the other man, and now me, is somehow not going to catch up with you?"

Hinson broke out in laughter.

"Oh, Allen, it doesn't matter if it catches up with me or not. All that matters is that you won't be the one who tells the world that Patricia and I are responsible for the killings. Let someone else try and figure it out."

With that statement, Hinson raised his gun, aimed at Allen Murphy's forehead and pulled the trigger.

105.

Dimitri Van Acker rang the doorbell at Julie Sutton's home. He wondered again why he had decided to move back to Georgia. The morning heat had already reached record breaking levels and he felt like he needed another shower. He looked behind him to the burned down remains of Susan's apartment. The autopsy had gone the way he expected it would go. Susan had been shot. He wondered if she'd seen her attacker. He doubted it, but then if she did, there had been nothing she could have done about it. His mind flashed back to the moments following the autopsy. Van Acker could understand that Hope was not happy with him for having taken the piece of fabric and leaving her in the dark about it. She must feel that he didn't trust her with that information. Then again, if his suspicions about Hinson were right, then he'd probably made the right decision about taking the fabric. Who knows what would have happened if Hope had told Hinson about it. At this point, he hoped that Hope would not go to Hinson with the information he'd shared with her and that she would not tell him about the piece of fabric.

Van Acker was brought back to reality when the front door opened and Julie called out his name.

"Hi Dimitri, how are you today?"

"Julie, hi, I'm sorry. My mind was not here for a moment."

"I understand. A lot of things have been going on lately. My mind has a hard time staying focused also. Why don't you come in?"

Van Acker followed Julie into the house and she led him into the living room. She motioned for him to take a seat opposite her by her reading table. He obliged.

"Well, Julie," Van Acker started, "where do we start?"

Julie unconsciously looked out the window towards her sister's apartment and felt an emptiness engulf her. She needed to know what had happened to Susan. She also needed to let Van Acker know that she had made up her mind to sue her father for what he'd done to the both of them.

"Why don't we start with Susan? Can you tell me what the autopsy revealed?"

Van Acker rubbed his chin and looked Julie directly in the eyes.

"Julie, it appears that Susan was shot in the chest before the apartment exploded. The Medical Examiner found a hole under her left breasts and the inside of her chest cavity showed signs of being shot. With those findings, it is safe to say the explosion wasn't accidental. Whoever shot Susan tried to cover it up by setting up the apartment to explode."

Julie had tears running down her face and Van Acker reached over to hold her hand and try to comfort her. She looked at her him and tried to compose herself.

"To tell you the truth, Dimitri, I knew that already."

Van Acker looked at her with questioning eyes.

"You knew she was shot?"

Julie looked down to the floor.

"I didn't necessary know that she was shot. Like I told you the other day, I knew that she'd been killed before the explosion. I sat in this very chair and watched everything going on that night."

Again, tears were flowing down her cheeks. She looked at Van Acker and asked:

"Does that make me an accessory? Does me sitting here and doing nothing make me just as guilty as the person who pulled the trigger?"

Van Acker was at a loss of words. Here he thought that he had no more leads in the case and out of the blue Julie tells him that she witnessed everything. Was there anything she could have done to stop Susan from getting killed? He seriously doubted it. It might have cleared up a lot of questions, but it wouldn't have saved Susan.

"No, Julie, it doesn't make you an accessory. I do have some follow up questions I want to ask you about that night."

"Okay, go ahead. I'll see what I can remember."

"Can you tell me if the person who entered the apartment was taller, smaller or about the same size as the person who came later and was almost killed by the explosion?"

Julie thought for a minute.

"I believe that I would have to say that they were both about the same height. It's hard to judge that when it's dark, but I think that they were about the same."

"Okay, that's good. Now, think about how the person moved. You said the person was athletic, right?"

487

Julie nodded agreeing.

"Okay, did the person move like a woman or a man?"

Julie had never thought about the difference between the movements of a man and the movements of a woman. She guessed there was a difference. Could she remember how the person moved? She realized that it would reveal a lot and narrow down the possibilities. The person did have a certain grace to its movements, not like a man would move with big movements but more like a woman with short controlled movements. Yeah, that's exactly the way that person moved.

"It was a woman!"

"Are you sure?"

"Yeah, I'm sure. Playing it back in my mind, the person didn't move like a man. A man would have had a longer stride in his step. This person had a shorter, more calculated stride, like a woman moves."

Van Acker just looked at Julie without being able to say a word. He had never thought about the difference in movements between a man and a woman, but when he thought about it and analyzed it, there was a difference.

"That is brilliant, Julie! You have no idea how much you have just pushed this investigation in the right direction."

"Glad I could help."

Van Acker thought hard for a moment, because his earlier conclusions suddenly didn't add up. He had been thinking that Hinson might have been the killer, but Julie's recollection of the events did not match with the way Hinson looked and moved. His dead witness had told him the tag light of the car the killer drove wasn't working.

"Julie, can you remember if there was anything that stood out about the car that the killer drove?"

Again Julie tried to think back. She didn't know much about cars. Maybe if she remembered what was different between the cars that she saw that night, she might be able to push the investigation a bit further in the right direction. Just then it hit her.

"There was something wrong with the car the killer drove. I couldn't see the tag in the back."

"You mean, there was no tag or there were no tag lights?"

"I don't know, I just didn't see the tag."

"It doesn't matter. It would be hard to tell which one it was. You helped me out enough with this."

"I'm sorry, that I can't remember. I know it's probably important."

"It is, but I have a corroborating witness to the tag story, a dead witness as he may be."

Both Julie and Van Acker felt silent for a moment as each was lost in their own thoughts. Julie was thinking about her other legal problems; and Van Acker was thinking about what he's been missing and how what Julie just told him didn't make it any clearer in his mind. He needed to jot his thoughts on paper and see if he could make them add up. Could it be they were dealing with two different killers, or maybe three? Was all this just a coincidence? No! There just was no way that it was that easy. Somehow everything was connected, but how?

Julie broke the silence.

"Dimitri, not the change directions here, but we have more to discuss than Susan's death. There's the matter of the lawsuit against my father, there is my divorce from Tom, and then there is something else that came up."

Dimitri Van Acker looked at her in disbelieve.

"Julie, you're trying to tell me that you will need my services for three different things?"

"I'm afraid so. I shot Tom! He'll be fine, I think, but I'm afraid that he'll try to come after me for attempted murder."

Julie told Van Acker in short of the events that had played out the night she shot Sutton and her fears about having to go to jail for trying to kill her husband. She also told Van Acker, while turning a deep red, about her meeting with Lester and the consequent tapes that were produced and how she ended up with both of them in her possession.

Van Acker told her that Tom did not have much of a case, especially with her having ownership of both of the incriminating tapes.

Van Acker's mind could not stay focused on their current discussion and he felt that he needed to excuse himself. Something was gnawing at his brain and he could not shake it.

"Julie, if it would be alright with you, could we discuss your father's lawsuit and the divorce some other time? There's something on my mind about Susan's death and I don't seem to be able to concentrate on the other issues. I know that they are also important but I need to clear my mind for a bit. Could we meet again tomorrow, if that works for you?"

Julie felt relieved that Van Acker wanted to reschedule the other issues. She knew that they were important but not pressing so much that it couldn't wait.

"Yes, tomorrow would be fine. I'm sure that I don't have anything pressing on my schedule. I guess it will be a couple of days before we can have Susan's funeral."

"Thank you and I apologize for the inconvenience."

Dimitri Van Acker got up and shook Julie's hand and showed himself out. On the porch, he looked towards the burned out apartment and tried to imagine what it would have looked like the night of the murder. He kept coming back to the black car with the missing tag lights. And then it hit him. Andrew Hinson! He knew he was missing something this morning when Hinson pulled out of the high school parking lot! He had turned his lights on and when pulling away, the tag lights were not working! So who was driving his car the night of the murder?

Van Acker walked to his car and dialed his cell phone. The call was answered on the first ring.

"Honey, does Hinson date anyone?"

106.

Hope Olson was sitting at her desk at the Sheriff's station. Even though Andrew Hinson had given her the day off, she had gone in to the office after she left the funeral home and was sorting through her thoughts on the Susan Knox case. After comparing notes with Van Acker, which she thought she should have been privy to from the get-go, she was trying to put everything together. Susan had been shot before the explosion; Shawn Joiner had clearly concluded that during the autopsy. Then to top it all off, Van Acker had revealed his little secret about the piece of fabric he had recovered the day Underwood had been killed. What bothered her more than him keeping it from her was that every answer to his questions about what was found on the piece of fabric pointed towards Andrew Hinson. Was this just a coincidence or did Hinson have something to do with Underwood's murder? Van Acker had pointed out that Hinson had a cut on his arm about the same height as where he had found the piece of fabric on the door frame. Again, was that a coincidence? She held her head in her hands and rubbed her eyes. There were too many coincidences. She felt uneasy knowing that her boss, the Sheriff of Dawson County, could be involved in any of this.

Hope thought about Hinson having been all too eager to lead the investigation into Underwood's death. In less than a day, it had been concluded that it had been a robbery gone bad. She had not been involved in the investigation at all. Her only involvement was finding the body. She wondered if proper procedure had been followed and if fingerprints had been taken at the crime scene. And there was one question mark left next to her list of thoughts that needed a name put next to it: blood type A-. Maybe she needed to do some spying inside the Sheriff's department. She got up and walked towards the dispatcher.

"Hi Debra."

"Hi Hope, is everything all right?"

"Oh yeah, just have a lot on my mind today. Listen, I am following up on some leads that may cross reference with another case we're working on. Do you know if there was a chain of evidence set up in the Joshua Underwood case?"

Debra started clicking away on her computer.

"Let's see. I'm sorry, but there's not a lot there. We've got a case number assigned to it. I don't see anything that suggests evidence was taken from the scene."

"Not even Underwood's wallet?"

"Nope."

"What about fingerprints?"

"If fingerprints were lifted, I don't have any notes about it. Either it wasn't done or whoever put the case together didn't enter it."

"Hinson was the lead on the investigation, wasn't he?"

"Let's see."

Debra clicked away on the keyboard some more and a frown appeared on her face.

"It appears that Hinson was the lead. The case was closed yesterday. Not enough supportive evidence to look any further than robbery. I guess that's it."

Hope scratched her chin. That was odd. Why would Hinson close the case this quickly, not pursuing the possibility that Underwood's killer was the same one as Susan Knox' killer? Unless...

"Debra, I've got one more question, and I don't know if you can help me with this or not."

"Okay, I'll see what I can do."

"Assume for just one minute that one of our deputies or Hinson gets shot in the line of duty. Wouldn't we have vital records on file to help with a speedy process in the emergency room? I'm thinking blood type information, diabetes, etc."

"We do keep that information on all of our employees. It's part of our personnel records. Hinson keeps those files in his office."

Hope smiled inwardly. She just needed an excuse to get in Hinson's office.

"Thanks Debra. You've been a great help."

"Anytime!"

Hope returned to her desk. Somehow she needed to find out what Hinson's blood type was. To do that, she needed to find an excuse to get in his office. She looked down at her notes again. She still couldn't believe that Hinson somehow was involved with what had been going on in town the last couple of days. Was he one of Susan's lovers? If he was, then he would be a suspect. Two of Susan's lovers were already dead. She was sure that Radcliff had not killed Susan. How about Scarboro? He was still a possibility, but she started to doubt that he was involved. The color of his car didn't match with the car involved. What about Tom Sutton? His car didn't match the description either. Then her head shot up and looked towards Hinson's office. Why had the thought never occurred to her? Hinson's personal car was a black coupe. It was an older model, but it was black. Could that have been the car she saw that night when she was returning to the station after her patrol? It was a possibility. That made one more checkmark next to Hinson's name. Hope Olson jumped as her thoughts were disturbed by her phone ringing.

"Hope Olson."

"Honey, does Hinson date anyone?"

"Eh, I honestly don't know. Why?"

"Just curious, because I have a witness who puts his car at Susan Knox' apartment the night of her murder. It was driven by a suspicious female, dressed in black, who entered Susan's apartment and is more than likely our killer."

"Are you sure about that?"

"I have an eyewitness who can testify to that, yes."

"May I ask who your witness is?"

"Sure. It's Julie Sutton. She was sitting in the dark behind her window the entire evening and watched everything that went on that night. The reason I know that it was Hinson's car is because those were the final word my dead witness told me before he was shot; a black coupe with missing tag lights. This morning when I went for my run, Hinson showed up at the high school to do some running too. We ran together, felt each other out and jerked each other around a bit before he got tired and left. When he drove off, he turned on his lights. It didn't hit me till just now that his tag lights were not working. Hope, whoever he's dating, and that's if he's dating anyone, is Susan's killer."

Hope couldn't believe her ears. It was still all very circumstantial and she didn't believe that any of this would hold up in court. She needed more prove. She also had a plan to get in

493

Hinson's office. Nobody needed to know that it was Dimitri calling her. As far as anyone was concerned, this could be Hinson calling her about a case. She would use the phone call as a way to get into Hinson's office.

"Listen, I don't know if that's enough evidence or not for an arrest. Let me consult the file on the case. I do believe it is still on your desk, right?"

There was silence on the other end of the phone. She smiled as she could see the confusion on Van Acker's face. She knew it wouldn't take long for him to catch on.

"If you say so, honey! Listen; see if you can find out if he's seeing anyone. I've got a sneaky suspicion that it may be Patricia Langston. She claimed that she let a friend borrow her Jeep, right? So her Jeep shows up in the same area of my witness' murder. Coincidence? I don't think so! I think that Hinson was covering up for his girlfriend by killing Underwood and my witness. Think about it and let's get together in a little bit. I'm gonna go by Patricia's and see if I can get her to talk to me."

Hope Olson couldn't believe what she was hearing. She thought it all a bit too farfetched, but then again, she'd heard more bizarre stories.

"Sure that will be fine. Let me look at the file and then I'll meet you later this afternoon. I think that I'll work today anyway and take off some other day. I need to get out some. I'll do some patrols this afternoon if that's okay with you."

She could hear Van Acker laughing on the other end.

"Sure you do that. I love you."

"You too. Bye."

She flushed as she almost uttered the words "I love you" to Van Acker. She'd caught herself just in time. If she'd done that, there might have been some interesting stares coming at her from her fellow employees. She got up and walked over to Debra.

"Debra that was Hinson; he needs me to look over some details on the drug bust we did last week. The file is on his desk. I'll be in there for just a bit looking over the details."

"That's fine."

Debra waived Hope off. It wasn't the first time one of the deputies would need to go into Hinson's office. They would always let her know about it. Everyone knew that Hinson did not like anybody to go into his office without his permission.

Hope walked in and looked around the room. There was only one window to the outside which was blocked with vinyl blinds. There was no other line of sight into the room except through the door. She found the filing cabinet that had "personnel" written on it. Quietly she opened it. There were maybe 20 files in it. They were placed inside the drawer alphabetically and it took her no time to find Hinson's name. She pulled the file out and opened it. There was not much in there, then again, why would there be, he was the boss after all. She found his medical assessment sheet and scanned over it. She found the blood type line. A-! Damn! It looked like Van Acker was right.

As quickly as she could she placed the file back in its proper place and closed the drawer. She walked to his desk and sat down for just a moment. She scanned the desk hoping to find anything that would link him with a woman. There was nothing out of the ordinary. Hinson didn't keep personal pictures on his desk or on his wall. His desk was neat and besides some files and his name plate was bare of any clutter. His desktop calendar had a few notes on it. She looked them over and found nothing of interest. She was about to get up when a piece of paper sticking out from underneath the calendar caught her attention. She pulled it out. Written on it was Patricia with a phone number along side of it. Hope quickly memorized the phone number, slid the paper back where she had found it, got up and walked out of Hinson's office.

She needed to get out. Hope looked at her watch and noticed that it was close to noon. It was time to go home and get ready for some patrolling. She gathered her notepad from her desk and announced to Debra that she was going home to change her clothes and would be on the road patrolling around two. Debra waved at Hope as she walked out the door, while answering the ringing phone.

"Sheriff's office."

"Debra, Hinson. Have you seen Hope?"

A confused look crossed over Debra's face.

"Well, yes sir. She just left from here. I thought you knew she was here since you talked to her about some details about the drug bust last week."

495

"I did what?"

"I'm sorry, sir. She got a phone call and she told me it was you. The way she talked it sure sounded like she had talked to you."

"What did she do after she supposedly talked to me?"

"Well she went into your office to look up some of your notes on the drug bust, I guess. She wasn't in there but a couple of minutes."

Debra heard the phone disconnect and looked at it with great curiosity. She shrugged her shoulders wondering what that was all about.

107.

Hinson slammed the phone down in the middle console of his car.

"Bitch!" he yelled.

In a way, he knew that he should be proud of Hope Olson for figuring out that she needed to check on him. If it was any other investigation, she would have done great, narrowing down the possible suspects and coming to the right conclusions. Of course, she had help from Van Acker. For some reason Van Acker had more information than he had thought. Right now he was a thorn in his side. It was time to get rid of him. He sincerely hoped that he would not have to kill anybody else but Van Acker. Allen Murphy had been necessary and would never be able to be pinned on him. It would be explained as another robbery gone wrong. First Underwood and then Murphy; it didn't look good for his department but if he could sway popular opinion that way, and they could somehow, miraculously find a suspect, things would settle down quick enough. If he wasn't mistaken he remembered seeing Jovanovich still hanging around town. Hinson smiled. Now that would be perfect. After eliminating Van Acker, he needed to put a plan into action to set Jovanovich up for the murder and robbery of Underwood and Murphy. It shouldn't be too hard.

Of course, there was still the issue of Hope Olson. He hated to get rid of her, but she knew too much. Could he set her and Van Acker up against each other? Whose information was Hope going on to come to her conclusions about his involvement in Susan's murder and then later Underwood's and Van Acker's witness? It had to have been Van Acker. How had he been able to put the pieces together he didn't know, but it seems like he stayed one step ahead of everything. He had underestimated him. But, it didn't matter any more. It was time to close the noose around his neck. He put his car in gear and started towards Patricia Langston's place. He picked up his phone and dialed Hope Olson's cell number.

***

Dimitri Van Acker smiled as he got in his car. It had taken

him a few seconds to catch onto what Hope was trying to do. He had asked her if she would be able to find out what Hinson's blood type was. Obviously she needed an excuse to get into Hinson's office. He hoped that her ruse had worked and that she would be able to confirm the last bid of information that would link Hinson to the murder of Joshua Underwood. On the way to Julie Sutton's he made a quick call to Sid Schumaker to ask if there was enough of the fabric left to do any further testing. Schumaker had assured Van Acker that any good forensic scientist would be able to find the same items on the fabric that he had and that he would send it back in overnight mail. Van Acker had given him Hope's address for the fabric to be sent to. He hoped that Hope would be able to make it part of the chain of evidence even though he feared the case was already closed.

Van Acker looked at his watch and decided that he would go talk to Patricia Langston before heading back to Hope's to have some lunch. He couldn't wait to hear how her little adventure inside the Sheriff's office played out. He cranked his car and headed towards Patricia Langston's place.

***

Hope Olson was almost home when her cell phone started ringing. She looked at the caller ID and saw that it was Andrew Hinson. She hesitated. Should she answer it or let it go to voicemail? What was the use, he would keep trying till he tracked her down anyways. She answered the call.

"Olson here."

"Hope, Andrew. I know I told you that you could take the day off, but I've got a situation brewing and I need you at Patricia Langston's house on the double. No need to come in the cruiser, you can just come in your car."

Hope's stomach contracted. What was going on? Van Acker was supposed to be on the way to Patricia's also.

"Can you fill me in on the situation, sir?" she asked, hoping the trembling in her voice couldn't be heard.

"All I can say is that you might have been right yesterday."

"You mean about her being involved with what happened at the cotton hangar?"

"Something like that. Just come over to her place and we'll sort it out from there."

"Yes, sir, I'll be there as soon as I can get there."

She disconnected the call. She didn't feel good about this. Why would Hinson want her over at Patricia's? From what Van Acker had deducted, Patricia might have been Susan's killer and then Hinson had been covering up for her by eliminating any possible witnesses or leads in the case. Still, why would she want to kill Susan and why would Hinson want to cover it up? Maybe they were an item, like Van Acker thought. But then why meet over there? Something just didn't seem right about this. She felt as if she was being set up. It was time to make some phone calls and set some things up herself.

Her first call was to the Sheriff's office.

"Sheriff's office."

"Debra, it's Hope. Can you tell me if Hinson tried to call me back?"

There was a short silence on the other end of the phone.

"Hope, I don't know what's going on but he did call and ask for you. It sounded like he had no recollection of your previous conversation."

"Did you tell him that I went into his office to look at the drug bust file?"

"I sure did."

"Okay, thanks Debra. I'm meeting with him in a little bit. I'll talk to him about what happened. See ya."

Hope disconnected the call. There's no way Hinson could know what she went into his office for; however, if he is guilty then he will figure that she's on his scent and that could be dangerous. He wasn't one who liked to be cornered. She needed to call to Van Acker. She dialed the number. The phone rang forever before there was finally an answer.

"Dimitri Van Acker speaking."

"Dimitri, it's Hope. Listen, a lot is going on right now and a lot is happening fast."

"Slow down, what are you talking about?"

Hope explained what had happened at the Sheriff's office and the resulting call from Hinson for her to meet him at Patricia

Langston's.

"He wants me there on the double. I don't have a good feeling about all of this. He said it had something to do with my suspicions from yesterday."

"What were those?"

"That Patricia Langston is involved with Susan's murder."

"You told him that?"

"Yes, and he told me that I was probably overreacting, that he would go have a talk with Patricia. Dimitri, if they are an item, then we're going to walk straight into a trap. If I were you, I'd wait to go by there till I find out more."

"Hope, I just drove up in her driveway."

"Shit! Can you make it look like you're turning around?"

"No, Patricia is walking out the door right now. Looks like I'm going to have to talk to her. Her Jeep is back by the way! That might be why Hinson couldn't make the autopsy."

"Okay, listen, make it short and see if you can get away from there before Hinson gets there. I don't want you there, got it?"

"I will try."

"Alright, I love you!"

"I love… Damn, Hinson just drove up behind me and blocked me in. He doesn't look too happy. I suggest you get here as fast as you can."

With that, Van Acker disconnected the call.

Hope looked at the phone and felt an uneasy feeling coming over her. She knew that things were getting out of hand, but she hadn't counted on them getting out of hand this fast. She had no idea at this point what Hinson was up to, but she feared that his dislike for Van Acker was going to make its way to the surface. She needed help in this and the only help she could figure on getting was an ally within the Sheriff's department. She grabbed her phone and dialed the number, hoping she had figured correctly on her ally.

"Hello?" a sleepy sounding voice answered.

"Gonzales, it's Hope. I need your help."

"Sure, what is it?"

Hope explained what Van Acker and she had found while investigating the Susan Knox death, Underwood's death, and the shooting at the old cotton hangar. She also filled him in on her

500

meeting Hinson at Patricia Langston's and that Van Acker and Hinson were already there. Gonzales quietly listened to everything Hope told him. Hope knew that Gonzales did not like Hinson and knew that he was her only ally within the department.

"What is it you need me to do?" Gonzales asked.

It took Hope Olson about 5 minutes to explain what she wanted him to do and what she was planning on doing. When she disconnected the call, she felt a little better. She hoped that things at Patricia Langston's weren't getting out of control too fast.

Hope drove into her driveway and rushed inside. She needed to get a few items before she took off towards Patricia Langston's. Five minutes later, dressed in her uniform, she ran out the door, cranked up her cruiser and with lights flashing she headed towards Patricia Langston's.

108.

Andrew Hinson slowly exited his car, leaving the door open and staying behind it for cover. He slowly reached behind his back and palmed his gun, cocked it, and pointed it at the driver's side door of Dimitri Van Acker's car. Everything he'd put in place was falling together and it was time to finish things up. He looked away from Van Acker's car to see what Patricia was planning on doing. He didn't like that she'd come out of the house, but he just would have to deal with that distraction. Depending on how things developed, she would be fine. If for some reason, it didn't start going the right way, as much as he hated it, he would have to eliminate her too. He couldn't afford any loose ends.

***

Patricia Langston who had come out to greet Van Acker froze when she saw Hinson drive up and park behind Van Acker, blocking him in. She felt her stomach drop when she saw Hinson open the driver's side door get out and take position behind the door drawing his gun. What in the world was going on? Had Van Acker done something to deserve this or had it something to do with her. From what she'd heard, Van Acker was Susan Knox' lawyer and was looking into what happened. Then it became clear to her. Hinson had probably been following Van Acker's progress through Olson. She realized there was only one way that she could escape being pinned for the murder and that was if Hinson eliminated everyone who knew anything about what had been happening the past days. This was becoming more than she could handle. She had never intended for anyone else to loose their lives. She had thought that Hinson would be able to keep her name out of it and that he might be able to make the explosion look like an accident without much investigation. Unfortunately that had not happened. She had no idea what he had been doing behind her back trying to cover for her. It was time to end this. She was guilty of Susan's murder and she was going to come clean. Hinson would have to deal with his killings on his own terms.

***

Dimitri Van Acker watched Hinson's movements and knew that he'd been right about his involvement in the events of the past couple of days. Hope and he had obviously gotten to close to the truth. He was curious to see how Hinson was going to talk or obviously shoot his way out of his predicament. He had a sick feeling that if there was shooting going to be involved, he was going to be on the receiving end of a bullet. Well, he wouldn't go out without a fight. Van Acker casually leaned forward and pulled his gun out of the scabbard. He checked the clip to make sure it was full. He slid the slide back and felt good knowing that a bullet was in the chamber; if it would help him survive or not, he didn't know. He decided that he would stay in his car until Hinson forced him one way or the other to open his door and step out. He was praying Hope would get here soon.

He looked over at Patricia and saw the frightened look in her eyes. She was obviously confused about what was going on in her front yard. The way she acted, he might have been wrong about her being involved with Hinson. He just didn't know. He tried to make eye contact with Patricia, but she was focused on Hinson.

***

Hinson wondered if Van Acker would step out of the car and confront him. He quietly hoped he would. It would work to his advantage. One wrong move and he would shoot him, no questions asked. He was sure that he could convince Patricia to stick to whatever story they came up with about why he had needed to take a shot at Van Acker. However, it didn't seem as if Van Acker had any intend of stepping out of the vehicle. His engine was still going and he was staying in the air-conditioning while Patricia and he stood in the hot July sun getting warmer by the minute. He glanced at his watch. It wouldn't be too long before Olson would make the scene if he figured his timing correctly.

He looked over at Patricia again and noticed that she didn't look so good. She had a look of defeat on her face and he was afraid that she was falling apart and was going to confess. He could not afford for her to do that as it would make everything he had done come to light. Not to mention it would make everything he had done be for nothing. He would have killed three people for nothing. That's not why he had killed those people. He had done it to protect her, so he could be with her. He looked down at the ground. God, how he loved her! He looked back up at her. A frown covered his face. Yes, he loved her, but he would still take her out if she threatened his freedom!

***

Patricia noticed the change in Hinson facial expression and when his eyes stared back at her, it was almost as if she didn't recognize the man who stood behind that door. What had happened to him? The look he gave her scared her and send chills up her spine even though she felt as if she was about to melt. She instinctively knew what he was thinking. If she confessed to killing Susan, everything he had done to protect her would have been for nothing. She knew that he would not be able to live with that. Would he shoot her? She couldn't tell. She hoped that her life meant something to him. Then again, Joshua Underwood's life had not meant anything to him or the man he shot by the old cotton hangar. Would she be next? She hoped not. Patricia took a step forward towards Van Acker's car. She had made up her mind. There was no going back. She motioned for Van Acker to roll his window down.

***

Dimitri Van Acker was trying to watch both Patricia's and Hinson's facial expressions. One was filled with fear, yet with a hint of determination; the other was filled with anger. Looking in his rearview mirror at Hinson, Dimitri knew that things were not going to end peacefully. Where was Hope? She should have been here by now. He looked back towards Patricia. She had taken a step closer to his car and was motioning with her hands to roll down the window. He looked back into his rearview mirror as his finger was trying to find the button to let the window down. Between his eyes moving away from Patricia and focusing on the rearview mirror, he caught movement in the bushes to the right of Patricia's house. It hadn't been much, but there had been movement there. There was nothing between his car and the bushes and pretending to look in the mirror, he focused on where he thought he had seen something. As he looked hard, he could barely make out the form of a person, crouched down behind the bushes. This was getting more and more interesting. He wondered if Hinson had brought reinforcements or if whoever was hiding in the bushes was one of Hope's little surprises. He doubted that Hinson had anyone else working with him. Too many witnesses would just make it harder for him to walk away clean, and Van Acker had decided that this was what was going on. Once everyone who was involved with trying to solve the Susan Knox case was eliminated or silenced, Hinson would be home free to make up whatever story he could come up with. He'd make himself out to be the hero and that would work miracles for his reelection. Somehow he had a feeling that Hope, even though she sounded concerned and not prepared on the phone, had managed to put something together to foil Hinson's little plan.

He jumped when his phone rang. He looked at the display. Hope! He pushed the connect button and then the speaker button so he didn't have to have the phone in his hands.

"Hope?"

"Dimitri, listen, I'm just around the corner. I know that you're in your car, that Patricia is standing between you and the house and that Hinson got you blocked in, standing behind his door with his gun trained on you."

Van Acker looked down at his phone in disbelieve. How in the world did she know all that? Then a smile covered his face. Of course! The person hiding in the bushes was with her. She had managed to get help from someone.

"Hope, that's the situation. I can tell that your scout has done a good job telling you what's going on here."

There was silence on the other end and Van Acker could barely hear her curse.

"Listen, don't get mad. I was barely able to spot him or her. Your help is positioned to where neither Patricia nor Hinson can see them. So you're still good to go. Just hurry up. I don't like the look on Hinson's face."

"Well sit tight honey, because here I come."

With that said he could hear sirens and saw the blue lights on top of Hope's cruiser flash before he noticed her pulling in, blocking the driveway.

Hope had left her phone active after telling Van Acker that she was coming. She drove into the driveway hard and parked her car sideways, blocking the drive way from anyone coming or going. She grabbed her rifle out of the rack and was out the cruiser and hidden behind her door in no time.

***

Everything had happened so fast that Hinson didn't know where to go. He was caught in open view to Olson. Again, he had to give her credit. She was full of surprises and nothing escaped her. He wondered how she had known where and how to park without having seen the scene. Was she that good or did she have help. Could it be that Van Acker had called her unnoticed and told her what the scene looked like? Quite possibly! Both she and Van Acker were a number. He'd underestimated both of them. He would not make that mistake again. Time to see how the chips were going to fall.

"Hope, it's about time you got here. I've got a situation on my hand." Hinson yelled out.

"Andrew, it's over. I know that you're the one who killed Underwood. We have evidence to back that up."

"I don't think so sweetheart. I have evidence that Van Acker is the one who killed Underwood. That's why I'm trying to make the arrest. Now if you would be so kind as to follow orders and quit making accusations, we might be able to wrap this up without anyone else getting hurt."

Hinson hoped that accusing Van Acker of Underwood's killing would at least mess with Hope's mind enough to throw her off.

"That's right, Hope. I need you to go to the passenger side of his car and reach under the seat. You will find the gun that was used to shoot Underwood."

"I'm sure I will. And how did it get there? Did you plant it?

506

Give me some credit Andrew and don't treat me like a rookie."

He smiled. Well it was worth a try. He was sure the gun he had planted was still there. He looked over at Van Acker's car and could see him trying to reach over to see if there was indeed a gun under the passenger seat. Good! Go ahead and reach for it! Make sure your fingerprints are on it!

***

Dimitri Van Acker could not believe how things were turning out. He thought Hope's little display of force would have thrown Hinson for a loop. Instead, he was as cool as he could be and now accused him of being in possession of Underwood's murder weapon. He reached over and while holding a handkerchief he kept handy just in cause his allergies acted up, felt under the seat to see if there was something there. Sure enough there was a gun there. He could hear Hope screaming at him not to touch it. He thought about pulling it out from underneath the seat, but decided that he'd better listen to her. If they survived he would have to live with her, so he decided to listen. He sat back up and looked over at Patricia. She hadn't moved since Hope had pulled up and he didn't know what to think of the way she was reacting to everything going on. He ventured a glance in the bushes, trying to see if anyone was still hiding but couldn't make out anything.

***

Hope knew that Hinson wasn't going to volunteer any information so she decided to see if she could get Patricia to talk.

"Patricia, honey, are you okay?" Hope asked keeping her eyes on Hinson.

She thought that she saw a small jerk of the head when she asked. Obviously, he hadn't expected the conversation to shift to her.

Patricia looked over in Hope's direction and nodded her head.

"I need to ask you a question and I need you to think hard before you answer it, okay?"

Again Patricia nodded her head.

507

"The night that Susan Knox' apartment exploded, did you get a phone call from her?"

Patricia didn't wait to think about the question. She knew the answer and she'd made up her mind that she was going to confess.

"Yes, ma'am, I did."

Hope looked briefly towards Patricia.

"Can you tell me what you two talked about?"

This time there was a little hesitation before Patricia responded.

"She called me to tell me that she was HIV positive and that it would be in my best interest to get tested for the virus also."

So far so good Hope thought. Now she decided to push a little harder.

"Patricia? Are you dating anyone now?"

She looked over at Hinson and saw his face turning red. His hand jerked slightly as he adjusted the grip on his gun.

"Don't you answer that Patricia!" he shouted.

"And why wouldn't she answer that, Andrew?" Hope shot back. "Is it because it is you she's dating?"

Patricia's face turned bloodred. How was it possible for them to have found out?

"Hope, this is none of your business. If we are dating then that is her and my business."

"So you two are dating then?"

Patricia couldn't stand it any longer.

"Yes damn it! We're dating; we have been dating for 8 months!"

***

Dimitri Van Acker had been listening to the exchange between Hope, Hinson and Patricia. He admired Hope for the way she was handling the situation. She was reading Patricia the way he was reading her and it was only a matter of time before they would get a confession. He wasn't surprised that Hinson didn't want her to answer the question about whether they were dating and looking in his rearview mirror could see that Hinson was getting more and more agitated. He decided to keep Hinson some more of balance.

Keeping his car running, he slowly opened the door.

***

"Stay in the car, Van Acker," he heard Hinson yell.

Van Acker looked over towards Hope, looking for a clue about what she wanted him to do. He was afraid that if Patricia started to confess everything that Hinson was going to shoot her. Being outside the car, he would be able to distract Hinson. His eyes trained on Hope he eased the door open a bit further. Hope gave him a small nod of the head, suggesting that he should get out of the car. Obviously she wanted Hinson distracted also. He eased the door open all the way but stayed seated, holding his gun in his right hand out of view from Hinson.

"Van Acker, I told you to stay in the car. I'm not going to warn you again."

Dimitri Van Acker couldn't resist.

"What? If I get out you going to shoot me too, like you shot Underwood and my witness?"

"You son of a bitch! I should have shot you in the head instead of your witness!"

***

Hope gasped as she realized the implications of what had just been said. Van Acker had been right all along. So far they had no confession on any of the killings, but Van Acker had plainly touched the right cord in Hinson. She looked over at Hinson and he had turned red in the face. He was barely able to control himself. She wondered if she would be able to get him to surrender his gun. Even if he managed to kill both Van Acker and her, which she doubted he could pull off, she had Gonzales recording everything that was being said. Now she needed to try to defuse the situation.

"Andrew, there's no need to make this any worse. We figured out that it was Patricia who killed Susan Knox and then tried to cover it up by blowing up the apartment. We also figured that you must have drove by the funeral home on Sunday and saw Underwood's truck in the parking lot. You thought that was strange and you had to investigate. I bet Underwood was so busy playing detective on Susan's body that he never heard you come in. You knew that he had found the bullet hole underneath Susan's breast and you just couldn't have that because your girlfriend was the one who killed her. Then you noticed this strange man hanging around town for a couple of days. I noticed him too by the way. I even talked to him and asked him what he was doing here. So when he turned up dead, I figured that Susan's killer or Underwood's killer was onto him also. At that point we hadn't figured out there were two people involved. What got us on the right track was a piece of fabric that I found at the funeral home."

Hope looked towards Dimitri and winked at him. Nobody needed to know that it wasn't her but Van Acker who had found the piece of fabric and had sent it off for analysis.

"It's amazing what kind of stuff attaches itself to our clothes. How's your arm by the way?"

Hope swallowed and looked towards Patricia.

"Patricia, now that we know that you and Hinson are an item, we have enough evidence to put you at the scene of the crime. We know you drove his car that night and not your Jeep. Hinson's car has the tag lights missing. That's what made us realize who was involved. There's not that many black coupe driving around with broken tag lights."

Hinson started laughing at the top of his lungs. Everybody turned their attention to him.

"You think you and your boyfriend are pretty smart don't you! I must say, I've got a great detective team running around town."

He busted out in more uncontrolled laughter.

"Well, you know what? You're right! I did kill Underwood and the other guy. But how do you know that's everybody? Maybe there are more idiots who got in the way who needed taking out!"

Hinson looked towards Van Acker.

"Hey hotshot! Haven't you wondered why you haven't heard from your little spy?"

Van Acker turned white. With everything that had been going on, he had forgotten that Allen Murphy had not called him to tell him what he had witnessed.

Hinson laughed even louder, obviously having lost all sense of clarity.

"Hey hotshot! You don't look so good suddenly. Yeah, you see, old Murphy, he thought he was pretty slick. Not slick enough though!"

"Tell me you didn't, you son of a bitch!" Van Acker screamed as he pushed himself out of the car and tried to level his gun.

"Dimitri, no!"

Hinson needed only a fraction of a second to put Van Acker's unprotected body in front of his gun sights before he pulled the trigger in rapid succession.

Dimitri Van Acker felt the first bullet hit him square in the chest. Before he hit the ground, he had no idea how many bullets had hit him.

Hope Olson leveled her rifle at Hinson's head. She already knew he was wearing a vest. Hinson was unloading the last of his bullets when the bullet coming from Hope's gun entered the back of his head and exploded out the front.

Patricia Langston who had stood by looking at the whole scene started to scream uncontrollably as she saw Hinson's head explode in front of her eyes. She rushed to his car and fell on her knees crying, looking at what was left of her boyfriend.

Gonzales got to Dimitri before Hope made it around her car and Hinson's car. By the time she got there, Gonzales was back on his feet and held Hope back.

"He's gone, Hope."

"No, he's not! Tell me he's not!"

109.

Six months later.

Hope Olson was standing in the county graveyard in front of Dimitri Van Acker's grave. Just as she had for the past six months, once a week, she came by to talk to him, laying a red rose on his grave. She had taken on the difficult task of calling his parents back in Belgium and asking what to do with his remains. It was decided since he loved the United States and since he had chosen the United States as his new homeland, he should be buried where he was happiest. So, she had buried him, next to his best friend Allen Murphy.

The aftermath of the shootout at Patricia Langston's hadn't been all that complicated. Patricia confessed to killing Susan Knox and rigging her apartment to create an explosion. Together with the taped confession that Officer Gonzales had been able to make during the stand-off, it was determined that Andrew Hinson was responsible for the murders of Joshua Underwood, former FBI agent and witness protection program participant Jerome Gerard, and Allen Murphy. Patricia Langston was currently incarcerated in the county jail awaiting trial. Andrew Hinson's body had been returned to his home state of Virginia where it was said, he was buried in an unmarked grave in the same cemetery where his parents where buried.

Hope Olson helped Julie Sutton get in touch with the law firm that Van Acker had worked for in Washington, DC. As it happened one of the partners was licensed to practice law in the State of Georgia. He agreed to represent Julie Sutton in both her divorce against Tom Sutton and in the law suit she filed against her father for child molestation.

Once Tom Sutton realized that Julie possessed both tapes of her meeting with Eddie "Lester" Jovanovich, and there was a taped confession of his involvement with Susan Knox, he decided the best option was to grand her an uncontested divorce. Judge Julia Snelgrove wasn't easy on him and Julie Sutton ended up with ownership of their home, her car, and alimony of $2,500.00 per month. Sutton was persuaded that any effort to file suite against Julie Sutton for attempted murder would go nowhere. Judge Snelgrove made it clear that she was not going to waste the time of her Grand Jurors with frivolous claims. Julie Sutton realizing that $2,500.00 of alimony was not going to keep her in her house and pay the electric, water and other bills, started looking for a job. Dr. Earl Scarboro, after carefully considering her situation decided to hire her to replace her sister's position. So far, it looked like Julie Sutton was enjoying her newfound freedom and independence. Hope made sure that she went to see her at least once a week to sit down and talk to her. Over the past few months, Julie seemed to be doing better. She was seeing a psychiatrist once a month and being able to talk about her bad experiences had seemed to help. Phyllis Knox was paying for the therapy her daughter was going through. It was way past due that Julie got some professional help.

James Knox, after the Grand Jury reviewed the tapes that Susan had made; and which Hope turned over to Judge Snelgrove after reviewing them with Julie Sutton, was promptly arrested. His trial was scheduled for the September docket, in Dawson County, even after several attempts of his lawyers requesting a change of venue. Judge Snelgrove made it clear that if the crimes were committed in Dawson County, then the people of Dawson County were going to judge those crimes.

Those were the things that Hope Olson came to the graveyard to talk to Van Acker about. She buttoned up her coat a little tighter. She smiled as she thought of the last time that she'd seen him alive. It had been one of the hottest summers Georgia had experienced. Now, January of the following year was one of the coldest on record in Georgia. How fitting, she thought. After Van Acker's death, Hope had felt into a depression. If only she could have acted quicker. If only she could have done something different. But she'd done everything she could have done. The Sheriff's department's psychiatrist had worked with her to get through and past her emotions. She had done well. She still had moments of deep sorrow, but of late she'd gotten better. Coming out here to talk to Van Acker had helped. Her weekly ritual of placing the red rose on his grave brought her peace.

Hope Olson had been in deep thought holding her weekly ritual that she had not seen Helen, Kelly, and Michelle Murphy approach her.

"Good morning, Sheriff."

Hope turned around and looked at the three women in front of her.

"Good morning, ladies. I'm glad that all of you could make it."

She had to get used to being called Sheriff. She'd only been sworn in a couple of days as the new Sheriff of Dawson County. She'd been appointed interim Sheriff until a special election was scheduled to let the voters decide who they wanted to represent them as Sheriff. Hope had been urged by all of her friends and coworkers to run for the office. After careful consideration, she'd accepted the challenge and here she was; Sheriff Hope Olson.

She reached out to Helen Murphy and gave her a big hug. She then repeated the gesture with both Kelly and Michelle. All of them held hands and silently prayed.

15578080R00273

Made in the USA
Lexington, KY
05 June 2012